TERROR TALES OF THE SEASIDE

Edited by Paul Finch

TERROR TALES OF THE SEASIDE

First published in 2013 by Gray Friar Press.
9 Abbey Terrace, Whitby,
North Yorkshire, YO21 3HQ, England.
Email: gary.fry@virgin.net
www.grayfriarpress.com

All stories copyright © 2013 retained by the original authors
Cover copyright © Steve Upham 2013

Typesetting and design by Paul Finch and Gary Fry

The moral rights of the author and illustrator have been asserted.
All rights reserved. No part of this publication may be
reproduced, stored in a retrieval system, or transmitted, in any
form or by any means, electronic, mechanical, photocopying,
recording or otherwise without the prior permission of
Gray Friar Press.

All characters in this book are fictitious, and any resemblance to
real persons, living or dead, is coincidental.

ISBN: 978-1-906331-37-5

TABLE OF CONTENTS

Holiday From Hell by Reggie Oliver 1

The Eerie Events At Castel Mare

The Causeway by Stephen Laws 17

The Kraken Wakes

The Magician Kelso Dennett by Stephen Volk 36

Forces Of Evil

A Prayer For The Morning by Joseph Freeman 61

Hotel Of Horror

The Jealous Sea by Sam Stone 77

The Ghosts Of Goodwin Sands

The Entertainment by Ramsey Campbell 90

The Horse And The Hag

The Poor Weather Crossings Company by Simon Kurt Unsworth 112

The Devil Dog Of Peel

Brighthelmstone by R.B. Russell 130

The Ghouls Of Bannane Head

Men With False Faces by Robert Spalding 142

This Beautiful, Terrible Place

GG LUVS PA by Gary Fry 160

In The Deep Dark Winter

The Incident At North Shore by Paul Finch 175

The Walking Dead

Shells by Paul Kane 204

Hellmouth

The Sands Are Magic by Kate Farrell 224

Wild Men Of The Sea

Broken Summer by Christopher Harman 235

HOLIDAY FROM HELL
Reggie Oliver

My friends thought it would be a holiday for me. I had been engaged for a summer season at the Majestic Theatre, Brightsea, acting and assistant stage managing. They didn't realise that acting and stage managing in weekly repertory, a new play to learn your lines and find props for every week, was no casual pastime. Not that I was complaining: it was my first professional engagement out of drama school. I felt it to be a critical moment in my existence, and I still do. The glamour and danger of it has been augmented by the creations of memory through the passing years.

When I arrived at Brightsea in the middle of June the theatre season had already begun. One thing I had not accounted for was the difficulty in finding somewhere to stay, or "digs" as we called them. This was in the days when people still went on holiday at the English seaside in large numbers and the town was full. I could have rented a room here or there for a week or two but I did not want to be constantly on the move. I wanted to put down roots in this strange place.

Brightsea is on the Wirrall Peninsula facing the Irish Sea and is a resort which is well-known and popular with some, Liverpudlians in particular. I confess I had never heard of it till I went to work there. There were sands, there was a pier and a bandstand; there were amusement arcades and bingo halls; curving round the bay there were sweeps of white stucco Victorian terraced houses, almost every one of which was a hotel or 'guest house'.

In my day there were, beside a pair of 'moderne' 1930s cinemas, two places of live entertainment: the Pier Pavilion for variety and the Majestic Theatre where I was bound.

I wanted to like Brightsea but, even at the height of the season when the resort teamed with holidaymakers, there always seemed to me something windswept and melancholy about it. Perhaps my difficulties in finding lodgings affected my impressions.

After sleeping on a fellow actor's sofa for a couple of nights I finally found a room of my own. In a side street off the main promenade I discovered a dingy looking three storey terraced house that called itself The Belleview Hotel, and for once I did not see the ubiquitous NO VACANCIES sign in its bay window. I knew I could not afford an ordinary hotel room, but this looked like no ordinary hotel.

The woman who answered the bell was tall and angular, in her late fifties I should guess, with a strongly marked face that might once have been handsome. Her hair was dyed a fierce black. Her name was Mrs Warlock and she told me there were no vacancies. I was not disposed to take her at her word.

"All my eight rooms are occupied this week," she said with an intonation that suggested considerable pride in this achievement, but also a certain distaste. I looked beyond her into the little hallway. It seemed clean enough, but the dark red patterned wallpaper relieved only by a few framed steel engravings of religious scenes would not be to everyone's taste. A dark mahogany hat and umbrella stand, embellished with bevelled mirrors, brooded over the space. Two black Homburg hats (one of them enormous) hung on the pegs; in the stand was an old fashioned baggy umbrella with an ebony handle carved to look like the head of a bird of prey.

I explained my position, that I was an impoverished actor who needed a small cheap place to stay in until October: anything would do, an attic would be fine. Mrs Warlock considered me for a long moment in silence then without a word led the way upstairs.

As she moved she jingled slightly from the numerous bracelets and trinkets she wore about her person. Most of them were silver. Several had astrological significance. I wondered vaguely if she might hold seances on the long winter evenings. It must be bleak and lonely in Brightsea at that time of the year.

The sombre decor of the hallway was repeated throughout the hotel, giving it a distinctly Victorian aspect. I noticed the absence of fire doors and wondered when the Hotel Safety Inspectors had last been.

An uncarpeted wooden staircase led up from the third floor to the attics of which she showed me one. It immediately appealed to me. I was a romantic then and it was exactly as I imagined those garrets to be like in Paris where artists lived *La vie de Bohème*. There was a dormer window from which I could look out across gleaming slate roofs to a blue band of sea. I remember its being blue that day.

Mrs Warlock, who seemed to have taken to me, quoted a very fair price and said I could make use of the bathroom on the third floor. I would have to have my meals out, except for breakfast which I could take with the other guests in the dining room at eight. Wishing to seal the arrangement on the spot I gave her a deposit in cash and said I would return later in the day with my stuff when rehearsals were over.

Mrs Warlock seemed to find my enthusiasm for her attic puzzling. She said she would have the bed made up by the time I came back. Then after a pause she added:

"All my other guests are very old. I hope you don't mind."

I shook my head.

"They come up from an Old People's Home in Diss."

"Diss in Norfolk?"

"I suppose so. There are seven of them and they come every year with the woman who looks after them: Miss Harriman."

"I didn't know people went on holiday from Old People's Homes," I said.

"Well these do. They'll probably be in bed by the time you get back from the theatre tonight. You'll meet them at breakfast tomorrow morning, though. I hope you don't make a lot of noise."

I shook my head. I was too dedicated to my chosen profession, too ambitious to be noisy.

At rehearsals that afternoon I reported that I had found digs. The rest of the cast seemed relieved and asked me where they were. When I told them one of the older actors, who was a regular in the Majestic seasons said:

"Good God! I thought the Belleview had closed down ages ago. Something to do with Health Regulations. Rats, I believe."

"Don't scare the lad," said Janet my fellow assistant stage manager. She was barely older than me but she took an almost maternal interest. I think I was in love with her.

"I'm not afraid of rats," I said.

After rehearsals I took my belongings to the Belleview. Mrs Warlock let me in and gave me a key to the front door, telling me that her other guests were out at the moment. Nothing stirred within, not even a rat.

Having unpacked and arranged the attic to my satisfaction I found I had a little time before I was due in for the evening performance, so I ventured out for a walk along the promenade.

It was the hour of the evening meal – shortly after six – and, in countless guest houses and hotels along the front, heads, pink from their day in the sun, were bent low over whatever was on offer. Restaurants and cafés too were doing a good trade. There would be time for a quick drink before they took their seats at the Pier Pavilion or the Majestic.

The tide was out and the broad sweep of sand in Brightsea Bay was almost deserted. A man threw a ball for his dog, but the dog's response was muted and unenthusiastic. A woman was dragging her screaming child towards the concrete steps up to the promenade. Far out, almost at the water's edge where the sand was smooth and shiny as a billiard ball, an odd group of people were walking along behind a tallish stout woman in a tweed skirt and a hat with a feather in it. The woman in front was middle aged and energetic, the group behind – there were seven of them, three women and four men – were elderly, mostly white or grey haired, and one of the men was grotesquely fat. They did not so much walk as shamble behind their leader who was accompanied by a black, barrel-bodied pug dog, its thin little legs trotting so fast that they were barely visible. It seemed an odd time to be out for a walk, and so far from the land proper. Westward the sun was beginning to fall behind a wrack of cloud towards the sea.

That night in the Green Room during the interval I told the company of my vision of Brightsea at eventide.

"Brightsea is the weirdest place," said Martin, one of our actors. "Have you noticed how ugly everyone is here? And overweight! All those chips, I suppose. I barely see a beautiful face until I get into the theatre and sit down in front of my dressing room mirror. My dear, you'd think the Berliner Ensemble had come to town."

That night we went after the show to a bar called *Sally's* where we could drink all night providing we paid, so it was late before I turned my steps to the Belleview. Janet seemed concerned about my new digs, which touched me, but I was determined to find myself in my solitude.

The Belleview was silent when I entered it. One dim forty watt bulb illuminated the hallway. I was relieved to find that the carpeted stairs did not creak. All sounds from the town outside were excluded and the silence was an enveloping force. I stopped on the first floor landing to confirm the silence within me.

It was true. Brightsea had not penetrated this house, but it had a life of its own, barely detectable but still present. Paradoxically I was most aware of it when I was not paying attention. Along the walls of the landing were framed engravings of the Inferno scenes from the Doré *Divine Comedy*. I was studying one of them when I first heard the faint sound of breathing. It came from no particular direction, but surrounded me as if I were inhabiting a vast lung. I turned my attention away from the engraving and the noise vanished: there was silence only. I turned back to the engravings and there again, at the corner of my consciousness, was the breathing.

After a while I had had enough of this and climbed the long stairs to my attic eyrie. There, I fell asleep quickly, only wakened the following morning by the distant old fashioned sound of a dinner gong. It was eight o'clock. I dressed and came down for breakfast.

In the hallway beside the hatstand was a basket in which was curled a black pug dog. When I reached the bottom of the stairs the dog opened one bulging malignant eye to stare at me. I heard a low growl. To my left the dining room door was open and I entered.

Seven pairs of eyes turned towards me. They belonged to seven aged people seated at four tables. They were in pairs apart from an immensely fat man who sat alone. I thought I had seen him on the beach the previous evening and I guessed now that they were all of that party, and that the severe woman with the deep-set eyes who had not looked up when I entered the room was their guardian from the Diss Old People's Home.

"Good Morning," I said. There was no reply.

The fat man was the first to look away and devote all his attention once again to the plate of bacon and eggs, garnished with a tinned plum tomato, baked beans, a sausage and a slice of fried bread. He pronged his food and put it into his mouth with quick, neat movements that reminded me of a bird or an insect. The face was broad and flat, like that of a frog, with a long slit of a mouth that closed in on each intake of food with the speed of a trap. The chewing movements were so quick they were almost convulsive.

Mrs Warlock came in to ask me if I would like tea or coffee. Having taken my order she said: "You've met the gang, have you?" There was a silence which she felt inclined to fill. She formally introduced her guests, beginning with the fat man who was called Clutton Gewler. All their names were slightly odd. Mrs Warlock seemed ill at ease with the situation, and her slightly stilted bonhomie did not make it any better.

When she was gone one of the old women, whom Mrs Warlock had introduced as Mona Covett said: "What are you doing here, young man?"

I explained that I was at the Majestic, but none of the old ones, not even my interrogator, seemed very interested. That was fine by me. I was young. I did not want to get involved in some long meandering conversation with an aged person. Nevertheless, I was curious and began to study them as covertly as I could.

How old were they? Infinitely old: in their eighties at least, I guessed and all had white hair except one who appeared to be wearing a toupee of a rich and unconvincing chocolate brown hue. Their faces had not disintegrated into the soft-focus shapelessness of some elderly people; on the contrary their features were very pronounced, strongly differentiated from one another, and yet curiously lacking in personality. Or should I say humanity? How can I explain? It looked as if each one of them were wearing a mask that had been cunningly stuck to their faces and had now taken over their whole being. The expression in their eyes was uncommunicative; at any rate not quite human.

"What are you looking at, young man," said Mona Covett. She was dressed in a pale green twin set with a grey skirt, and she seemed even older than the others. Her face looked as if it had been crushed in a vice to make it thinner and her cranium was surrounded by a cloud of fine white hair that did not wholly hide the yellow, wrinkled skin that papered her skull.

"Nothing, Mrs Covett"

"*Miss* Covett."

"I was in the theatre once, you know," said the man in the chocolate toupee who sat at her table. His name was Valentine Pryde. "You may have heard of me." He wore a velvet jacket that had once been black but was now faded and greenish in parts and a brightly coloured foulard scarf at his neck. I suspected make-up on his chiselled features. It only served to accentuate his age.

At another table Franz Pigritz and Eira Gruffyd, a red-faced woman, were bickering. I only heard a few words.

"Would you mind pouring me another cup of tea, dear Mrs Gruffyd?" said Mr. Pigritz, a flabby somnolent old gentleman in grey. I detected a slight accent: Austrian perhaps.

"What's the matter with you, Franz?" said Mrs Gruffyd (Welsh accent). "Pour your own fucking tea! You've got arms, haven't you? You can reach." The young are easily shocked, but I am still not quite comfortable when I hear words like that coming out of old mouths.

Mr. Pigritz disconsolately flapped his arms which were short and plump. He made no attempt to pour the tea himself. His companion's fierce attack seemed to have daunted him. I felt half inclined to go to his rescue, but something about Mrs Gruffyd intimidated me as well.

The third couple, in the table most distant to me, seemed an even more ill-assorted pair. The man, called Talbot Lavard, gaunt and grey in a black suit, was studying the back page of the *Financial Times*, half moon spectacles perched on his beak of a nose while the woman opposite him, flamboyantly dressed with dyed red hair, was muttering at him words I could not catch. Mrs Warlock had introduced her to me as Venetia Lustig and I had not cared for the predatory way in which she had looked at me. Lavard took no notice of her, and the utter steadfastness with which he ignored her had a kind of passive violence to it. Once, to attract his attention, she took a page of his paper between finger and thumb and gave it a little shake. In silent fury he withdrew it from her reach. Mrs Lustig was big, old and clumsily shaped, but in such a way that suggested voluptuous contours formerly.

The person who intrigued me most was the only one who had ignored me when I came in. This was Miss Eve Harriman, the overseer of the old people. She wore a neat black coat and skirt and a white blouse. Her reddish hair was scraped back from a rather nondescript face on which the lines of authority and absence of humour had been deeply etched. Nevertheless there was something magnetic about her, attractive even, in the way that power attracts almost in spite of itself. She drank black tea and nibbled dry toast with puritan dedication.

I left the dining room and went upstairs to fetch a script. Mrs Harriman's pug in the hall opened its eye and growled once more. When I reached my room I found that I was trembling. I was hoping that I would not meet any of them in the hall on the way out and that the black pug had been removed.

I paused long on the first floor landing before coming down stairs, listening. From the dining room came a low murmur, not quite like that of human conversation. Or, so it seemed to me. It was like the buzzing of a hive of angry bees, or the grunt of pigs herded together. I began to be ashamed of myself for lingering so long. I must run the gauntlet.

At the bottom of the stairs I encountered Mrs Harriman who had come out of the dining room to attach a lead to her pug's collar. Without looking at me she said:

"I wouldn't touch him."

"I have no intention of doing so. What's his name?"

"Pluto." The dog growled. Mrs Harriman looked at me for the first time. Like those of her charges, Mrs Harriman's face seemed like a kind of mask but a more inscrutable one than theirs. "What is the play you're doing this week at the Majestic?"

"*Murder Most Deadly*," I said. "But I'm not in it this week. I'm only stage managing."

For a moment a little mocking smile was on her lips. "I think we might come tonight. My boys and girls like a good murder. You're quite ambitious aren't you?"

"I suppose so."

"Want to be a big star? I could help you. I know quite a few people in the business, believe it or not."

"Can I get you some complimentary seats?"

"No need. But we'll have another talk. There may be some things you can do for me."

I had no idea what she meant. Perhaps she was mad. I left for rehearsals.

In the afternoon I was sent to go round the town looking for props for the next play, *Night Must Fall*. It was bright and hot; the streets were crowded; the sea was full of the splash and cry of children. There was something flamboyant, almost frighteningly so, about Brightsea that day. I kept seeing Mrs Harriman's old people in different places about the town. Mr. Gewler was sitting in the window of one of the sea-front cafes demolishing a huge plate of chips. He seemed to be in his element, surrounded by equally corpulent customers, some of them children. Those around him ate as he did with a morose dedication, occasionally glancing at Mr Gewler, as if for reassurance.

I passed a jeweller's shop into which a young couple were staring. Behind them stood Mona Covett, though why I could not see her reflected like them in the glass of the shop front I don't know. The couple were holding hands tightly, convulsively. Miss Covett little fists clenched and unclenched in time with theirs.

There was a Punch and Judy show on the sands. Each time Punch knocked Judy with his stick it seemed to be with increasing violence and the children sitting crossed legged in front of the little theatre screamed ever louder. I did not notice at first that an adult was also watching the performance because she was buried up to the neck in sand. But the head that emerged from this makeshift grave was the red and white one of Mrs Gruffyd. Her face was not unlike that of Mr Punch himself.

Halfway along the promenade I saw Martin, one of the actors in our company, leaning against the railings and talking to Valentine Pryde. There was a strange symmetry in their swaying movements. If Pryde made a gesture, Martin unconsciously followed suit, reminding me somehow of a flightless avian courtship ritual.

Just below the promenade's rampart I saw Mr Pigritz slumbering on a deck chair in its shade. A little child came up and urinated against his leg. Pigritz slumbered on. In the distance I spotted Mrs Lustig staring into a parked car. I began to feel dizzy.

"Are you all right?" My fellow stage manager Janet was suddenly standing beside me.

I looked again towards the parked car but Mrs Lustig had gone. "It's too hot," I said as if excusing myself. Men and women drifted like brightly coloured balloons along the afternoon promenade. Nothing was quite real, except the theatre. It was time to go there and make ready for the evening performance.

That night the performance of *Murder Most Deadly* was unusually well received by a near capacity audience. It was a poor play but full of the kind of routine moments that some people find reassuring:

"Inspector, are you accusing me of -?"

"I'm not accusing anyone, Colonel Anstruther, I'm just trying to get at the truth ..."

Before the performance I looked through the gauze peephole in the curtain at the auditorium. There is always a strange excitement to be had from looking at 'your' audience, even if you are only the stage manager. The people coming into the theatre seemed livelier than normally: not the usual blue rinsers, though there were some of them too. There was even a bit of a scuffle and some raised voices over one of the seats in the stalls.

I looked in vain for Mrs Harriman and her seven charges, but when the play had begun I did see them. I was 'working the corner', as they say, in other words I was sitting in the wings on the left hand side of the stage, prompting if necessary and giving the sound and lighting cues. There were not many of those in the play and everyone knew their lines this week so I had time to wonder. From my vantage point I could see a section of the stalls, the circle and the stage box almost opposite me. There was just enough illumination reflected out from the brightly lit stage for me to see that there were four dim figures in the box. I almost missed a doorbell cue trying to work out who they were. It was Mr. Pigritz, Mrs Gruffyd, Mr Lavard and Mrs Lustig. Mr. Pigritz was forever nodding off whereupon Mrs Gruffyd would give him a sharp dig in the ribs. It was only during the interval that I was able to ascertain that the other four of my fellow guests at the Belleview were occupying the stage box on the prompt side of the auditorium. I looked at them as much as I dared during the rest of the performance but they barely moved and I could not see their expressions clearly enough to tell whether they were enjoying themselves or not.

At the end of the play during the curtain calls I looked up at the box again, but the four had gone.

After the show, as Janet and I were restoring the set for the following evening's performance, I began to stare again at the two stage boxes. It was obviously pure fancy, but it seemed to me that a dark mist hung about their interior, as if their occupants had not quite gone from the place.

"There's something funny about those boxes, isn't there?" said Janet. "I rather think you're like me. You're a bit of a sensitive. Did you know that for some reason the Management never sells tickets for the boxes, not even if it's a full house?"

"Well they did tonight. I saw. They were both occupied."

Janet gave me an anxious look, her head on one side. "I don't think so," she said.

I made no further comment. We finished our work quickly. When we got to the stage door we looked out to find that there was a small crowd outside and that the rest of the cast were signing programs and autograph books. Among them I was astonished to see my fellow guests at the Belleview. Only Mrs Harriman held back, watching the others with an inscrutable expression. The seven were pressing insistently through the throng, thrusting their programs at the actors to be signed. Their faces carried no expression that I could tell, only the pronounced characters of their mask-like features.

"They won't want our autographs," said Janet. "Let's go out through the front of house and avoid the fuss."

For some reason we ran giggling and hand in hand through the darkened theatre and out through the foyer. The front of house manager who was just locking up the box office eyed us with disapproval. We were still holding hands when we were out in the free night air under the theatre entrance canopy with its flickering coloured bulbs.

"That was very odd," I said, "I've never seen autograph hunters outside the stage door before."

"Just a bunch of kids," said Janet. "They were probably having a laugh."

"Oh, they weren't all kids. There were at least seven adults there."

"So you saw them too, did you?"

"What do you mean by that?"

Janet squeezed my hand. "Let's go and have a drink at *Sally's*," she said.

The rest of the cast joined us at *Sally's*, seemingly rather out of sorts after their signing session. I was not drunk when I left Sally's because I had been talking more than drinking. What about? Nothing. Nonsense. I think I had told Janet that I was in love with her and she had taken my declaration with gentle equanimity. Whatever had happened I was feeling light-headed as I returned to the Belleview, but not incapable.

I opened the door of the hotel as quietly as I could. There was no light on in the hallway but some illumination was coming through the fanlight from the street lights outside. I shut the door quietly and paused to listen. Once again I was conscious of a breathing sound in the house. To my right the dining room door was closed, but opposite the door to the 'lounge' was open. Dim light from the street filtered through the net curtains of its bay window into the room. On its armchairs and sofas seven dark figures were seated. When I saw them the shock deprived me of movement.

They seemed motionless but the unison of their breathing gave me an illusion of movement. But they were not asleep, Mrs Harriman's seven old people. I knew that because I could just see that their eyes were open. The eyes glowed slightly in the dark, a dull, luminous red like the dying embers of a fire. Seven pairs of eyes were watching me in the dark.

I might have stayed there all night because the terror of it was absolute, the rigid motionless terror of eternity. My lungs seemed to contract. I could only take tiny shallow breaths. Then a scuffling sound roused me from paralysis. I broke away and ran upstairs to my room.

I switched on the light but the bulb flashed and died with a little pop. I was in the dark again. There was something in the room, something that pattered and snarled.

A reading lamp stood on the bedside table. If I could get to that and turn it on I thought I could be safe. I felt my way towards it, but before I reached it I tripped over something. It yelped and I felt its teeth sink into my leg. Biting back a shriek of pain I stretched out my hand for the lamp and turned it on. The dim forty watt Mazda bulb, made dimmer by its parchment shade, revealed that I had stumbled over Pluto. I stared at the little curled black thing and it stared malevolently back like a slug with eyes. It began to whine with pain, then dragged itself to its feet. One leg was obviously damaged. Slowly, then with increasing urgency it circled the room, apparently searching for something. Having found it beneath a chair, it picked it up with its teeth and carried it into the faded penumbra cast by the bedside lamp, still limping and in agony. It dropped the object at my feet.

At first it looked to me like a part of a doll. I reached for it, slowly tentatively, uncertain whether Pluto might not make a savage bid for its recovery, but he just stood there staring at me with his glassily malignant eyes. I picked it up and almost instantly dropped it. It was soft and cold, a real dead thing. It was a severed child's hand.

Pluto and I looked at each other, then, suddenly, anticipating my vicious reaction perhaps, the pug was scrambling painfully for the door. The next moment it was through and I heard it scrambling down the stairs. A scuffle, a thump and an agonised yelp indicated that at one point it had had a fall. I was alone with the severed hand.

It lay there quietly while I studied it. I had never seen such a thing before. It no longer filled me with horror because in itself it was only accidental and innocent. How had it got here? To whom did it belong? But these were not the pressing questions. The most urgent matter to decide was what I should do with the thing.

I found a *Kwiksave* supermarket bag and wrapped it tightly in that. After some indecision I decided to put it in my jacket pocket. Then, when I went out the following morning, I would not have forgotten it, and could dispose of it as I thought best. I am not sure I slept at all that night.

Early the next morning I crept out of the house and went for a walk. I could not face breakfast with Miss Harriman and her crew. The early light was fresh; Brightsea was deserted. The water glittered under Brightsea pier, its web of iron struts that supported it, looking like the finest lace. Everything seemed pure to me; all of the previous day's vulgarity washed clean by the dawn.

I considered the bag in my pocket. Should I bury it in the sand? Should I merely drop it in one of the many waste bins that the municipality had thoughtfully provided?

Just then I heard a siren. A police car, its blue light flashing, swept out of a side street and onto the main boulevard along the front. It was hurrying in the direction of the pier. I decided to postpone the question of the bag and find myself some breakfast.

When I got to the theatre later that morning some of the company were agog with a murder that had just been reported in the town.

The mutilated corpse of a girl had been discovered that morning in the pier toilets. (Ladies or Gents?, you may ask. I forget.) I went straight to my dressing room and put the child's hand in its bag into the bottom of my make-up box, and there it remained for many years.

It is now – forty years later – withered and desiccated, barely recognisable as part of a once living human being, but I still have it with me. I carry it now in a special black leather pouch that I had made for it. In fact I am never without it in my trailer on a film set, or in my star dressing room. I believe it to be talisman of great power. It accounts for the spectacular success of my career: that and my phenomenal talent, of course.

On that day of days the company began rehearsals for the next play, in which I had a part. I was going to play Dan in *Night Must Fall*.

Later, towards evening, I was walking along the promenade with Janet. We were vaguely looking for somewhere to have a bite to eat before the show. I think we had had a slight argument about the nature of reality or some such. I was quite philosophical in those days. I believe I was maintaining that all experience was subjective and that there was no such thing as absolute truth. It was all quite amiable, though.

The beach before us was almost deserted and the tide was on the turn. Fat grey clouds threatened overhead and the few holidaymakers that remained were making a hurried retreat from the shore, carrying their beach paraphernalia with them like so many refugees. Disgruntled fragments of conversation drifted up to us.

"If you don't stop bellyaching, Sydney, I'll give your legs such a smack …" "If I've told you once, I've told you a thousand times, you shouldn't go guzzling beer on an empty stomach …" "If you've got sand up your botty hole it's your own fault …"

At the shoreline only eight figures remained: eight and a barrel-chested, limping black dog. Pluto, despite his impediment, was dancing round the seven old people as if he were a sheepdog gathering the herd together.

Miss Harriman turned towards the sea and the setting sun that was glaring like a red eye from under the brow of clouds. Her seven charges had by now been shuffled into a weary platoon behind her. There was a brief pause and then Miss Harriman began to walk into the sea, the seven following her. Pluto dashed ahead of them into the waves and was rapidly engulfed. Soon the eight were up to their waists in water but still they went on. I was invaded by an overwhelming feeling of horror, not so much at what I saw as at the possibility that I was hallucinating and mad in consequence. I took Janet's hand.

"Can you see what I am seeing?" I asked.

"Oh, yes. I think so …"

"Thank God for that."

By this time they were up to their necks. What would they do next? Would they swim? Would they turn round? The next moment their heads had sunk beneath the surface of the sea which bubbled a little as they went down. For a few seconds an exhalation of greyish steam went up from the bubbles into the darkening sky, then all was still again. I noticed that there were once more people walking along the promenade. It was, despite the threat of a storm, "a beauteous evening, calm and free."

It began to rain and I realised I had forgotten my script. So Janet and I parted at the bandstand and I returned to the Belleview. When I met my landlady in the hallway she told me that Miss Harriman and her seven old people had gone back to Diss that afternoon. Their holiday was over.

"I'm not sorry they've gone," said Mrs Warlock. "Old Mr. Pigritz soiled the bed every night, and there were stains on Mrs Lustig's sheets that I shouldn't like to discuss in polite company."

THE EERIE EVENTS AT CASTEL MARE

It's a sad truth that many British seaside towns in the early 21st century are mainly famous for having gone to seed. Numerous exclusive coastal resorts, which in Regency days were a fashionable destination for the independently wealthy, boomed during the Industrial Revolution when they became a summertime Mecca for the working classes. However, in the era after World War Two, with the slow decline of industry and the arrival on the scene of cheap package deals abroad, the British seaside underwent a slow change for the worse. Many traditional holiday towns struggled to find customers; despondency and dereliction set in; most became shadows of their former selves.

But not all.

Several of Britain's more famous resorts had never catered purely for blue-collar clients, but had continued to offer genteel entertainments and expensive hotels, seeking to attract both the upper and the middle classes. One such was the spa town, Torquay, on Devon's sunny south coast.

Today, Torquay still has a distinguished air and is a thriving tourist centre (it is not known as the 'English Riviera' for nothing). But even Torquay has its fair share of eerie tales to tell, none more so than that of Castel a Mare, an old abandoned house notorious for being haunted by entities that would physically and violently attack intruders.

Castel a Mare was built in Victorian times; the exact date of its construction is unknown, but it occupied extensive grounds in the town's upmarket Warberry Road. When, in the early 20th century, stories first began to circulate that it was haunted, it had been empty and in a dilapidated condition for some considerable time, possibly since as far back as the 1880s.

The first recorded incidents date from 1912, when local people reported unnerving noises in the house at night: female screams, the relentless opening and closing of doors and, more alarming still, the sound of heavy feet running back and forth up and down the stairs and along the decrepit landings. Shortly after this, the First World War began and, with its colossal death toll, proved a catalyst for increased fascination with spiritualism. Inevitably, Castel a Mare became the focus of many séances and all-night vigils. Numerous 'contacts' were reported, including brutal attacks on investigators, either via the agency of a medium who had become possessed or through poltergeist activity. In all cases, the victims were left badly shaken, though one or two were also injured. During the course of this, a picture was gradually constructed of the entities supposedly dwelling in the house. There were believed to be two of them, and they were male and female. One was said to be the ghost of a maid who was beaten to death in Castel a Mare when she learned that her master, a doctor, was responsible for other murders. Far from being a passive and persecuted spirit, this maid was described as angry and threatening, though nothing like as threatening as the male. He was supposedly the source of all the violence, and his reign of terror would culminate in a truly spectacular manifestation, which was not only the most dramatic incident to occur at Castel a Mare, but also the most authentically attested to as it was witnessed by the respected journalist, Beverley Nichols (who went on to pen 60 books and work as a columnist for 'Women's Own' from 1946 until 1967).

Nichols was 19 in 1917, when, late one night, he and two other companions commenced an impromptu ghost-hunting expedition at Castel a Mare. Nichols himself experienced nothing out of the ordinary, except that he began to feel ill and had to leave the building early. One of the others soon joined him, leaving one lad, Peter St. Aubries, upstairs in the house alone. St. Aubries, who had also seen nothing odd up to this point, was bored and also about to leave when he was suddenly confronted by a terrifying figure – a hulking man with no face. St. Aubries shrieked for help, but the figure grabbed hold of him and administered a vicious beating. When the unfortunate lad finally fought his way outside, he was battered, bruised, covered in dirt and dust, and promptly fainted at the feet of his pals, neither of whom, perhaps understandably, were inclined to go back inside to investigate.

Castel a Mare was finally demolished in the 1920s, and though in later years another house was built in its place, there were no further reports of disturbances. Since then, no-one has been able either to verify or dismiss the many spooky incidents associated with it. Photographs of the house remain, but depict a pleasant villa of a sort typical in wealthy seaside resorts of that era. An unnamed doctor did indeed live there in the 19th century, but is believed to have moved away around 1870 – he is not known to have been accused of murder or investigated for any crime. The name itself, Castel a Mare, is not as sinister as is often imagined. One persistent assumption was that it was an abbreviation of 'Castle Nightmare', but though the specific meaning has never been established, most likely it meant 'Castle by the Sea'.

In truth, the Castel a Mare case is a textbook haunting with all the classic components: rumours that a mass murderer once lived there (unconvincing attempts have even been made to link him to Jack the Ripper); the presence of both female and male entities, possibly one of the murder victims and her murderer; incident-strewn séances and vigils; the alarming possession of mediums and other visitors; the final appearance of a truly gruesome spectre ... and of course it all comes to us from that golden age of haunted houses and paranormal investigation, so much of which was later discredited because of the numerous hoaxes that were perpetrated.

Only the Beverley Nichols account gives it credibility, but that is a significant credibility nonetheless.

As a final and rather curious footnote, interest in Castel a Mare was briefly reawakened in the 1960s, when US toy company, Aurora, released a series of glow-in-the-dark model kits based on famous Hollywood monsters, including Dracula, Frankenstein, the Wolf Man, the Mummy and so on. One of these, rather mysteriously, was 'the Forgotten Prisoner of Castel-Mare', and it wasn't actually a monster, it was a skeleton standing upright in chains. Though it was speculated on at the time, there is apparently no connection between the two. The 'Forgotten Prisoner' was entirely an Aurora invention, possibly derived from Edgar Allan Poe's classic horror tale, 'The Cask Of Amontillado'. It is doubtful its creators had ever heard of Castel a Mare in Torquay, England.

THE CAUSEWAY
Stephen Laws

When Hugh began to slow the car, Pauline didn't speak. She just gave him one of her looks. The one he referred to as the 'withering' look. He couldn't see it because he was keeping his eye on the causeway, but he could feel it. He ignored her, tried to keep his face as straight as possible as the car finally rolled to a halt, right at the foot of the rescue station, a wake of sandy water furling around the tyres.

The station itself was set in a concrete base, rising to fifty feet above the pitted roadway. A rusted steel ladder, mottled and leprous with peeling white paint was stapled to the side of that base with rusted stanchions. A narrow platform at the top gave access to the actual shelter; a simple, square concrete cabin with a flat roof – perhaps fifty feet square and with one salt-encrusted window looking out across the flat expanse of sand to their destination – Pitcher's Island.

Pauline turned in the passenger seat to look at Hugh, waiting for the answer to her unasked question. Hugh was craning to look up through the side window at the sea-stained concrete pillar. When he looked back at her again, he was smiling.

"So why have we stopped?" croaked Pauline, anger flaring again. The words came out in a gargle. Her mouth was still full of the peanut brittle she had been eating these last twenty minutes. Still smiling, Hugh took one of her hands in both of his own; his eyes never leaving her face. Ordinarily, Pauline would have dragged free and berated him. But this apparent act of affection was so out of character, so unexpected, that it took her completely by surprise.

"What ...?" she began again.

And then Hugh clamped the handcuffs on her right wrist.

Pauline stopped chewing, looked vacantly at the manacle – and then back at Hugh again as, still smiling, he fastened the other handcuff onto the steering wheel. He sat back, admiring his handiwork. Pauline worked the peanut brittle around in her mouth so that she could ask just what the hell he was playing at; looked back at the handcuffs again and saw that each cuff had a protective layer of spongy linen wrapped around the fastening bracelets so that her wrist, and the steering wheel, wouldn't suffer abrasion.

"Goodbye darling," said Hugh matter-of-factly.

And when Pauline finally swallowed the brittle, turning to look at him again, Hugh smiled and quickly climbed out of the car.

Pauline began to make sounds then. But thanks to the operation on her larynx as a child, and the fact that she couldn't raise that voice above a croak, there was no way that any of the sounds would carry – a fact that Hugh had taken fully into account. When he closed the door, Hugh didn't look back. Instead, he took a deep breath of the salted evening air and looked back with satisfaction through the quickly descending darkness; back down the twisting and rutted causeway along which they had travelled. It wasn't possible to see the landwards shore now. Very soon, darkness would envelop everything and the sea would rush in over the causeway between the mainland and the island.

The car was shaking furiously on its suspension as Pauline struggled in vain to free herself from the steering wheel. But Hugh still didn't look back into the car. A great feeling of peace had come over him as he turned now to look out across the glinting black-and-white of the bay. The water was rushing in fast now. Could it be that it had reached his ankles in the short time that it had taken to stop the car and do the deed? He steadied his hand on the roof, felt it shuddering and shaking. Far away, down that twisting and winding road, he could see twinkling lights from the few habitations on Pitcher's Island. No one would be heading this way now – or from the mainland. Much too late to risk it, as anyone who checked the tidal timetables would know.

Hugh, of course, had checked them well. He had been very careful about that; checking the tide shifts and timetables down to the very last detail. Leaving it until just the right moment. He'd been up here several times in the past year, telling Pauline that he had been on business. And, of course, he had been on business of sorts. But not the kind that Pauline could have dreamed of in a million years. He had studied the times, sat in his car and watched the tide come in. He had watched the comings and goings of the islanders and the tourists who visited Pitcher's Island. He had deliberately picked the most opportune time, when the tourist season was over, to suggest the need for a holiday break. Pauline had believed that hotel accommodation was waiting for them on the island.

She was wrong.

Night was falling fast – the tide was coming in even faster.

In twenty minutes at the most, the causeway would be under twelve feet of water, and his problems would be all over.

Whistling a jaunty tune and with not so much as a backward glance, Hugh began to climb the rusted ladder leading up to the rescue station. Water began to swirl under the wheel trims as he ascended. From within the car, the muted and strangled sounds of anger suddenly ceased.

When they began again moments later, those horror-stricken but muted sounds no longer seemed human.

*

Hugh unscrewed the top from his half-bottle of whisky, savoured the moment – and took a deep swallow. It tasted of fire and achievement and a job well done. He checked his watch and settled back on the wooden bench to survey his surroundings. From his pocket, he retrieved a pencil thin flashlight, bought especially for that evening, and used it now to reacquaint himself with his surroundings. He was already familiar with the layout of this concrete bunker-on-stilts. He had spent several afternoons pacing the solid floor, looking down through the small circular aperture that served for drainage in bad weather; or looking out through the salt-encrusted window to sea. The walls were bare, apart from faded graffiti. Back in 1984, Jane would do anything for a fiver, Ken loved Gillian 24/7 and Newcastle United Were Crap (True). There was a notice board facing the main door that gave tide times, and instructions on what to do in the event of car breakdown or similar misfortune. First and foremost, it directed attention to the red telephone set into the wall at the left. From here it would be possible to ring the mainland and alert the coastguard.

But Hugh had made other plans.

It took three concerted yanks to pull the telephone out of the wall and discard it on the concrete floor.

It was lying there like that when we came in. Bloody vandals. If only someone had checked on it, Pauline might still be alive ...

"Must remember to sob at that point," Hugh said aloud, and took another swallow.

His attention turned to the window, and he quickly switched off the flashlight. If he could see lights from the island, then someone might see a glimmer of light from the rescue station cabin no matter how small. Best take no chances.

Settling back, he thought back to their conversation in the car, en route to the causeway.

*

It can't be good for you, Pauline. All that sweet stuff you cram into yourself all the time.

Is that right, my darling husband? Is that RIGHT?

I'm only saying ... for your own good ... you need to cut down.

You think you're here to tell me what to do? Is that it? You think that just because we're married, I'm supposed to do everything that you tell me?

It's not like that, sweetheart ...

Don't sweetheart me, you hypocrite. Don't you think I know why your married me?

I married you because I ...

Don't you DARE say it! Don't you dare say: 'Because I love you.' Because, Hughie love, we both know why you married me. And it wasn't because I was an oil painting was it?

That's not fair ...

Oh, so it was because of my sweet disposition then? The way I adored you. The way that I took to you straightaway.

I don't know what you mean ...

Mun-eee, my darling. Daddy's money. Isn't that why you pursued me?

Money never came into my thinking.

Seems to me that the little bird of untruth is perched on your shoulder, Hughie. Don't you think that there were others? All thinking they could get to Daddy's wonderful, green crinkly stuff through me?

All of which was true, of course. Never in a million years would he have looked her way if it hadn't been for the fact that her old man was worth a small fortune. And at a time when he was at the lowest point on his life, he felt sure that this was the way to go. Make a beeline for the daughter. Back then, she had been an awkward cow; but he felt that he could handle it, could get to the Number One position; twist her around his finger, because no other sod on earth would have her. Now, it seemed after four years of hell that he was in Position One Hundred and Forty.

*

Suddenly, Hugh realised that he had drunk half of the whisky, and in the time he had been thinking back, darkness had closed completely around the refuge station. He put the bottle back in his inside pocket, walked to the window and looked out. There was no moon, and only the merest ripples of light on the water. Miles away, specks of light shone steadily from the houses on the island at the other side of the causeway.

Somewhere to the right, out of the window's sight line, the car was submerged.

There was no sound.

Hugh was pleasantly surprised to discover that he had no feelings about that, at all. He would have to work up some degree of emotion, of course. For the police and for Pauline's family. But he had been living a lie for such a long time, he felt sure that he could lie about her tragic end very convincingly. Hugh returned to the bench and lay full length on it, staring up at the pockmarked concrete ceiling.

She fell.

It was horrible.

I told her that we shouldn't try to cross – that the tide was coming in fast. But she insisted.

We'd just reached the rescue station, and the water was coming in under the doors. So we stopped, and you could see the water rising fast as we climbed the stairs. Then, of course, the telephone was out of order. Vandalised. And that's when Pauline remembered that she'd left the mobile phone in the glove compartment of the car. I went back – and the water was at the windows. I started down, but Pauline held me back; didn't want me to risk it. She was holding my arms and then – well – then she must have leaned against the wooden rail. It snapped – God, that sound! And she went right over, into the water. I jumped in after her, but in the dark I couldn't see where she'd gone and ... and ...

The wooden rail at the top of the platform stairs.

Hugh rose quickly, yanked open the door and stood out on the platform.

There was no reflection on the water, not even the merest clue that there was a submerged car down there at the foot of the stairs.

Leaning in close, he yanked at the wooden rail.

When he'd visited that station two weeks ago, he had seen the deep unrepaired crack there – and had got the key part of his plan already worked out. The wood screeched, but the rail would not break. Standing back, he kicked hard. The rail splintered. On his second kick, a three-foot section fell away and made a satisfying splash in the darkness. Grinning, Hugh looked out into the night – then back down to where the car lay.

I jumped in after her ...

Calmly, keeping his hand firmly on the station's concrete wall, Hugh made his way down the semi-submerged stairs.

He kept walking, entered the water; breath hissing at the cold. Waist-deep, chest-deep.

And now, he could not bring himself to look in the direction that he knew the car lay; did not want to think that his hateful wife was only a few yards away in the darkness. Eyes bulging, mouth frozen open in a drowned scream. Hair flowing like seaweed around her head.

Hugh ducked his head under; exploded back out of the water and clambered quickly back up the stairs, chest heaving as the icy cold invaded his body. He did not look back when he slammed the station door behind him.

Back on the bench, he drank more whisky.

It was going to be a long, uncomfortable night.

But it was going to be worth it.

*

Cold, shivering and wet – Hugh had still managed to drift off into a shallow sleep. And in that shallow place, he remembered:

So how do you really feel about me, sweetheart? Go on – tell me again how much you love me, and how you didn't marry me because you wanted to get a foot in the family business?

Pauline – you keep saying that, and it's not true.

Well we might be married, but that doesn't mean you're family, sonny.

For God's sake ...

God's got nothing to do with it. Quite the opposite.

You've had a lot to drink, darling. Don't open another bottle ...

Piss off, Hughie! Remember when you called my mother a witch?

Look, I'm sorry. She shouldn't have ...

Shouldn't, couldn't, wouldn't! What if I told you that she IS a witch? What if I told you that Daddy's a warlock? That I'M a witch, Hugh-ee? Got my croaky little witch's voice, haven't I? Shame I don't have a wart and a hooked nose, isn't it? What if I told you that the whole family are witches and warlocks? That the reason we've got money is that we use it in business to make more money. What then? Maybe I can read minds, lover boy. Thought of that? Maybe I know – really KNOW – why you married me.

Hugh smiled and hugged himself.

"Didn't read my mind tonight though. Did you, bitch?"

He dreamed of insurance money, other women, family money and more women.

*

A river of money, a river of sympathy, and acceptance at last into the arms of a wealthy family. In dream, Hugh saw and felt Pauline's rich industrialist father put an arm around his shoulders.

We never said anything about what you must have suffered at home, Hugh. After all, no one should come between a wife and husband – but we could see what you were having to put up with, you know. Pauline was always demanding, even as a child. You're broken-hearted now, but I promise – you'll stay as big a part of the family now as you always were. We'll see to you. Don't worry. We'll see to you ...

Now there was only Hugh, standing alone in the centre of a flurrying whirl of leaves.

But they weren't leaves. They were twenty-pound notes, swirling and spinning around him. He began to grab for them, stuffing them into his pockets. As fast as he could catch them, clouds more of them were swirling around his body. Thick and fast and – now suffocating. There was too much, the swirling was taking away his breath. Something was going wrong with this dream. Because now they weren't twenty-pound notes anymore. They really were leaves – brown-parchment autumn leaves that crumbled into ash in his hands and pockets.

The swirling wind became swirling water.

In that swirling murk, Hugh saw the car – its roof just below the surface.

The passenger door jerked wide open in a flurry of bubbles and oily water.

"Hugh–eee ..." gargled a familiar, clogged voice.

And Hugh was instantly awake with a scream in his throat.

For a moment, it seemed that he could still hear that drowned but horribly living voice, but when his own strangled scream faded, the silence seemed smothering and claustrophobic. The moon had emerged from behind cloud cover in the time that he had slept, and its thin light etched the interior of the rescue station cabin. Teeth chattering at the cold, and with his damp clothes somehow restricting his breathing, Hugh listened. There was no sound. Only the throbbing of his own heart, that internal sound seeming to pulse in his ears. He pulled himself to his feet, made his way to the window and looked out across the causeway to the island. Moonlight etched silver ridges on the waves. Distant household lights burned steadily.

It was no use. It had only been a dream. But he had to go and look.

Outside, on the platform looking down the stairs, black-silver waves lapped around the rescue station. Even if the car door had really opened, he would not be able to see beneath the surface.

"What the hell am I ...?" began Hugh out loud, but the sound of his own voice was unnerving. *What the hell am I doing?* he continued in thought. *It was just a bloody dream. I'm free of her, and I've got to keep my nerve. Just a few more hours until the tide goes out. It'll still be dark. I'll get down there when the water lowers. Get the handcuffs off. Drag the bitch out of the car – and then launch her. With any luck the tide might take her right out.*

Back in the cabin, Hugh reached for the whisky bottle and found that it was empty. With an expression of disgust, he walked to the small hole in the centre of the floor, positioned the bottle – and dropped it. Best get rid of it.

There was no splash.

Hugh gritted his teeth and stared at the hole.

Leaning forward he peered down and saw only darkness.

Anxiety was cramping his stomach again.

There should have been a splash. Why wasn't there a splash? It was only twenty feet or so down to the water.

So you didn't hear a splash? So what?

Because it's so quiet. That's why so what. It's so quiet, I should have heard that bottle hit the water.

Unless someone or something down there caught the bottle as it fell ...?

"No, no, no!" muttered Hugh, disgusted with himself and with such stupid thoughts. Taking the pencil-torch from his pocket, he shone it down the hole and saw only seawater reflected back. He remembered his previous concern about any light, no matter how small, being seen from the island – and switched off again. But he couldn't get rid of a bad feeling. Deliberately making noise, deliberately breaking the smothering silence inside the concrete cabin, he walked around in a circle, flapping his arms at his side to try and regain some warmth; now slapping one wall as he passed, then another. "No, no, *no!*"

And at the sound of his last exclamation, something somewhere made a slow and deliberate *scratch*.

Hugh froze.

After a while, he moved to the hole in the floor. Only darkness down there, and no further sound.

"Come on, come on. Pull yourself together ..."

A muffled *thump* came from somewhere outside.

Perhaps something in the water, bumping against one of the supporting pillars?

Or perhaps a first trodden tread on the steps leading up to the cabin?

Using anger to overcome fear, Hugh lunged to the cabin door and flung it open. He refused to allow the unbidden image of what he might see emerging from the water, hand-over-hand on the stair rail, to deter him. But the crash of the door almost made him scream as he threw himself onto the platform in a defiant rage.

There was nothing emerging from the water.

Nothing on the stairs.

Just the glistening black water furling around the struts of the rescue station and lapping at the semi-submerged staircase.

And now, because of the recently emerged moon, the barely visible top of the car – perhaps twelve inches below the surface.

Hugh slammed back into the cabin, realised that he was now looking for something to jam under the handle of the door and cursed himself for a stupid, bloody fool.

It's okay! It's all right! I can use this! I can use these stupid fears for when I'm rescued. Yeah, that's it. This will all convince them how distraught I am. That's because ... because ... I AM distraught. I've just killed my wife. That's a big thing. It's affecting me. Strung me out. I mean, got to be expected, hasn't it ...?

The thin, barely audible scratching sound came again.

A single, deliberate sound.

Hugh had been facing in its direction this time, and he knew where it came from. Not from the door, or the stairs outside. But from the opposite wall, somewhere outside. And this time, he screwed his eyes shut and convinced himself that it was imagination. Not the sound – which could be anything at all. A stress in the concrete wall. An iron stanchion making that sound as the water lapped against it. No, he wasn't imagining the sound. But he was imagining what that sound reminded him of, and he knew that was why he had to pull himself together.

That long, single scratching like a fingernail on a blackboard.

A sound that reminded him of Pauline's disgusting long, black fingernails.

And the thought ... the thought ...

... *pull yourself together, Hugh* ...

... that she was somehow out there, climbing up the stanchion from the water; somehow free of the car, somehow now climbing the side of the rescue station with seaweed hair hanging in her eyes and with a horrible, inhuman grace.

A shuffle and a bump from above.

She's on the roof. Oh my good God, she's reached the roof. How could she climb up there like that?

Hugh remembered her words: *"I'm a witch, Hugh – eee..."*

"Pauline!"

The sound of his own voice startled him. It was muffled and somehow bounced back at him from the concrete walls. Might his voice sound like that if he was calling out from his own coffin? The moment that he had called out, he cursed himself for his lack of control, his stupidity and his ridiculous imagination. But all of this would somehow not obviate the crawling feel of terror in his gut. Hugh backed off to the wall, staring up in the moon-etched darkness, waiting for any further sound.

Five long minutes passed – then ten.

There was no further sound.

Just the voice in Hugh's head that sounded like him, but somehow was also *not* his voice.

You haven't thought this all through, have you? Like an anxiety-laden twin, deep inside. Some horrible internal Siamese twin brother, who wouldn't shut up.

Those handcuffs had foam rubber. But she had a free hand, didn't she?

What do you mean?

Well, she'd have clawed at her wrist as the water came in. She'd have clawed with those horrible black fingernails in her panic. I bet she's clawed great gouges out of her skin in her terror, trying to get free. Not much point in your foam coverings then, is there? What's the post-mortem going to reveal? Think about the questions they're going to ask.

Shut up! Shut the hell up! Even if she had – it could be anything. She could have got jammed up against the stanchions. Or fish could have got at her, or ...

They'll find fragments of her own skin under her fingernails, Hugh. They'll put two and two together – and they'll come up with the right answer – you.

Something shuffled and slithered overhead.

Clothes still drenched in cold seawater, Hugh nevertheless broke out into a horrid sweat.

"Can't have it both ways, you bastard! She's either down there in the car right now or ..."

He couldn't bring himself to say: *Out there on the roof.*

And here's another thing. What about the handcuffs? Even if she hasn't clawed her wrist, even if there are no marks – what are you going to do with them when you've got them off?

I'll walk to the island when the tide's out. It'll still be dark. I'll find somewhere to hide them on the way.

What if someone comes before then? Maybe someone will spot the car when the water level drops. Maybe from the island, maybe from the mainland? Perhaps even from the air. There's a coastguard helicopter that flies regular patrols over the causeway. I should think they'd spot the car before anyone. Have someone down on a winch in a jiffy, don't you think? They might send someone out to rescue you before you've had a chance to get back in the car and get those handcuffs off.

Hugh felt as if he might throw up.

The logic of the voice inside could not be denied. He had to know one way or the other, had to get those cuffs. Why wait too long? The top of the car was just a few inches from the surface, and the bitch had been dead for a long time. It couldn't be too difficult to get that door open, get the cuffs off and kick her out. Even if help came quickly, he wouldn't be searched for bloody handcuffs, would he? Lots of time to get rid of them.

There was another scuffle on the roof, way off to the right.

Hugh edged across the cabin to the window. If he got down low and angled up through the top right hand corner, he was sure he'd be able to see what was up there.

It's not Pauline. How can it possibly be Pauline? She's down there, in the car. And I've got to get down there and get those cuffs off!

But he had to rationalise what was going on. Just the sight of a loose-flapping section of roofing, perhaps. A piece of wire hanging out from corroded concrete, scratching against the side of the building.

Hugh reached the window, saw the moon sailing through clouds and crouched low beneath the frame. Glancing back to where he thought the noise had come from on the ceiling, he began to crane his neck around as he rose from his haunches, straining to see if there was anything out there on the side of the building. Should he use the torch again and risk it or …?

A face leered down through the window at him.

In shock, Hugh cried out and sank to the floor.

And then laughed, heart hammering.

In the black screen behind the eyelids of his screwed-up eyes, he could still see the image of that face.

It was his own, reflected back at him by the moon – through the pane.

Somehow reassured and just wanting to look, Hugh rose quickly again and peered through the glass, cupping his hand over his eyes and straining to see.

The window exploded inwards, and something hellish clawed and gouged at his eyes.

Shrieking, Hugh fell back from the shattered aperture, shards of glass lacerating his hands, his face and his neck. When he hit the floor, the thing was still raking and clawing at his face. Writhing, screaming, Hugh ripped it away, feeling the skin of one cheek tearing like cloth; hearing the thing's own shrieking as he flung it away from him across the cabin. Heedless of the shards of glass puncturing his forearms and elbows, Hugh scrabbled on his back like a crab until he had slammed into the cabin wall. There was blood in his eyes, and a terrible squawking thing was scrabbling and thrashing on the floor, not six feet away.

Hugh cleared the blood from his eyes, shrinking back against the wall – and saw his attacker clearly for the first time.

It was a seagull.

One wing had shattered as it crashed through the window, its back broken as Hugh had clawed it from his face.

Squawking, spinning in a broken circle, it scattered feathers on the cabin floor.

Hugh could see that a broken shard of window-frame had impaled the bird right through the mid-section of its body. Its beak flapped and stabbed furiously at the concrete floor as it spun.

The scratching. The rustling and bumping on the roof. It was the bloody seagull, flying and landing. Circling – then smashing through the bloody window because it's just a stupid bloody seabird and I thought it was Pauline and I should just ...

Hugh saw the blood on his hands, became aware of the lacerations on his face and arms.

"Wring its bloody neck!"

In a moment, he was on his feet again, crunching through the broken glass underfoot – and stamping down hard, again and again, as the seagull spun and squawked and flapped. The bird pecked and jabbed at his legs, and the further rage that this drew out of Hugh drove him to ferocious endeavour. Feathers flew as he stamped, as if a pillowcase had been burst in the cabin.

When the flat of his foot connected with the bird's head, the spinning stopped.

The broken wings fluttered feebly.

And Hugh kept on stamping until the greater part of the seagull's body had become nothing but a bloody, feathered smear.

Breathless, sobbing, Hugh fell back against the rescue station wall.

No opening car door, no Pauline catching whisky bottles, or coming up the stairs or climbing on the roof.

Just a blasted seagull, and a voice in the head that was now suddenly silent.

The handcuffs ...

This time it was most definitely Hugh's voice in his head – and not the voice of his mischievous, evil twin.

Pausing only to kick the wreckage of the seagull across the cabin floor, Hugh staggered to the door and pulled it open. This time he had no anxiety about looking down the staircase, for fear of what he might see. The bitch-witch was in the car, and this time his luck was coming back on course, because the tide was on its slow way out. The moon was low now, and he could see the top of the car. Steadying himself against the cabin door, he sucked in the salt air – and started down.

The fear was gone – and the resolve with which he had first started this plan to change his life had returned.

He descended.

The water on his legs seemed even colder than before. He gritted his teeth and continued on.

"Alright Pauline, my love. Here comes Daddy …"

Waist deep now, and oh so very, very cold.

"Get it over with. Get it done. Get her out and away. And get back to the cabin."

Hugh carefully pulled out the handcuff keys from his pocket, his hand clenched tightly. After everything that had happened that night, he was not about to drop the key in the icy water and ruin his plans.

"No chance. No chance, at *all*."

Chest-deep and the cold water was taking his breath away. The sand beneath his feet hardly seemed solid at all, and he refused to allow himself the thought that he might – after all – be swept away into the darkness and suffer his wife's fate at the last. Wading, gasping, and with arms held high – he reached the car and braced his key-hand fist on the roof.

He knew that he was going to have to go under, and resolved to have this over with in an instant: One-two-three.

But first, the door.

By touch, one handed, teeth squeaking as he gritted them in the cold, he found the handle.

With anger at wanting this over and done with – Hugh twisted and yanked.

The door would not budge.

It's not locked! It's not! It's the water pressure against the door, that's all. Keeping it closed.

Hugh raised a frozen leg and braced it on the car panel to pull the side of the door. Keeping his chin above water and one fist clenched tightly around the key, he twisted and tugged at the door handle and pushed hard at the panel with his foot.

The door came open in a rushing surge of murky bubbles.

"*Hughhhh!*" said an underwater voice from the car.

Hugh fell back in the water, enveloped in the surge, his head going under. There was a roaring of the deep in his ears and now he was being sucked back to the car. He flailed and kicked, exploding from the water and sobbing for air. His feet found the sandy bottom again and he jabbed both feet down hard, feeling soft purchase and flailing again to regain his balance as the water-surge eddied.

"Not her ... not ... not ..."

He was not going to lose control again.

There had been air in the car when he pulled open the door. Not much, but some. And the air rushing out, together with the water rushing in to completely fill those small crevices in the automobile, had made the sound; that *glooping* sound which had been so much like Pauline calling out his name.

Hugh pushed back. The door had semi-closed again, but when he pulled it this time, it came all the way easily back to its hinges. The car rocked gently on the sandy bottom. He paused only briefly, feeling the reassuring metal of the handcuff key clenched in his hand. He was gripping it so tightly it was cutting into his skin. Only then did he feel the sting of the salt water on his hands, neck and face from the shattered cabin window. That pain was meaningless. Once this part of the plan was over, he was almost ... *hah! Home and dry.*

Hugh looked down into the car – and could see nothing.

He thought of the pencil-torch but when he felt for it, the torch was gone. Probably lost when he fell back in the water.

Might not have worked anyway.

This would have to be done by touch.

Easy enough to find the steering wheel, and the manacle.

Pauline was in the passenger seat. With luck he might not feel anything but her arm and hand. If he felt anything else, he could bear it.

Hugh leaned in, one arm grasping for the wheel – the other reaching for a hand or a lock.

He steeled himself, ducked his head under the water to get better purchase, dared to open his eyes – and could see the shape of something.

Round, like the steering wheel – but blurred and indistinct.

He pushed inward and forward – reaching.

Something came fully into view before him.

The bubbles that exploded in that flooded space came from his own mouth.

*

The car was spotted by the coastguard helicopter on its first early morning sweep, the vehicle's fenders catching the rising sun.

Coastguard patrol had its station two miles away and responded immediately to the report, with a patrol car en route within minutes. The helicopter circled but could not ascertain whether the car had occupants, not being able to put down on the causeway until the tide had completely gone out and because the vehicle was covered in seaweed mess and encrustation.

Seawater furled around the wheels of the patrol car as it made its way slowly down the causeway.

It stopped behind the stranded vehicle. Bert Shefter and Paul Sawtell climbed out simultaneously.

There hadn't been a drowning on this stretch these last two years, but with thirty years experience between them both men had never got used to the stupidity of some people who simply ignored every warning sign you could put in their way; constantly marvelling at the lack of any common sense when it came to cars and large bodies of water. Why the hell would anyone want to take a risk like driving on a causeway at night?

"Hello up there in the station!" called Shefter.

When there was no answer, they exchanged glances – and started wearily towards the car.

The back windscreen was completely obscured by seaweed.

Sawtell reached the driver's side, wiped away a clump of sea-crap and, despite his expectation, training and experience, recoiled from what he saw inside.

"Jesus!"

Shefter moved to the front of the car and saw it too, as seaweed slithered from the front windscreen. He hung his head, sighed and looked briefly out to sea. "Better get on the radio."

"Suicide?"

"Yes, I think so. My god, what a way to go ..."

From the passenger seat, Pauline's dead arm was wrapped around Hugh's neck; hugging him in a close embrace. Her face, obscured by tangled hair, was squashed up against his cheek. Both men had the same thought and struggled to forget it. It looked not so much as if she was kissing him, more like she had been trying to eat him.

In the driving seat, Hugh sat bolt upright, eyes open.

But the crabs and fishes had visited.

Those empty sockets gazed straight ahead through the sea-smeared windscreen, his face a mask of horror.

"God," said Shefter, bracing his hands on the hood, forcing himself to look back inside. "They must have really loved each other."

When Sawtell searched his face for further meaning, Shefter nodded down to Hugh's lap.

They had handcuffed themselves together.

THE KRAKEN WAKES

Boaters and bathers are rarely endangered by Britain's native sea-life.

The waters off the United Kingdom contain a swarming multitude of creatures, but most of them are relatively benign; in fact, given the British population's voracious appetite for seafood, it is a far bigger risk for the fishes to come inshore than it is for us. Of course that isn't the whole story. The Portuguese man-o-war is a large species of jellyfish with a severe sting, which, though not native to the northwest Atlantic, inhabits the Northern Gulf Stream, and so during stormy periods can sometimes be found along Britain's western coast. Sharks, the most maligned of all sea creatures, only tend to be seasonal visitors to Britain, and for the most part these are the relatively harmless basking sharks and blue sharks. Hammerheads have occasionally been sighted, but extremely rarely, while these too have no interest in attacking large prey like humans. In fact, according to the statistics, only two assaults by sharks have ever been recorded off the British Isles, and neither of these had a fatal outcome.

On the whole therefore, you can paddle off Britain's beaches and swim in Britain's seas with a sense of almost complete safety. There is absolutely nothing down there to give you cause for alarm.

Nine times out of ten.

In the 1860s, southern English newspapers were filled with stories concerning a Channel Island fisherman's chance encounter with a truly horrific beast, which, if it occurred today would likely decimate the local tourist industry. The unfortunate fisherman had been out in his boat alone in the bay of Brecqhou, which is part of the island of Sark but in modern times falls under the jurisdiction of Guernsey. While the fisherman was reeling in his catch, the tide took his small vessel close to the mouth of a cave from out of which there came a sudden immense turbulence. The fisherman almost over-balanced and fell into the water. In his struggles to stay aboard, he didn't notice the ghastly shape now unravelling beneath his boat – a second later he was assailed from all sides by a mass of writhing, fleshy tentacles, which onlookers described as being almost 40 feet in length. The fisherman had no chance of survival. The gigantic octopus, which he had disturbed, pulled both himself and his boat beneath the surface and neither were ever seen again.

So goes the sensational story, though even detailed research in the modern day is unable to turn up an exact date for this event or a name for the tragic victim. However, at the time it was widely known about and discussed. French novelist Victor Hugo was so impressed by the story that he travelled to Brecqhou and witnessed the creature for himself, as it swam across the bay. He later included the incident in his 1866 novel, 'Toilers of the Sea', setting it in Guernsey and describing a fierce battle between his hero, Gilliat, and a giant octopus, though in this case the human triumphed.

There seems little doubt that such an event actually did happen, though it is wreathed in mystery. The terrifying multi-tentacled devil of the deep has been a staple of horror and fantasy fiction throughout history. The legendary kraken is the ultimate marine nightmare, primarily because we know it is based on truth. Early Scandinavian stories about the ship-devouring horrors Hafgufa and Lyngbakr are not just myths; they clearly relate to instances when early seafarers ran into trouble with Architeuthis, the Giant Squid, though this aggressive carnivore, whose maximum tentacle length has been measured to at least 43 feet, tends to be a denizen of extreme depth, which explains why encounters with it are thankfully so rare. In general we also have little to fear from Enteroctopus dofleini, the Giant Pacific Octopus, some of whose tentacles have been observed to reach 23 feet (though this would be unusual – most members of the species are significantly smaller). Whereas the Giant Squid is rarely a threat to humanity because it exists in the deep ocean, the Giant Octopus dwells in coastal waters and not necessarily at great depth, but it is not a belligerent animal. There have been occasions when divers have got too close and have been attacked because the creature was frightened, but the danger here has mostly involved the octopus damaging or yanking away the diver's breathing apparatus rather than because it was trying to eat him.

All of this makes the dreadful incident at Brecqhou even more baffling.

These days the Channel Islands, an archipelago of British Crown Dependencies not officially part of the United Kingdom but often regarded as the most southerly point of the British Isles, are a holiday haven and host hundreds of thousands of visitors every summer: swimming, snorkelling, yachting, scuba-diving and waterskiing are all hugely popular past-times, which means that the Common Octopus, who lives in abundance in this region, is regularly seen and photographed. But none of its larger cousins have been reported, and certainly there have been no other attacks.

It is not impossible that what happened off Guernsey back in the 1860s did not involve a Giant Octopus, but a Giant Squid, which had somehow migrated from out of the Atlantic into relatively shallow waters. This has happened before – in 1775, a dead squid reputedly over 60 feet in length was washed up on the Isle of Bute, and in fact, Victor Hugo's monster, which he initially described as shooting through the water like "a closed umbrella without a handle", sounds much more like a squid than an octopus.

So on the whole there is nothing to fear. These creatures exist in nature. Science recognises and understands them. And they only appear off the British seaside once in a blue moon. Bathers and paddlers need not be concerned. Nine times out of ten.

THE MAGICIAN KELSO DENNETT
Stephen Volk

All tricks, all illusions, funnel down to a few basic misdirections, at the end of the day. The majority of it is the patter, the *spiel*, the storytelling. The gift of the gab. Taking someone on a journey, but a journey that goes somewhere they don't expect, in a way they didn't expect it.

I was born in Seagate and I've lived here all my life. It's strange that people flock here for holidays, or used to, and used to have smiles on their faces and happiness in their hearts at the thought of going somewhere different. To me Seagate was never different, never fun-loving or exotic in any way, never a place to get away from it all and have a good time. It was simply my home. I suppose at times I've envied the little families I saw inside the ice cream parlour on the sea front, or sitting with their fish and chips in newspaper on the benches facing the sea. But to be honest most of the time I thought they were stupid for thinking this place was in any way special just because there were sticks of rock with its name going down the middle. It certainly wasn't special to me. It was a dump.

The fun fair I remember being seedy ever since my childhood is derelict now, segregated by a massive chain-link fence and guard dogs, its name – *Wonderland* – nothing but a sick joke. The only people who have 'fun' there are the pill-heads and drug dealers whose scooters whine around the Esplanade from mini-roundabout to mini-roundabout touting their wares. Up on Cliffe Road a whole run of grand Victorian-era hotels lie abandoned, semi-restored by property developers who inevitably ran out of cash.

Sometimes you see a light on inside one at night time and wonder if it's a solitary owner living under a bare light bulb eating beans on toast, or a bunch of junkie squatters shoving needles in their veins. This is the image of the resort now, not candy floss and deck chairs, but inflatable li-los flapping in a bitter wind outside beach-side shops that get more money from selling lottery tickets.

When they announced a big, new, posh art gallery was going to be built at the old fish market near the harbour, a lot of London people argued it would bring much-needed prosperity to the town. Predictably, the locals didn't want it. In fact they gathered hundreds of signatures on a petition about the loss of a car park where old ladies came in coaches to buy cups of tea and go home again. But that was typical. Seagaters have no interest in the outside world. They just want to keep all the things that made a crappy 1950s seaside resort crappy, even though it's dying on its feet. Anyway, the art gallery happened, with a bistro-style café offering Mediterranean stuffed peppers and risottos of the day. Meanwhile the most artistic thing you were likely to see two streets away on the High Street was a wino coughing his guts up outside an amusement arcade or pound shop.

Sorry for not having a rose-tinted view of the great British seaside town, but I'm not the Tourist Information Centre. I live here. And I've spent all my life listening to people telling me I'm lucky – I'm not.

I guess when I heard that Kelso Dennett was coming, I thought that might change.

And it did.

*

I work in a hotel, though I don't have any professional qualifications. When my grandmother died, my dad had enough money to give up teaching, which he hated, and invest in a hotel, the White Hill – two AA stars, fuck knows how – on one of the narrow streets off Quayne Square leading steeply down to the sea. That's where I was born and that's my day job, setting the tables for breakfast and dinner. Serving hard, crusty rolls with watery, micro-waved soup so hot it gives you mouth blisters. My father's made a profession of being pleased with himself. What he has to be smug about I have no idea.

What is he? The owner of a shitty hotel in a shitty little town, and there he is, sounding the gong to call people down for dinner like it's the Ritz? What a loser. Still, he's happy running his little empire, and I've seen that gleam in his eye when he tells people he's fully booked. It's power, that's all that is. It's pathetic, but in the present economic meltdown, in this armpit of the universe, there's precious little to give you any feeling of power over anything.

The power to change. To make things better. It's always seemed almost impossible. Yet there was one person in the world who was regularly telling us that *anything* was possible. That 'the impossible' was just a mindset to be overcome.

And suddenly, according to *The Advertiser*, he was coming to Seagate – to perform his most outrageous stunt ever.

*

Everyone knew that Kelso Dennett was a Seagate boy. Or, more accurately, from The Links – which, I remember from my childhood was the 'rough part' of town, which was synonymous with the poor part. You didn't want to mix with boys from the Links, my mum used to say. They were always kids who used to smoke in the street, and that said it all. To her mind, anyway.

It was also well known that the TV star's return to his home town was being touted as something of a gesture of thanks to the residents. Though the fact he said he was looking forward to it either meant he had lived in blissful ignorance of how much the place had gone tits-up (to put it mildly) or that the sentiment was complete PR bullshit to get the locals on side. After all, he had a reputation as a master manipulator. He was hardly going to rubbish the place. He was too much of a canny operator for that. He wouldn't have done it in Seagate if there wasn't something in it for him. As everyone who watched his television shows knew, there was always more than meets the eye. That was the attraction. That, and the prospect of real physical or mental harm.

Within days of the official announcement, the production company took out ads looking for runners. No prior experience necessary, but good local knowledge a bonus. I reckoned I was in with a chance, and my dad could find a temporary replacement or get stuffed, so I applied and got an interview. The form I had to fill in was about thirty pages long.

"Nick Ambler." My name.

"28." My age.

"Single." My status.

The girl with the razor-sharp marmalade fringe asked if I had a relationship.

"Sort of. A girlfriend. But only sort of." She asked her name and I said Cyd, spelt that way. "After Cyd Charisse. The dancer? *Singing in the Rain* and shit?"

She nodded in a vacant, prosperous kind of way and see-sawed her expensive roll-point pen as she asked the all-important question about local knowledge.

"I have that." I shrugged. "I've lived here all my life."

"Then you're perfect." She brightened, nodding again. "Nice town."

I thought, "You haven't lived here."

She showed a lot of teeth but was pleasant enough, though the guy next to her, black guy – I mean *really* black, like ink – didn't say a word. But they must've liked me, because later, in The Bear, I got a text saying I'd got it.

The teaser ads were already going out between programmes, so it was no secret this was going to be a *Kelso Dennett Special*, as they called them now. This one, leaving very little to the imagination, and full of succinct, if dubious, promise, was called *Buried Alive*. (No prizes for guessing its central premise.)

The magician was planning to be buried in a wooden coffin six feet under on the beach at Seagate – his most daring stunt to date – with no means of escape or communication, and no access to food or drink for the entire period. He would be sealed in the casket and that would be it, until they dug him up forty days and forty nights later.

As soon as they'd heard about it, certain corners of the media were, predictably, incendiary with outrage. It was shocking, yes. Audacious, yes. Mad, yes. But, frankly, you'd hardly expect anything less. Pushing boundaries – not only physical boundaries, but boundaries of what was acceptable as popular entertainment – was his stock-in-trade. 'Going too far' had rapidly become his business model.

Previous 'specials,' which had involved apparent decapitation, invisibility, and even a poltergeist haunting, always caused controversy. It was almost part of the Kelso Dennett 'brand' – but now there was a new element, the element not just of jeopardy, or of harm, but of death.

From the moment it was announced there was a great deal of conjecture as to whether what he was attempting to do, and survive, was even medically possible. Was consummate showman Kelso Dennett really simply tarting up weary old illusions in new clothes (always the accusation), or genuinely (as he claimed in this case) forcing his physiological and psychological endurance to the absolute limit? It was, of course, impossible to tell.

Certainly, as a TV viewer, it was always hard to know exactly what methods he was using to achieve his mindboggling effects. You definitely couldn't trust what he *said* he was doing. His sometimes wild, irrelevant gestures or pseudoscientific preambles may be just that – irrelevant. And just because he said he wasn't using stooges, did that really mean he wasn't? His previous compulsive extravaganzas had relied on not just trickery but the use of techniques such as hypnosis and suggestibility – or did they? The paranormal waffle might just be window dressing for a gag no more complex than Chase the Lady or Tommy Cooper's bottle/glass routine.

Was the poor guy who thought he'd been in a time machine, or the couple who were convinced a serial killer was hunting them down, actually in on the joke all along? You always sensed that your eyes, and ears, were on the wrong thing – which was exactly where Kelso Dennett wanted them.

*

My job was to keep an eye on the assembled crowds standing at the rail on the Promenade – to keep them at bay. 'At bay' is probably too strong a phrase. But I had a Hi-Viz vest and a walkie-talkie which kept me in direct contact with the Third Assistant Director in case some of the locals wanted to get a closer look at the set before the team wanted them to. I watched them setting up a white tent on the beach above the high-tide mark. The crew were busy in their various capacities, but I had little idea what most of them did. There seemed to be a lot of quilted windbreakers, a lot of pointing, a lot of coffee in polystyrene cups, and a lot of talk.

The production company, for their own convenience, were putting me up in the hotel where they were based. I told my dad my shifts would be weird so wouldn't be back to lay breakfast or wait at tables for dinner, and I squared it with Cyd I might not be around much too. In view of what happened, that was just as well, on my part. You might even think it was forward planning. It wasn't. I wasn't planning anything. All I was planning was earning some money.

*

I watched them digging the grave with a JCB. It wasn't like digging into soil, and the sand was dry, but eventually they managed to get a fairly good, rectangular hole without the walls crumbling or it filling with water. For some reason the police were in attendance, and so were the fire brigade. Possibly to do with Health and Safety. Probably to do with just seeing themselves on TV. We were going live at 10pm and everything was stressed to the hilt.

On the far side of the beach I saw somebody talking to the man who did the donkey rides. Whether they were asking him to get into shot or get out of shot I couldn't tell. In the end he just stood there.

The crane shot went up beside me so that the crowd, which had now increased to several hundreds if not thousands on the Promenade and down the length of the pier, could see a high angle view of themselves on the big screens erected on the beach.

A second camera panned along the route of a hearse down the High Street. Security men parted the throng to allow it to drive down a slipway to a flat bed of concrete normally kept clear for use by the lifeboat crew and ambulances. Five undertakers got out and I was surprised to see that they weren't actors but the family firm that had operated in town for as long as I could remember – adding a macabre dimension of authenticity. Four acted as pallbearers, sliding a pale teak coffin from the back, hoisting it to their shoulders and following the fifth with complete solemnity towards the grave. The dignity of the enactment seemed to make people forget they were watching an entertainment programme and the strangely reverential silence that fell continued as the undertakers lowered the coffin onto a rustling purple tarpaulin laid flat beside the grave, then stood aside with their heads bowed. The sense of anticipation was electric.

Similarly followed by street cameras, a black Mercedes with tinted windows glided through town and descended the slipway. A chauffeur opened the back door and Kelso Dennett stepped out – fashionably mixed race, distinctive shaved head. Small. Tiny. I hadn't seen him in the flesh before, but it was weird. I've heard people famous from TV have a presence when you meet them in real life, a kind of vivid familiarity because we feel we know them, we're intimate with them, I don't know, or maybe it was the make-up or the lighting – but he seemed to *glow*. His skin seemed literally *golden* against the black zippered tracksuit one of the tabloids later said gave the proceedings a "dark Olympics" vibe. Anyway, the crowd went mental. If I didn't have a job to do, I think I might've gone mental too.

Calmly taking a microphone from a production assistant, he thanked everyone for coming and said in a high, surprisingly boyish voice he'd do his utmost to reward them for their faith and their patience. He faltered a little, very slightly giving away his nerves (unless that was part of the act), finishing by saying he got "succour and strength from their love and their prayers." He almost made it sound like a prayer itself.

Then, according to the voice-over, he was off into the graveside Winnebago "to mentally prepare for the greatest challenge of his magical career."

While he did, and while forensic experts from the Navy and RAF examined the coffin inside and out, a pre-prepared VT about the Victorian fear of premature burial played to the gathered fans, with an obligatory nod to Edgar Allan Poe. It quoted from a hundred-year-old article in the *British Medical Journal* about human hibernation, in which it was said Russian peasants in the Pskov Governance survived famine "since time immemorial" by sleeping for half the year in a condition they called *lotska*, while James Braid (father of hypnotherapy) wrote in his 1850 book *Observations of Trance* that he had seen, in the presence of the English Governor Sir Claude Wade, an Indian fakir buried alive for several months before being exhumed in full health and consciousness. More recent findings came from a 1998 paper in *Physiology* which described a yogi going into a state of "deep bodily rest and lowered metabolism" with "no ill effects of tachycardia or hyperpnea" for ten hours. Another study, on a sixty-year-old adept named Satyamurti, recorded that he emerged from confinement in a sealed underground pit after eight days in a state of "Samadhi" or deep meditation, during which time electrocardiogram results showed his heart rate fell below the "measurably sensitivity of the recording instruments."

Kelso Dennett, in ten-foot high close-up, then gave chapter and verse on the techniques perfected by such mystics and gurus to cut down their bodily activity to the frighteningly bare minimum. The essence of hatha yoga, he said, is the maximization of physical health as the necessary basis for self-realisation – the purification and strengthening of the body as the means to effectively channel powerful but subtle forces (*prana*) – in this case, to slow the processes down to an extremely low rate, and so achieve a state of physiological suspension. "But this terminology and classification is multi-layered and elusive – not easily open to standard observation and measurement. The concepts are far from being embraced into mainstream biology and science. Some might say that makes them *primitive* or *superstitious*, but turning it the other way round, maybe science has got a lot to learn." A tiny light reflected in his dark irises. "My hope is to replicate these physical states – to hover on the very brink between life and death – and test them to the ultimate limit of what is humanly possible. I have prepared for this event not just for months, but for years. Perhaps even my whole life. Now I believe I am ready to successfully attempt it. But do the experts?"

As we were about to be told, clearly not.

The medical professionals interviewed were unanimous that the enterprise was foolhardy to the point of insane recklessness. As if to confirm this, we saw footage of Kelso Dennett training for long periods in a sensory deprivation tank – but only for as long as *eleven* days, after which he sounded the alarm and was lifted out, gasping, dripping, shielding his eyes from the camera light. This time there would be no alarm button. No microphone. Nothing. For *forty* days.

The coffin having been pronounced tamper-free, a disembodied voice asked the crowd to remain absolutely quiet when the star emerged from the trailer so as not to disturb his intense level of concentration. The murmuring drained to a complete hush. He emerged barefoot and stripped to the waist, distinctive sleeve of tattoos up his left arm, pentagram on his right shoulder, astrological symbols inked all over his back, pure muscle, but wiry, a runner's physique, wearing only a pair of black lycra shorts.

A woman wearing a fur coat, tight jeans, thigh-length boots and shades threw her arms round him, and he kissed her. I saw she didn't want to let go of his hand. It looked as though she genuinely didn't want him to go through with it. She seemed upset but trying to control it. He hugged her and held her by the shoulders for a moment and looked into her eyes and she obediently backed away, tucking lariats of blonde hair behind her ears.

Everyone knew who she was. His wife, Annabelle Fox – most famous from a fish fingers commercial when she was five years old. Not done much since, other than date famous boyfriends, rock stars or actors, from what I could tell.

We waited patiently in the freezing wind as the supervising medical team fitted him up to their biofeedback machines, attaching electrodes wired to their contraptions, the EEG and ECG. Immediately flickering wavy lines appeared on the big screens and we could hear the magician's amplified heartbeat coming from the gigantic speakers. We were told it was forty beats per minute. A normal basal heart rate is sixty to a hundred. Under sixty is called bradycardia and can be dangerous, but it's not unusual for an athlete to show a normal rate as low as forty – and Kelso Dennett was certainly as fit as an athlete.

He put his hands together over his chest in an attitude of prayer and gave a miniscule nod to the crowd, Hindu fashion. He climbed into the coffin and lay flat as the undertakers screwed the lid back into place.

The crowd remained silent and still as the pallbearers lowered it into the bespoke grave. Sand was first piled in by a bulldozer, then flattened by spades – an irrationally or perhaps rationally disturbing experience for those of us watching, resembling as it did some laboriously drawn-out execution in some far-off barbaric fundamentalist dictatorship. Later on some bright spark had the theory that there was an escape hatch to a fully-fitted underground apartment kitted with plentiful food and drink, though how a 'fully fitted apartment' could have been constructed under the beach of a popular English holiday resort without anybody noticing is anybody's guess.

Barely seconds after the spot was marked by a wooden cross, the magician's face appeared back on the massive screens, showing us in a pre-recorded message that he had written something down and put it in a sealed envelope, handed to the

Mayor of Seagate to place in a safe deposit box in a bank of his choice.

Close-up. "This envelope contains something vitally important – but it must only be revealed when the coffin has been removed from the grave after forty days and forty nights. Not before." Finally, and movingly, he said he believed he could perform the superhuman task he has set for himself, but Fate might have other plans – and that if he failed, he wanted his family to know that he loved them very much. "And Annabelle, what can I say? You are my rock, my sun, my moon. I will see you in forty days and forty nights, my darling, or I will see you in the afterlife. God bless you all."

The end credits rolled – no music – as the camera tracked back from the grave, cross-fading to the ECG.

The woman with wind-tossed hair watched. Eyes behind sunglasses. Cheeks white. Lipstick red.

That night, when the crowds had dispersed and the production crew had drinks and canapés on the beach to celebrate, she left early. It must've been quite an ordeal for her, so I wasn't that surprised. It must've been a strange sort of thing to celebrate, if you were her. I watched her cross the beach alone, leaving the penumbra of the television lights, her husband's heart still pulsing with an even monotony in the air. When I went back to the hotel, there was no sign of her.

*

The next morning the cross was at an angle. Messages had been left there. Flowers, predictably. I guess security let them through the cordon. A trail of thin wires led from the grave to the trailer where the scientists had their equipment. The bass throb of the magician's heart was still beating loud from the speakers. It had become slower over the first twenty-four hours, imperceptibly at first, the number in the corner of the screen flashing thirty beats per minute – technically well into bradycardia. Near it I saw Annabelle Fox drinking one of the coffees in polystyrene cups. She was surrounded by members of the production team, but she looked terribly alone.

Eventually I plucked up courage to sit next to her in the hotel bar, because nobody else did. She didn't know my name, but knew I was one of the runners. I'd brought her those coffees enough times. She said she thought she needed coffee right now.

"I love his shows." I ignored the fact she was tipsy. "What a great man."

She laughed. "Nothing is what it seems." She could see I didn't know why she said that, so changed the subject. Or did she? "You know, people talk about *charisma*, but they don't really know what charisma means. Charisma is power. The power to make the other person, the weaker person, to do exactly what you want."

"Is it?"

"Look at Aleister Crowley. You've heard of Aleister Crowley? Frater Perdurabo. Ipsissimus. Master Therion." I tried not to look blank. "Magick with a 'k'. The Great Beast 666. Crowley wasn't particularly attractive. Pretty fucking far from it. He was a repulsive, pot-bellied old goat – but he was *charismatic* in spades." Her eyelids were heavy. "He'd say to a friend, 'Watch this.' And he'd follow a person down the street, make them faint to the floor by just *willing* them to. Just by staring at the back of their head. That's *real* magic. Through Crowley – through Thelema. Tantric rituals... Sex magic..." She looked at me lopsidedly. "My husband is really, *really* interested in sex." Then she held me with a steady gaze, rolling ice cubes in her glass. "You're interested in sex, right?"

"Yes." I said without thinking.

She rose and swayed and pronounced the need to go to bed. My room was on the same floor as hers and I said I was tired too. By the time we got out of the lift I wasn't sure what I'd heard or why I'd heard it.

"Do you want to come in for a ..." She paused before the last word. "... chat? I was going to say 'drink', but I think I've had more than enough of that."

Immediately I was through the door she started to undress and so did I. The bedside lights were on and neither of us switched them off. I told her I'd never felt so hard before. She laughed and pressed me down on my back, and knelt beside me and slipped a Durex over me with her fingertips. I came almost immediately but she kept me erect, a smile on her face the whole time. We switched positions and I felt her cold hands stroking my lower back then gripping hard as I drove in. She covered her mouth so that nobody could hear, but I snatched her hand away and held her lips with mine until we ran out of breath.

*

Afterwards I lay inside her and said I wanted to lie that way all night. She laughed like it was a childish but nice thing to imagine. Her skin burned against mine, but her hands and feet were like ice from a day on the beach. The soft thrum of his heartbeat touched the window panes as we lay in each other's arms.

She said she didn't like hotel rooms. They made her a bit crazy. I grinned, saying you can do crazy things in hotel rooms. She said Kelso liked the anonymity. The fact nobody could tell anything about you because a hotel room contained none of your belongings. None of your history.

"He doesn't like people knowing things about him. He's a bit paranoid like that. He's worried about the *paparazzi*, yes. It's enough to make anyone think they're being watched, bugged, hacked. It's a terrible feeling. But it's more than the Press, to him. They're not the enemy any more. *Everybody's* the enemy. *I'm* the enemy. He likes me to stay indoors as much as possible, or know exactly where I am every second of the day."

"Why?"

"He thinks I might give away his secrets."

"What secrets?"

"All kinds."

She went and crouched at the mini bar, a sprig of damp pubic hair visible in the gap between her buttocks. She returned with shorts of whisky emptied into tea cups from the hospitality tray.

"When we were on honeymoon in Rome we woke up one morning and the bells were chiming in St Peter's Square. We'd asked for breakfast to be delivered to our room, and pastries and coffee arrived piping hot. He got up, stark naked, and put crumbs on the windowsill. I asked him what he was doing. He said he could control which bird would peck it up. I giggled, but he said he meant it. He came back and sat cross-legged on the bed next to me. I waited for seconds, minutes. Then he smiled at me and clicked his fingers and right at that moment – that *exact* moment, a bird landed and started eating up the crumbs."

"What first attracted you to millionaire Kelso Dennett?" I ran kisses up her arm.

She smiled. "Maybe his – manual dexterity…" She took my hand and placed it over her private parts, guiding my middle finger towards her clitoris.

"Obviously he likes to be in control."

"That's what magic is. The ultimate control of the external world."

"Well," I said. "He can't control you now."

I arched over to kiss her on the lips, but she stiffened.

"I think you should go." She held my face in her hands. "I'm enjoying this too much."

"So am I."

"I mean it."

She got off the bed and put her dressing gown on, pointlessly, not moving as she watched me dress.

"What's your name again?"

"Nick."

"Nick, this never happened."

"Pff. Gone," I whispered before closing the door.

My own room was significantly colder than hers, so I turned up the thermostat. My mind was racing. I knew I wouldn't sleep so I put on the bedside light to read, but the bulb was dead. I switched it off and on again, mystified, because it hadn't been dead earlier.

*

I saw Kelso's wife again at breakfast but she didn't acknowledge me with so much as a glance. I also saw her later in the catering wagon – a converted double-decked bus. I wanted to sit with her, in fact I had a fantasy of touching her up under the table, or her touching me up – but that was impossible. There was no way any of these people could find out what had happened between us. What was I thinking? That she would call a meeting? Announce it from the rooftops?

I looked at the rota. I stood at my allotted station, by the coin-operated telescope overlooking the sweep of the bay.

The grave had almost lost any delineation against the rest of the sand. You wouldn't have known where it was, if not for the circle of footsteps around the small cross, the fence of plastic ribbon attached to iron rods, the trailer containing the equipment, and of course the video projection screens and tall, angled spotlights, the kind you often pass on motorways when they have road works at night.

People gathered occasionally in small groups, pointing or taking snapshots or videos with their camcorders. Then they'd move on, or linger, sometimes not moving or speaking. Typical British holidaymakers with their anorak hoods up, peering around like meerkats, not wondering for a second about the metaphysics of life and death, wondering where to go to get a two course lunch for under a tenner.

As well as the channel's news programme, which gave it a minute slot every day, there were teams from most of the terrestrial and cable networks, a few from America – where Kelso was big – and Japan, where he was even bigger. Then there was the locked-off CCTV cam pointed at the grave itself, uploading to the Internet on a dedicated website, buriedalive.co.uk, where you could watch 24/7. The fact there was very little to watch was irrelevant. It was already going viral on twitter, with endless comments and retweets – ("OMG loving @buriedalive"; "KD #completenutterorgenius?"; "Cant watch 2 spookie"; "Diggin the Kels") – the numbers exceeding even the broadcasters' high expectations. It was quickly obvious that this wasn't just 'event' television, it was a national event, period.

The tall lights came on as the sunlight faded. The slippery rocks where Dad and I used to catch crabs reflected a shiny glow. The men in Hi-Viz vests protected the twelve-foot cordon around the grave, but they let through a little girl in a sky blue parka and matching wellies who stuck her little windmill in the ground next to the flowers before running back to her mum and dad.

*

When my shift was over I went to the hotel bar. Kelso's wife wasn't there. I waited. She didn't appear.

I went to my room. Drifting to sleep, I started to hear scratching, like a small animal trapped in the cavity wall behind the head board. A bird but bigger than a bird. Perhaps a squirrel. Wings or paws scurried as if desperate to escape. I was annoyed because I knew it would keep me awake. Obviously something had fallen down the chimney and got trapped – then I heard a sudden bang, like a door slamming, and it stopped completely.

I pulled on my jeans and went out into the corridor. Nobody else was out there. Surely the person in the next room must've heard it too? I raised a fist to knock on the room next to me, but I could hear the TV on. They were listening to the live coverage of *Buried Alive*. I looked down the corridor to the far end. For some reason I expected Kelso's wife to be standing there, but she wasn't.

*

The next day I saw her overlooking the beach. I went up to her and leaned on the rail beside her. I wondered if she felt guilty and might move away, but she didn't. It was almost as if I wasn't there. Her eyes were fixed on the circus – by which I mean, her husband's grave.

"It's getting to people," I said. "Anticipation."

"That's what it's all about." She took a deep drag on her cigarette. I wondered if it warmed her. "Will people lose interest, d'you think?"

"They adore him. Look at the viewing figures."

"Things can change."

"Can they?"

"Have you read the newspapers today?"

"They can't get enough of him."

She exhaled a short, sharp breath. "You know what the papers are like. They build people up and up, then they like to knock them down. He's a cash cow right now, yes. But they could turn against him without batting a fucking eyelid." She sucked the cigarette like an addict.

"Are you afraid?"

"For him? Yes, of course. Always. But he knows what he's doing. He *always* knows what he's doing, don't worry. He plans it to the nth degree. You have no idea. He leaves nothing to chance, my husband the magician. He knows everything, absolutely everything that can happen, and will happen."

"That's what I mean. Does that scare you, ever?"

"What do you think?"

She crushed dead ash on the balustrade and brushed it off into the wind, her hair flickering and lashing like the torn shreds of a flag. I heard a rasping voice in my walkie-talkie and switched it off.

"The woman from *Hello* magazine is waiting to do an interview. She says she waited all day yesterday, with her photographer. The office are hassling me to hassle you, but if you don't want to do it, don't do it. Fuck them. I'll tell them you're not feeling well."

"Thank you."

Over the next few days I decided not to intrude into her space. In my spare hours I slept or when I couldn't sleep I watched old DVDs of Kelso Dennett's magic shows: *Bamboozler* and *Scaremongering* and *MindF****. You probably remember them all. I know I do. The man who wakes up to find all the doors and windows of his house have been bricked in. The girl made to think she can bend spoons. Even more astonishingly, the guy who wakes up in what he thinks is the past, thirty years ago, and meets *himself* as a child, having been hypnotised to think a lookalike boy actor was literally him.

This one set the tone for the outrageously ambitious and controversial 'specials' to come, some of the greatest 'did you see?' TV moments of all time. *Abduction* – inducing a UFO abduction experience. *Guillotine* – inviting an audience who believes in the death penalty to witness a beheading. *Invisible* – making a young woman think she is invisible for a day. *Sleepwalkers* – getting a dozen people to sleepwalk at exactly the same time, on the same night – making them climb onto roofs across the London skyline – a stunning image caught by a helicopter camera as the sun came up. In the minds of many it was the culmination of the use of technology and sense of 'event' that had become Kelso Dennett's hallmark.

Then there was the infamous Easter special, *Crucifixion*. Not hard to see why Christian groups were immediately up in arms. Badgered by the Press, the magician explained he simply wanted to find out whether the experience was as truly transcendental as some claimed. No slight to any religion intended. Nevertheless, lobby groups found a loophole in the broadcaster's charter and the transmission was cancelled. It was rumoured that he went to Philippines anyway, going through with the ritual without the presence of cameras. However there *were* cameras at Heathrow on his return, to film him – as I saw now – getting off the plane, hobbling, and with bandages round his hands.

I paused the picture as the phone rang. It was Annabelle's voice asking me to come to her room. I left the DVD in the player and went. She was already naked and her first kiss as she captured me in it tasted strongly of white wine. She almost gnawed off my lips, tore out my tongue. I wanted to do it the same way as before but she had different ideas and got onto the bed on all fours.

As we lay afterwards in our salty sweat, I asked her how she'd got the long, puckered scar I'd felt across her shoulder blade. She said her mother always told the story that when she was born she shot out so quickly she hit the bed post.

"Unlikely."

"All right then. My father said I was an angel come down to earth. And that's where they had to cut off my wings so that nobody would notice. You prefer my father's version?"

"What about the other wing?"

She laughed and kissed my bare chest. I thought I could hear my own heart beating, but it wasn't. She didn't need to say anything.

I sat up and pulled on my socks and underpants. The sliding door of the closet was half open. Beyond my bisected reflection I could see a row of Kelso Dennett's suits on hangers, all black, all identical. Black patent leather shoes arranged perfectly on the floor.

"Nick? Stay."

*

On sentry duty, I looked down at the grave, a mandala-type geometry incised around it by a myriad of footprints, now. The print place in Church Street had the enterprising thought of printing *Buried Alive* T-shirts and were doing a roaring trade from a stall next to the fishing boats and cockle vendor. Groupies descended, some booking into B&Bs for the whole forty days. Others, the vultures of the tabloids for instance, seemed to be hovering in morbid expectation, eager for him to fail, to die. I thought about him dying too. I thought about him lying in complete darkness in that coffin under the sand and not coming out. I thought about that a lot.

When I passed a camera crew one day, a female student from Israel was saying, "People are tweeting he's dead, but he isn't. That's just evil. He's not dead. He wouldn't leave us like that. He'll come back, I know he will."

*

On day twelve I asked permission to take Annabelle away from the set. I said I thought she needed it, and they bought that. They gave me petty cash to get a hire car. We drove somewhere, only about twenty miles away, but a nice place with a spa, and stayed overnight. We swam in the heated swimming pool. Booked two rooms but slept in one. Didn't even set foot outside the door one day. Made love ridiculously, non stop. I called room service and ordered more champagne.

"Are you paying for this? You can't afford this."

I told her it was all on the production company's dime. Her expression changed completely. I crawled across the bed towards her, said it didn't matter, did it? "So what?"

She prowled the room for her smokes, then said she'd like to drive back to Seagate after lunch.

I said "Fine."

We didn't converse over the food. Picking at her salad, she was dived on my some spotty lad from the local rag who asked her about the rumours her husband is dead, that the television company knew it and were covering it up. Annabelle seemed to tighten and wither, covering her face with her hands. I told the moron to get out and get lost, following him through to reception to make sure he did. Outside I caught another guy taking photos through the dining room window with a hefty lens. The two of them stood back and stared me out, like cornered rats, afraid of nothing. *Cunts*. That explained it. I'd had a weird feeling all day. I'd sensed somebody watching us at the poolside while we swam. I'd thought I saw somebody, back-lit with the sun behind them, but when I'd wiped the water from my eyes they were gone. Like I say, that explained it.

We drove back in silence. When we were five minutes from the hotel Annabelle placed her hand on my thigh.

That evening I couldn't stand the laughter and music in the bar. I stood overlooking the beach, listening to the sombre toll of his heartbeat coming from the speakers, seeing the iridescent green lines of the projected ECG. Thirty people or more were gathered down there with candles, though whether they were Christians praying for his wellbeing or avid fans I couldn't tell. Were they proper visitors at all, or was it pre-arranged? You couldn't take anything at face value any more. What was genuine public reaction and what was part of the *schtick*? The channel was after ratings, but they were legally culpable too, weren't they? Wasn't there some kind of professional duty of care? Could they be sued if he *didn't* come out alive? And if something went disastrously wrong, wouldn't they do everything they could to bluff it out, play for time – just like the reporter was saying?

Children played hopscotch on the sand near the giraffe lights and generator. I shivered at the unbidden fantasy that the trucks would move away, the electrics and machinery towed off, and he'd be left down there though lack of interest, a victim of the viewing public's fickle apathy. I shivered because I found myself almost willing it to happen.

"He's strong." Annabelle's voice, right behind me. "You have no idea how strong. He'll never let down his public. Never. They made him who he is. He'll never forget that. Never."

I held out my hand. Pale as paper, she took it. Pressed her lips against mine. When she stepped back she must've seen my eyes flicker.

"Nobody can see us."

"I know." I turned up my jacket collar and we walked to somewhere out of the icy wind, the little gift shop by the turnstile to the pier that sold fishing bait and postcards.

My teeth were chattering. "What are we going to tell him?"

"When?"

"When? When he comes out. What do you think I mean?"

"We tell him nothing, of course. Why would we?" She looked at me like I was the stupidest, most naïve idiot in the world. "Oh, Nick…"

"Don't be a fucking bitch, all right?" I turned my back to her.

"Well, what are *you* going to do? Tell your girlfriend?"

"Yes."

"No you're not."

"I *will*. I'm prepared to."

"To do what? Throw away what you've got?"

I barked a laugh. "Got? What have I 'got'? I've got nothing. You're kidding. This place? This life? In this dump? It means fuck-all to me."

"You don't mean that."

"I fucking do. And don't act as though all this is bollocks, what we've been doing together for the last twelve days, because I know – "

"Oh, grow up! You've had good sex. I've had good sex. I'm not saying I haven't enjoyed – "

"Oh, thanks a fucking – "

"I just don't want to take away – "

"You're not taking away *anything*!" I turned on her. I'd had enough. "For fuck's sake, you're *bringing*. Bringing me everything I've ever wanted! Christ. I've never felt so…"

"What?"

I choked back the word, then thought, fuck it. "So … *alive*."

Her eyes filled up and her lip curled. "Go. Go."

*

I knew I wouldn't be invited to her hotel room that night. I thought I may even have blown it completely. I sat in my room and sobbed. I felt like doing a Keith Moon and tearing the room apart, disgusted with myself that I was so fucking well brought up I'd never do anything that would embarrass my parents. I thought, fuck my parents! I looked down at the ghost-written biography of Kelso Dennett I'd thrown at the wall. It had fallen open at a photograph taken in India. He was fire walking. Everybody was grinning. He was taking Annabelle by the hand. She was doing it with him, stepping barefoot onto the coals, but she looked frightened to death.

I heard a rap at the door. She took me by the hand and led me down to the beach. She found a secluded spot out of sight of the men in Hi-Viz jackets, under the shadow of the lip of the Promenade, not far from the concrete slipway. She knelt and took me into her mouth. The mixture of hot and cold was explosive. I almost passed out in a shuddering fit. My fingers ran through her hair. It was the colour of seaweed in the spill of artificial lighting. I cried, "No." I said, "No." I was facing the grave and she wasn't. I turned my cheek to the wall and shut my eyes.

*

At the twenty day mark, I thought things would settle into a routine as far as the stunt was concerned, but I couldn't have been more wrong. The tension, far from easing off, was ratcheting up unimaginably. Everyone could feel it, and the callous metronome of those insidiously slow heartbeats – fifteen beats per minute now – did nothing to calm anybody's nerves.

I was getting blinding headaches. Maybe it was because I was existing on Red Bull to pep me up through a whiskey hangover most of the time, or maybe the pressure of lying to Cyd was getting to me. I was flying off the handle and giving excuses why I couldn't sleep at her grotty one-bedroom flat, cuddled up on stinking nylon sheets. I blamed it on the job, but the truth was I couldn't stand the sight of her any more with her M&S cardigan and lank, boring hair. I'd say I was going for a walk, but I wasn't going for a walk, I was going to her. To Annabelle Fox from the fish fingers commercial I used to watch when I was seven years old.

*

"Did he really spend months at a Tibetan monastery?"

"No. Not months. Years." She was sitting up, twisted in crisp white sheets in the afterglow. "See, what people don't understand is his body doesn't matter to him. It's just an instrument. The mind is what matters. That's how he got into tattoos and scarification and body modification. Medicine men who put needles through their cheeks and don't feel a thing. It's all about physical extremities, pain, distress, fear – whatever – anything to remove you from your sense of self, your sense of mortality."

"I'd have thought his mortality would be all too important to him, down there in the dark, alone."

She looked at her own reflection. "That's because you're not him."

"Good."

She didn't turn to me. "It *is* good."

We fucked again, deliciously, freer now, and while I was in the bathroom disposing of my used Durex I heard the sound of a glass smashing. I shouted but Annabelle didn't answer. When I came back into the bedroom she said it was an accident, she'd dropped it. Although she was in bed and the glass was over on the coffee table. I didn't say anything, but I had a strange feeling that wasn't what had happened at all.

*

Later that night I woke up in the dark of the room. It must've been four or five in the morning, but really I had no idea. It scared me that my heart was drumming in my chest. It was inside my ears and it made me think of the heartbeat coming from the speakers down on the beach. At the same time I had a definite, overwhelming sense of a presence. Of someone in the room. Luckily my eyes had opened because if I'd had to open them I wouldn't have.

A spill of intense yellow came from the bathroom – one of us must've left the light on. Illuminated by it stood a figure. A man standing there, arms hanging at his side, simply looking at me. Looking down at the bed. It was Kelso Dennett, dressed exactly as he was when he stepped into the coffin. Naked to the waist, lycra pants, sleeve of tattoos, pentagram, shaved head.

I switched on bedside light.

"Wha?" Annabelle rubbed her eyes, contorting against her pillow. "Nick? Jesus …" I was blinking too, inevitably – the sudden brightness flooding my vision, a complete searing white-out. "What the hell?"

But by the time my eyes had got accustomed to the glare, there was nothing to tell her, because there was nobody there. "Fuck. Nightmare. Really bad. Shit. Sorry. Sorry." I kissed her. "Sorry. It's gone. Gone…"

But it didn't go.

It didn't go at all.

*

The next night I sensed him in the room again. In the exact same place, like a replay. Like the image from the DVD. Except this time I didn't turn and face him, and this time I could feel him walking slowly towards the bed.

I didn't open my eyes.

He stayed there for several minutes, but it seemed like hours. Perhaps it *was* hours. I have no idea.

And I thought: *How long has he been there? How many times before and I haven't noticed?* And I tried to close my eyes even tighter, and shut out the sound of his beating heart, but it only seemed to get louder.

*

The days come, and the nights, and I haven't told Annabelle what I saw standing by the bathroom door, not that I'm sure what I saw, or even if I saw it. When you think about what you did yesterday, it's like a dream, isn't it? If somebody told you it didn't happen, or it happened differently, you wouldn't be able to contradict them, would you? All you could say is – well, what *would* you say? I don't know.

I don't know what to say to her. I don't know whether to ask her to come to my room instead of me going to hers, or whether that will even make any difference. Why should it?

Now, I hardly sleep anyway because I can't bear the thought of waking in the middle of that night with that feeling of panic in my chest. I can't bear it because I know who will be there, looking down at me.

Jesus Christ. Jesus Christ.

*

Twenty-nine days now. Thirty tomorrow.

I count them like a prison sentence. With my unblinking eyes fixed on it, the digital clock at the bedside moves past midnight. I can hear her gentle breathing inches away from my back. I feel the aura of another warm body next to me. I cling to her the way a child clings to its mother, and she strokes my hair. She has no idea what is inside my head. She has no idea what is in the room. Now it's my secret. It's all about *my* secret now.

*

Day thirty-six.

The headaches are worse than ever. I need to go to the doctor. The doctor has to give me something for this. It's not normal. It just isn't.

And I know the viewing public is getting excited, but I'm starting to spend all my waking hours thinking what they are going to find when they dig down and bring up his coffin. My stomach knots on a regular basis. Is he going to be dead? Is that his last, greatest trick, after all? The great almighty fuck-you? Then, at other times, I become absolutely certain that when they dig him up, the coffin will be empty.

I'm not sure which of the two eventualities terrifies me the most.

Which is why I dare not sleep any more. I can go four nights without sleep, can't I? Just four nights. Of course I can. I'll make sure I can.

Then it will all be over.

I dare not close my eyes. Because shutting them means opening them – and opening them... what the *fuck* will I see?

*

BBC News (UK)

BAFFLING TV 'STUNT' ENDS IN HORROR: MYSTERY OF MAGICIAN'S 'FINAL TRICK'

Thursday 11 April 2013 12.44 BST

DNA tests are expected to confirm that the body found under Seagate beach yesterday – buried in a coffin as part of a stunt by an acclaimed television illusionist – is that of local man Nick Ambler.

Mr Ambler, 28, was the son of hotel proprietor Stuart Ambler and his wife Corinne, and had been working on the production as a runner.

Detectives have said they want as a priority to interview TV magician Kelso Dennett, whose present whereabouts are unknown. They are also urgently seeking his wife, actress Annabelle Fox, to help them with their inquiries.

Famous for controversial and sometimes blasphemous stunts, the showman had returned to his home town claiming, in typically audacious fashion, that he would survive being buried alive for forty days and forty nights. It was only when the coffin was exhumed yesterday that the body of the dead man was discovered.

A spokesperson for Kent Police said: "Initial findings indicate that the young man had been in the coffin for the entire forty days. Scratches on the inside of the lid, together with broken fingernails, indicate a desperate and no doubt prolonged and agonising attempt to escape."

Last night, in the glare of the news cameras, a visibly shaken Mayor of Seagate opened the sealed envelope entrusted to him by Kelso Dennett before he stepped into the coffin forty days earlier. It contained a single sheet of paper, folded once, on which was written just two words in block capitals – the name of the deceased.

FORCES OF EVIL

The atrocities committed in England during the age of the witch-hunts are well documented, but there were an equal number in Scotland during the same era, most of which were appallingly gruesome even by the normal standards of the period. To begin with, Scottish witch-hunters had more brutal methods legally available to them: torture was entirely permissible, and in Scotland it wasn't necessary, as it was in England, to prove that death or injury had been caused by sorcery in order to impose capital punishment – the use of witchcraft for any purpose carried the ultimate sanction.

As with the cases in England, there were numerous Scottish witch-trials that illustrate the cruel injustices resulting from ignorance and superstition, but there were also a few containing elements of mystery, which suggest that maybe the dark arts were not entirely imaginary. Two perfect examples of these juxtaposed 'realities' come from Scotland's southeast coast, on the facing shores of the Firth of Forth.

In 1705, the small fishing village of Pittenweem, north of the Firth, became the focus of a witch scare that exemplified the worst kind of paranoia-driven brutality. When Patrick Morton, a young blacksmith's boy, accused, among others, a well-to-do local woman, Beatrix Laing, of sending evil spirits to make him ill, an official investigation was launched with the full approval of the Scottish Privy Council. No-one seems to have considered that the ignorant Morton had grown up strongly influenced by a local fanatical minister, or that he and Mrs. Laing were at odds over a business contract, or that there had been no suspicion of witch activity in Pittenweem for over 60 years.

The unfortunate Laing was imprisoned for five months on the say-so of the youth, and tortured repeatedly until she confessed and named several 'accomplices'. On her release – which possibly occurred because of her high social status – she fled to St. Andrew's, where she died in ignominy and shame. However, the real horror at Pittenweem was only just beginning. One of Laing's fellow-accused, Thomas Brown, was also imprisoned on the lad's word, but he wouldn't confess and so was denied food until he died of starvation. Another, Janet Corphat, was taken from her cell by an angry crowd, hanged on the village seafront, stoned, cut down while still alive and placed beneath a door upon which rocks were piled until she was pressed to death. To ensure *'the witch' was dead, a carter then drove his horse, pulling a loaded sledge, back and forth over her corpse.*

Though Morton was later discredited as an inveterate liar, nobody was ever brought to justice for these acts, which even under the legal auspices of the time amounted to homicide by lynching. That there was not even an enquiry indicates how deeply rooted was the fear and loathing felt for so-called witches in that community.

One possible cause of this may be found on the south shore of the Firth, roughly one century earlier, when there was an equally unnerving case of Scottish 'witch-lore', though this tragedy was touched by more sensational and bizarre circumstances.

In 1590, King James VI of Scotland (later James I of England), was returning home from Denmark with his new bride, Princess Anne, when he experienced a sea-storm so fierce that many in his court thought it unnatural. He was forced to take shelter in a Norwegian harbour and thus survived, but others were not so fortunate. One ship, closely resembling the royal vessel, was not far from the Scottish harbour town of Leith, once again on the Firth, when it succumbed to the tempest and sank with all hands.

Scotland had hosted no major witch-trials up to this point, but accusations were made by certain Danish nobles that witchcraft had created the storm. Similar rumours spread in Scotland, fuelled by one David Seaton, deputy-bailiff of Tranent, East Lothian, who had long suspected that his maid, Gilly Duncan, led a double-life. Under terrible torture, Duncan revealed that she was part of a coven headed by Francis Hepburn, the famously superstitious Earl of Bothwell, who had been attempting to murder the king.

The denunciation of Bothwell surprised no-one; he was a malcontent of long-standing, but some 200 others were also accused, four of whom – John Fian, Euphema McLayan, Barbara Napier, and Agnes Sampson – were brought to trial. Viciously tortured, they described blasphemous ceremonies in St. Andrew's Auld Kirk, in the coastal town of North Berwick, and macabre rituals at which a demonic presence had manifested. King James himself assisted in the interrogations, and heard how the witches had invoked the North Sea storm that nearly killed him by sacrificing a cat in Leith harbour. Gilly Duncan played a tune to the king on a Jew's harp, to which she said the hellish cohorts had danced, and Agnes Sampson gave him intimate details of a conversation he had held with his new bride on their wedding night, which left him stunned.

On conviction, Fian, McLayan and Sampson were strangled and burned on Castle Hill in Edinburgh. Bothwell meanwhile, after many rebellious shenanigans, escaped to Italy, where, though he lived in poverty, he is supposed to have practiced witchcraft until his dying day. Whether this latter detail amounts to mere propaganda is unknown. Though cousins, James and Bothwell were diehard enemies, so it is not impossible that the rebel earl might have sought to use black magic to kill the childless monarch in order to clear his way to the throne. It also seems evident that sabbats of some sort – possibly festivals of the 'Old Religion' – were being held at the Auld Kirk under cover of darkness. But there are more mundane explanations as well. At this stage of his career, it was politically expedient for James to root out his enemies once and for all, blackening the name of Bothwell in the most irreversible way possible, and at the same time reinforcing his own declarations on the 'Divine Right of Kings' by casting himself as the ruler who literally beat the Devil.

A PRAYER FOR THE MORNING
Joseph Freeman

"Mummy is this where the leopard hospital was?"

"It's *leper* hospital, darling. Don't take your seat belt off until we've parked."

"What's a leper, mummy? Daddy hurry up and park."

"I'm trying to, love. Won't be long now."

"It's an ill person, darling. Bits of them fall off."

"Eurrrrgh!"

Dunning smiled to himself at the conversation as he guided the BMW slowly along the increasingly narrow country lanes. Trees stooped down from the grassy banks as though checking his speed. A very tight turn made him slow even further, but then he saw the signpost outside the picturesque cottage that had once been a village post office, and he knew they were almost at the beach.

"Is that true?" he asked his wife, as they picked up speed again, on a straight lane that should lead them to a car park. "There was really a leper hospital right here?"

Kate had a knowing smile on her face; her green eyes caught the sunlight like prisms. "Not any more, before you ask if we can go visit, but yes there was. A long time ago now, I think."

"Before your time, eh?" The lane had narrowed again, and up ahead a troop of walkers were marching towards him like they had nothing to fear. "I think here's a bunch now."

"Mummy, are they lepers? Do their bits fall off?"

"No Charlotte, your father's being silly again. Best not to believe anything he says."

"Don't listen to her Charlotte, at least not about not listening to me. Where would we be then?"

A couple of metres from the car, the walkers grudgingly formed a single file line along the side of the lane. The man in front had a nose so bulbous that it looked like a raindrop waiting to fall.

"Come on, come on," Dunning muttered. "If you don't clear the way I'll make some bloody bits fall off you."

"Daddy! You did a swear!"

"Well, your mother told you not to listen to me didn't she?"

Charlotte giggled to herself from the backseat, and Kate rubbed a hand along his thigh and into his crotch, whether to calm him down or to shock the bulb-nosed walker who was peering into the car he didn't know and didn't care. They drove past the stragglers and turned into the car park, and he looked across at her. She mouthed an obscene promise to him, and he smiled his receipt and looked forward to returning to the holiday cottage later that evening.

The car park was a large expanse of uneven waste ground leading to the dunes on one side, and a long wooden shack that promised TEAS ICES REFRESHMENTS on the other. He navigated the rough ground carefully, but they were still thoroughly shaken about by the time he found a nice spot and switched off the engine.

"All out, boys and girls," he called, unclipping his seatbelt.

Charlotte was already out, and standing beside his door. "There's no boys here, are there mummy? Just girls."

"That's right. And naughty ones at that." He climbed out and locked the car behind him. Kate sidled alongside him and slipped a hand into the rear pocket of his jeans, casting him a look that was the right kind of dirty over the top of her sunglasses. Charlotte lost interest, as she always did whenever she sensed anything that might lead to boring grown-up yucky kissing, and ran off towards the beach.

"Enjoying yourself, Mrs D?" Dunning asked as they followed her at a lingering pace. On the benches outside the refreshment shack, middle-aged people were resting their cumbersome stomachs on their knees.

"A delightful time," Kate replied, "thank you."

"Has much of it changed since you were a girl?"

"A lot of things look different but still very familiar. I guess your memories fade over the years, or get changed."

"Getting old, eh? It'll happen to me one day."

"You be careful, I'm only four years older than you."

"And in much better condition and improving with every year, unlike me. Perhaps I should've booked myself into the leper camp. Sorry, you were saying?"

"It's just strange how our perceptions of places, events, even people can be totally different from the reality. You convince yourself that something was one way and when you go back to check, it really wasn't. Does that make sense?"

Dunning saw the sea as they reached the cliff-top path. It seemed like a reflection of the sky above that had turned angry and was trying to drag itself along the beach with claws of foamy waves. Though it was hardly heat-wave weather, or even a particularly nice summer's day, children and dogs were running splashing through it, whilst their respective parents and owners lay like driftwood on the pebbles.

"Sure," he told her as they trudged down the steps to where Charlotte waited, waving, on the beach. "The mind is a natural, organic thing after all, and memories are hardly incorruptible. They're like … like ghosts …"

"You mean they swoop around graveyards going 'Woooooo'?" Kate teased him, waving her arms menacingly above him. Charlotte giggled, waiting for them patiently now she saw they weren't kissing.

Dunning slapped his wife's bottom gently. "No, you know what I mean. Memories are not a definite thing. They're hardly a perfect record. They're too sensitive, too subject to influence by so many other things." They reached the bottom of the steps and he smiled down at his daughter. "I guess bits drop off them, too."

"Yuck, you're talking about leopards again!" Charlotte screwed up her face. Dunning realised that whenever she did so she looked exactly how he remembered Kate's mother in her old age, wrapped in a tartan rug by the fireplace and her face twisted into a permanent grimace of distaste, usually at him. Behind her the sea crashed and splintered. A highland terrier became increasingly enraged by the waves, leaping into them and yapping loudly.

"Mummy will you race me along the beach?"

"Let's ask your father if he wants to join us first."

"He won't. Daddy's too slow."

"Well, how about it?" Kate asked him, "Fancy working up a sweat?"

"I have to save myself for later, thanks. Besides, I'm too slow."

He smiled as they ran away together along the beach, beneath the overhanging cliffs where once a whole city had stood. Over the years the sea had claimed it for its own, and whatever remained of it now was deep beneath the waves. The very idea had fascinated him ever since Kate told him the story, and the legends and myths which had quite naturally grown around it. Kate had grown up thirty miles along the coast; until her parents had separated when she'd been thirteen and her mother had taken her to live in the Midlands. This holiday, some thirty years later, was the first time she'd returned.

His previous experience of the English coast was pretty much limited to awful bank holiday excursions to Blackpool with his parents as a boy, and a couple of later trips when he'd been old enough to know better. When he gazed along this picturesque stretch of coast, he smiled to think how much he'd enjoyed trudging along the litter-strewn, windswept and grimy beach way back then.

He'd first started to suspect the mysteries of adulthood when, at six years of age, he'd found a condom in the sand he was using to build a castle. It felt strange to remember that now, after all these years, and almost unsettling that he had nobody to share the memory with. A few hundred yards along the coast, his wife and child were miniature versions of themselves, as though his family were being rendered much less significant. He tried to march quickly towards them, and outpace the morbid notion.

He'd already left most of the other people behind; perhaps they didn't want to stray too far from the car park, or from the refreshments. To his left, the sea hissed as it rushed at the beach; to his right, the cliff face looked angrily gouged. He tried to imagine huge chunks of the land crashing into the sea, bringing with them houses, homes, lives. He doubted anybody had died in such a manner – surely the erosion of the land was much too gradual for that to happen? But nevertheless, it was a singularly lonely thought, a lonely place. In some uncertain way, it appealed to some uncertain part of him.

He was glad when Charlotte and Kate were near enough for him to reach out to, and then to hold onto. "You can't be tired already, surely?" he asked his daughter, scruffing up her hair which made her twist her already panting face into even more of a grimace.

"It's hard running on beaches," she informed him, "It's like being on the moon."

"And how would you know what that's like?"

The three of them walked together to where the waves were darkening the sand, stepping forwards and backwards in a laughing line to dare the water. Dunning himself was the first to get splashed, and he dragged the other two with him, until they squealed and pulled him away, almost overbalancing him. They spent the rest of the afternoon trudging back along the beach, and then along the cliff-tops, until Dunning felt as though they were looking for something not easily apparent at first glance. They found a good site to sit and rest before heading off to find something to eat and drink, and Kate told him about the nearby cathedral ruins – now little more than a jagged wall, but once a mighty and magnificent building which had sat some miles in from the coast.

"I still find it incredible to believe that so much land could be lost," he confessed "Just to look out there and think that a whole town is missing …" He shook his head as he gazed towards the point where the land fell away to the sea, a solitary tombstone like a bad tooth all that remained of a large graveyard. He thought about the land being pulled apart by the sea, a notion haunting enough by itself. There was no need for him to think of the bodies disturbed as they were torn from the ground where they'd been laid to rest.

"Worked up an appetite yet?" Kate asked him.

"Yeah, but perhaps not fish and chips anymore."

Kate watched him carefully until he realised that he was frowning, and reassured her with a quick grin. Charlotte was running around the ruins; he would catch the occasional glimpse of her flitting by like a ghost. Beyond the ruins were the heath and the woodland. A breeze stirred and brushed by him. The sky above the sea darkened a shade, and where the two met, clouds were gathering.

"Looks like we're in for a summer shower," Kate told him, reaching forward to grab his hand as if he were the only protection she could ever need. "Let's go and get some dinner and then we can get this one home to bed."

He didn't know whether she'd meant herself or Charlotte, but presumably an early night would mean different things in either case. He stood up with a smile, feeling genuinely good, any haunting morbid thoughts that may have been stirred in his mind had no place there on such a beautiful day. He was a lucky man. Kate called Charlotte out of hiding, and as they were waiting for her to run across from the cathedral ruins she told him another story.

"There were a few churches here in the past."

"Really? It was that big a place?"

"Yes. There is a story you'll enjoy, and I don't know how likely this is, that sometimes when it's quiet you can hear the church bells ringing from beneath the sea."

Though the idea intrigued him, Dunning couldn't help but shudder. Charlotte bounded up to them, tireless as a puppy dog, and he gathered his family in his arms and started to stroll back along the cliff-tops towards the car. The storm gathering over the sea was sending darker waves towards the shore. He wondered what they might be stirring up.

"What did you think, Charlotte? Isn't this place great?"

"I liked the broken church, and I liked the beach, but I saw a funny man."

"Funnier than me? Where was he then?"

"Behind the broken church. I think he'd come up from the sea."

Kate laughed affectionately. "You mean he came up from the beach?"

"He came up from the beach and then he went into the trees."

"I hope you didn't follow him," Dunning warned good-naturedly. "Men who go into trees stop being men and often turn back into monkeys."

"He was wearing a white blanket. I could only see his hands sticking out, and a bit of his face. He didn't look very well."

"Well perhaps he'd been bathing in the sea, dear, and he'd had enough for now," Kate answered, her smile showing her amusement at the child's inquisitive mind.

"Perhaps he'd got sunstroke, like when you fell asleep in the garden last summer and we thought you'd been boiled."

They reached the car park and he unlocked the doors to usher them in. Charlotte was frowning, and before he shut her into the back of the car he heard her murmur: "He didn't have much of a suntan. He was as white as snow."

The rain started as they pulled out of the car park. They'd escaped just in time but the glum faces lined up on benches and plastic seats outside the café, and the outraged shrieks coming from the direction of the beach betrayed many others that hadn't been so lucky. The clouds darkened as though a lid had been lowered on the sky, and Dunning switched on the radio to replace the drumming of rain on the car. Charlotte was quiet. Surely she couldn't be tired already? Dunning watched her in the rear view mirror, her tiny face tightened in concentration, pressed up against the window, but there were only trees out there.

"Will you be joining us for dinner, madam?" he asked, to bring her back to them.

The light rain followed them several miles inland where they found a large country inn in front of an open-air aviation museum. Dunning parked the car behind the building, beneath an overhanging canopy of dripping trees, and as he switched off the engine the sky was rent apart with an echoing crash, and the rain began in earnest. They sprinted across the car park for the safety of the inn; jet planes were washed into blurs beside them. Inside, everything was warmth and good cheer. They found one of the few unoccupied corners of the oak-beamed dining room, and as Dunning queued at the bar to place their order he was watched over by a stag's head above the fireplace. Two hours later, stuffed with fine food and drinks, they started back towards the holiday cottage.

The rain had stopped, and the sun had returned for the last part of the day. As they drove along the coast road, smooth jazz playing softly, they saw the sunlight scattered across the silver sea like pieces of a jigsaw puzzle. Charlotte, who'd seemed to reanimate herself during dinner, was now on the verge of falling asleep, and Kate was leaning against his shoulder, drunk from the wine she'd had, and smiling contentedly.

Back at the holiday cottage he saw them both to bed. Charlotte first, a sleepily murmuring bundle in his arms whom he lowered into her bed and checked she was comfortable before leaving her to find the perfect end to her day in dreams. Dunning found Kate in the main bedroom, silhouetted against the soft evening light through the window. He pushed the bedroom door shut behind him, and Kate pulled him towards her. Her mouth was hungry, her taste sweet and instantly arousing. He could feel himself stiffening as her hands roamed across his body. He held her close, the heat from her body made him want her so badly, made him feel so alive.

Despite, or more probably because of, their years of marriage and intimate knowledge of the best and worst of one another, removing each other's clothes was as exciting as it had ever been. She took pleasure in the strength of his arms, the hair on his chest, the taste and smell of his bare skin. He was thrilled by her long, smooth, graceful limbs, her full and heavy breasts and the way that, naked, she looked more innocent and beautiful than at any other time.

They fell onto the bed and ate hungrily of one another; writhing and moaning, filling their every sense: a lovemaking so hungry that it was as though they were both afraid it would be the last time, and feeling so close that they may as well have blurred into one, until a ferocious orgasm shattered them both into a million electric pieces.

They lay holding one another, looking into one another's eyes as the summer evening darkened outside. "I love you," Dunning said, and, more than words, he meant it with his heart and soul and every fibre of his being.

"I love you too," Kate replied, her eyes luminous in the dimming shadows. "So deeply. We have a wonderful life."

"We certainly do. You look tired."

"A little. I think I'll have a rest for a while and then I can make us some dinner."

"Don't worry yourself. If you're tired, you get some sleep and I'll fix myself something to eat later. I thought about going for a drive, soak up some moonlight and some of this delicious peace and quiet."

Kate had her eyes half-closed now, and was murmuring sleepily. "Okay. Be safe. I've had such a lovely day."

"Me too. I love you."

"I love you. See you in the morning."

"Bye."

The evening was beautiful. Dunning drove with the window down, soft smooth music playing and a breeze billowing his linen shirt. The carriageway was almost empty, a wide open stretch of road beneath a beautiful sky of velvet purples and vivid pinks.

He knew where he was heading. The remnants of the coastal town had been haunting him ever since that morning: he'd wondered what it would be like without the dogs, the children, the tourists, even the sunlight. He'd thought of standing on the cliffs, bathed in silvery moonlight thick as paint and hearing the sound of drowned church bells from beneath a sea that covered so many secrets.

Dunning drove along the long, curving stretch of road that was interspersed only occasionally with increasingly small villages. By the time he saw the sign he'd been looking for, the day was catching up to him and with a yawn that stretched his face, he was growing tired. He wouldn't stay long, he promised himself; back at the cottage there was a warm bed and his loving wife, but he knew that if he didn't make this trip he'd regret it.

In the twilight, the forests beyond the heath had solidified into one dark mass. On impulse, he switched off the CD player. Beyond the noise of the car were the sounds of the night: a gentle breeze, something racing through the undergrowth away from, or even towards the car. In the forest, something cried out – a lonely sound that touched his heart – and beyond all that he fancied he could hear the secretive whispering of the sea.

The heath was studded by picnic areas; that must have one been one of them he was driving past, but as it was swept away behind him he thought he must have made a mistake. It was unlikely there would be a small group of people out here feeding at this hour, unless they were as strange as he was beginning to feel he must be.

Besides, even the moonlight couldn't have made people quite so pale. What he'd seen must have been tree stumps, for there were several more on the heath just beyond the reach of the headlights.

He pulled into the car park and switched off the engine, and then the lights. The night fell in upon the car, and he felt a much smaller part of the world than he had previously. He had to smile at himself, driving all this way out here romanticising the place only to be so easily spooked. On that note, he pushed himself out of the car and into the night. He could hear the sea crashing and whispering beyond the car park, beyond the cliffs. There was a beautiful full moon, like a disc of perfect white innocence in a sky the colour of velvet sin. At his back, the heath and the trees beyond it seemed alive with whisperings of their own. In his lightweight linen shirt he felt colder now the day's heat had faded but he hadn't brought a jacket. And he had to remind himself that, whatever his fancies, he was probably far safer and less likely to come to harm out here than he was in a busy city centre.

As his eyes adjusted slowly to the darkness, Dunning marched across the car park; the gravel crunching seemed to compete with the sea and the forest to produce something like a voice without words. He reached the cliff-top and looked down over the moonlit beach, and his heart skipped a beat when he saw a bone-white figure staring back up at him.

He stepped back from the edge of the cliff, both startled and embarrassed. Even when his mind had settled enough to tell him that only driftwood could look so stripped and incomplete, he was loath to venture back. Instead he set off walking along the cliff-top, ground which had once been a mile or so inland: a thought that served to remind him of all that lay beneath the cold and whispering sea.

Trees creaked in a sudden wind, the long grass rustled as if something had broken out of hiding towards him. Of course there was nothing that he could see; only, now that his eyes had adjusted to the night, he could see thin, twisted, pale figures amongst the trees.

Silver birches, no doubt, but the illusion was an unpleasant one. The sea crashed down below, the land here was like a leper, he thought, bits dropping off it. He smiled to himself, and then something deep in the woods cried out again, and one of the pale figures moved out of sight amongst the trees.

Dunning paused, but it seemed darker over there than before. Could he really be certain that something had moved, rather than a trick of perspective as he walked making it appear to? And even if so, what of it? Had anyone else less right to be out here than he had? He set off walking again, but his nerves were taut and he promised himself that he would go only as far as the cathedral ruins before heading back.

Though the night had music of its own, Dunning himself felt so soundless as to be a ghost. He wanted to make some noise, as if to prove his own substance, but he felt foolish thinking about it, and even a little wary of attracting the attention of anything that might be sharing the darkness with him. When he heard a clattering along the cliff-face not far below his feet, he knew he must have dislodged some lose rock, but his mind was full of the image of an incomplete figure as pale as drowned flesh clambering up from the beach towards him.

Here were the ruins, just ahead. If he'd been any less foolish he could have enjoyed the walk as much as he'd expected to. He had to smile at least, imagining how amused Kate would be in the morning as he recounted his misadventures, as she pictured him blundering around white as a sheet and jumping at his own shadow. He picked his way across the grass to make a circuit of the ruin; the churchyard's last remaining gravestone seemed a good enough warning to venture no further. In the clear moonlight the ruins were crisply outlined in silver, an ethereal and dreamlike image. As he watched, something darted from the trees and out of sight behind the ruins.

It was a dog, it had to be, to be so thin that its ribcage was visible, and to move on all fours like that. But Dunning was uneasy and far from reassured. He could have sworn that the creature had dropped onto all fours from a standing position.

Whatever he'd seen, it was time to go and he had to admit that he would be safer taking the long way round through the trees than walking along the cliff-top in plain sight. His heart was hammering his chest like a fist and blood roared in his ears as though bringing the sea into him. He kept glancing warily at the ruins as he approached the cover of the trees. He really wasn't far from his car, he must remember that, he would soon be safe and heading back to his family and probably, if he could find sleep, the best nightmare he'd ever had.

Stepping into the woods felt like letting the dark claim him. Some nocturnal creature wailed and he wished he knew enough to tell himself what it was. Things were moving about deeper amongst the trees, but that needn't worry him as their step sounded much lighter than a human's would be. He hadn't realised how bright the moonlight had been back out in the open until he'd stepped out of it. The trees nearest to him were merely sketched in what little light there was, and those further away could have been anything, or nothing. He had to be careful – he'd come in here to be safe, not to do himself some harm. He watched his step as best as he could, and reached out a hand to steady himself against a tree.

Only, what he touched didn't feel so much like a tree as something soft and pulpy, less than flesh. He snatched his hand away in disgust and shock, only to find strands of whatever he'd touched come away on his fingers.

Dunning didn't think; he just shoved himself away from whatever it was that he'd touched, rubbing his hand against his leg until his fingers ached. When he regained his composure, he realised he'd sent himself deeper into the woods. He could no longer see the heath. He no longer knew which way he was facing.

If swearing could have oriented him, he would have been fine. When he'd finished cursing, the noises of the woods were all around. Things snapping. The breeze being broken into something like a voice by the trees. Other, less easily identified sounds.

How easy it had been for him to become lost, how quickly it had happened. What the hell was he supposed to do now? Indecision held him dumbly immobile. A step in any direction might lead him towards freedom, or a night in the woods. His own fears had chased him in here, and had pushed him into becoming lost. Perhaps facing up to them might be his escape.

"Is there anybody there?" he called out, and then again when his voice could make a better pretence of sounding sure of itself. "Hello?"

There was a rustling in the trees behind that made him feel as if all he'd done was alert something to his presence which he would have rather kept away from. He couldn't have wandered that far into the woods, and if he was sensible he could easily find his way out. All he had to do was take a dozen steps in each direction and then back again, and he would find the way out within a couple of minutes.

He started forward, measuring his strides carefully. With every yard gained he felt as though something was backing away from him, an idea that was not in the least reassuring. It felt like forever before he counted his twelfth step, and beyond that lay only more darkness. He had to resist the urge to take just one more step, then one more, and then keep going. The way out might be right behind him. Carefully he doubled back on himself, but before he'd moved more than a few yards, he swore again.

There was a tree in his path. He wouldn't let this one startle him into idiocy – at least this one felt the way a tree should feel. But it also meant that he couldn't have been heading back along the same path, and his idea had fallen through. There was no way out. Anger made him lash out, but it was something else that made a barely audible chuckling sound, a sound like something with a mouth full of mud, or worse.

Dunning pushed himself off the tree and he stepped into utter blackness beyond it, his hands held out before him to warn him of any possible collision. A strange hand took his, in the darkness, and when he pulled back with a cry it peeled away in his grasp like an empty glove.

Give me a hand, he thought crazily, and spluttered a laugh as he backed away. There had to be a way out of this, and he would find it, whatever it took. He only wished that the morning wasn't so far away, that it would come quickly to chase away anything he need fear. Trees surrounded him, though some of what he told himself were trees shook and stumbled. He daren't look upon them, any less than he dared to stop moving. He pushed himself past more trees, and then past a form that he might have had more chance of recognising if there had been more of it. Whatever he touched now in the darkness, he mustn't let it stop him. However many of them there were, they were still less than he was. The morning would arrive, and as long as he didn't stop moving it would find him back with his wife and daughter, he could hold onto that at least.

Too late, he feared that they were not converging on him so much as herding him. He raised his head long enough to help himself find an escape, and was unable to lower it even when he realised there was none. They were all around, crawling, shambling, limping between the trees, their broken and incomplete forms making an abomination of their ability to move. He only saw them from the corner of his eye, because he was unable to look away from what was waiting for him just ahead.

It stood between the trees, white as the moon and worse than naked. Its outstretched arms could only reach the trees because they were too long for its spindly body, its fingers almost half as long as the arms they grew from. It raised a blank, featureless globe that served as a head, and began to grin blindly – only it wasn't reminiscent of a natural smile so much as dough tearing.

In that moment, a terror that he might never see his family again outweighed any fears for his own safety.

Rage made him cry out, but he was echoed by several voices that had infinitely more of that emotion, if much less of the physical means to express it. He was moving, running towards the apparition that was blocking his path. If it could tear itself apart so easily then by Christ, wait until he got a hold of it. There was little ground between them; he would be upon it in an instant. Its mouth stretched wider, wider than any mouth should, wide enough to swallow his head if he let it. It raised its ridiculously long arms towards him, though whether to warn him off or to embrace him, he couldn't tell.

When it came, the thing had even less physical presence than he'd imagined. Dunning felt something settling over him like a wadded curtain of diseased flesh. As he started to tear with his hands, his eyes screwed shut, the feelings that washed over him were brief but vivid enough almost to make him surrender to his fate. He smelled flesh gone bad, and then rotten. He smelled the sea, felt a vast expanse of it weigh down upon him.

He felt an ageless agony rack his body and mind, an agony so intense that it seemed intent upon wiping away any human emotion he'd ever had. None of it was enough to stop clawing at the thing, tearing into it until his hands felt caked in something he dared not imagine.

When he opened his eyes, the rage that almost filled his mind allowed him to confront the others. If need be he would tear and bite at every one of them until he gained his freedom or lost his mind. But rather than moving towards him, they were retreating amongst the trees, fading into the darkness, leaving parts of themselves behind like a trail to follow. The one nearest hid much of itself behind a tree that was too thin to conceal any natural form, though the part that it showed was bad enough. With what passed for its arm, it beckoned him to join them.

Dunning looked down at himself, but that no longer helped as much as it should have done. "No," he said, and tried to repeat it but his voice was even less certain now. "No, I'm not one of you."

He turned away from the ruined face that watched him with more sympathy than he would have feared, and though a fire burned his veins and it hurt to move, he began walking. He wanted to run, but he didn't have the power or trust the whole of his body to obey him. However tired he became though, he would never stop walking, not until he found his family. The night no longer held anything for him to fear – let the trees shake and the creatures of the night cry out, but the darkness wouldn't last forever. He shut these things out; and whatever else was happening to his physical state.

As long as he had legs he could walk, and it would take even more than the loss of those to keep him from his family now. His one remaining fear was that by the time he got home to them, there would not be enough left of him for them to recognise.

HOTEL OF HORROR

'The Haunted House of Horror' was a low-budget British horror film released in 1969; it was produced by Tigon Films and written and directed by Michael Armstrong.

It wasn't exactly a seminal movie, but it was notable for several reasons: firstly because, despite its title, it was actually an early example of the 'slasher flick', the main antagonist being a crazed killer rather than a ghost or monster; secondly because it was explicitly gory for its era – it raised many a prudish eyebrow at the time; but mainly because it was filmed at one of the most haunted locations in the whole of the United Kingdom, the Birkdale Palace Hotel in Southport, on the Merseyside coast.

With or without 'The Haunted House of Horror', the Birkdale Palace, which was demolished shortly after filming in 1969, boasted a grim history and was associated with mysterious and brutal deaths throughout the 103 years of its existence.

It was constructed in 1866 in what was then a burgeoning holiday resort. Southport, like so many other seaside towns in England, had first come to the attention of the wider public in the 18th century as a spa town. The well-to-do, particularly those convalescing from illness, would travel there to bathe, relax, and enjoy the fresh air and the quiet coastal scenery. In the age of industrialisation, Southport went the same way as its other main rivals on England's northwest coast – Blackpool, Fleetwood and Morecambe – by throwing open its once exclusive doors to the working classes of Lancashire, though all through that era it strove hard, and with some success, to maintain its aura of quaintness.

The Birkdale Palace was very much in keeping with this, an ornate and luxurious building, boasting over 75 plush bedrooms, which was viewed as the town's crowning glory until well into the 20th century. However, from the beginning the Birkdale Palace was dogged by unfortunate incidents.

The first untimely death to occur there was reputedly that of its architect, who arrived at the site on completion of the hotel – only to find that it had been built the wrong way around. It was facing inland instead of out into the Irish Sea, as he had planned. So distraught was he to find his Gothic masterpiece tainted in this way that he threw himself down the hotel's main lift-shaft.

Other grisly events followed. For reasons unknown, two young girls committed suicide together in the hotel. In 1961, the corpse of another young girl, Amanda Jane Graham, who was *only six, was found under one of the beds after she had been abducted and murdered by one of the hotel porters.*

It should be pointed out that stories like this, of which there are many connected with the Birkdale Palace, could easily be urban myths. Few details are ever given by folklorists – such as the names of the two girls who supposedly killed themselves, the name of the murderous porter, what happened to him afterwards and so forth. But one disaster connected with the hotel which definitely did occur was that of the Eliza Fernley, a local lifeboat that went down in December 1886 while coming to the aid of the sailing ship Mexico, which had run aground nearby. Some 14 drowned crewmen were later brought ashore and laid out in a temporary mortuary at the hotel.

Equally undeniable are the multiple reports of paranormal activity at the Birkdale Palace, which have allegedly stemmed from these tragedies.

During the time of its existence, every kind of disembodied voice was heard in the Birkdale Palace: groans, laughter, screams, shouts, the sound of children crying. Much poltergeist activity was also reported – doors and windows opening and closing of their own accord, objects flying through the air. Perhaps most frightening of all are those incidents connected to the lift. Disturbed guests reported feeling an eerie presence inside it, especially if – as sometimes happened – the lift jammed between floors and its lights unaccountably dimmed. But perhaps the most spectacular event of all involving the lift occurred in the hotel's final days. It was 1969, and a demolition team was in the process of dismantling the property. Even though all the power was cut, the lift, which weighed approximately four tons, apparently began to move up and down the shaft under its own power – and several workmen were witness to this. Checks were made to see if anyone was fooling around with the winching system, but apparently nobody ever was. The Manchester-based demolition team were extremely unnerved by this incident, and were quoted widely in the local press at the time, convinced they'd experienced the supernatural.

Paranormal investigators visited the Birkdale Palace many times, both while it was in use and afterwards, but were never able to provide easy explanations for the plethora of bizarre phenomena. One group, who were normally known for their skepticism, openly stated that they believed the hotel to be filled with restless spirits.

Today, the only part of the structure remaining is The Fishermen's Rest pub, which was once the hotel's posh Coach House bar. This too is allegedly haunted, though the sole apparition sighted there is that of a little girl sitting alone in a corner. The rest of the grand hotel is no more than a memory, though not a particularly ugly one. Southport is still a holiday resort, albeit a little quieter now than it was in its heyday, but its general atmosphere of gaiety makes it difficult for anything to engender a sense of fear.

"The Palace was a great old place," a garrulous regular of The Fishermen's Rest commented. "I was only a lad back then, but I knew it was haunted. When it was coming down, me and the other youngsters used to dare each other to go inside. It was very scary, and sometimes you heard strange things. But we were all a bit proud of it. It's not everyone who can say they once had England's most haunted hotel at the end of their garden."

THE JEALOUS SEA
Sam Stone

"The signs are so cute," Angela said.

Garrick laughed; she had said this about every sign they had seen since crossing the border into Wales.

The promenade was deserted as they reached Rhyl. It was six in the evening, in the middle of summer, yet the sky was overcast and the sea wild. It was as though it knew a storm was on its way. They passed a huge theatre with the Welsh name of *Theatr Y Pafiliwn*. Thankfully the signs were also in English and so Angela immediately translated this to *Pavilion Theatre*.

As they approached a small roundabout Angela could see there was a cluster of colourful structures, which housed children's rides, farther up on the left. The area resembled a fairy tale village but was still tacky nonetheless. To the right was a White Rose Shopping Centre,

And, as they crossed the roundabout, a long row of arcades lined the promenade. It was all so dreary that Angela felt her mood plummet at the thought of staying there – even if it was only for one night.

"Why?" she murmured.

"I told you, everywhere else was booked at this time of year. It's only a pit-stop," Garrick said.

"It's seedy."

Garrick sighed but said nothing more as the SatNav told him to take the next left. He turned the car into a small side-street, and a bright neon sign illuminated the way to their bed-and-breakfast.

"There," said Angela.

Garrick took a right turn just after the hotel and they found a very small but underused car park.

He pulled up near to the rear entrance and both he and Angela climbed out. It had been a long drive and they were happy to stretch their legs.

Garrick took their overnight bag from the boot. He ignored the frown on Angela's face as she glanced around at the broken bottles, empty cans and litter that was scattered on the ground.

"This looks okay," he said as they passed through a back corridor into a large reception. To Angela the place looked anything but okay. It was dirty, old and lacklustre. It reminded her of some bad comedy sketch she had once seen, but couldn't fully remember.

"As long as the sheets are clean ..." she said.

They approached the old wooden desk. Angela thought it was corny that there was a bell-push, but she said nothing as Garrick hit the top with his palm and the loud *ring* echoed through the hollow emptiness of the hotel reception and out into the obscure back room.

Angela looked around while they waited and noticed a cabinet full of stuffed animals at the other side of the room. She shivered when she saw the large fish in a glass cabinet hung from the wall. "That's horrible ..."

"Can I help you?"

The woman was a cliché of bed-and-breakfast landladies the world over. She had silver hair scraped back into a bun and a scowl that seemed to be etched permanently on her face. Everything about Rhyl screamed mundane, grubby and above all 'chavy'.

"Mr and Mrs Briant," Garrick said. "We have a reservation."

The woman frowned at an old book that lay open on the desk and then nodded.

"Honeymoon is it?" she asked.

"No. We're travelling to see relatives. Thought we'd take the scenic route."

The landlady failed to see the irony in Garrick's words, but Angela giggled behind him.

The landlady frowned. "Only one night then, is it?"

Garrick nodded.

She told him the price and waited as Garrick fished out his credit card to pay for the room. Angela was surprised when the woman dutifully retrieved a wireless card machine from under the desk; she had half expected her to have one of the old imprint machines, or not to be able to take the card at all.

"That will be an extra charge of one percent," the woman said.

She held out a key with a thick block of wood attached to the end, and after a few vague directions, Angela and Garrick found themselves on the third floor in front of a thick oak door.

"It's like *Fawlty Towers*," Angela giggled. "I'm not expecting this bed to be very comfortable."

"It's just one night," Garrick reminded her as he opened the door.

The room was unexpectedly clean, with a large four-poster bed in the centre. It was surrounded by matching furniture, and a bright red rug took up the centre. There was even a flat screen television on one of the chests of drawers.

"We hit lucky," said Garrick as he opened a door beside the free-standing, oak wardrobe. "En suite bathroom. The website said they only had a few. Looks like we got the best room in the place."

Angela felt a little better. She hadn't relished the idea of tripping out onto the landing to find the nearest bathroom. She sat down on the bed and found it to be comfortable.

"This isn't that bad actually," she said.

After they freshened up they went back downstairs and wandered out to look for a place to eat. The town centre was quiet and as deserted as the promenade had been.

"Where is everyone?" asked Angela. "Thought it was the holiday season down here?"

The air was suffocating and the light was starting to fade. Heavy clouds gathered over head and the sound of the sea dominated the empty streets as the waves rose and fell against the promenade. Angela could feel pre-storm tension in the atmosphere. She felt like a diver in a pressure chamber, waiting to hear the bad news that she was suffering from the bends.

They passed by one of the arcades. Above the loud music Angela could make out the sounds of machines working. She saw a group of teenagers gathered around a racing car game. In the back of the shop an old man staggered from one machine to another holding a plastic cup from which he retrieved two pence coins.

They passed a pub and sounds of revelry issued from the door as it opened for a young man with sleeve tattoos on both arms. He lit a cigarette and stared out towards the sea.

"Danny?" said a girl from the doorway. "Don't stay out too long. You know it's going to be a bad night."

Garrick took Angela's hand as they weaved inwards towards the main shopping complex. It was now around seven thirty in the evening and so all of the shops were closed for trading. But Angela noted how many had whitened glass and had shut down permanently.

"Here's a pub that serves food. Should we try this?" Garrick asked.

"Yes," Angela said.

They went inside and despite the outward appearance the pub was cheery and the menu varied. It was also quite busy. There were more people inside than they had seen since they arrived in Rhyl. Even so, they managed to find a small table in the corner by the window.

"You're not from around here, are you?" asked the waitress as she approached.

"No. But then I suppose not many people are in a seaside town," Garrick said, smiling.

The waitress was young but serious. Her hair was jet black and pulled back severely into a high ponytail. She wore a name badge that said she was 'Aimee'.

"Staying somewhere nearby?" Aimee asked.

Garrick nodded.

Aimee said nothing more but quietly took their order. When she had gone Angela leaned over the table and took Garrick's hand.

"She was a bit chavy wasn't she? Liverpool face-lift and all."

Angela's snobbery sometimes grated on him, but this time Garrick laughed. "This place is a bit ... okay it's seedy. I know. But it's kind of fun too."

Angela leaned over and kissed him. "Anywhere is fun when we're together."

The food arrived after only a short wait. They ate in silence but Angela couldn't help looking around at the people who were in the pub. There was a family sitting on the next table: husband, wife and two children, one a boy, the other a girl. All of them were wearing football shirts supporting the same team. The son was a clone of the father, even down to the shaved head and the mean expression on his face.

A group of young men were gathered around one of the tables. They talked excessively loud as they swigged from pints of beer, interspersed with shots of pale blue liquid. Angela frowned over at their rowdiness. They were so like groups they had seen before. Even down to the razor-patterned haircuts.

The door opened and a gaggle of girls entered – all wearing ridiculous heels, skirts that were too short and clip-in hair extensions. Angela tried not to stare. They all seemed so stereotypical of this sort of resort, and she couldn't shake the feeling that she was in the middle of some kind of stage play that was being given for their benefit.

As Garrick paid the bill Angela went to the ladies room. As she passed each group of loudly chattering diners she found that they were speaking gobbledegook. At first she thought it was the sheer loudness of the chatter that made it indecipherable, but as she paused beside a family of four she began to believe that they weren't talking at all. It was just noise. Almost like elevated white noise. She tried to listen in again, make sense of the din, but a blast of music from an old juke-box made it impossible.

Angela felt the stirrings of a headache, which gathered behind her eyes just as the brewing storm arrived outside.

"I need to get out of here," she said as she met Garrick by the door. 'It's too loud.'

Garrick nodded. "I know."

"You're not going outside on a night like this, are you?" asked Aimee appearing behind them.

"Of course. A night like this is exactly what we look for," Angela said.

They passed through the shopping precinct once more and headed for the sea. The wind was pounding the land and the water beat against the promenade as though it were a giant living beast that would consume anyone who dared to confront it.

"It's beautiful," said Angela. Her eyes reflected the dark storm, turning them from blue to grey.

Garrick frowned.

They walked the promenade, daring the waves to reach for them, but it was a game Garrick disliked. Rain beat down on the flagged pavement and the sky cracked with lightning. Across the road the arcade music grew louder as though it was trying to compete with the storm. The smell of burnt onions wafted towards them. Angela wished there was a pier at this resort. It would have been fun to walk out and tease the sea a little more.

"What are you doing?" asked Garrick as Angela leaned over the rail and stared down at the angry waves.

"It can't get us Garrick. No matter how hard it tries."

Garrick took her arm and pulled her away from the edge. "One of these days it will. You shouldn't mess around like this. It's dangerous."

They walked back across the road. Angela was elated by the storm. The spray from the sea had energised her and her eyes glowed with a green, sub-aqua light.

Garrick's concern deepened. Her eyes always reflected her inner calm or, alternatively, her inner turmoil. Now they showed change.

"Let's go back to the hotel," Garrick said.

"Not yet," Angela said.

She was drunk on the storm. It made her presence outside all the more perilous.

"Come," he insisted.

Back in their room Angela was still glowing as she rubbed her hair dry. Even the blonde looked brighter and her hair appeared to have grown. It was flowing around her like sun bleached seaweed. Her clothes were soaked but she barely noticed.

Garrick was afraid. He felt the chill of the sea. The dark cold beckoned him, but never broke through his resolve to stay on land. Angela was a different story; the sea called to her despite their promise to shun it forever. Part of her wanted its possessive arm to swoop her back. The seaside trips made the torment both wonderful and torturous to them both. But Garrick loved the land more than the water. Angela had left the sea for him. He often feared that one day she would lose the battle and be called back into its jealous embrace, leaving him desperate and alone.

"What?" Angela said as though reading his thoughts.

"This was a bad idea. It was too dangerous. Plus this place ... it's not normal. Not like the other seaside resorts."

"What are you saying?"

"Back there, in the pub. You noticed it, didn't you? The people were ... different."

"They looked like the people we find in all of these places," Angela said.

"Yes. They did. They looked *exactly* like them. That group of girls ... didn't we see them in Newquay? That family wearing football shirts ... I'm sure they were the same people we saw in Blackpool ... They were caricatures, Ang. Don't you see?"

There was rising panic in his voice but Angela said nothing. Instead she stripped away her wet clothes and began to dry her damp skin. Garrick tried not to notice the green scales that patterned her stomach, thighs and legs. He was relieved to see the telltale sign of change disappear as the towel soaked up the last drops of salty water.

"I might take a bath," she said.

That is a good idea, he thought. The sea's saline poison would be washed away by the clean land water. Angela would be calmed. Garrick went into the bathroom and began to run the warm tap into the large bath.

As he poured in the bubble bath he heard the outer door open and close.

Garrick hurried back into the bedroom. Angela was gone and so were her wet clothes. He pulled on his water-proof coat. His heart burned with fear. Since they had returned to the room the storm had stopped raging. The jealous sea had rapidly forgotten their proximity and Garrick had thought the danger past.

As he reached the reception he saw the old woman standing behind the counter. It was as though she had been waiting there all this time, without moving – just for him.

"Have you seen my wife?" he asked.

The old woman's scowl turned into a smile. Her teeth were razor sharp.

Garrick's terror increased. He hurried out into the storm, ran along the street and crossed the empty road to the promenade. The wind buffeted him as though it were trying to stop his progress. Garrick screamed into the night in frustration.

He saw Angela by the railings. As he crossed the road, she walked away, crossing back towards the arcades.

Garrick felt a momentary relief. At least she had left the shore and was walking back to safety. The rain lashed at him as he crossed the road and followed Angela into the arcade. As he paused at the door the man they had seen earlier was still feeding coins into the machines. His movements were stiff and he moved in rhythm with the overly loud music.

Angela walked passed him and Garrick hurried forward.

"*Ang! Wait!*"

Angela disappeared round the corner as Garrick reached the man. He glanced at the machine – it appeared to be a cardboard cut-out and the man was nothing more than an automaton.

"What's going on here?"

He reached the back of the arcade just in time to see Angela slip out through the back exit.

He found himself in an alley. The emergency exit door closed behind him and the sound of the arcade faded completely. As his eyes adjusted to the darkness, he saw Angela's red coat lying over a dumpster. He picked it up and looked around. Angela was at the end of the alley and turning back onto the strip.

"*Angela? Stop! What are you doing?*"

As he left the alley he found himself back on the row of deserted shops. Angela was nowhere to be seen but he turned towards the strip, just as she had.

He saw the young man with the sleeve tattoos, still standing outside the pub, cigarette in hand. As Garrick approached he remained like a frozen statue, even as the elements beat against his already soaked skin and clothing. The cigarette disintegrated under the onslaught, dropping from his fingers in thick brown tears. "You shouldn't be outside on a night like this," said a female voice from the doorway.

Garrick glanced up, half expecting to see yet another fake person. Instead he came face to face with the waitress, Aimee, from the pub.

"Come inside, quickly," she said.

She grabbed his arm and Garrick felt the will to resist leave him.

"Have you seen my wife?" he said.

Inside, the pub was full of cardboard figures.

"What's happening?" Garrick asked.

Aimee's hair was no longer in the tight ponytail; it flowed around her shoulders, the colour of octopus ink.

"You aren't human?" he said.

"Anyone who can move around here right now is like us," she said. "When did you escape?"

"We've been on dry land about five years," Garrick replied.

"And you?"

"Fifty."

"That's a long time."

"Yes. And I plan to stay dry. But every few years it sends something to find us," Aimee said. "You are lucky you haven't been caught so far."

Garrick sat down at a small round table. There were two pints of bitter standing in a sticky mass. The pub smelt of spilled, stale beer. It permeated the carpets and curtains.

"I need to find Angela," Garrick said.

"I ... I think it's too late for her ... She went too close. The sea got her."

"No ..." Garrick said. "I saw her on land. In the arcade."

"You don't understand. On nights like this ... the sea has power on land too. It got her as soon as you drove up the promenade. I could smell it on her when you came in the restaurant. What do you think has happened to all of these people here?"

Garrick shook his head.

"They are *inbetween*. They won't even remember this ... All they will remember is a bad storm."

"What do you mean 'inbetween'?"

"It's a place where the sea is on land and the land is in the sea. Both have merged."

"How?" Garrick asked.

"How did it keep you prisoner in the first place? How did the greedy, jealous sea hold onto us for so long? It has power. But you know that or you wouldn't have woken and left in the first place."

"The land seduced us ... me first. Then Angela came with me. I was never sure she really wanted to leave."

The door of the pub rattled as though a hand were trying the handle.

Garrick stood, but Aimee caught his arm.

"It's looking for us."

A gust of wind huffed against the door but it didn't open.

"As long as we stay inside we will be safe," Aimee said. "The storm will pass in a few hours."

"*Garrick*?" The door rattled again.

"That's Angela! I have to let her in!"

"No!"

Garrick was at the door before Aimee could stop him.

Angela stood in the doorway wet and bedraggled. Seaweed clung to her clothing, and through the outline of her skirt, Garrick detected the faint shape of legs reforming from a tail. It was as though she had pulled herself once more from the bottom of the sea.

"It tried to take me, but I couldn't go back without you," she gasped.

Garrick pulled her inside. He turned to look at Aimee, but the girl had backed away as far as she could from the door.

"Help me," he said. "We need to dry her. Get the salt off."

Aimee hurried to the ladies toilets and returned with a large wad of paper towels. Garrick began to pat Angela dry. Aimee backed away again, frowning.

"A drink. Get her some brandy. She's freezing cold to the touch."

Garrick took off his own coat and placed it around Angela's bare legs. The scales were receding again but Angela was shivering.

Aimee placed a drink on the small table as Garrick sat Angela down, and pulled her close to help warm her. He picked up the glass and held it to Angela's lips. He noticed how blue they were and remembered the first time her saw her underwater. Her pale yellow hair was like the sunlight he had glimpsed shimmering on the ocean, and her scales were the palest green.

"We were happy in the ocean then ..." said Angela as though she could read his mind.

She had stopped shivering and was watching him carefully.

"It can be good again," she continued.

"We made a pact," Garrick said.

"Put her outside," Aimee said. "The storm is almost over, but it won't end until it takes her back."

"She can't go out there!" Garrick said. "What is *wrong* with you?"

Garrick hugged Angela to him as he glared at Aimee. He didn't see the smile that spread over his wife's lips, only the terror this expression brought to the other girl's face.

"She's not your wife anymore. Can't you see that?" Aimee said backing away until she was behind the bar.

He felt the splash of salty water on his feet first. He looked down. The bar was filling with the water from outside. He stood, pulling Angela up.

"Come on. Stand on the bench. It's flooding in."

Aimee was crying as she climbed up onto the bar before the water could reach her. "I'm not going back. I'm not. I should never have helped you."

Garrick looked around, confused. He couldn't see where the water was coming from.

"It's not your wife!" Aimee said again. "You let it in. You let the *inbetween* in!"

Garrick turned to Angela. Water poured from her mouth and out into the room. He stepped away afraid, and tumbled from the bench down into water now waist deep. He could feel the salt sinking through his clothes and into his skin. His legs began to change. It hurt. It hurt a lot.

It was like the first time he had pulled himself out of the sea and lay on the beach. The sun had dried him, soaking up the salty liquid until he wept with pain. The heat was agony after the constant cold of the sea and he felt his blood burn in his veins. That day he was born into humanity and he had lived in their world ever since.

Now, the hurt was reversed. He felt the cold seeping back into him. Destroying the warmth he had learned to enjoy. It was far worse than the burn of the sun had ever been. This was dying, not living. And Garrick screamed, even as the water came above his head and forced its way into his lungs. He choked it in, suffocated on his salty poison.

Then he felt Angela's arms. Her hair wrapped around him when he tried to resist. She pulled him out through the door. They swam through the flooded streets out towards the ocean with the *inbetween* following them as it released its hold on the town and the storm drifted away.

Life fell back into normality. The streets of Rhyl were vibrant and bustling. The arcades were alive with loud music and the sounds of coins falling as the machines paid out. The flat two-dimensional people, filled out, moved, and stretched their tight limbs, unaware of their strange paralysis. The gaggle of girls, the beer swilling youths and the football-shirt wearing family faded back into the distant memory of a merman who once escaped the sea to enjoy time on land.

Aimee stood in the doorway of the pub looking out at the cloud that drifted over the water. The jealous sea was satisfied for now, but it would send the *inbetween* again and again until it snatched back all of its wayward children. Aimee knew it was only a matter of time before it reached her too.

Still, there would be more like Garrick and Angela. Every season brought one or two of them to the seashore. They would look out at the water, daring it to take them back. And as long as there were sacrifices Aimee would be safe. The sea would back away with its prizes like a tourist with an inconsequential toy, never realising it had missed out on the biggest prize of all.

It was several hundred years since Aimee had left the water, not fifty.

"I'm not going back. Not now, not ever," she murmured.

The cloud huffed, the wind rattled along the promenade, but it was nothing more than posturing. The power had receded. The ocean could do nothing more that day. But it knew she was there and wouldn't be satisfied for long.

THE GHOSTS OF GOODWIN SANDS

Goodwin Sands, a submerged ten-mile sandbank six miles off the Kent coast, is one of the most dangerous obstacles in the busy shipping lanes of the English Channel. At least 2,000 vessels are rumoured to have been wrecked there over the centuries and as many as 50,000 lives lost.

But there is more to Goodwin Sands than tales of maritime tragedy. Legend tells how it is all that remains of the now sunken isle of Lomea, once an agricultural paradise in the tenancy of Earl Godwin (father of King Harold Godwinson, who was killed at the battle of Hastings), and later the property of St. Augustine's Abbey, the occupants of which allowed the sea to inundate it sometime around 1092 as they neglected to maintain its coastal defences (the abbey bells are still said to toll beneath the foaming waves).

There is persistent historical and geological debate on the matter of Lomea, most modern scholars feeling there is insufficient proof that the island ever existed. But if the monks of the St. Augustine's chapter did not perish on Goodwin Sands, there were many others who definitely did. In 1624, a severe storm drove a number of merchantmen onto its perilous shoals. In 1703, a similar tempest wrecked a fleet of warships there, costing nearly 3,000 lives. In 1851, the Mary White sank off the Sands, and the paddle-steamer SS Violet went down in 1857, both with multiple fatalities. The sandbank's 20th century tally of destruction included the SS Cape Copez in 1907, the SS Mahratta in 1909 and the pirate radio ship, Ross Revenge, in 1991.

It is no surprise that numerous ghostly ships have been reported in the vicinity, or that eerie voices have been heard calling from the Sands when the sea-fogs come down. In 1939, the Ramsgate lifeboat was summoned when a paddle-steamer identical to the SS Violet, wrecked 82 years earlier, was sighted going down to a chorus of lamentation. Not only did the lifeboat crew find no survivors, they found no bodies either, no wreckage and no reports that any craft had gone missing in the area.

But perhaps the most famous Goodwin Sands ghost story concerns a ship which it is not even certain existed to begin with. The schooner Lady Lovibond allegedly sank on February 13th 1743, when first-mate John Rivers, driven mad with jealousy as the skipper, Simon Reed, had just married the woman of his dreams, deliberately steered the ship onto the shoals. Every 50 years afterwards, a phantom version of the Lovibond – giving off *a spooky greenish glow – is said to reappear and re-enact the tragedy, and this is not just wild rumour. In both 1798 and 1848 rescue services were launched from nearby Deal in response to reports of a wreck on the Sands, and in neither case was any trace of a damaged or endangered vessel discovered.*

This mystery has only deepened with time. When curious journalists took a boat out to the Sands on February 13th 1998, and failed to spot any spectral craft, they looked into the story more closely and no contemporary accounts of the Lovibond disaster were uncovered. Not only that, there is no mention of any vessel called Lady Lovibond in the Lloyd's Register, though this doesn't mean that she was never launched.

Beacons and buoys now ensure that Goodwin Sands is avoided by most shipping, but there are still those who occasionally stray near, usually in the midst of those all-enveloping sea-frets so common to England's southeast coast, and afterwards report curious sounds from the Sands: despairing cries and the cracking of timbers. Some even claim to have witnessed glowing, semi-translucent craft gliding silently through the vapours.

THE ENTERTAINMENT
Ramsey Campbell

By the time Shone found himself back in Westingsea he was able to distinguish only snatches of the road as the wipers strove to fend off the downpour. The promenade where he'd seen pensioners wheeled out for an early dose of sunshine, and backpackers piling into coaches that would take them inland to the Lakes, was waving isolated trees that looked too young to be out by themselves at a grey sea baring hundreds of edges of foam. Through a mixture of static and the hiss on the windscreen a local radio station advised drivers to stay off the roads, and he felt he was being offered a chance. Once he had a room he could phone Ruth. At the end of the promenade he swung the Cavalier around an old stone soldier drenched almost black and coasted alongside the seafront hotels.

There wasn't a welcome in sight. A sign in front of the largest and whitest hotel said NO, apparently having lost the patience to light up its second word. He turned along the first of the narrow streets of boarding houses, in an unidentifiable one of which he'd stayed with his parents most of fifty years ago, but the placards in the windows were just as uninviting. Some of the streets he remembered having been composed of small hotels had fewer buildings now, all of them care homes for the elderly. He had to lower his window to read the signs across the roads, and before he'd finished his right side was soaked. He needed a room for the night – he hadn't the energy to drive back to London. Half an hour would take him to the motorway, near which he was bound to find a hotel. But he had only reached the edge of town, and was braking at a junction, when he saw hands adjusting a notice in the window of a broad three-storey house.

He squinted in the mirror to confirm he wasn't in anyone's way, then inched his window down. The notice had either fallen or been removed, but the parking area at the end of the short drive was unoccupied, and above the high thick streaming wall a signboard that frantic bushes were doing their best to obscure appeared to say most of HOTEL. He veered between the gateposts and came close to touching the right breast of the house.

He couldn't distinguish much through the bay window. At least one layer of net curtains was keeping the room to itself. Beyond heavy purple curtains trapping moisture against the glass, a light was suddenly extinguished. He grabbed his overnight bag from the rear seat and dashed for the open porch.

The rain kept him company as he poked the round brass bellpush next to the tall front door. There was no longer a button, only a socket harbouring a large bedraggled spider that recoiled almost as violently as his finger did. He hadn't laid hold of the rusty knocker above the neutral grimace of the letter-slot when a woman called a warning or a salutation as she hauled the door open. "Here's someone now."

She was in her seventies but wore a dress that failed to cover her mottled toadstools of knees. She stooped as though the weight of her loose throat was bringing her face, which was almost as white as her hair, to meet his. "Are you the entertainment?" she said.

Behind her a hall more than twice his height and darkly papered with a pattern of embossed vines not unlike arteries led to a central staircase that vanished under the next floor up. Beside her a long-legged table was strewn with crumpled brochures for local attractions; above it a pay telephone with no number in the middle of its dial clung to the wall. Shone was trying to decide if this was indeed a hotel when the question caught up with him. "Am I..."

"Don't worry, there's a room waiting." She scowled past him and shook her head like a wet dog. "And there'd be dinner and a breakfast for anyone who settles them down."

He assumed this referred to the argument that had started or recommenced in the room where the light he'd seen switched off had been relit. Having lost count of the number of arguments he'd dealt with in the Hackney kindergarten where he worked, he didn't see why this should be any different. "I'll have a stab," he said, and marched into the room.

Despite its size, it was full of just two women – of the breaths of one at least as wide as her bright pink dress, who was struggling to lever herself up from an armchair with a knuckly stick and collapsing red-faced, and of the antics of her companion, a lanky woman in the flapping jacket of a dark blue suit and the skirt of a greyer outfit, who'd bustled away from the light-switch to flutter the pages of a television listings magazine before scurrying fast as the cartoon squirrel on the television to twitch the cord of the velvet curtains, an activity Shone took to have dislodged whatever notice had been in the window. Both women were at least as old as the person who'd admitted him, but he didn't let that daunt him. "What seems to be the problem?" he said, and immediately had to say "I can't hear you if you both talk at once."

"The light's in my eyes," the woman in the chair complained, though of the six bulbs in the chandelier one was dead, another missing. "Unity keeps putting it on when she knows I'm watching."

"Amelia's had her cartoons on all afternoon," Unity said, darting at the television, then drumming her knuckles on top of an armchair instead. "I want to see what's happening in the world."

"Shall we let Unity watch the news now, Amelia? If it isn't something you like watching you won't mind if the light's on."

Amelia glowered before delving into her cleavage for an object that she flung at him. Just in time to field it he identified it as the remote control. Unity ran to snatch it from him, and as a newsreader appeared with a war behind him Shone withdrew. He was lingering over closing the door while he attempted to judge whether the mountainous landscapes on the walls were vague with mist or dust when a man at his back murmured "Come out, quick, and shut it."

He was a little too thin for his suit that was grey as his sparse hair. Though his pinkish eyes looked harassed, and he kept shrugging his shoulders as though to displace a shiver, he succeeded in producing enough of a grateful smile to part his teeth. "By gum, Daph said you'd sort them out, and you have. You can stay," he said.

Among the questions Shone was trying to resolve was why the man seemed familiar, but a gust of rain so fierce it strayed under the front door made the offer irresistible. "Overnight, you mean," he thought it best to check.

"That's the least," the manager presumably only began, and twisted round to find the stooped woman. "Daph will show you up, Mr..."

"Shone."

"Who is he?" Daph said as if preparing to announce him.

"Tom Shone," Shone told her.

"Mr Thomson?"

"Tom Shone. First name Tom."

"Mr Tom Thomson."

He might have suspected a joke if it hadn't been for her earnestness, and so he appealed to the manager. "Do you need my signature?"

"Later, don't you fret," the manager assured him, receding along the hall.

"And as for payment..."

"Just room and board. That's always the arrangement."

"You mean you want me to..."

"Enjoy yourself," the manager called, and disappeared beyond the stairs into somewhere that smelled of an imminent dinner.

Shone felt his overnight bag leave his shoulder. Daph had relieved him of the burden and was striding upstairs, turning in a crouch to see that he followed. "He's forever off somewhere, Mr Snell," she said, and repeated "Mr Snell."

Shone wondered if he was being invited to reply with a joke until she added "Don't worry, we know what it's like to forget your name."

She was saying he, not she, had been confused about it. If she hadn't cantered out of sight his response would have been as sharp as the rebukes he gave his pupils when they were too childish. Above the middle floor the staircase bent towards the front of the house, and he saw how unexpectedly far the place went back. Perhaps nobody was staying in that section, since the corridor was dark and smelled old. He grabbed the banister to speed himself up, only to discover it wasn't much less sticky than a sucked lollipop. By the time he arrived at the top of the house he was furious to find himself panting.

Daph had halted at the far end of a passage lit, if that was the word, by infrequent bulbs in glass flowers sprouting from the walls. Around them shadows fattened the veins of the paper. "This'll be you," Daph said and pushed open a door.

Beside a small window under a yellowing light bulb the ceiling angled almost to the carpet brown as mud. A narrow bed stood in the angle, opposite a wardrobe and dressing-table and a sink beneath a dingy mirror. At least there was a phone on a shelf by the sink. Daph passed him his bag as he ventured into the room. "You'll be fetched when it's time," she told him.

"Time? Time..."

"For dinner and all the fun, silly," she said, with a laugh so shrill his ears wanted to flinch.

She was halfway to the stairs when he thought to call after her "Aren't I supposed to have a key?"

"Mr Snell will have it. Mr Snell," she reminded him, and was gone.

He had to phone Ruth as soon as he was dry and changed. There must be a bathroom somewhere near. He hooked his bag over his shoulder with a finger and stepped into the twilight of the corridor. He'd advanced only a few paces when Daph's head poked over the edge of the floor. "You're never leaving us."

He felt absurdly guilty. "Just after the bathroom."

"It's where you're going," she said, firmly enough to be commanding rather than advising him, and vanished down the hole that was the stairs.

She couldn't have meant the room next to his. When he succeeded in coaxing the sticky plastic knob to turn, using the tips of a finger and thumb, he found a room much like his, except that the window was in the angled roof. Seated on the bed in the dimness on its way to dark was a figure in a toddler's blue overall – a Teddy bear with large black ragged eyes or perhaps none. The bed in the adjacent room was strewn with photographs so blurred that he could distinguish only the grin every one of them bore. Someone had been knitting in the next room, but had apparently lost concentration, since one arm of the mauve sweater was at least twice the size of the other. A knitting needle pinned each arm to the bed. Now Shone was at the stairs, beyond which the rear of the house was as dark as that section of the floor below. Surely Daph would have told him if he was on the wrong side of the corridor, and the area past the stairs wasn't as abandoned as it looked: he could hear a high-pitched muttering from the dark, a voice gabbling a plea almost too fast for words, praying with such urgency the speaker seemed to have no time to pause for breath. Shone hurried past the banisters that enclosed three sides of the top of the stairs, and pushed open the door immediately beyond them. There was the bath, and inside the plastic curtains that someone had left closed would be a shower. He elbowed the door wide, and the shower curtains shifted to acknowledge him.

Not only they had. As he tugged the frayed cord to kindle the bare bulb, he heard a muffled giggle from the region of the bath. He threw his bag onto the hook on the door and yanked the shower curtains apart. A naked woman so scrawny he could see not just her ribs but the shape of bones inside her buttocks was crouching on all fours in the bath. She peered wide-eyed over one splayed knobbly hand at him, then dropped the hand to reveal a nose half the width of her face and a gleeful mouth devoid of teeth as she sprang past him. She was out of the room before he could avoid seeing her shrunken disused breasts and pendulous grey-bearded stomach. He heard her run into a room at the dark end of the corridor, calling out "For it now" or perhaps "You're it now." He didn't know if the words were intended for him. He was too busy noticing that the door was boltless.

He wedged his shoes against the corner below the hinges and piled his sodden clothes on top, then padded across the sticky linoleum to the bath. It was cold as stone, and sank at least half an inch with a loud creak as he stepped into it under the blind brass eye of the shower. When he twisted the reluctant squeaky taps it felt at first as though the rain had got in, but swiftly grew so hot he backed into the clammy plastic. He had to press himself against the cold tiled wall to reach the taps, and had just reduced the temperature to bearable when he heard the doorknob rattle. "Taken," he shouted. "Someone's in here."

"My turn."

The voice was so close the speaker's mouth must be pressed against the door. When the rattling increased in vigour Shone yelled "I won't be long. Ten minutes."

"My turn."

It wasn't the same voice. Either the speaker had deepened his pitch in an attempt to daunt Shone or there was more than one person at the door. Shone reached for the sliver of soap in the dish protruding from the tiles, but contented himself with pivoting beneath the shower once he saw the soap was coated with grey hair. "Wait out there," he shouted. "I've nearly finished. No, don't wait. Come back in five minutes."

The rattling ceased, and at least one body dealt the door a large soft thump. Shone wrenched the curtains open in time to see his clothes spill across the linoleum. "Stop that," he roared, and heard someone retreat – either a spectacularly crippled person or two people bumping into the walls as they carried on a struggle down the corridor. A door slammed, then slammed again, unless there were two. By then he was out of the bath and grabbing the solitary bath-towel from the shaky rack. A spider with legs like long grey hairs and a wobbling body as big as Shone's thumbnail scuttled out of the towel and hid under the bath.

He hadn't brought a towel with him. He would have been able to borrow one of Ruth's. He held the towel at arm's length by two corners and shook it over the bath. When nothing else emerged, he rubbed his hair and the rest of him as swiftly as he could. He unzipped his case and donned the clothes he would have sported for dining with Ruth. He hadn't brought a change of shoes, and when he tried on those he'd worn, they squelched. He gathered up his soaked clothes and heaped them with the shoes on his bag, and padded quickly to his room.

As he kneed the door open he heard sounds beyond it: a gasp, another, and then voices spilling into the dark. Before he crossed the room, having dumped his soggy clothes and bag in the wardrobe that, like the rest of the furniture, was secured to a wall and the floor, he heard the voices stream into the house. They must belong to a coach party – brakes and doors had been the sources of the gasps. On the basis of his experiences so far, the influx of residents lacked appeal for him, and made him all the more anxious to speak to Ruth. Propping his shoes against the ribs of the tepid radiator, he sat on the underfed pillow and lifted the sticky receiver.

As soon as he obtained a tone he began to dial. He was more than halfway through Ruth's eleven digits when Snell's voice interrupted. "Who do you want?"

"Long distance."

"You can't get out from the rooms, I'm afraid. There's a phone down here in the hall. Everything else as you want it, Mr Thomson? Only I've got people coming in."

Shone heard some of them outside his room. They were silent except for an unsteady shuffling and the hushed sounds of a number of doors. He could only assume they had been told not to disturb him. "There were people playing games up here," he said.

"They'll be getting ready for tonight. They do work themselves up, some of them. Everything else satisfactory?"

"There's nobody hiding in my room, if that's what you mean."

"Nobody but you."

That struck Shone as well past enough, and he was about to make his feelings clear while asking for his key when the manager said "We'll see you down shortly, then." The line died at once, leaving Shone to attempt an incredulous grin at the events so far. He intended to share it with his reflection above the sink, but hadn't realised until now that the mirror was covered with cracks or a cobweb. The lines appeared to pinch his face thin, to discolour his flesh and add wrinkles. When he leaned closer to persuade himself that was merely an illusion, he saw movement in the sink. An object he'd taken to be a long grey hair was snatched into the plughole, and he glimpsed the body it belonged to squeezing itself out of sight down the pipe. He had to remind himself to transfer his wallet and loose coins and keys from his wet clothes to his current pockets before he hastened out of the room.

The carpet in the passage was damp with footprints, more of which he would have avoided if he hadn't been distracted by sounds in the rooms. Where he'd seen the Teddy bear someone was murmuring "Up you come to mummy. Gummy gum." Next door a voice was crooning "There you all are", presumably to the photographs, and Shone was glad to hear no words from the site of the lopsided knitting, only a clicking so rapid it sounded mechanical. Rather than attempt to interpret any of the muffled noises from the rooms off the darker section of the corridor, he padded downstairs so fast he almost missed his footing twice.

Nothing was moving in the hall except rain under the front door. Several conversations were ignoring one another in the television lounge. He picked up the receiver and thrust coins into the box, and his finger faltered over the zero on the dial. Perhaps because he was distracted by the sudden hush, he couldn't remember Ruth's number.

He dragged the hole of the zero around the dial as far as it would go in case that brought him the rest of the number, and as the hole whirred back to its starting point, it did. Ten more turns of the dial won him a ringing padded with static, and he felt as if the entire house was waiting for Ruth to answer. It took six pairs of rings – longer than she needed to cross her flat – to make her say "Ruth Lawson."

"It's me, Ruth." When there was silence he tried reviving their joke. "Old Ruthless."

"What now, Tom?"

He'd let himself hope for at least a dutiful laugh, but its absence threw him less than the reaction from within the television lounge: a titter, then several. "I just wanted you to know – "

"You're mumbling again. I can't hear you."

He was only seeking to be inaudible to anyone but her. "I say I wanted you to know I really did get the day wrong," he said louder. "I really thought I was supposed to be coming up today."

"Since when has your memory been that bad?"

"Since, I don't know, today, it seems like. No, fair enough, you'll be thinking of your birthday. I know I forgot that too."

A wave of mirth escaped past the ajar door across the hall. Surely however many residents were in there must be laughing at the television with the sound turned down, he told himself as Ruth retorted "If you can forget that you'll forget anything."

"I'm sorry."

"I'm sorrier."

"I'm sorriest," he risked saying, and immediately wished he hadn't completed their routine, not only since it no longer earned him the least response from her but because of the roars of laughter from the television lounge. "Look, I just wanted to be sure you knew I wasn't trying to catch you out, that's all."

"Tom."

All at once her voice was sympathetic, the way it might have sounded at an aged relative's bedside. "Ruth," he said, and almost as stupidly "What?"

"You might as well have been."

"I might... you mean I might..."

"I mean you nearly did."

"Oh." After a pause as hollow as he felt he repeated the syllable, this time not with disappointment but with all the surprise he could summon up. He might have uttered yet another version of the sound, despite or even because of the latest outburst of amusement across the hall, if Ruth hadn't spoken. "I'm talking to him now."

"Talking to who?"

Before the words had finished leaving him Shone understood that she hadn't been speaking to him but about him, because he could hear a man's voice in her flat. Its tone was a good deal more than friendly to her, and it was significantly younger than his. "Good luck to you both," he said, less ironically and more maturely than he would have preferred, and snagged the hook with the receiver.

A single coin trickled down the chute and hit the carpet with a plop. Amidst hilarity in the television lounge several women were crying "To who, to who" like a flock of owls. "He's good, isn't he," someone else remarked, and Shone was trying to decide where to take his confusion bordering on panic when a bell began to toll as it advanced out of the dark part of the house.

It was a small but resonant gong wielded by the manager. Shone heard an eager rumble of footsteps in the television lounge, and more of the same overhead. As he hesitated Daph dodged around the manager towards him. "Let's get you sat down before they start their fuss," she said.

"I'll just fetch my shoes from my room."

"You don't want to bump into the old lot up there. They'll be wet, won't they?"

"Who?" Shone demanded, then regained enough sense of himself to answer his own question with a weak laugh. "My shoes, you mean. They're the only ones I've brought with me."

"I'll find you something once you're in your place," she said, opening the door opposite the television lounge, and stooped lower to hurry him. As soon as he trailed after her she bustled the length of the dining-room and patted a small isolated table until he accepted its solitary straight chair. This faced the room and was boxed in by three long tables, each place at which was set like his with a plastic fork and spoon. Beyond the table opposite him velvet curtains shifted impotently as the windows trembled with rain. Signed photographs covered much of the walls – portraits of comedians he couldn't say he recognised, looking jolly or amusingly lugubrious. "We've had them all," Daph said. "They kept us going. It's having fun keeps the old lot alive." Some of this might have been addressed not just to him, because she was on her way out of the room. He barely had time to observe that the plates on the Welsh dresser to his left were painted on the wood, presumably to obviate breakage, before the residents crowded in.

A disagreement over the order of entry ceased at the sight of him. Some of the diners were scarcely able to locate their places for gazing at him rather more intently than he cared to reciprocate. Several of them were so inflated that he was unable to determine their gender except by their clothes, and not even thus in the case of the most generously trousered of them, whose face appeared to be sinking into a nest of flesh. Contrast was provided by a man so emaciated his handless wristwatch kept sliding down to his knuckles. Unity and Amelia sat facing Shone, and then, to his dismay, the last of the eighteen seats was occupied by the woman he'd found in the bath, presently covered from neck to ankles in a black sweater and slacks. When she regarded him with an expression of never having seen him before and delight at doing so now he tried to feel some relief, but he was mostly experiencing how all the diners seemed to be awaiting some action from him. Their attention had started to paralyse him when Daph and Mr Snell reappeared through a door Shone hadn't noticed beside the Welsh dresser.

The manager set about serving the left-hand table with bowls of soup while Daph hurried over, brandishing an especially capacious pair of the white cloth slippers Shone saw all the residents were wearing. "We've only these," she said, dropping them at his feet. "They're dry, that's the main thing. See how they feel."

Shone could almost have inserted both feet into either of them. "I'll feel a bit of a clown, to tell you the truth."

"Never mind, you won't be going anywhere."

Shone poked his feet into the slippers and lifted them to discover whether the footwear had any chance of staying on. At once all the residents burst out laughing. Some of them stamped as a form of applause, and even Snell produced a fleeting grateful smile as he and Daph retreated to the kitchen. Shone let his feet drop, which was apparently worth another round of merriment. It faded as Daph and Snell came out with more soup, a bowl of which the manager brought Shone, lowering it over the guest's shoulder before spreading his fingers on either side of him. "Here's Tommy Thomson for you," he announced, and leaned down to murmur in Shone's ear "That'll be all right, won't it? Sounds better."

At that moment Shone's name was among his lesser concerns. Instead he gestured at the plastic cutlery. "Do you think I could –"

Before he had time to ask for metal utensils with a knife among them, Snell moved away as though the applause and the coos of joy his announcement had drawn were propelling him. "Just be yourself," he mouthed at Shone.

The spoon was the size Shone would have used to stir tea if the doctor hadn't recently forbidden him sugar. As he picked it up there was instant silence. He lowered it into the thin broth, where he failed to find anything solid, and raised it to his lips. The brownish liquid tasted of some unidentifiable meat with a rusty undertaste. He was too old to be finicky about food that had been served to everyone. He swallowed, and when his body raised no protest he set about spooning the broth into himself as fast as he could without spilling it, to finish the task.

He'd barely signalled his intentions when the residents began to cheer and stamp. Some of them imitated his style with the broth while others demonstrated how much more theatrically they could drink theirs; those closest to the hall emitted so much noise that he could have thought part of the slurping came from outside the room. When he frowned in that direction, the residents chortled as though he'd made another of the jokes he couldn't avoid making.

He dropped the spoon in the bowl at last, only to have Daph return it to the table with a briskness not far short of a rebuke. While she and Snell were in the kitchen everyone else gazed at Shone, who felt compelled to raise his eyebrows and hold out his hands. One of the expanded people nudged another, and both of them wobbled gleefully, and then all the residents were overcome by laughter that continued during the arrival of the main course, as if this was a joke they were eager for him to see. His plate proved to bear three heaps of mush, white and pale green and a glistening brown. "What is it?" he dared to ask Daph.

"What we always have," she said as if to a child or to someone who'd reverted to that state. "It's what we need to keep us going."

The heaps were of potatoes and vegetables and some kind of mince with an increased flavour of the broth. He did his utmost to eat naturally, despite the round of applause this brought him. Once his innards began to feel heavy he lined up the utensils on his by no means clear plate, attracting Daph to stoop vigorously at him. "I've finished," he said.

"Not yet."

When she stuck out her hands he thought she was going to return the fork and spoon to either side of his plate. Instead she removed it and began to clear the next table. While he'd been concentrating on hiding his reaction to his food the residents had gobbled theirs, he saw. The plates were borne off to the kitchen, leaving an expectant silence broken only by a restless shuffling. Wherever he glanced, he could see nobody's feet moving, and he told himself the sounds had been Daph's as she emerged from the kitchen with a large cake iced white as a memorial. "Daph's done it again," the hugest resident piped.

Shone took that to refer to the portrait in icing of a clown on top of the cake. He couldn't share the general enthusiasm for it; the clown looked undernourished and blotchily red-faced, and not at all certain what shape his wide twisted gaping lips should form. Snell brought in a pile of plates on which Daph placed slices of cake, having cut it in half and removed the clown's head from his shoulders in the process, but the distribution of slices caused some debate. "Give Tommy Thomson my eye," a man with bleary bloodshot eyeballs said.

"He can have my nose," offered the woman he'd seen in the bath.

"I'm giving him the hat," Daph said, which met with hoots of approval. The piece of cake she gave him followed the outline almost precisely of the clown's sagging pointed cap. At least it would bring dinner to an end, he thought, and nothing much could be wrong with a cake. He didn't expect it to taste faintly of the flavour of the rest of the meal. Perhaps that was why, provoking a tumult of jollity, he began to cough and then choke on a crumb. Far too eventually Daph brought him a glass of water in which he thought he detected the same taste. "Thanks," he gasped anyway, and as his coughs and the applause subsided, managed to say "Thanks. All over now. If you'll excuse me, I think I'll take myself off to bed."

The noise the residents had made so far was nothing to the uproar with which they greeted this. "We haven't had the entertainment yet," Unity protested, jumping to her feet and looking more than ready to dart the length of the room. "Got to sing for your supper, Tommy Thomson."

"We don't want any songs and we don't want any speeches," Amelia declared. "We always have the show."

"The show," all the diners began to chant, and clapped and stamped in time with it, led by the thumping of Amelia's stick. "The show. The show."

The manager leaned across Shone's table. His eyes were pinker than ever, and blinking several times a second. "Better put it on for them or you'll get no rest," he muttered. "You won't need to be anything special."

Perhaps it was the way Snell was leaning down to him that let Shone see why he seemed familiar. Could he really have run the hotel where Shone had stayed with his parents nearly fifty years ago? How old would he have to be? Shone had no chance to wonder while the question was "What are you asking me to do?"

"Nothing much. Nothing someone of your age can't cope with. Come on and I'll show you before they start wanting to play their games."

It wasn't clear how much of a threat this was meant to be. Just now Shone was mostly grateful to be ushered away from the stamping and the chant. Retreating upstairs had ceased to tempt him, and fleeing to his car made no sense when he could hardly shuffle across the carpet for trying to keep his feet in the slippers. Instead he shambled after the manager to the doorway of the television lounge. "Go in there," Snell urged, and gave him a wincing smile. "Just stand in it. Here they come."

The room had been more than rearranged. The number of seats had been increased to eighteen by the addition of several folding chairs. All the seats faced the television, in front of which a small portable theatre not unlike the site of a Punch and Judy show had been erected. Above the deserted ledge of a stage rose a tall pointed roof that reminded Shone of the clown's hat. Whatever words had been inscribed across the base of the gable were as faded as the many colours of the frontage. He'd managed to decipher only ENTER HERE when he found himself hobbling towards the theatre, driven by the chanting that had emerged into the hall.

The rear of the theatre was a heavy velvet curtain, black where it wasn't greenish. A slit had been cut in it up to a height of about four feet. As he ducked underneath, the mouldy velvet clung to the nape of his neck. A smell of damp and staleness enclosed him when he straightened up. His elbows knocked against the sides of the box, disturbing the two figures that lay on a shelf under the stage, their empty bodies sprawling, their faces nestling together upside down as though they had dragged themselves close for companionship. He turned the faces upwards and saw that the figures, whose fixed grins and eyes were almost too wide for amusement, were supposed to be a man and a woman, although only a few tufts of grey hair clung to each dusty skull. He was nerving himself to insert his hands in the gloves of the bodies when the residents stamped chanting into the room.

Unity ran to a chair and then, restless with excitement, to another. Amelia dumped herself in the middle of a sofa and inched groaning to one end. Several of the jumbo residents lowered themselves onto folding chairs that looked immediately endangered. At least the seating of the audience put paid to the chant, but everyone's gaze fastened on Shone until he seemed to feel it clinging to the nerves of his face. Beyond the residents Snell mouthed "Just slip them on."

Shone pulled the open ends of the puppets towards him and poked them gingerly wider, dreading the emergence of some denizen from inside one or both. They appeared to be uninhabited, however, and so he thrust his hands in, trying to think which of his kindergarten stories he might adapt for the occasion. The brownish material fitted itself easily over his hands, almost as snug as the skin it resembled, and before he was ready each thumb was a puppet's arm, the little fingers too, and three fingers were shakily raising each head as if the performers were being roused from sleep. The spectators were already cheering, a response that seemed to entice the tufted skulls above the stage. Their entrance was welcomed by a clamour in which requests gradually became audible. "Let's see them knock each other about like the young lot do these days."

"Football with the baby."

"Make them go like animals."

"Smash their heads together."

They must be thinking of Punch and Judy, Shone told himself – and then a wish succeeded in quelling the rest. "Let's have Old Ruthless."

"Old Ruthless" was the chant as the stamping renewed itself – as his hands sprang onto the stage to wag the puppets at each other. All at once everything he'd been through that day seemed to have concentrated itself in his hands, and perhaps that was the only way he could be rid of it. He nodded the man that was his right hand at the balding female and uttered a petulant croak. "What do you mean, it's not my day?"

He shook the woman and gave her a squeaky voice. "What day do you think it is?"

"It's Wednesday, isn't it? Thursday, rather. Hang on, it's Friday, of course. Saturday, I mean."

"It's Sunday. Can't you hear the bells?"

"I thought they were for us to be married. Hey, what are you hiding there? I didn't know you had a baby yet."

"That's no baby, that's my boyfriend."

Shone twisted the figures to face the audience. The puppets might have been waiting for guffaws or even groans at the echo of an old joke: certainly he was. The residents were staring at him with, at best, bemusement. Since he'd begun the performance the only noise had been the sidling of the puppets along the stage and the voices that caught harshly in his throat. The manager and Daph were gazing at him over the heads of the residents; both of them seemed to have forgotten how to blink or grin. Shone turned the puppets away from the spectators as he would have liked to turn himself. "What's up with us?" he squeaked, wagging the woman's head. "We aren't going down very well."

"Never mind, I still love you. Give us a kiss," he croaked, and made the other puppet totter a couple of steps before it fell on its face. The loud crack of the fall took him off guard, as did the way the impact trapped his fingers in the puppet's head. The figure's ungainly attempts to stand up weren't nearly as simulated as he would have preferred. "It's these clown's shoes. You can't expect anyone to walk in them," he grumbled. "Never mind looking as if I'm an embarrassment."

"You're nothing else, are you? You'll be forgetting your own name next."

"Don't be daft," he croaked, no longer understanding why he continued to perform, unless to fend off the silence that was dragging words and antics out of him. "We both know what my name is."

"Not after that crack you fetched your head. You won't be able to keep anything in there now."

"Well, that's where you couldn't be wronger. My name..." He meant the puppet's, not his own: that was why he was finding it hard to produce. "It's, you know, you know perfectly well. You know it as well as I do."

"See, it's gone."

"Tell me or I'll thump you till you can't stand up," Shone snarled in a rage that was no longer solely the puppet's, and brought the helplessly grinning heads together with a sound like the snapping of bone. The audience began to cheer at last, but he was scarcely aware of them. The collision had split the faces open, releasing the top joints of his fingers only to trap them in the splintered gaps. The clammy bodies of the puppets clung to him as his hands wrenched at each other. Abruptly something gave, and the female head flew off as the body tore open. His right elbow hit the wall of the theatre, and the structure lurched at him. As he tried to steady it, the head of the puppet rolled under his feet. He tumbled backwards into the mouldy curtains. The theatre reeled with him, and the room tipped up.

He was lying on his back, and his breath was somewhere else. In trying to prevent the front of the theatre from striking him he'd punched himself on the temple with the cracked male head. Through the proscenium he saw the ceiling high above him and heard the appreciation of the audience. More time passed than he thought necessary before several of them approached.

Either the theatre was heavier than he'd realised or his fall had weakened him. Even once he succeeded in peeling Old Ruthless off his hand he was unable to lift the theatre off himself as the puppet lay like a deflated baby on his chest. At last Amelia lowered herself towards him, and he was terrified that she intended to sit on him. Instead she thrust a hand that looked boiled almost into his face to grab the proscenium and haul the theatre off him. As someone else bore it away she seized his lapels and, despite the creaking of her stick, yanked him upright while several hands helped raise him from behind. "Are you fit?" she wheezed.

"I'll be fine," Shone said before he knew. All the chairs had been pushed back against the windows, he saw. "We'll show you one of our games now," Unity said behind him.

"You deserve it after all that," said Amelia, gathering the fragments of the puppets to hug them to her breasts.

"I think I'd like – "

"That's right, you will. We'll show you how we play. Who's got the hood?"

"Me," Unity cried. "Someone do it up for me."

Shone turned to see her flourishing a black cap. As she raised it over her head, he found he was again robbed of breath. When she tugged it down he realised that it was designed to cover the player's eyes, more like a magician's prop than an element of any game. The man with the handless watch dangling from his wrist pulled the cords of the hood tight behind her head and tied them in a bow, then twirled her round several times, each of which drew from her a squeal only just of pleasure. She wobbled around once more as, having released her, he tiptoed to join the other residents against the walls of the room.

She had her back to Shone, who had stayed by the chairs, beyond which the noise of rain had ceased. She darted away from him, her slippered feet patting the carpet, then lurched sideways towards nobody in particular and cocked her head. She was well out of the way of Shone's route to the door, where Daph and the manager looked poised to sneak out. He only had to avoid the blinded woman and he would be straight up to his room, either to barricade himself in or to retrieve his belongings and head for the car. He edged one foot forward into the toe of the slipper, and Unity swung towards him. "Caught you. I know who that is, Mr Tommy Thomson."

"No you don't," Shone protested in a rage at everything that had led to the moment, but Unity swooped at him. She closed her bony hands around his cheeks and held on tight far longer than seemed reasonable before undoing the bow of the hood with her right hand while gripping and stroking his chin with the other. "Now it's your turn to go in the dark."

"I think I've had enough for one day, if you'll excuse – "

This brought a commotion of protests not far short of outrage. "You aren't done yet, a young thing like you." "She's older than you and she didn't make a fuss." "You've been caught, you have to play." "If you don't it won't be fair." The manager had retreated into the doorway and was pushing air at Shone with his outstretched hands as Daph mouthed "It's supposed to be the old lot's time." Her words and the rising chant of "Be fair" infected Shone with guilt, aggravated when Unity uncovered her reproachful eyes and held out the hood. He'd disappointed Ruth, he didn't need to let these old folk down too. "Fair enough, I'll play," he said. "Just don't twist me too hard."

He hadn't finished speaking when Unity planted the hood on his scalp and drew the material over his brows. It felt like the clammy bodies of the puppets. Before he had a chance to shudder it was dragging his eyelids down, and he could see nothing but darkness. The hood moulded itself to his cheekbones as rapid fingers tied the cords behind his head. "Not too – " he gasped at whoever started twirling him across the room.

He felt as if he'd been caught by a vortex of cheering and hooting, but it included murmurs too. "He played with me in the bath." "He wouldn't let us in there." "He made me miss my cartoons." "That's right, and he tried to take the control off us." He was being whirled so fast he no longer knew where he was. "Enough," he cried, and was answered by an instant hush. Several hands shoved him staggering forward, and a door closed stealthily behind him.

At first he thought the room had grown colder and damper. Then, as his giddiness steadied, he understood that he was in a different room, further towards the rear of the house. He felt the patchy lack of carpet through his slippers, though that seemed insufficient reason for the faint scraping of feet he could hear surrounding him to sound so harsh. He thought he heard a whisper or the rattling of some object within a hollow container level with his head. Suddenly, in a panic that flared like white blindness inside the hood, he knew Daph's last remark hadn't been addressed to him, nor had it referred to anyone he'd seen so far. His hands flew to untie the hood – not to see where he was and with whom, but which way to run.

He was so terrified to find the cord immovably knotted that it took him seconds to locate the loose ends of the bow. A tug at them released it. He was forcing his fingertips under the edge of the hood when he heard light dry footsteps scuttle towards him, and an article that he tried to think of as a hand groped at his face. He staggered backwards, blindly fending off whatever was there. His fingers encountered ribs barer than they ought to be, and poked between them to meet the twitching contents of the bony cage. The whole of him convulsed as he snatched off the hood and flung it away.

The room was either too dark or not quite dark enough. It was at least the size of the one he'd left, and contained half a dozen sagging armchairs that glistened with moisture, and more than twice as many figures. Some were sprawled like loose bundles of sticks topped with grimacing masks on the chairs, but nonetheless doing their feeble best to clap their tattered hands. Even those that were swaying around him appeared to have left portions of themselves elsewhere. All of them were attached to strings or threads that glimmered in the murk and led his reluctant gaze to the darkest corner of the room.

A restless mass crouched in it – a body with too many limbs, or a huddle of bodies that had grown inextricably entangled by the process of withering. Some of its movement, though not all, was of shapes that swarmed many-legged out of the midst of it, constructing parts of it or bearing away fragments or extending more threads to the other figures in the room. It took an effort that shrivelled his mind before he was able to distinguish anything else: a thin gap between curtains, a barred window beyond – to his left, the outline of a door to the hall. As the figure nearest to him bowed so close he saw the very little it had in the way of eyes peering through the hair it had stretched coquettishly over its face, Shone bolted for the hall.

The door veered aside as his dizziness swept it away. His slippers snagged a patch of carpet and almost threw him on his face. The doorknob refused to turn in his sweaty grasp, even when he gripped it with both hands. Then it yielded, and as the floor at his back resounded with a mass of uneven yet purposeful shuffling, the door juddered open. He hauled himself around it and fled awkwardly, slippers flapping, out of the dark part of the hall.

Every room was shut. Other than the scratching of nails or of the ends of fingers at the door behind him, there was silence. He dashed along the hall, striving to keep the slippers on, not knowing why, knowing only that he had to reach the front door. He seized the latch and flung the door wide and slammed it as he floundered out of the house.

The rain had ceased except for dripping of foliage. The gravel glittered like the bottom of a stream. The coach he'd heard arriving – an old private coach spattered with mud – was parked across the rear of his car, so close it practically touched the bumper. He could never manoeuvre out of that trap. He almost knocked on the window of the television lounge, but instead limped over the gravel and into the street, towards the quiet hotels. He had no idea where he was going except away from the house. He'd hobbled just a few paces, his slippers growing more sodden and his feet sorer at each step, when headlamps sped out of the town.

They belonged to a police car. It halted beside him, its hazard lights twitching, and a uniformed policeman was out of the passenger seat before Shone could speak. The man's slightly chubby concerned face was a wholesome pink beneath a streetlamp. "Can you help me?" Shone pleaded. "I – "

"Don't get yourself in a state, old man. We saw where you came from."

"They boxed me in. My car, I mean, look. If you can just tell them to let me out – "

The driver moved to Shone's other side. He might have been trying to outdo his colleague's caring look. "Calm down now. We'll see to everything for you. What have you done to your head?"

"Banged it. Hit it with, you wouldn't believe me, it doesn't matter. I'll be fine. If I can just fetch my stuff – "

"What have you lost? Won't it be in the house?"

"That's right, at the top. My shoes are."

"Feet hurting, are they? No wonder with you wandering around like that on a night like this. Here, get his other arm." The driver had taken Shone's right elbow in a firm grip, and now he and his partner easily lifted Shone and bore him towards the house. "What's your name, sir?" the driver enquired.

"Not Thomson, whatever anyone says. Not Tommy Thomson or Tom either. Or rather, it's Tom all right, but Tom Shone. That doesn't sound like Thomson, does it? Shone as in shine. I used to know someone who said I still shone for her, you still shine for me, she'd say. Been to see her today as a matter of fact." He was aware of talking too much as the policemen kept nodding at him and the house with its two lit windows – the television lounge's and his – reared over him. "Anyway, the point is the name's Shone," he said. "Ess aitch, not haitch as some youngsters won't be told it isn't, oh en ee. Shone."

"We've got you." The driver reached for the empty bellpush, then pounded on the front door. It swung inwards almost at once, revealing the manager. "Is this gentleman a guest of yours, Mr Snell?" the driver's colleague said.

"Mr Thomson. We thought we'd lost you," Snell declared, and pushed the door wide. All the people from the television lounge were lining the hall like spectators at a parade. "Tommy Thomson," they chanted.

"That's not me," Shone protested, pedalling helplessly in the air until his slippers flew into the hall. "I told you – "

"You did, sir," the driver murmured, and his partner said even lower "Where do you want us to take you?"

"To the top, just to – "

"We know," the driver said conspiratorially. The next moment Shone was sailing to the stairs and up them, with the briefest pause as the policemen retrieved a slipper each. The chant from the hall faded, giving way to a silence that seemed most breathlessly expectant in the darkest sections of the house. He had the police with him, Shone reassured himself. "I can walk now," he said, only to be borne faster to the termination of the stairs. "Where the door's open?" the driver suggested. "Where the light is?"

"That's me. Not me really, anything but, I mean – "

They swung him through the doorway by his elbows and deposited him on the carpet. "It couldn't be anybody else's room," the driver said, dropping the slippers in front of Shone. "See, you're already here."

Shone looked where the policemen were gazing with such sympathy it felt like a weight that was pressing him into the room. A photograph of himself and Ruth, arms around each other's shoulders with a distant mountain behind, had been removed from his drenched suit and propped on the shelf in place of the telephone. "I just brought that," he protested, "you can see how wet it was," and limped across the room to don his shoes. He hadn't reached them when he saw himself in the mirror.

He stood swaying a little, unable to retreat from the sight. He heard the policemen murmur together and withdraw, and their descent of the stairs, and eventually the dual slam of car doors and the departure of the vehicle. His reflection still hadn't allowed him to move. It was no use his telling himself that some of the tangle of wrinkles might be cobwebs, not when his hair was no longer greying but white. "All right, I see it," he yelled – he had no idea at whom. "I'm old. I'm old."

"Soon," said a whisper like an escape of gas in the corridor, along which darkness was approaching as the lamps failed one by one. "You'll be plenty of fun yet," the remains of another voice said somewhere in his room. Before he could bring himself to look for its source, an item at the end of most of an arm fumbled around the door and switched out the light. The dark felt as though his vision was abandoning him, but he knew it was the start of another game. Soon he would know if it was worse than hide and seek – worse than the first sticky unseen touch of the web of the house on his face.

THE HORSE AND THE HAG

Minster-in-Sheppey, on the north coast of the Isle of Sheppey, in Kent, is one of southern England's oldest centres of Christian pilgrimage. A monastery was first constructed there in the Dark Ages, around 670 AD, by Queen Seaxburh in honour of her late husband, King Eorconberht, once a feared pagan warrior but a man who later converted to Christianity, threw down the many idols for which this district was famous, and created the first Saxon archbishop. Saexburh would later go on to become an abbess in her own right and a saint, and her tomb at Ely was venerated for many centuries.

It is perhaps a surprise, therefore, that a story of fearsome and apparent supernatural vengeance is also associated with Minster-in-Sheppey. Whether it owes to the anger of God, as some have assumed, or is simply a tale of ill-luck and unfortunate coincidence, it is impossible to determine.

It concerns Sir Robert de Shurland, a famous knight and local land owner, who seems to have had a fairly fractious relationship with the monks of Minster-in-Sheppey. This came to a head in the year 1300, when for whatever reason – the causes of the dispute are not recorded – Sir Robert killed one of his ecclesiastical neighbours. Some tales tell how, in a fit of rage, he drew his sword and cut the fellow down during an argument. But other accounts claim that Sir Robert actually kidnapped his victim and buried him alive. Either way, news of the incident was soon circling, and the High Sheriff of Kent, Henry de Cobham, issued an arrest-warrant. Sir Robert knew that he was in serious trouble – one did not slay priests or monks in the Middle Ages. As fate would have it, a fleet of ships was passing the coast at that time, one of them the royal flagship of the king, Edward I, who was en route to Europe. Sir Robert had served King Edward ably upon the battlefield, and many times had been promised a reward – he now sought to call this in, though it wouldn't be easy.

The king's ship was over two miles from shore when Sir Robert, mounted on his strongest battle-steed, rode into the waves. Incredibly, he urged the animal into ever deeper water until soon it was swimming, and even then he spurred it relentlessly on. The crew of the ship reacted in amazement when he finally came up alongside them, and King Edward was so impressed by this feat of daring that he heard Sir Robert out and afterwards granted him an unconditional pardon. Of course, the ordeal was far from over. If they didn't want to participate in the *king's latest French war, Sir Robert and his horse now had to return to shore the same way they had left it. But once again the dauntless duo was successful. The loyal animal made it back to the beach with its master on its back, whereupon both collapsed on the sand, exhausted.*

Only after several minutes did Sir Robert realise that he wasn't alone. On looking up, he spied a hideous hag nearby. Cackling, the hag assured him that, though his steed had saved his life on this occasion, in due course it would be the reason for his death. Sir Robert drew his sword in an effort to force the hag to tell him more, but she had now withdrawn into the woods beyond the dunes. He searched, but was unable to find her. Brooding and frightened, Sir Robert returned to the beach. Seeing no other way to prevent his horse being the death of him, he drew his steel again and beheaded the noble brute.

Decades later, Sir Robert, who had not lived a happy life, was wandering disconsolately along the same stretch of shore, when he heard that familiar cackling laugh. He spun around and beheld the same hag – who by now should have died from old age – sitting on a rock. When he demanded an explanation, she replied that his time was nigh. He responded in his usual way, by drawing his sword and running at her. The hag promptly vanished, revealing that 'the rock' she had been seated upon was the skull of the horse he had beheaded all those years earlier. Furious and frustrated, Sir Robert kicked at the skull and it shattered, only for one of its teeth to penetrate his leather boot and sink into his toe.

Sir Robert limped home, but over the next few days fell into a fever from which he never recovered. Within weeks he was dead, accounted for either by blood poisoning or gangrene depending which version of the tale one reads.

How much truth this story contains remains open to conjecture, but it was well known throughout Kent for many centuries. Sir Robert de Shurland certainly existed in real life and is known to have died as the result of an injury to his foot. His resting place can still be seen in the abbey church at Minster-in-Sheppey, the effigy on his tomb portraying an archetypical knight of that era, though with one unusual addition – next to his right foot lies a horse's severed head.

THE POOR WEATHER CROSSINGS COMPANY
Simon Kurt Unsworth

SEE THE BAY AS IT SHOULD BE SEEN!

FOR A SINGLE EVENING ONLY THE POOR WEATHER CROSSINGS COMPANY IS SOON RETURNING TO MORECAMBE! BOOK NOW TO CROSS THE BAY IN THE WORST OF WEATHERS AND SEE ITS TERRIBLE MAJESTY AND PURPOSE AT CLOSE HAND. FOR A SELECT FEW, THIS IS A ONCE IN A LIFETIME OPPORTUNITY, AS THE COMPANY HAS NO PLANS TO RETURN TO AREA FOR MANY YEARS. WALK WITH THE KING'S GUIDE TO THE SANDS AND HAVE THE EXPERIENCE OF YOUR LIFE!

Sykes found the advert on a night out towards the end of summer, in one of the pubs on the seafront thick with noise and sweat and the odours of stale beer and cheap perfume. It was a hand-printed poster stuck to the wall, the sort of thing that he always thought of as American: an A4 sheet with details printed across most of the paper's face but with the bottom sliced into fingers to tear away, each with the number to call printed along its length.

He tore a finger off and stuffed it in his pocket, not really intending to do anything about it, and found it the next morning, crumpled and beer-stained, in amongst his change and masses of other flyers and leaflets. He looked at the number for a moment and then picked up his mobile. *What can it hurt*, he thought? *It's something new to do, after all*.

*

"Welcome, welcome!" cried the little man, doing an odd hopping, skipping dance in front of the small crowd as he spoke. "You are most welcome!"

They had called Sykes out of the blue that day, almost two months after he had registered with them, telling him that the crossing was to be that night. At first he was going to turn them down but then he thought, *What else will I be doing? Sitting in front of the television watching programmes about houses or antiques? Sitting in a bar I don't like, drinking with people I don't really know? Walking like a ghost through Morecambe, wishing I was somewhere else?* And, almost without intending to, he heard himself agree to go and nodding when they told him where to meet the rest of the walkers.

As well as Sykes, there were three Japanese students waiting by the side of the road, an old man wearing a bright yellow raincoat and a sou'wester, a couple with a child who looked to be about nine, all three wrapped up in wet weather gear that creaked with newness, and a group of five that he thought might be from one of the seafront hotels that specialised in coach holidays for retirees. Around them the autumn night squalled, spraying them with rain as fine as exhaled breath, cold and tasting of brine and sand.

And there was the man.

He was small, not even reaching Sykes' shoulder, and dressed in a pair of black trousers whose cuffs he had rolled to his knees, a white granddad-collared shirt and dark waistcoat, and a cape that looked old, made of oilcloth. His hair was long, falling from a balding pate in straggles, and he had muttonchops that dripped with rain. He was barefoot.

"Ladies, gentlemen and young folk," the man called, "if I can have your attention. Shortly, we will set off across the bay, but first: rules! There are always rules, are there not? Rules to obey, rules to know! You must stay close to me, and do not wander off. Stay within sight of me and each other. Do what I say, go where I go, for the bay is filled with quicksand and has a voracious appetite for those who stray, and it would be a terrible shame to lose any of you before our purpose is fulfilled."

"Is it safe?" asked the female half of the couple, putting her hand on the child's shoulder. She was American, her accent rich with nasal cadences. "I mean, it's getting dark. How will we see where we're going?"

"Madam, the bay is lit by the lights of moon and stars and by my knowledge," said the man, "and as King's Guide, your passage to your destination is mine to oversee." Sykes looked up; the sky was a swirling mass of grey/brown clouds and leaden distance and spiralling, white narwhal tusks of rain. He couldn't imagine the stars or moon would be visible tonight.

"I thought it was the Queen's Guide to the Sands," said the old man, his sou'wester rustling like liquid rolling over tarpaulin. "He's written books. I have one of them."

"Ah, yes, that fellow," said the little man. "He is the Queen's Guide, yes, to take people safely across the sand. Cedric is an honourable and venerable man and he does sterling work, has done for many a year, but he walks the daytime hours through the light of good weathers, taking the masses across the bay. Mine is a much older, more exclusive position. We only walk the seas in the worst of conditions, with small groups, and only ever as evening falls. I, friends, am Mister Calcraft, and I am the King's Guide to the Sands; not just these sands, but all the sands there are. Now, shall we go?"

They were at Hest Bank, on the gravelled car park above the foreshore. Behind them, the fence separating them from the tracks of the West Coast railway line murmured to itself in metallic whispers. The beachfront café, shutters down, was silent, an uneven apron of the parking areas almost empty of vehicles. Calcraft set off, walking down the steps to the foreshore, an expanse of seagrass and rocks that stretched out to either side and in front of the group, fringing the mudflats that started out in the bay proper. Instead of heading out into towards the distant humps of Barrow, however, Calcraft turned and began to walk parallel to the coastline, his cape fluttering about him, his hair dancing in the increasing breeze.

"The bay is one of this country's great natural events," he called back over his shoulder, "nearly two hundred square miles of intertidal mudflats and sand connecting Barrow all the way around to Heysham, and its history is long and its produce bountiful."

The group passed a small square of chain-link fence enclosing a stream emerging from the bank that dropped from the foreshore to the mudflats. "The Red Bank Outflow," said Calcraft brightly. "Allowing exit for the water that runs down from the hills, channelled through the earth to prevent erosion of the roads that line the shore. Two workmen died in its creation when an incorrectly supported wall slipped and smothered them. They were trapped for hours, in the mud, before they were found suffocated, their fingers raw and their mouths full of filth from their struggles to live."

The rain fell harder, furring Calcraft's words in a low caul of noise. The little man stepped nimbly across the ground, leaping over obstacles with apparent ease, dancing ahead of the group; the tide had done odd things to the earth here, cutting it down so that chunks of solidified mud protruded like giant building blocks from the ground, surrounded by small sinkhole pools whose surfaces constantly fractured and reformed, reflecting what little light there was. The group moved past two old fisherman's cottages, closed and empty, and then they were away from the buildings and there was simply open ground to their right and the bay to their left, flat and painted in shades of darkness. Sykes looked back over his shoulder as Calcraft began to lead them out over the fractured landscape and towards the deceptive smoothness of the sands beyond. The buildings behind them were little more than hunched, shadowed shapes against the sky and for a moment, he didn't like it; it felt as though they were walking away from civilisation.

No, worse; it felt as though civilisation had turned its back on them.

*

Sykes had done one of the more normal cross bay walks when he first moved to Morecambe, back when he and Dee were together and Morecambe had been his hopeful place and not just a grey jumble that lay around him, as cloying as an old coat. What he remembered most about it was the way the mud rose up his legs and clung, working its way inside shoes that had been so filthy after the walk that he had had to throw them away, and the way the bay had opened up around them the further out into it they had gone. The Barrow headlands ahead of them and the costal stretch of Morecambe and Heysham to their rear had wrapped around the long line of people like sunlit, comforting arms, leaving them to walk across (or, more accurately, through) a flat expanse of mud and sand that was cut by huge yet oddly gentle upheavals and valleys, and channels of fast flowing water. With the sun above him and the distant hills of the Lake District to his face, Sykes had felt tiny and insignificant and yet curiously cheered, like some explorer walking the plains of some vast and new land, discovering with every step something that he would carry with him forever.

This walk was nothing like that.

For a start, there were so few of them; whereas before he had been part of a huge snake of hundreds of people, holding Dee's hand as they waded and strode and shuffled and stared about them like tourists (which, he supposed, they had been), now there was only Calcraft and the little group. Its smallness meant that they were soon strung like beads on wire, Calcraft lithe at their head and the rest of them dragging behind him. The sound of the rain was a constant aggressive susurrus, pattering against the damp earth and the waterproof materials of coats and trousers, the air smelling of seaweed and something else, something thick and faintly rancid; old fish, or vegetation exposed by the retreat of the tide, or deep water, Sykes supposed. And then there was the view.

Or rather, there wasn't. The distances opening up between the people on the walk were filling with rain that drifted like smoke, and thickening brown darkness in which darker patches emerged and then faded. It hemmed them in, reducing Sykes's vision to a ragged circle around him, not the coming of night because that was an hour or two away yet, but the obstruction of the evening by clouds that stretched all the way from sky to earth. By his reckoning, Sykes could see maybe two or three hundred feet, and could make out nothing of Barrow or Heysham and little of the closer land behind them or to their side. Most of what he could see was featureless and brown, mottled and shifting as though somewhere just beyond his view something was moving through the bay alongside them. Even the air was a dripping, sullen khaki, stained to a watercolour blandness by the weather.

"The oceans are this planet's lungs and heart and soul," Calcraft called from ahead of them. "Mankind has investigated almost none of the water's lightless depths, choosing for the most part to remain on its fragile surface and pretend that it is his domain and that he has mastery of it. Even on land we are surrounded, though, never far from water, and the earth has millions of miles of coastline, places where the seas breathe in and out to reveal something of themselves and the things they cover. Sometimes, like tonight, some of us are allowed glimpses of the things that the oceans normally keep hidden."

Somewhere behind Sykes someone called out but when he turned back there was simply a line of eleven shuffling figures, following in the widening, blurring footprints of Calcraft, drab in the gloom.

"The coast here is a treacherous one," Calcraft continued. "As far back as maritime records go, the bay has taken its share of sustenance from the land and from those that try to work its beds and surfaces. Gales come in from the Irish Sea, tearing the surface to violent shreds, and its bed is uneven, littered with hidden banks and beset by fast-flowing tides and cross currents. In the days of sail, it was as dangerous when the gales died away and boats were left becalmed, drifting towards obstacles with slow, inexorable grace.

"The first wreck of note here was up at Fleetwood, when a vessel whose name most have forgotten but that was called the *Geomerung* was caught on a bank and then routed and set afire by royalists. Its crew were all killed, of course, their bones and the skeleton of the ship itself long since swallowed by the mud.

"Morecambe became 'Morecambe' in 1844; prior to that it was Poulton, and it was mentioned in the Domesday Book, although then it was called Poltune, and until 1820 it was a port town. That was the year the first recorded tourists arrived, responding to an advertisement offering a cottage for hire as an excellent base for sea fishing. Until then, the relationship between the inhabitants of the sea and those of the land was clear; when tourists began to arrive, however, things became somewhat confused."

They were far out into the bay now, Calcraft taking a path that led them slowly right, curving northwards. They came to a channel of water, flowing quickly. "As people who didn't understand the contract between the water and the land, who didn't live each day holding the water in their hearts and being held in its, arrived at the coast, boundaries blurred and became fractured, broken. The sea became another commodity, to be used rather than respected. And thus does change begin."

The group had come back together at the edge of the channel, waiting. The rain was harder here, heavier, a shimmering wall around them that sounded like dropping coins and tearing card.

"Look around you," said Calcraft. "This is how very few people see the bay. This is how very few ever see any ocean; dark, torn by poor weather, its lips drawn back and its teeth exposed, tongue writhing around them. Imagine this place as it was before the arrival of tourism, the skears rising from the water and topped by sickly trees, the low waters around them covering great mussel beds, a home for crabs and migratory seabirds, fished by locals who used coracles to get to them and who would return to the mainland as the tides came in, dragging sacks of the ocean's bounty for sale or to feed themselves and their families. For thousands of years, settlers in the area have used the skears for food, and their voices filled the airs and their thanks were heard at the greatest of heights and the lowest of depths. Now, onwards!"

Calcraft stepped out into the channel, the water breaking against his legs in small waves. "Follow, please," he said, his voice loud and clear now that Sykes was closer to him. "This cut isn't deep but the waters flow fast. Be confident and hold each other for safety if you wish. Madam," the guide said, turning to look at the family, "you might wish to hold your child's hand for the next few moments. Such flesh as he might easily be swept away if it is not anchored by a mother's love and solid grip!"

And then they were off again. The water was cold, but not as cold as Sykes expected. It pushed against his legs, insistent rather than bullying, and his feet sank into mud where he put them down; the sensation was strangely reassuring, as though he were creating temporary foundations for himself against the pressures of the tide. He stayed close to Calcraft, attempting to keep up, interested in the near-constant litany coming from the guide, ignoring what sounded like raised voices from behind him. "There are one hundred square miles of intertidal zone in the bay, one hundred square miles of land that is periodically exposed and then lost again by the movement of the tides, a hinterland between the twin kingdoms of water and land. What nature fills and empties twice a day without thought would take a modern tap running at full flow over twenty million years to fill."

The water was up to the man's waist now, was brushing at Sykes at about mid-thigh, and Calcraft was speeding up. He was over half way across the channel, a small dark shape ahead of Sykes, still talking as he went, his voice all around them. The rain had softened slightly, falling now almost as mist, fingers of it spiralling down in the distance and glimmering silver against the browns and blacks of the approaching night, its sound a throaty whisper. When Sykes looked back, the group was once again spread out, the couple and child closest to him, both adults holding the child's hands and making him walk between them. The boy stared at Sykes from inside his tubular hood and Sykes grinned at him and winked. The boy smiled back briefly and then dropped his eyes.

Beyond the family, the Japanese students were walking together and behind them, three of the coach party were strung out, perhaps five feet apart and moving through the water like bobbing dinghies.

There was a flash of lightning as Sykes turned back towards Calcraft, and for a moment the distant mass of the Barrow headlands were black solidities against the moving, sodden sky. Silvered light leapt about them, coating the channel and the wet mud of its far bank like smearing nitrate, and then it was gone, leaving behind after-image phantasms of itself in Sykes' eyes. Someone behind Sykes made a noise that might have been surprise or fear, or even an appreciative groan, and then fell silent again.

On the far side of the channel, Calcraft stopped once more, turning back to his party, still following him through the water. "From here, the esteemed Cedric would begin to curl us back in towards the waiting safety of Arnside, but we are made of sterner stuff, are we not, and have to go further out before we can come back in. The charter of the Poor Weather Crossings Company, of the King's Guide, is to show the bay at it most elemental, out in the places where people do not usually go. We carry this task out across the world, our destinations dependent on weather and date and the darting of the schools of the silvery fish and the lazy shift of whales, and it is my humble honour to be its Guide and to fulfil its responsibilities."

As Sykes came up the bank of the channel, Calcraft had already reached its upper edge and was heading away. Sykes waited, offering the couple and the boy his arm to come up the slope, and then ushering them past him and waiting for the three students to offer them help as well. Two were female, one male, he saw, and all smiled at him. "He's too quick," said one of the girls in perfect, accentless English, nodding at the receding figure of Calcraft.

"Yes," said Sykes, thinking about Calcraft's instructions to stay in sight of each other, of the old man in the yellow slicker, wondering if he'd be able to keep up, wondering about the coach party group and how safe this little jaunt really was.

"Will you ... ?" said the male student, interrupting Sykes's thoughts by holding out his camera. Sykes nodded, glancing at the still in sight Calcraft, and took it.

He stepped back and took several photographs of the three standing together at the edge of the strip of flowing water. After the lightning, the camera's flash seemed puny and faint, its pallid light catching the students and freezing them into the tiny screen on the camera's rear. Behind them, the flash showed Sykes the group of three from the coach party just beginning to make their way up the bank.

There was no sign of the man with the yellow sou'wester.

Actually, there was no sign of the man with the sou'wester, or the other two from the coach party. Sykes went back to the edge of the water, ignoring the student's attempt to take back his camera, and held it up high. He took several photographs and then looked at them on the tiny screen in its rear; the pictures weren't good, the flash struggling against the expanse of the bay, catching the fragmenting glitter of rain, but they all showed essentially the same thing: the expanse of water, visible across most of its width, uninterrupted by wading humans. "Shit," he muttered.

The student tapped Sykes on his shoulder, his smile faltering, and Sykes handed him his camera back. Leaving the boy and his friends he went quickly away from the channel, looking for Calcraft.

There was a shape moving through the mist ahead of him but it looked too large to be the guide, a shadow that stretched up above Sykes's head and then melted away as he pushed forward, seeming to slip sidelong and vanish into the fluttering ribbons of water. The constantly shifting mist and rain and spray was doing odd things to the light, what little there was of it, creating dancing figures at his sides that kept pace with him and distorted shapes ahead of him, smaller and more distant. Where was Calcraft? Where were the others?

There.

The guide was still walking briskly along, his feet doing little more than indent the mud that Sykes' feet were sinking into, and he was still talking. "Of course, it's not simply the bay that takes its toll, the whole coast here, the coast *everywhere*, it levies a cost, a price, that we must pay. The sailors of the yawl *Arlette* found that out in 1920 at Walney, as did the crew of the *Crystal* at Horse Bank, and a thousand others over the years. The *Vanadis* went down in the next bay along the coast early last century and its skeleton can still be seen at low tides such as we have tonight, the ribs of it blackened and its cargo of hard wood from Norway long since floated free." The little man skipped up a shallow rise, his feet kicking up licks of spray, as Sykes finally caught him up.

"You have to stop," he said. "We've lost someone. A few people, I think."

Calcraft wheeled about. From atop the rise, he looked down at Sykes, his edges blurring in the rain. It had thickened again suddenly, was so heavy now that the falling water was kicking up a secondary splashes as it hit the water-logged earth, curled skeins that lifted in the wind before merging with each other like tangled pleats of cord.

"Lost someone?" repeated Calcraft. Gradually, the rest of the people on the crossing were closing in, gathering around the man. "No, I don't think so; no one is lost. Everyone is precisely where they should be."

"The old man in yellow," said Sykes. "Some of the group that arrived together. I don't know their names. Are they ahead of us?" He turned to the approaching group. "Where are your friends?" he called. "There were five of you at first. Who's missing?"

"We weren't together," said the first of them, an older man who had mud spattered across his skin and who looked tired, his face a pale moon of worry in the darkness. "I mean, we're on the tour together but we aren't friends, none of us really know each other. They were behind us and now they're not, it's all I know."

Calcraft didn't speak. Instead, he walked down the short slope and moved back towards the channel. In the scoured light the shadows coalesced into moving shapes and then fragmented again and for a moment something huge seemed to be capering just out of sight, given form by a trick of gleam and water, and then it was gone. The wind lifted its voice, became the choral song of something moaning through lips that were inflexible and taut, the rain the sound of tombstone teeth grinding, and then it, too, was gone.

"Well," said Calcraft after he reached the water's edge. "I see nothing to concern us here."

"What?" said Sykes. "There are people missing! You need to call someone!" Behind Calcraft, the family pulled closer together, the mother's arms sneaking around her child, keeping him pressed flat back to her belly. The students had also clustered to each other, forming a little tableau like the statues in military graveyards.

"There's no need to call anyone," said Calcraft. "They are not missing."

"Then where are they?"

"The full crossing is not for everyone," said Calcraft. "All along its length, people who struggle, those who fall behind, are collected."

"You mean you have helpers?" asked Sykes, relaxing slightly. *Outriders, on those little quad bikes, or a tractor maybe?* He'd seen then in the distance, sometimes, harrying the edges of the walks that went across the bay in the daytime, shepherding people back to the column or letting them ride on the rear of the vehicles if they were getting tired. That would explain the figures that he kept seeing at the edge of his view, just out of sight but not out of perception, moving fast around them.

"Oh, no," said Calcraft, "not 'helpers'. I am their assistant, not they mine. I am the goat of the crossings, the King's Guide, a mere servant to their masters."

"Are they safe?" said Sykes, growing irritated with Calcraft's florid oratory. "Are *we* safe?"

"They are gathered together," said Calcraft. "And as for you, you are my ward, sir." He tuned again, heading on. After a moment, Sykes and the others followed.

*

"Fishing has changed, as all things do," said Calcraft as he walked. It was harder going here, the earth slick with water and clumps of grey/green seaweed that lay in wide, dank tangles. The earth itself was the consistency of thick mud, the boundaries between earth and pool less clear, and Sykes's feet were permanently under the surface of water so that walking was more like a skier's shuffle. Sykes was moving as fast as he could, trying to keep Calcraft in sight, the man a fluttering shape in the space ahead of him, his voice a thread that Sykes and the others followed.

"Catches came to be taken from further out, dragged from the depths into the bellies of ships that were made of steel rather than wood. Tourism spread its fingers further out from the coasts, across the waters themselves, in yachts and liners of increasing grandeur and opulence, safe and fast and clean and steady. Yet even now, safety is not assured; the ocean can reach out and fish even as it is fished, crews dragged from the fishing boats or the boats themselves dragged under, vast liners or tramp ferries sometimes gored or overturned, spitting their passengers into freezing seas or polluted estuarine deltas. In the wars, crafts as sleek as sharks and as stealthy as the tides themselves proved little protection for the men that crewed them, the seas remaining as demanding a master as they had ever been. Even now, in the lightless deeps, their metal skeletons sit quiet and abandoned, their corridors patrolled only by creatures that have never seen the surface of the world they inhabit.

"Trawlers still fished these waters in the war, sometimes catching unexpected cargoes, ships like the *Murielle,* torn open and sunk with all hands lost by a mine near the Morecambe Bay Lightship. No more was it a simple trade of fish for man; now, complexities multiplied and the Company was called upon more and more often to lead its tours to places rarely seen."

Sykes was exhausted, trying to keep up with the little bastard; the man seemed to be fucking *dancing* over the pitted earth, skipping through water and mud alike without appearing to even notice it. He seemed almost dry where Sykes was soaked to his belly, cold and anxious, and what about the others? Turning, he saw the students and the family close by, heads all down and churning forwards, and behind them the members of the holiday group. Only two of them were in sight now, pallid shapes in the distance against a background that constantly writhed and rippled. Even as he watched, the rain and turmoil thickened, coagulating into something solid, and came closer, seeming to reach out and swallow the rearmost of the two. Sykes waited for the weather to loosen its grip and release the figure, but it did not.

Something splashed off to his side, big enough to be heard over the constant rain. Sykes looked but saw nothing; nothing except air the colour and texture of saturated muslin. He turned about, losing Calcraft in the distance and then finding him again. He was on the edge of Sykes's vision, tiny and indistinct, still darting along. The family and the students were up ahead of Sykes as well, having both passed him as he looked back. They were hunched in to each other in two small groups, the students closer and slower, their wet-weather gear turning them into reflective pepper-pot shapes in the gloom. Sykes peered up; high above, the clouds were tearing apart and reforming and then tearing apart again, revealing patches of inky sky. There were no stars.

There was another flash of lightning and then, like an echo, the students' camera flash went off. Caught between the two flares, Sykes's eyes clenched. Something flashed again, puncturing his eyelids with glare, and then it was gone. He opened his eyes cautiously, his vision dancing with yet more movement, black and red patches shifting in among the brown and silver shimmer around him. Rain rolled around the rim of his hood, gathering and spilling inside his coat, snaking down his neck in cold trails. Calcraft and the family were even further away and he hurried after them, stepping around increasingly dark pools and slick, greasy ridges of mud.

The camera was on the ground, half buried.

Sykes only saw it because it was facedown and the power LED was on, a tiny red dot in the night. He bent and picked it up, looking around. Was that the students ahead and to the side, shadows in the downpour?

There seemed to be more than three. Had they found some of the elderly group? Joined up with them? He blinked, trying to clear his vision, but it didn't help.

"Hey!" he called, hoping to attract their attention, holding their camera up. The figures faded away, their shapes lost again. He started to jog, his feet splashing through the water, the tang of salt in his nose. The skin of his face felt tight and stiff, as though he was wearing a mask that constantly cracked and resealed itself. "Hey," he called again but his voice sounded tiny and depthless against the noise of the bay, swallowed by the wind and the tattoo beat of the rain.

The students appeared again in the distance as he came closer, distorted, magnified by some trick of the water and wind so that they appeared to be tall, taller than the houses they had left behind them on the shore, and then they were gone. Sykes broke into a run.

There was no land now, just mud covered by a thin but deepening layer of water. How far out had they come? Calcraft was up ahead, still walking on, apparently impervious to the weather. The little bastard was still speaking, Sykes heard, carrying on oblivious as Sykes tried to catch his breath to call him.

"Out here, the bay is still fecund despite the years of depredation," Calcraft was saying. "Huge beds of cockles line the ocean's floor, exposed at low tides such as these. The bay, generous as ever, offers itself to man. The *seas* offer themselves to man, and they ask little in return except that they are occasionally acknowledged."

"Calcraft," called Sykes. "We have to go back, this is getting dangerous."

Calcraft stopped and turned, beckoning the family and Sykes in to him. They came together in a huddle, gathering around the little man. Sykes was far taller than him, was looking down at the man's dripping scalp, pale under worms of hair.

"The tides here are quick, moving like quicksilver to surround the unwary. The waters have become crafty in how they take their reward, have *had* to become crafty, subtle in their appetites. They bay tries to take offerings most years, is sometimes successful and sometimes not. It almost took three children and their dog in 1967 but was beaten by the speed of the helicopters of the coastguard, has missed others who were more wary or simply luckier, morsels missed or spat out, but it would be a mistake to underestimate the grand majesty of the water. It takes fishermen looking for worms and tourists unused to its terrible speed, swimmers caught by riptides as strong as the hands of the devil himself. Not much, we might think, for how much it gives, and we would be right but remember; occasionally its hunger is voracious. Think of those twenty-three Chinese cocklers, their last moments on earth not on earth at all but in water, thousands of miles from home and their loved ones, all around them cold and grey and the stink of brine in their noses and the taste of the ocean in their mouths as they screamed their last."

"Did you hear me?" asked Sykes, holding out the camera to Calcraft. "We need to go back. This weather, it's too dangerous for us to stay out here." The father said something that Sykes didn't hear and tried to grasp Calcraft's arm but the man pirouetted out of the way.

"From the beginning, the creatures of the land and the creatures of the sea have had a contract, ancient, forgotten by almost all," said Calcraft as though Sykes and the father had not spoken. "By almost all, but not by all. Even if man forgets, the King remembers."

"For Christ's sake," said Sykes and then the rain shifted, solidified and the darkness reached out and lifted the child off his feet and snapped him away.

The mother screamed, the sound stopping abruptly as something that might have been a tentacle but might equally have been an arm or a finger or a fin wrapped around her and sucked her back into the night's mouth. Sykes cried out, trying to run but stumbled, falling to his knees in a spray of brine and wet, clinging sand, which sprayed up around his face and neck, and then he was up.

Someone behind him shrieked, the noise of it long and ululating, rising in pitch as it fell in volume until it was gone, and then the only sound was Sykes's own breathing and the fall of his feet into earth that was more liquid than solid. His clothes were cold and wet, chafing and tugging as he ran, as though he was wearing someone else's skin, old and ill-fitting. The air curled about him, given shape by the rain and spray, twists dragging about his feet, the liquid slathering his face, dripping into his eyes and mouth. Where was he running? Away from Calcraft, but was he headed back to the shore? Sykes didn't know, just ran.

It was hard, the ground uneven, pools opening up before him at the last moment so that he had to dodge clumsily to their sides or run through them, slow and irregular. There was no moon above, nor stars, yet there was a luminescence in the air around him, the dank rain lit as though from within by a queasy sepia glow.

"Random chance selected you the moment you called us," said a voice from by Sykes's ear.

He yelped, staggered in surprise and stumbled again, falling and rolling through a patch of weed that smelled of salt and decay. Cursing, he clutched at the plant and hauled himself up, running on.

Calcraft ran at his side.

"At its heart the contract remains simple, even if the methods of implementing its conditions have become more complicated," said the small man. He ran as nimbly as he had walked, seemed to shiver across the surface of the puddles and skate over the undulating earth like an insect. His voice was conversational, neither breathless nor ragged. "The seas provided and occasionally they took, reaching out with a wave or a storm to swallow down boats and sometimes the crews. A reciprocal arrangement, fishermen and fished, neat and tidy.

Sykes leaped over a tussock, landing heavily the other side in water that came to his waist, thinking briefly that he might have to swim before the footing underneath him became solid enough to hold his weight.

"But there are fewer fishermen and fewer boats, and those that take to the water are larger, harder to take to the bottom than the coracles or longboats or wooden schooners of the years gone by. What were my masters to do? The contract changed, not by them but by you, taking more and more and giving less and less, and so the Poor Weather Crossings Company was born. I am the King's

Guide and I lead you out, I entice you with tales of wondrous views and of not-to-be-missed opportunities, I tell desperate immigrants of cockle-beds where fortunes lie simply waiting to be claimed, I whisper in drunken ears in public houses that night-time swims can be so much fun, I encourage dogs to jump into stormy seas so that their owners might follow. I am Calcraft, the King's Guide to the sands, the Judas Goat, and I serve my master well."

All around Calcraft, figures swarmed through the rising tide, half-seen and blank-eyed.

"Your sacrifice will keep the seas at bay, protecting those on the shore. Be honoured," said Calcraft, running closer to Sykes. Sykes lashed out, missed and fell, his clothes ballooning with water, the weight of it holding him, rolling him onto his back so that he was staring up into a sky that seemed only feet above him, the colour and texture of decaying shrouds. He fumbled in his pocket, rooting through sodden layers for his phone. His fingers were cold, lost their grip on it as he pulled it out and it fell into the water. The slight noise of it entering the tide sounded huge, echoing, curling around Sykes's rising moan and carrying it up into the clouds where it was lost in the wraiths of rain. Calcraft leaned into his vision, smiling.

"It wouldn't have worked anyway," he said. "Out here, you are beyond the reach of technology and there are only the truths of history and a covenant made when the first man lifted a fish from the water on the end of hook or spear. We have shown you the bay at its most glorious, shown you the seas laid out in a way that few ever see them, rewarded you for the offering you will make, but now the tour is done and the sacrifice due. We must finish, for the Company is needed elsewhere."

Over Calcraft's shoulder the rain fell harder, thicker, the water forming shapes that stretched to the ceiling of clouds above. The little man stepped back, nodding a last time, leaning back and opening his mouth to the rain and drinking the drops down. Sykes opened his mouth to scream but the tide flowed over his lips and choked his voice to nothing, and then the King was above him and taking hold of him and he was gone to the court where no light ever shows.

THE DEVIL DOG OF PEEL

A truly unnerving tale is connected with Peel Castle, in the port of Peel on the Isle of Man. It concerns a demon hound, which, like so many of its ilk, has long been viewed as a portent of doom. But this particular hound, the 'Mawtha Doo' as it is known in the Manx tongue, has some especially chilling antecedents.

Peel Castle is located on St. Patrick's Isle, which lies just offshore, but is easily reachable via a causeway. Peel itself is the third largest town on Man, and its busiest fishing port, but it has a long past steeped in eerie tradition. Pagan beliefs told how the island was protected in ancient times by the sea god, Manannan mac Lir, a powerful being who was outraged when Christianity took root there, punishing the locality with mists and storms. Likewise, the island is home to several mythical monsters – the Glashtyn and Buggane for example – not to mention all kinds of bogey beasts drawn from faerie lore. Like so many other parts of the British Isles, it has also experienced witchcraft and boasts a legion of home-grown ghosts.

The castle was first constructed as a timber fortress by Vikings in the ninth century, the invaders having displaced a Celtic monastic community existing there beforehand (which might well have seen another deity angered). However, the Norsemen were not on Man purely to destroy. They were in the process of settling the island, viewing it as an ideal staging-post for their raids upon Britain and Ireland, but also as a kingdom in its own right. The town of Peel thus developed as both a market and a fishing port. Much present day Manx culture is attributable to the Norsemen, but while in charge there they fought each other incessantly, and in due course were so weakened by this internal strife that they lost the island to Scottish suzerainty in 1266. It was declared a lordship of England in 1399, and when finally purchased by the British Crown in 1764, it assumed the status it enjoys today as a self-governing Crown Dependency. Peel Castle, which had been much rebuilt during the medieval era, in particular with impressive stone ramparts, remained a viable military outpost until well into the 19th century.

It was during this later period, when the English had a military presence on Man, that rumours concerning the Mawtha Doo first began to emerge. Initially it was reported as a shadowy, dog-like form that prowled the castle corridors and battlements after dark. On some occasions, it was heard growling in the *dungeons or howling from the high towers, but things took a turn for the infinitely more frightening one night during the reign of Charles II (1660-1685), when a young guardsman decided to challenge the beast. By this time, the Mawtha Doo was regarded as a real-life entity rather than a legend, which was increasingly antagonistic to the soldiers stationed there. The state of affairs had become so bad that even seasoned troopers sought any posting rather than Peel Castle, and those who were sent there would not move around the passages at night unless they were in company (some were reportedly so afraid that they wouldn't even leave their guardrooms).*

On the night in question, one particularly brash youngster, emboldened by drink, loaded his pistol and vowed to dispatch the monster. Leaving his comrades crammed around their brazier, he set off alone into the darkness. Within a very short time, they heard his shrieks, first filled with anger but then with terror. The sound of a pistol shot finally roused his mates from their fear. They investigated, and found the brash guardsman crawling feebly up an unlit stair towards them. He'd encountered something so dreadful that in the space of a few minutes it had withered him to great age. His hair had turned grey, his skin was wrinkled and his body wasted and knotted. More to the point, his mind had gone. He could do no more than mumble incoherently for the next three days, at which point, even though he had suffered no visible injury, he died.

No other incidents as extreme as this one were reported again, but further encounters with the shadowy hound were still said to cause death in some form or other. To this day, with the castle now a Visitors Centre owned by Manx National Heritage, the stories persist, though no sightings of the Mawtha Doo have been made in recent times.

The potential source of such an entity, or at least the source of the story, has been speculated on for a considerable time. Could its origins lie in the island's distant past, when the ancient British gods sought vengeance for their abandonment? Was it a device of the marauding Vikings? – many of Britain's mythical black dogs were believed to have been unleashed by the Norsemen as Dark Age weapons of mass destruction. Another theory concerns Duchess Eleanor of Gloucester, who in 1443 was found guilty of using sorcery in an attempt to kill King Henry VI, and was jailed at Peel Castle for the rest of her life; she died there 14 years later.

As with so many modern seaside towns, such ghostly tales have done little to put off the tourists. Peel may not be the warmest coastal resort, and it is definitely one of the stormiest –

perhaps it was one of Manannan mac Lir's bad moods that saw the destruction of the Cathedral of St. German within the castle walls in 1824 – but the turbulent history of the island is part of its attraction, as the annual Viking Festival will attest. No-one celebrates the memory of the Mawtha Doo, of course ... perhaps because they don't believe in it.

That could be a mistake.

BRIGHTHELMSTONE
R.B. Russell

I am not sure how old I was when I visited Brighton with my mother; I could only have been about ten or eleven. My father had been dead for about a year and I recall it as the first holiday that we took without him. I remember that I didn't want to go to Brighton. I didn't want to go anywhere. Essentially, I couldn't see the point to anything. I still hated my mother at that time. I think that I blamed her for my father's death, which was completely unfair; his car accident was his own fault. But I was feeling very sorry for myself. My mother's unhappiness angered me: I didn't believe that anybody else had the right to be as upset as I was, and so I took it out on her.

We stayed in a guest house called *Brighthelmstone*, which was on East Street, a narrow, busy thoroughfare just off the seafront, close to the Palace Pier.

"It's a stupid name," I said petulantly as we waited for the landlady to answer the door.

"It's what Brighton used to be called," my mother patiently explained.

We were on the top floor, necessitating a climb of four flights of stairs, and, naturally, I hated that too. For reasons of economy I had to share a room with my mother; a room with two single beds. Whenever we'd been on holiday before, my parents had booked one room for themselves and I'd had another of my own. Now, I resented the lack of privacy, and the unwanted intimacy. My mother appalled me and my refusal to let her even touch me must have added to her agony. I was being profoundly selfish, I can see that now.

After we had been shown to our room, the first thing my mother did was unpack a framed photograph of her and my father, which she set up on the dressing table. It showed them when they were quite young; before I had been born. Then she laid out her never-ending array of chemicals, powders, ointments and sprays. These had fascinated me; at one time I had delighted in watching her use them. I was drawn to them, I know, because they all seemed improbably exotic. Each one was different, but most had their names printed in gold script on the labels, and all claimed that they had been made in France or other foreign countries. She loved to hear me read out to her the lists of outlandish ingredients they contained. I know now that they were probably all bought at Boots, but they had once seemed so glamorous. By the time we were in Brighton, though, it turned my stomach to see her rubbing the stuff into her skin and painting her face, all in an attempt to make herself look like the younger woman in the picture with my father. And to make it worse, I was always being told how poor we were, and I presumed that these things were expensive. It seemed, therefore not only a waste of time but knowingly wasteful.

When she started using her creams, powders and paints in Brighton I had to look away. I took pleasure in going to the window and opening it wide. I knew that my mother hated me to sit on the low sill, hanging out, high above the busy street. It was dangerous, and I suppose I was taunting her, although it pains me now to admit this. I would pretend not to hear her calling me to be careful, or see her walking slowly over to me, not wanting to startle me in case I fell out. I thought that was a good game.

*

On our first day in Brighton we sat on the beach, which was boring because there were only pebbles; no sand. Under the pier it stank of rotting stuff, but *on* the pier it was more enjoyable. I wouldn't admit this to my mother, though. After a couple of days, because the holiday was going so badly, we took a bus out to some village on the South Downs and walked over interminably dull hills in a light drizzle. I was sure that we were both marking time, waiting for the holiday to end.

And then, one evening, as we walked along Kings Road, we happened to wander into a brash, noisy, brightly-lit amusement arcade near the pier, and for the first time since my father's death I found something that really fascinated me; a large track which allowed up to eight people to race model cars together in slots. It seemed expensive at ten pence a time, but my mother supplied me with the money for several goes and I was outrageously happy. I'm ashamed to acknowledge that in an instant my apparently profound, overwhelming grief was entirely forgotten.

When my money ran out I immediately considered going to my mother to cajole more from her, but, instead, I waited, watching others using the game, and I found that I was perfectly content to observe. I fantasised that I was driving the slot cars, travelling at incredible speeds, often having spectacular crashes. In fact, I realised that operating the cars was actually less enjoyable than watching others play with them. When I was controlling the car I had to concentrate on speeding up and slowing down, keeping my car on the track, and if it came out of the slot I would have to run around and put it back on again. All this spoiled the fantasies.

On that first evening I spent all my time by the slot racing cars, oblivious to the world around me. Finally I wondered what had happened to my mother, and I reluctantly went to find her. To my surprise she was at the back of the arcade playing bingo. She was sitting in a chair with a strange, mechanical board in front of her, while a bald man in a sparkling suit called out numbers from a raised, glazed booth. There must have been room for fifty to join in the game, but there were only five or six other people playing. I asked my mother what she was doing and she said, without looking at me, "Trying to concentrate."

I watched the game finish, and immediately she put more coins into the slot which reset her board with new, random numbers. As it did so she had time to explain to me, excitedly, that she had won the very first game she had played, and she said she wasn't going to give up on her run of luck. She asked if I was happy amusing myself, and if I had enough "pennies", so I said yes to the first question, and no to the second, which meant that she handed over more coins.

I went back to the slot cars quite contentedly, and watched them until I was hungry. When I returned to my mother she handed me some more money and told me to go next door and buy some fish and chips for myself. This was quite a novelty; I'd not bought food in a café, on my own, before, but I went and ordered a large bag of chips to take away. I also asked for a cream soda, which I'd always wanted to taste, but had never had the opportunity to try. I soaked my chips in vinegar and salt, which I was not normally allowed to do, and because food wasn't allowed in the amusement arcade, I sat out on the pavement in the garish light of the canopy and enjoyed my dinner.

It was getting dark and the sea beyond the promenade and beach was black and restless. There were a few lights on the horizon, from passing ships, I assumed. By then it had become so much later than we had ever stayed out on previous nights, and I was very surprised to see all the shops still open. They looked so enticing and quite magical in the artificial light, whereas earlier that day they'd looked tawdry and down-at-heel.

After I had eaten, I contented myself with watching the slot cars for the rest of the evening. I stood at strategic points around the track, putting people's cars back on when they flew off at corners. I was unaware of the passing time, but then my mother appeared and we went back to the boarding house. It was gone eleven o'clock and I was thrilled to be going home so late. I lay in bed watching my mother with the usual competing emotions of fascination and horror as she got ready, sitting at the dressing table with all her bottles. I also watched the hands of the bedside clock moving closer and closer to twelve, and, finally, my mother finished at the dressing table. She got into the adjoining bed and switched off the light. It was just past midnight, and I felt that some kind of milestone had been passed.

*

The following morning we went, once again, to the amusement arcade. My mother pressed some more money into my hands and went to the bingo at the back, leaving me standing by the slot cars. I had one go on them, but, as I already knew, the excitement wasn't quite the same as when I was watching other people operate them. The arcade was not yet very busy, though, and as nobody else was playing with the cars I decided to wander off and return later.

It seemed to me to be a very daring thing to do. I had it in mind to visit some of the shops that had looked so enticing the previous evening. After all, I now had money to spend, but suddenly the shops didn't look as wonderful as they had all lit-up in the night. I wandered around an emporium that offered dull rubber rings and plastic windmills on the outside, but inside there was rather more to tempt me. I spent so long trying to decide between a die-cast model aeroplane that caught my eye, and a secret agent kit, that I soon realised it was lunchtime and I was worried that my mother would be looking for me. I hurried out having bought nothing at all and ran back to the arcade. Just inside, walking towards me was my mother.

"I wondered where you were," she said, but she was not angry with me. She must have only just thought to come looking for me, so I said I'd popped outside for some fresh air.

We went to a slightly tatty restaurant and had a set three-course meal for what my mother said was a bargain price. It was dark and brown inside, and I suspected that this was to hide the fact that the cutlery and crockery were not quite clean. I liked the idea of a three-course meal, though; it struck me as grown-up. It was worryingly quiet inside, though, compared to the cafés I'd visited before. I decided that it was because the elderly diners would probably complain, no matter what background music was played, at whatever volume.

In a whisper I asked my mother whether she was good at bingo and she laughed. She said that nobody was 'good' at it; it was down to luck. Yesterday she had been lucky. That morning less so, but in the afternoon she knew she would be winning again... She asked if I minded being left on my own and I said no, and that I loved the slot cars, as I honestly did.

When we returned to the arcade, she again she gave me some cash to play on the cars. I counted up all the money I had when she was gone and there was several pounds in silver. It was more than I'd ever handled before, except for my last birthday, when I'd been made to put it all into my Post Office savings account. I was about to pocket it when a woman asked if I would change her one pound note for ten of my ten pence pieces. There was a queue to get change, she said, and so I warily gave her the coins and she went away. I was staring at the note she had given me in exchange, when a young man came up to me and snatched at it.

I describe him as a young man because, in retrospect, I think he could only have been about fifteen or sixteen. I thought of him as fully-grown then, and frightening at that. He wore a tight-fitting suit, and he had a face that I might have ordinarily liked, but he smelt sour and looked angry.

"Give that to me, and empty out your pockets," he snarled, pushing me towards the wall.

I looked around for help, but suddenly that part of the amusement arcade was empty. I was backed up between two machines offering fluffy toys as prizes for anyone who could operate the crane inside them. I had nowhere to run, and to compound my fear he needlessly produced a knife.

My legs seemed to fail me and I couldn't breathe. I clung to the wall as he jabbed the knife in my direction. Although he didn't quite touch me with it, I was sure I was going to die. I put all of my money into the man's open left hand, dropping some of the coins in my rush to end the ordeal. But this wasn't enough for him.

"Pick them up," he spat, and I did as I was told.

"That's not enough," he said, looking at what I had given him, before stuffing it all into his pocket anyway. "You a holiday-maker?"

I nodded, unable to talk.

"Where you staying?"

"A g-guest house," I finally stuttered.

"Anybody there now, in your rooms?"

"No, my m-mother's playing bingo."

He explained that I was to take him to where I was staying.

"If anyone says anything, we're friends ... If anyone asks, my name's Tom."

"But I don't have a key," I said, clutching at a valid excuse that made my heart leap with unwarranted hope.

"I don't need keys," he said with a scowl. "We'll walk side by side, like we know each other. And if you try and run I'll knife you."

I didn't doubt him. I hated the idea of taking him back to the guest house, but at least there was very little there for him to steal, and then he would have to leave – my torment would be over.

And so we walked out, just as he said, with his knife concealed under his jacket. I could hardly make my legs move, I was so scared. There were people around us, and I hoped that somebody would look at me and see my fear and growing despair. I wanted somebody to stop us and ask if I was okay. Was I unwell? Where was my mother?

But nobody seemed to notice us. Wildly, I even thought of taking him to a different guest house, perhaps saying I was confused, but I was certain that Tom, if that was his real name, would use his knife if he wanted to. Because he was so much bigger and stronger, I knew that if I tried to slip away, he would catch me in a moment.

Tom complained that it was too far, even though there were only a couple of roads to cross as we walked along the seafront. In East Street I took him to the door.

"*Brighthelmstone?*" he said. "That's a stupid name."

"It's what Brighton used to be called."

I had said the words quietly, remembering my mother's reply to my own similar statement.

The front door of the guest house was on the latch and we entered without anybody challenging us. On the way up he swore at all the stairs, and then fiddled with the lock to our room. He was using his knife, and I assumed he knew how to open the door, like crooks on the television did, but soon he gave up. He looked over the bannisters, to make sure nobody was around, and then shoulder-charged the door. It burst open and he fell inside, onto the floor.

That was my chance to run – I knew it – while he was on the ground, struggling. But to my shame I didn't. He got up, came out onto the landing and dragged me roughly inside.

With the door shut behind us I gave up all hope. I was bitterly regretting not having tried to get away. If he was going to kill me, I decided, it should have been while I was escaping; if I was going to die, it ought to be heroically. I was feeling sorrier for myself than I had ever done before.

"Where's the jewellery?" he asked. He threw the knife in the air and caught it by the handle after a couple of rotations. I told him to look for a blue box in the bottom drawer of the dresser. I felt a traitor, but I told myself that he'd have eventually found it anyway. He knelt down and pulled it out, turning his nose up at what he saw inside. He threw the box casually on the bed; his attention had been taken by the picture of my mother and father.

"Money," he said, distracted. "Where's the money?"

"There isn't any."

I was going to add that it was all in my mother's purse, but I didn't think it would do any good to explain.

"Who's that?" he asked, picking up the photo.

"My mum and dad." I don't know what compelled me to tell him, "My dad's dead."

"She's a looker, alright. And available, eh?"

I didn't know what he meant. He now pulled open the top drawer of the dresser and was staring at my mother's underwear. At first I was embarrassed that he had seen it, but to my horror he pulled out a handful of items and then held them to his face and sniffed them. A moment later he had dropped them on the floor and was going over to the wardrobe. There he pulled one of her dresses off the hanger and put his face to where her breasts would be when she wore it.

"Lovely," he said.

"Don't do that!" I told him, and he came out of his reverie.

He grinned at me and ran the blade down the dress. He wasn't cutting it, but that was obviously the threat.

"Please don't do that," I said.

"Or what?" he asked, now letting the blade take the full weight of the dress, and caressing it with his free hand.

I said, "She doesn't look like her photograph anymore. She's all old and wrinkly."

I knew just how horrible it was to say that, and I immediately regretted it. It was so rude, and, really, so wrong. My mother still looked young and beautiful, but I wanted to be cruel to her as well as to him. The effect my words had on Tom, though, was only half-anticipated, and half-understood.

He was angry. He stuffed the dress violently back into the wardrobe, knocking the other clothes off the hangers. Then he swept everything off the top of the dresser; all of my mother's bottles and tubs of exotic creams and powders, her brushes, hairspray and eye pencils. I backed away towards the window which had been left slightly open. I knew there was no escape that way; I'd stared out of it often enough so that I didn't have to watch my mother at the dresser.

"You're not getting away," said the young man, thinking he'd read my thoughts. In a second he was across the room and, holding me by the neck with one hand, he pressed the blade of his knife into my stomach. The point cut me only slightly, but it felt like a searing flame to my flesh. And then he hauled me up and pushed the top half of my body out of the window. I was balanced right on the edge of the sill, looking up at the eaves of the building and at the sky. I assumed the worst. Gulls were crying above me, and vehicles were roaring far down in the street below. In an absolute agony of fear, I lost control of my bowels. A moment later he swore and let go of me.

For a few seconds I did not know if I was going to fall. The billowing net curtain came to hand and I pulled myself round, grabbed the window frame and got back inside.

"Did you shit yourself?" asked the young man, laughing. "I ought to chuck you out the window to get rid of the smell."

He leant out to get a good look at the street below.

"And it's a long, long way down," he called back to me. He only had one foot on the floor and said something about the air being fresher outside. With all my anger and all my might I pushed him.

*

He must have fallen quickly, because by the time I looked out the window he was a mess of arms and legs on the top of a passing lorry. From that distance he looked like a spider after our cat had played with it. And then the lorry was turning left at the end of the street, onto the seafront, and was gone.

I didn't know what to think of what I'd done, but I decided that the most important thing was to make good the damage to the room. I tidied everything up very hurriedly, putting my mother's things back in place. And then I took a clean set of my clothes down to the bathroom, stripped-off, and washed myself thoroughly. When I left the guest house ten minutes later I bundled up my soiled clothes and put them into a rubbish bin on the promenade.

I was shaking when I found my mother, still in the same seat, still playing bingo. There were a lot more people there now, and the blaring pop music sounded louder, and the bald announcer's voice more oily. The endless flashing lights threatened to completely disorientate me, but my mother gave me more money for my dinner and I was able to run back out of the amusement arcade. I promptly threw up on the pavement, and walked unhappily back to the guest house.

*

I found that I could open the door to our room by pushing on it hard. The lock was still in place, but very loose. Inside it was getting dark, and when I switched on the light I could clearly see that everything was still a mess, despite my earlier attempt at tidying. I don't know how I thought my mother could have come back and not noticed that anything was amiss. Now I took the time, and the utmost care, to put everything properly into what I hoped was its proper place.

I thought that the bottles and brushes, powders and sprays on the dresser would be the hardest to arrange convincingly. But when I closed my eyes I could remember quite clearly how they had been set out. I managed to make them look orderly and organised.

More difficult were the clothes in the wardrobe. I had put them back on their hangers, but it seemed to take forever to make them look neat. I also had to go through the drawers, folding up the clothes as I hoped my mother would have done. By the time I was satisfied that there was nothing more I could do, it was late, and I rushed back to the amusement arcade.

My mother was standing outside, looking worried. But by then I was quite calm; it seemed to have been a long time since I had pushed Tom out of the window, and my only real concern was that my mother would not realise that anything untoward had happened back in our room.

"I was about to call the police," she said.

"There's no need,' I smiled at her, and though my apparent calm was false, so was hers. "Did you win?" I asked her.

"Yes," she beamed at me. "But when I went to find you, so we could celebrate, you weren't there. And that was when I realised how silly I'd been to get so carried away with such a stupid game. What would you like to do next? The choice is yours... Anything..."

I asked if we could take the train back home, and she was surprised, but after making sure that was really what I wanted, she agreed. We went back to the guest house and packed, and my mother never said a word about anything not being just as it should have been.

THE GHOULS OF BANNANE HEAD

Walk along southwest Scotland's scenic Ayrshire coast these days and you'll see many caves. Some of them are flooded by the sea at high tide; some open onto the dunes; others lie hidden in tranquil coves. None, as yet, has been named definitively as the entrance to the underground refuge in which Sawney Bean and his cannibal tribe resided, even though it was supposedly located at Bannane Head, midway between Girvan and Ballantrae.

The tale of Sawney Bean is an age-old Scottish tradition. It is at least 16th century in origin, maybe much older, though it actually has more in keeping with the gruesome 'video nasties' of the modern era.

A pair of newly-weds who had just attended a nearby fair were journeying along the lonely coastal road when they were set upon by a horde of ragged ruffians, both men and women, who emerged shrieking from an isolated cave-mouth. The first assumption was that these assailants were simple brigands, and though the husband was a former soldier who was armed with a sword and pistol, he was half-minded to hand over his purse without resistance. However, when he saw the devilish horde bear his wife from her horse and tear her open, drinking her blood with deranged gusto, he cut his way free and rode hell-for-leather inland, raising hue and cry at every town and village.

Initially there was disbelief among local folk, but then it was recollected that, not only had a number of travellers been reported missing on this coast, but that fragments of humanity – body parts and internal organs – had occasionally been washed up on nearby beaches without explanation. This hadn't stopped the accusation of a number of suspects – some of them innkeepers at whose houses the disappeared had been guests – but now it seemed that the real culprits had at last been discovered. Word of the atrocities reached the court of King James VI, who authorised an investigation which, in his own inimitable way, he elected to lead personally.

With an army of 400 soldiers, the intrigued monarch scoured the coast for several days until at last the murderers' cave was located. Inside was a scene which even the most battle-hardened troopers in James's retinue could never have imagined: eviscerated corpses and dismembered limbs hanging from meat hooks; buckets and jars in which other human remains had been pickled as though in preparation for a demonic banquet; gnawed *human bones strewing the bloodstained floor; and heaps of stolen goods, which had been wrested from countless victims.*

The felons, a filthied tribe of inbred ghouls, were found cowering in one of the cave's deeper recesses. All were taken into custody and an explanation quickly forced out of them. The head of the fiendish clan was one Alexander 'Sawney' Bean, a former ditch-digger from East Lothian, who, while still a teenager, had decided that an honest living was not for him. He'd thus absconded across country with his common-law wife, committing innumerable petty crimes en route. Here, on what was then the Galloway coast, he found the perfect hideout – a cave which at high tide was inaccessible. Once installed there, he and his woman set to raising a family, which over a period of about 25 years amounted to 48 children and grandchildren, all conceived through incest. To survive, they preyed on lonely travellers, looting their goods, and then killing them and devouring their flesh.

There was no attempt by the criminals to hide their guilt, and no remorse was noted. The entire family was tried in Edinburgh, and not surprisingly, all were found guilty and sentenced to die. The men and boys, Bean included, had their limbs hacked off and were left to bleed to death in the market square at Leith (possibly the town of Sawney's birth). At the same time, their women were bound together in twos and threes and flung alive onto several large bonfires.

Thus passed the depraved cannibal, Sawney Bean.

That, of course, was the pious tone in which the famous story was often told, but how much truth in it was there?

There is no legal record from the reign of James VI of any person called 'Bean' being tried for murder. The earliest written accounts of the story can be found in mid-18th century pamphlets and broadsheets circulated in England, which has led to suspicion among some historians that, as the Jacobite rebellion had just been suppressed, this was an entirely fictional event created to demonise the Scottish nation. Indeed, a famous early sketch of Sawney Bean appears to show him as a Scottish country gentleman clad in tartan, rather than a savage cannibal. However, the less skeptical have pointed out that other pamphlets of the time are just as filled with English highwaymen and murderers, and give equally lurid accounts of their crimes and executions, which would suggest that anti-Scottish xenophobia was not to the fore.

Many scholars today believe that if Bean and his monstrous family existed, it was in a much earlier era, perhaps deep in the Middle Ages, when details of the crime might not have been *recorded but the appalling folk memory would linger. One possible prototype is Christie Cleek, a 14th century Highlander said to have reverted to murder and cannibalism during a time of famine, though it is also possible that both these fiendish characters, Bean and Cleek, are derived from the same source – an eater of human flesh whose name is now forgotten. Of course, until someone actually finds a coastal cave containing a few rusted iron hooks and maybe the odd chewed bone, there will always be doubt that something like this ever happened. But it is interesting that even today this alluring stretch of the Ayrshire coast can have an aura of menace, especially at night, when the sea moans and the wind sighs amid its lonely rocks and caves.*

MEN WITH FALSE FACES
Robert Spalding

The sea breeze blew the tangy vinegar scent of the fish and chips into Gary's face and set his mouth watering. Two months ago he couldn't have imagined such a reaction.

He'd only been living in the seaside town of Bognor Regis for seven weeks, and up until he had moved down he had never been fond of the so-called national dish. Perhaps it was the presumed freshness of the fish he got now, maybe it was the sense of eating it while looking out at the former home of his dinner; Gary didn't know. What was certain though was that he had made his regular Friday dinner a large haddock and chips, one pickled egg and plenty of salt and vinegar.

He walked briskly along the seafront promenade, enjoying the feel of the early summer wind and the slight salt taste it left in his mouth. So clear and clean; much nicer than the air in Slough. He reminded himself that he hadn't thought the air in his former home town had been that bad, it was simply that it couldn't match up to the sea breeze.

The pier shrieked out its electronic 'come hither', the claw games, two penny pushers and fruit machines all jangling their enticements. On another night, without his dinner growing colder in his hand, he might have spent a little time at one of the fruities. But tonight was reserved for fish and chips accompanied by a cold can of lager.

The slow setting sun glinted off the small waves rolling towards the stony beach; a high tide. One wave caught the sun at just the right angle to momentarily blind him. Blinking the white spots away, Gary put his hand on the sea wall for support

His fingers found a deep, jagged groove.

Looking down, he saw that the groove was actually part of a word, carved in cursive script into the stone of the sea wall.

The loops and whirls of the letters appeared almost alive, shifting and dancing. For a moment he felt as if the words were trying to hide their meaning from him, and the more he stared the less he could make out. What had at first seemed to be individual letters and words now looked like looping graffiti.

Everything in him said that he should look away, that this was no more than some kid's nonsensical vandalism. But something else, deep in his mind, said he should keep looking, that he stay just a little longer.

Gary caught the tip of his finger on one of the rough edges. The cut was shallow, and after a moment of sucking his finger he found the blood had stopped escaping.

He looked down for one final check on the carved graffiti and felt a sense of relief when the words were fully legible.

Beware Men with False Faces

The work of a very angry teenage girl, no doubt. The flowing script, so violently dug into the stone, it had to be a seriously pissed off young lady.

Gary smiled. "I hope your next boyfriend isn't so much of a shit, love."

He picked up his dinner from where he had placed it on the wall. It was still hot. What had felt like an age of staring at the words had been seconds at best. It had been the reflection off the sea, Gary reasoned; that was what had disturbed his eyes. If he hadn't been so blinded in the first place he would have seen the angry shout at the world for what it was straight away.

Gary started for home, thinking of the cold beers in his fridge. He didn't notice when he first began to whistle.

His fish supper was everything he needed it to be and the cold beers consumed while shooting people in far flung countries via his Xbox left a smile on his face. The only real blips on his Friday night were the occasional complaints over his headset from both the random opponents and his mate Alec about his whistling. He'd apologise but then be caught doing it again an hour later. Eventually he tired of all the whining and decided to call it a night.

*

Saturday was a lazy day, a time to relax and unwind. Gary had planned to spend it on the beach with a cold box full of beer and a couple of good books. His flat was only five minutes from the beach and he'd found a good spot that didn't get overrun by excitable children. It was his place and he was looking forward to it.

As he crossed the road a poster on a lamppost caught his eye. It was large, mostly blue, and dominating it was a clown with red lips, a white face and maniacal eyes. He wore a smile that seemed, for some inexplicable reason, to promise cruelty. Behind the huge, cruel clown there were others, balancing plates and juggling sticks, but in all their eyes Gary could see something malevolent.

"Men with False Faces." The phrase leapt from his lips and made him stagger back. The words 'World Famous Bognor Clown Convention' caught his attention.

A clown convention? Hundreds of men hiding behind their false faces, painted-on smiles attempting to hide their sinister intent?

Gary felt his legs give way and he landed hard on his tailbone. An electric shock of pain raced up his spine to punch him in the head. The pain hurt but also blasted the thoughts from his mind.

When he stood up again, his sudden fear of the clowns had receded. The larger clown on the poster appeared no more menacing than a kitten. Gary glanced at the other, smaller sign on the lamppost; it was another 'Have You Seen Me' notice. One of the many Polish migrants in the town had gone missing. Gary suspected there was a group of locals responsible. How often had he sat in the town's pubs and heard the mumbles and complaints that Bognor was becoming the third largest Polish town; that the Polish shops wouldn't serve you if you were English? Enough to have been curious about the second claim and find it to be lies.

Gary picked up his cooler and turned to the beach, hoping the poor fellow had just gone home and nothing more sinister.

His relaxing afternoon wouldn't come. The face of the clown leering out from the poster kept flashing into his mind and after two hours he'd barely read ten pages of the book. The pain in his tail kept him from finding a comfortable seat, adding to his disappointment. Annoyed with himself, Gary packed his things up and made his way home. He deliberately avoided looking at the poster, but he felt the clown's eyes watching him as he hurried past it.

In such a rush to be away from it, Gary stepped into the road without looking and was rewarded with a screech of brakes and the honking of a car horn. The red Focus had come to a stop barely three inches from him. The driver was a large, shaven-headed man who was yelling obscenities through the windscreen.

Sheepishly, Gary raised a hand in apology and scurried past, another blast of the horn followed by a revving engine sending him on his way.

Back home, he tried to unwind by going online and shooting people again. It soon became apparent that two things were going to stop him enjoying his game. The first was that his adrenaline rush from being nearly hit refused to subside, making his hands shake and his heart race so much that his aim was completely off. The second was that once again he was told off repeatedly for whistling, something he swore to them all he was not doing.

"Yesterday it was a tuneless mess," Alec finally told him. "Today I recognise a tune. But mate, it's bloody annoying. Would you just cut it out?"

Gary stared at the lobby screen, trying to listen to himself. "I'm not whistling, Alec."

"Yes you are. It's low at the moment, but if you aren't speaking you're whistling."

Gary couldn't hear it. Concentrating on holding his mouth shut, he muttered, "How about now?"

"No, not right now."

Gary let out a sigh of relief.

Five seconds later Alec's voice yelled in his ear, "But now you are! Jesus mate, just stop, alright?"

Gary quit the game and stared blankly at the console's home page.

*

There was nothing on the telly on Sunday morning and while Gary owned a decent amount of DVDs and Blu Rays, he found that none of them really captured his attention. Boredom was creeping up.

That was when he heard the whistling.

Gary slapped his hands across his mouth in shock, but this time the whistling continued. It was faint, almost at the edge of his hearing but it was there: a tune that he recognised but could not place. Holding his breath and turning about as slowly as he could so as to not make any noise, he listened for the source.

It was elusive, the noise slipping from his right ear to his left and back again, giving the impression that it was swirling around him.

Straining harder and harder to hear, Gary jumped as a clear note sounded. Now the sound was everywhere, the tune familiar and catchy but still he was unable to place it. He pulled his right hand to his mouth to cover it once again, and felt a chill of horror as his warm breath brushed his palm.

He *had* been whistling.

Gary clamped his lips shut and curled up on the floor, his arms about his head, blocking his ears. Apart from his weeping, there was blessed silence.

*

Monday brought work and all of the distractions that came with it. There were papers to be filed, information to be entered into databases and customers to talk to. Gary hurled himself into his work with a furious determination, always giving himself something to be doing.

His manic devotion was the result of a short break for coffee. He had been sat sipping the hot dark brew when Jasmine had poked her head around the door. Twenty years old, hoop earrings that were just about the right side of an acceptable size and dark green eye-shadow, she was about typical of the girls in town, in Gary's uncharitable opinion.

"Well someone seems cheery today."

"What do you mean?"

She gave him what he supposed was meant to be a knowing wink and a smile. "Because you've never sat there whistling before. Got some over the weekend did you? Finally got your end away? Good for you."

The coffee glued itself to the inside of Gary's throat, choking off his air. There was a moment of panic followed by relief as he coughed his drink over the desk.

"Go away and do your work. Just crawl away."

Jasmine looked hurt, her eyes moist with tears as she turned away but Gary didn't care. *He'd been whistling again!*

The rest of the day was consumed by his work; he had to ration catching up on his emails as it was too easy to let his mind slip while reading them.

Dave, the office manager, stepped into Gary's office five minutes before the end of the day and closed the door. Gary felt like a trapped animal, sweat beading on his forehead as he tried hard not to look at the closed door. Open, it gave him a view out into the world where there were other people. Shut, it was him and his mind, a mind he was convinced had started to betray him.

"I've had Jasmine in tears. Did you really tell her to crawl away like a bug?"

Gary shook his head, at first to clear it a little, then faster to indicate a negative. "I certainly did not."

"Gary, she's claiming you called her an insect and that she should crawl away like a bug because she wasn't worth your time."

That got to Gary. "What utter bullshit. Sorry about the language, but bollocks. I was having a coffee and she comes in and starts going on about did I get laid over the weekend. It's none of her business or anyone else's in this office if I do or don't shag anyone when I'm not here. I told her to go away and work. I may have said slink off or shuffle off but I would never say crawl. As for calling her a bug or insect, never. I didn't say that many words to her."

Dave was nodding. "That's what I thought. She does this. People tell her no or tell her off and all of a sudden it's a big old storm and people think she's worthless. I'll have a word."

Dave stood up, walked to the door and opened it. Relief swam through the opening along with the fluorescent light of the rest of the office. "Call it a day, Gary. See you tomorrow." Then he was gone.

Gary found himself gaping like a goldfish. Go home? He wanted to stay, to work. But no, that silly little slapper had to talk shit and now he was going to be left alone with that tune. That tune which for the first time since Saturday was nowhere to be found in his mind. His anger must have pushed it clean away.

Like a drowning man whose only hope of survival is a plank of wood covered in rusty nails, Gary clung to his anger. It was only going to cause him pain, but for now it was keeping him afloat. He stormed out of the office, throwing a vicious glare Jasmine's way as he went – her renewed sobbing followed him out of the door.

The thickening air of the Bognor summer hit him as soon as he was outside. Sweat beaded across his brow, tiny pinpricks of irritation.

Although Gary normally caught a bus from the office to the seafront, his ride would not arrive for another twenty minutes, so he decided to walk.

Sweat drenched his shirt, as what should have been a twenty minute walk had become something much longer. It wasn't the heat, though that was making him breathe a little harder. In addition, while he hadn't been looking, posters for the Clown Convention had gone up everywhere.

No matter which road he walked down, the leering clown with his terrifying smile was there. Gary cut back and forth through the residential roads, trying to find a route without the eyes of the false-faced man watching him, but there were none. Occasionally, another yellow poster for a missing person broke the flow of the clowns. Whether it was the same Polish man or not he didn't know, but Gary came to rely on the stern features of the missing man to provide him with a break from the clowns.

Eventually the houses in front of him dwindled away and the blue sea was visible. A small park in a close of tall, multi-home houses was his quickest path from here, so Gary decided to cut through. The entrance to the park was an archway of bushes on a wooden lattice. Normally when he came here, Gary felt as though he had found a little oasis of country in the middle of town, but as he approached it today there was an ear stuck on either side of the arch's apex.

It had to be a joke, Gary tried to convince himself. Had to be? Other people would have noticed, wouldn't they? Body parts growing on foliage was not an everyday occurrence in a seaside town, at least as far as he knew.

Fake, obviously fake.

Gary took deep, slow breaths and waited for his heart to slow its heavy metal beat. He squinted at the nearest ear.

So fake. He nodded to himself.

What if it's not?

Gary cursed his own mind; he wanted, *needed*, to leave the ear alone. To let it be someone else's problem. He couldn't bear the thought of being caught by such an obvious practical joke, certain that the perpetrators were no doubt even now watching him and laughing their arses off.

And yet, *and yet*, didn't it look just a little real? Just a touch too gooey, a smidge too weathered?

"Little shits!" he hissed, wanting to yell but not looking to draw more attention to himself. He sucked up a lungful of air, strode to the arch quickly and reached up.

Just as his fingers touched plastic, voices screamed in his ear.

Gary whirled and lashed out.

The teenager holding his mobile phone up to film the moment was caught by surprise as Gary's blow knocked him clear off of his feet. The other lad had a moment of shock and looked to Gary like he was about to get involved in some retribution.

"You little fuckers!" Gary screamed in the standing lad's face, causing all fight to stream out of him like urine down a leg. "Think that's funny? Do you? I'll give you funny!"

The lad had helped his friend up by the time Gary noticed he had his arm cocked back to deliver a punch. The two of them vanished out of the other end of the park before Gary heard their laughter begin.

He slumped to the floor and began to cry.

*

An hour later, Gary had chilled out a little.

He was on the beach, shoes off with his socks neatly tucked inside, letting the lapping waves wash over his feet. He curled his index finger around the edge of the stone, just like he had been taught, and with a flicking motion, sent it spinning towards the sea.

It clipped the top of an incoming wave and skipped off, still almost perfectly flat; again it hit the crest of a wave, this time launching itself higher but remaining flat. Gary smiled as the stone managed another four skips before sinking below the surface. He looked at the pile of flat stones next to him; some were more rounded than Tom had suggested, but they looked flat enough. He hadn't been able to find many of the broken flint ones, the stones that Tom insisted flew straightest and skipped the best, but he was pleased with his little pile.

It had been a few weeks after moving to Bognor that Gary had met Tom in one of the local pubs. Gary was still having a little trouble adjusting and had been feeling down. Tom had noticed and in the way that drunken philosophers do, decided he knew exactly what Gary needed.

So at three in the morning, under the light of a half moon, Tom had spent two hours showing Gary how to skim a stone, how to find the smooth missiles that would fly the best and generally how to relax with a simple bit of fun.

Now it was working for him. It had become a part of his life to come down to the beach and skim stones whenever things got a little on top of him. That he could get such calming enjoyment from something so simple as flicking his wrist was a source of constant surprise.

Something heavy splashed right at his feet sending a shock of cold seawater up his front and into his eyes. In surprise, Gary slipped over and landed on his backside, aggravating the healing bruise from his previous fall. Rubbing the saltwater out of his eyes, he heard whistling; that tune again, but slower and more mournful than before.

As Gary looked around he saw the boy he had smacked earlier holding a large rock in each hand. That was bad enough but what made Gary shake was the bright red smile the lad had drawn on his face in blood red lipstick.

A clown's smile, Gary thought.

The bloody smile widened and the boy threw one of the rocks at Gary's feet, causing stones to explode like shrapnel. Gary yelped in pain as one of the fragments scored a cut across his foot – just before the sea rolled back in and washed it with stinging saltwater.

The youth's smile widened so much that Gary feared it would split his face clean across. Gary felt a shiver of fear. They were alone on the beach; he'd deliberately looked for somewhere where there weren't a lot of people so that he wouldn't be disturbed. Now he was trapped, his back to the sea and a grinning lunatic with a deadly weapon in front of him. He darted his eyes to his shoes and socks, trying to ignore the renewed stinging every time a wave rolled in.

The lad saw Gary's eyes move and brought up the index finger of his now empty hand to wag it. *No, no, no.*

Gary felt sweat bead on his forehead as the threatening figure began to whistle again. It was the same tune Gary had found himself whistling before, but now all the joy and bounce that it had contained was gone; it was flattened out, elongated into something sinister.

And still Gary could not place it.

"What do you want?" It was a lame question, but it was the best he could manage.

To his immense shock, the youth began to caper in front of him, waggling his head and rolling his eyes, but never letting go of the rock or lowering it.

He did it all without ceasing to whistle the now melancholy tune.

The hairs on Gary's neck felt connected by tiny electrical sparks, snapping and frying his skin. A hot flush crept up and down his skin as he watched the bizarre performance. Without knowing why, he began to match the boy's whistling.

The red smile widened.

Bracing himself for an attack he was sure was coming, Gary increased the speed of his whistling. The youth did the same, somehow managing to maintain the smile.

When the tune was being whistled at what felt like the correct speed, the teenager suddenly dropped the rock, bowed, and walked back up the beach to the road, where he was soon gone from sight.

Gary was rooted to the spot as he watched him go. All the time whistling.

*

He called in sick for the next two days, citing a summer cold. Dave was understanding, but told him to take a couple of his holiday days as well.

"Make it a week off, enjoy yourself. Things aren't too hectic at the moment and you being out isn't going to cause a major crisis."

Gary spent the days huddled in his duvet on his settee, despite the heat outside as summer came marching on. Watching daytime TV and catching up on DVD box-sets, he tried to keep his mind distracted. He ate when he remembered and mostly drank bottles of cold beer from the fridge, but couldn't make himself drunk, despite his efforts to get there.

Instead he concentrated fully on the screen, the dialogue, the sound effects; he kept his ears busy because every time his concentration lapsed, the tune was there again. Either escaping from his own lips or floating through the walls. Bouncy, joyous and familiar, but devastatingly omnipresent.

The third morning when he awoke, the tune was gone. He wasn't whistling it; it wasn't coming from the walls, through the letterbox or under the door.

Silence, blessed silence, reigned.

Gary felt tears prickle at his eyes. Then his stomach growled, making him wince. How long since he had last eaten properly?

He decided that he deserved fish and chips. After everything that had been going on, it felt like just the thing to pick him up.

Gary made his way to his favourite fish and chip shop; the one just past the pier, with the open doors looking out onto the sea. The girl working behind the counter was quick and efficient, and favoured him with a bright smile that lifted his spirits. She was the kind of girl he could see himself dating if he ever actually got around to asking a girl out. Stepping out into the soft breeze, Gary inhaled deeply, revelling in the mixture of vinegar and the salty air. He knew his dinner wasn't going to wait until he got home, so he decided to find himself a spot nearby where he could enjoy it.

Passing the pier, which was now full of yelling children mingled in with the sounds of coin pushers and arcade machines, Gary spotted a girl sitting on the sea wall, right at the spot where he'd found the strange carving.

The girl waved him over. Gary checked to see if maybe she was beckoning to one of her friends, but he was the only person walking her way.

Her waving grew more insistent, more forceful.

Gary soon found himself in front of the girl.

"Hello mister, how are you today?"

"I'm fine, thank you." Gary looked at the wall, but the carved words were nowhere to be seen. He was in the right place, he was quite certain of it, but the words were gone and there was no sign that they had ever been there. Likewise, there were no signs of work done to cover them up or fill them in.

"Are you ignoring Bobo?" the girl demanded. "Say hello to him."

Gary looked at the girl. She was on the cusp of teenage-hood. Blonde hair, bright blue eyes that seemed to stare far away.

"Say hello to Bobo," she repeated.

"I beg your pardon?"

151

She gestured to the empty air next to her. "Bobo." Her tone implied that he should know what she meant. "He's an eighteen-inch tall, invisible clown with razor sharp teeth."

Gary took an involuntary step backwards. "He's a what?"

The girl stroked the air next to her, petting her invisible friend as she reprised the description.

Gary felt a smile stretch his face unnaturally.

"Bobo!" the girl squealed. "You can't say that. It would leave a horrible mess and we'd never clean it all up."

"That's a nice joke," Gary said. "But it doesn't scare me."

The girl shrugged and bent to kiss the invisible clown. Then she turned back to him. Blood dribbled from her lips and as she smiled; he saw a ruin of a tongue in her blood-filled mouth.

"Hith teeth urgh tho very tharp," she mumbled.

Gary's dinner slipped from his nerveless fingers and he sprinted away, her girlish giggle following him down the road.

He ran for town, for people. Needing to be around normal everyday people.

He heard the noise coming from the town centre long before he saw what made it. Cheers, laughter and loud children were the main sounds. Then he heard horns and vehicles and a whole cacophony.

A huge crowd for the size of the town lined the sides of the road, cheering and laughing. Gary felt like he knew what they were looking at, but he had to see for himself. He pushed his way through the press of people, driven on by this determination. He'd got most of the way through before he saw what everyone was looking at, and his blood ran cold.

Clowns.

Hundreds of clowns marching along the road. A rally of clowns, squirting water from fake flowers, throwing brightly wrapped sweets to children, and all of them with huge painted smiles on their deathly white faces.

The crowd shifted around him and Gary found himself right at the front. Sweat covered his brow and hands. The clowns were coming for him. Three of them arrowed straight at him. One with a narrow orange smile squirted him with his buttonhole flower. The next had a sad face with black lips, and he threw a bucket of confetti, while the third, who had the largest smile of any of them, got right up into Gary's face and hooted with laughter.

"What do you want?" Gary screamed.

For a second the clown looked taken aback, and then presented him with a wilting blue flower before dancing back into the parade.

All around him the people of the crowd laughed at Gary's reaction. He saw small children pointing while their parents looked on with a mixture of amusement and disapproval at his outburst.

Gary tried to back away from the road, but the crowd was holding him in place. More clowns came past, most turning to give a wave. The unintentional menace of their false faces made him shake. He needed to pee, he needed to run. He needed to be anywhere but here. Yet he was stuck; the only way out of this would be to run into the parade, to surround himself with fake smiles and lined eyes: pale faces that betrayed no real emotion, just projected unnatural happiness or weird melancholy.

He couldn't do it, couldn't stay there a second longer. The heat from the crowd, the mindless, braying laughter of his fellow humans at the capering fools before them.

Gary drove an elbow backwards, hearing a gasp of pain and shock. The crowd pressure lessened a little and he began to fight his way back into it. He didn't care how; he pushed and punched, kicked and scratched.

The crowd took notice and parted to let this violent idiot through.

Gary couldn't care less what they thought of him; he just had to get away, had to be away from the parade and the crush of people.

With a last frantic shove, he was clear of the crush. The high street lay mostly open in front of him. There were still a few shoppers wandering in and out of the stores, and the coffee shops looked to be full, with a number of people relaxing at outdoor tables. Gary massaged his forehead, trying to drive away the pain building behind his right eye. Then music began to play from the parade. A fanfare of trumpets, horns and drums.

Gary recognised the tune.

It was the one that had been playing in his head all week. The one he had been whistling. The one the dancing teenager had mockingly whistled at him.

It was the song of the clowns, the entrance music for a circus. He remembered the title. *Entrance of the Gladiators*.

He had once found it amusing; the idea that clowns would consider themselves gladiators, that the circus tent was an arena.

Now it was the confirmation of every fear he'd endured in the past few days. Gary spun around to scream at the parade, wanting them to shut up.

The words of fear and anger died in his throat.

A mime was standing a few paces behind, staring at him.

Gary turned again and began to walk. A quick glance over his shoulder showed the mime matching him step for step, keeping exactly the same distance.

He increased his pace, letting out a muffled whimper when he realised the mime wasn't going away. Terror began to pluck at his thoughts, mixing them up. Gary decided then he would make a stand; that he would take it no more.

Spinning around to face the mime, who now pretended to be in a box, Gary bellowed at him, not caring that the other people in the street were looking.

"Go away! I've had a shit week and the last thing I need is some fake Marcel Marceau following me down the street. Piss off!"

The mime cocked his head and tapped against his box. He shrugged his shoulders and cupped a hand to his ear.

Fury engulfed Gary. "You are not in a fucking box! You heard me perfectly well, now bugger off before I kick your head in!"

The mime appeared to find a handle on his box, twisted it and stepped through a door. He smiled at Gary.

"You heard me. Go away."

The mime held up one finger, asking Gary to wait a moment. Then he lifted his shirt to show a knife sheath without a knife in.

"An empty sheath? Is that really supposed to scare me?"

The mime made as though he was drawing the knife and waved it in front of him menacingly.

Gary took a step towards him. "There's nothing there, you maniac. Now leave before I hurt you."

The mime clenched his other hand around where the blade should be before pulling it upwards. Blood ran down his arm from a cut in the centre of his palm. He advanced on Gary once more.

With a scream, Gary fled.

He ran down the high street, the bloody mime chasing him the whole way, past the train station and up to the old *Picturedrome* cinema. Standing at the entrance to the cinema was another mime. Thus mime waved and walked towards him.

With another yelp, Gary ran left, heading towards the sea.

A glance behind showed him the mimes shoulder to shoulder, sprinting hard after him. Gary felt the strength and power of fear flow into his legs. It took only a minute of pelting along, but then he was round a bend in the road and the mimes were lost to view. He raced towards the beach and the pier. Hoping to lose himself amongst the crowds drawn in by the fruit machines, claw games and electronic noises, he ran as hard as he could manage. His lungs burned and he found his breath getting harder and harder to catch. But his goal was in sight.

He paused at the pedestrian crossing, willing the little red man to transform into his green counterpart, when he saw something that shattered his plans.

Three clowns stood outside the pier, talking and smoking cigarettes.

He couldn't go past them; they would know where he was and tell the others. The clowns would come for him and do whatever it was they had been plotting for so long. No, he couldn't go into the pier. But he had to stop running soon; his legs screamed at him to rest.

Gary used the last of his energy to dash across the road, clamber over the sea wall and duck round to hide *underneath* the pier.

Scrambling across the loose stones, he made his way into the murky light that filtered through the support struts and down from the planks above. He made his way into what he thought was the centre of the pier, facing rolling waves that broke ten feet in front of him.

There, his legs gave out and he was forced to lie down. As he did, his legs shook uncontrollably, the shaking passing up into his body. It was a combination of exertion, fear and bewilderment. He closed his eyes to rest.

"My, doesn't he look tired. A shame. Now he can't run away again."

The voice gurgled, liquid and thick. Whoever was speaking may have been using English, but it was not their native language.

Gary's eyes snapped open again.

To his surprise he could only see the pier above him. He'd expected to see the speaker standing there. He sat up, but there was no-one between him and the sea.

Turning slowly, knowing that whoever had spoken had to be behind him, Gary braced himself. Or tried to.

He could not have made himself ready for what he saw.

Three men in shabby suits stood before him, one wore grey, the second a dirty brown, the third black. The grey man and brown man had drooping faces that looked somehow familiar. Their skin seemed to sag in the wrong places: a lower eyelid drooping or a forehead that looked to be dripping downwards. Each of them would absentmindedly reach up and push the skin of his face around, as though melding it back into place. The man in black was another story. His face was ragged. His skin looked like paper and Gary could see little rips in it when he spoke. When the rips widened, Gary could see the muscles underneath.

"Why, I think you are ready," the man in black said. "Are you not ready for me? I think you are."

Gary got up and backed away. "Ready for you? How can I be ready for you?"

The paper-faced man chuckled, and it was a vile sound. "We've been preparing you."

Then all three of them began to whistle that damned tune again. This time it burrowed into Gary's mind and stayed there, becoming part of him, forcing him to hum along. In a panic, he turned to run, but stopped as he saw all his escape routes from under the pier blocked. To his right, the two mimes were waving. To his left, the teenage boys from the park and the girl with the invisible clown friend smiled menacingly.

Gary looked back at the men, numb, shuddering with horror.

"Who are you? Who are they?"

The man in black gestured. "These are our little agents of terror. Don't you think they've done a good job? Have they not suffused your soul with fear?"

The three men laughed; a liquid sound reminiscent of someone vomiting.

"As for us ... we are the Men with False Faces. Who did you think we were?"

Gary shook his head. "No ... clowns are men with false faces. They paint them on."

The trio nodded.

"True," Black said. "But they take them off, and then still have a real face." He reached under his chin and pulled at his own flesh. It peeled away, tearing and flaking like parchment, revealing the musculature beneath. "But us ... we have no real faces. We take new ones, new ones made supple by fear. New ones like yours."

As Grey and Brown pushed their faces back into place Gary knew where he recognised them from: the Polish men he had seen on the 'missing' posters.

As his legs buckled beneath him, the mimes and teenage boys raced in to hold him down. "But why that song? Why choose the clown song?"

Black shrugged. "We like it. It speaks to us."

Gary began to laugh, his mind shying away from the reality. Black slapped him and then pushed his skinless visage right down into Gary's "No laughing ... you will stretch my new face the wrong way."

"Your new face?" Had Gary known what must be coming, what they had planned, but had refused to accept it? As Black pulled a large, sharp knife from his trousers, the blade stained brown with years of dried blood, he could deny it no more.

Gary screamed.

"Excellent ... your screams make my new face last longer." Black grinned and began his work.

THIS BEAUTIFUL, TERRIBLE PLACE

In the annals of folklore there are many seaside cliffs where, because of past suicides, there is reputed ghostly activity. But no high point on the British coast can compare in this regard with Beachy Head, a chalk escarpment close to the town of Eastbourne in East Sussex.

Originally named for being a beautiful headland – 'Beaucheif' in medieval French – the cliff at Beachy Head is sheer and plunges approximately 530 feet onto rocks which, even at high tide, are only partially submerged. For anyone who goes over the edge here, either by accident or design, death is certain. Perhaps this is why so many suicides are reported; several a month at one estimation. It may also be a contributory factor that all around Beachy Head lies bleak, windswept down-land, which means there is rarely anyone close enough to interfere without their being spotted well in advance. However, not every lonely sojourn to this sad place has a calamitous ending. One such occurred in the late 1980s, when an elderly local man, who was in the habit of taking bracing cliff-top walks, attempted to do his good deed for the day.

It was late evening in summer, and the man was approaching the suicides' point, when he spied a black-clad figure loitering there. Assuming this was another troubled soul seeking to end their suffering, he hurried forward, hoping to talk them out of it – but when he drew close, he realised that he was facing more than simple misery.

The figure, which was crooked in shape – he later described it as "malformed" – and wearing what looked like a black habit and a black monastic cowl, turned slowly to look at him. Though he couldn't see its face in the deep shadow under the hood, it regarded him with what he said was chilling intensity. It then pointed a gnarled, dirty finger over the cliff edge. To his horror, the would-be Good Samaritan realised that he was being urged to jump. He then noticed something else, and this frightened him even more: though a strong southerly breeze was blowing, the figure's voluminous garments were not moving in the least.

The man later said that he knew he was in the presence of "a terrible evil" and possibly the cause of so many tragic deaths. He challenged the creature, demanding to know why it sought his destruction. It made no answer, but continued to point down at the frothing waves. Angry, the man continued along the path, but *gave the figure wide berth. When he glanced back, it was still positioned as before, still pointing over the edge.*

Despite his advancing years, the man reportedly ran the rest of the way back to Eastbourne, where he related the event to acquaintances in his local pub. There was an amazed response, not least because others there had heard similar stories about a black monk-like figure haunting the high rocks at Beachy Head, apparently urging anyone who came past to kill themselves. These tales went back to Victorian times and even beyond.

There is no satisfactory explanation behind this alarming story, but it is taken seriously and many Eastbourne folk avoid the Beachy Head footpath, especially at night. Allegedly, the black monk isn't its only supernatural visitant. Many spectral forms in the garb of centuries past are supposedly sighted traipsing across the downs and leaping from the cliff, only to vanish before striking the rocks. But the monk has the most malevolent aura. There were monastic houses all over East Sussex in the Middle Ages. The monks of St. Benedict wore a distinctive black habit and cowl, but despite modernist views that religious folk of that era were untrustworthy and self-serving, the vast majority did much good among the poor and downtrodden. If any monk or nun had been of so evil a disposition that his or her tortured soul would linger afterwards seeking the demise of others, they would likely have been named and shamed by folklorists (Marie Lairre for example, at Borley Rectory in Essex).

Another, perhaps even more disturbing possibility is that the black monk of Beachy Head is not dead at all, but a malicious person wearing a disguise and deriving enjoyment from the suffering of traumatised individuals.

Despite the many reported sightings, there has been no police investigation into this curious phenomenon. Maybe it is time there was.

GG LUVS PA
Gary Fry

Neil enjoyed living on the coast. His part-time job with Middlesbrough's social services paid just enough to cover the rent of a one-bedroom apartment in Sandsend. He was even able to work from home, monitoring welfare benefits applications. And during the evenings he took fine walks along the beaches, soaking up an atmosphere for which his city-self had yearned the better part of fifty years.

It was especially pleasant at this time of year, late autumn, when hordes of tourists stayed inland, saving money to return the following summer and ruin Neil's solitude all over again. But he wouldn't think about. He experienced enough duress at work but now had a few weeks off to recuperate.

The tide was out this afternoon, and he paced along its frothy margins, watching water strangle pebbles and sink into soft patches of sand. It was all so *clean* – unpolluted nature. He loved this as much as his rigorous filing systems at the office; it gave him a sense of order in a world he'd often found chaotic. Looking now at towering cliffs and the picture-postcard village carved amid them, Neil couldn't help thinking that he'd done pretty well for himself.

Further ahead, he spotted some markings on the beach. Using his walking stick – he was far from infirm, but this helped him negotiate awkward terrain – he paced across to the violation, his head tilting to make sense of it. It was a message inscribed in the sand, rather like a semi-literate proclamation by sentimental young lovers. Neil felt queasy reading such large letters, but noticed there was only one word. It read nothing like BAZ LUVS TRISH nor had two sets of initials followed by that foolish over-commitment FOREVER. The message simply read:

WHY?

It was as if it had been etched with a stick considerably thinner than Neil's fat cane. He stooped to run one hand over the grooves that formed the shakily written letters. Had the author been drunk while composing this message? The word, along with the slipshod question-mark, was two foot high and three wide: WHY? Neil glanced up at the heavens and felt as if the question was about the nature of existence.

He wasn't averse to metaphysical speculation, having read philosophy as an undergraduate before switching to a more practical subject in the hope of gaining reliable employment. But now, with time to spare, he enjoyed toying with deep contemplation and investigative enquiry. His father had died a few years ago and his mother was being cared for in a nearby rest home. It wouldn't be long before death became curious about Neil, too. And when it made its approach, he was determined to be as prepared as possible.

In the throes of such thoughts, he responded intuitively to the message on the beach by writing two similarly sized words directly beneath.

WHY WHAT?

Then he chuckled in self-rebuke and moved on. There were no footprints other than his own around this burgeoning conversation; just erratic scribbles in the sand that resembled the marks of thuggish seagulls after a fight for food. These led all the way to the sea, lending credence to this interpretation. After all, no person could be that light-footed, nor bear so little that resembled firm flesh.

*

The message in the sand – almost certainly now erased by the sea, along with his impromptu response – troubled him all night, ruining his usual eight hours of sleep. How had it been written when there was no evidence of anyone standing nearby? More to the point, what had it meant?

WHY? he thought upon waking early the following morning. And just as he'd asked at the time, he wondered: WHY WHAT?

He didn't plan on spending his fortnight break out walking; he also had interests in local history. After breakfast, he took a bus to Whitby and accessed its library, perusing microfiche articles on unusual sea-life. He chanced upon many horrifying pictures that turned his stomach, graphic photographs of wounds sustained by swimmers in the North Sea, just off the town's coast. Marine creatures could do terrible things to a body – strip flesh to the bone, nibble away faces. Only morbid curiosity forced Neil to continue examining these shots.

That was one of the reasons he rarely visited his mother in her rest home; he'd always been queasy about human frailty. When his father had died of a sudden heart attack, Neil had been relieved. The two of them had never got on, but that wasn't why he'd been grateful; he'd simply felt unable to cope with extended suffering.

People got little help with such matters from the state. Neil's job in social services had offered him such insight. In troubled times, a man must look after himself, and if that meant making sacrifices, so be it. While strolling back along the beach to Sandsend, Neil reflected on not marrying or having children. Then his parents came to mind, his father work-weary and pessimistic, his mother a mass of overprotective neuroticism. None of this appealed to Neil. His salary was modest, but had allowed him to tuck away a hundred-thousand, generating a steady income to supplement his wage. The sum was a backstop against future duress; few people had such a luxury these days, though Neil refused to describe it this way. After all, it had arisen from avoiding the kind of things many desired, most of it acquired through irresponsible spending. That was why the world was so unforgiving these days, wasn't it?

WHY? he thought again, approaching his home village. And then: WHY WHAT?

And after nearing the spot he'd chanced upon the day before, he noticed that, although the two other comments had vanished, an answer to his casual enquiry was now available:

DID YOU FORSAKE ME?

Neil felt his heart run a little faster, but he wasn't sure what the source of his arousal could be. Was he frightened ... excited ... intrigued? Whatever the truth was, it appeared as if someone was engaging with him, without the personal interaction that always made him uncomfortable. He glanced around, looking for onlookers on the beach or in the windows of the few residential properties that could be seen from here. But there was nobody. The area was deserted, a sharp breeze sweeping across the sand and bringing flecks of incipient rainfall.

He glanced again at the reply on the ground ... if indeed it *was* a reply, and not simply a random utterance from some inebriated prankster. The writing was as shaky as the message yesterday, clearly carved by the same sticklike object. And there was ambiguity in its meaning, surely. Divorced from his question, the statement seemed to invite a yes / no response. "Did you forsake me? Well, *did* you?" he heard a woman say in his mind, and in the absence of any other in his life, her voice sounded like his mother's. Nevertheless, if the question was a reply to his enquiry, the focus was different: "Why did you forsake me?" that mother-voice said, even though Neil tried to make it sound younger, and not the raddled husk the older woman used in her rest home. "Can you explain why you did such a terrible thing?"

But all this was foolish. The message wasn't intended for him, was it? How could it be when the person who'd carved the words in the sand had never even met him?

Neil turned to walk away, his racing pulse settling, but then he recalled something he'd observed yesterday. He twisted back, his body numb, and after shaking off a twinge in one knee, he re-examined the sand around the latest message.

It would be too generous to call the haphazard shapes leading away *footprints*. They looked like marks made by bony instruments, each bereft of substance or form. Ragged scratches at the thicker ends of these unevenly spaced disturbances could hardly have been caused by toes, could they? No, it was more likely that, despite meandering towards the sea in pairs, the prints were a residue of birdlife in the area, squabbling over food.

And so who had written the latest message? Indeed, who had composed yesterday's?

Neil was unwilling to be troubled by this issue, yet remained rooted to the spot. Rain was thumping down, driving all but the most furtive onlookers indoors. And this offered him enough privacy to add another irrepressible question to the sand with his stick.

WHO DO YOU THINK I AM?

*

Neil had been born in the 1960s, the so-called promiscuous decade, when women had revelled in newfound liberation and men had remained much the way they'd always been.

He'd long believed that this cultural phenomenon had bypassed his own family. His mother had clung desperately to Neil while his father had worked nightshifts, the only employment available at the time for skilled manual workers in the north east. Neil had seen too much of one parent, and not enough of the other. But later in life, he'd witnessed far worse in his role at the council. He considered himself lucky, as well as immunised psychologically against reckless behaviour, against the way a life could run askew with even tiny twists of fate.

That question on the beach dogged him all morning: DID YOU FORSAKE ME? Its Biblical undercurrent appealed to his chaste soul, even though he'd never had much religious inclination. While cooking lunch – fat-free and brain-enhancing, with a view to living as long as possible – he reconsidered his reply: WHO DO YOU THINK I AM?

Everything that had occurred – a disjointed conversation with an elusive being – had taken the form of questions. Maybe one or the other communicant would soon provide information, inviting trust in their developing relationship. With little experience of such matters, Neil imagined this was how young lovers conducted the first stages of a love affair. The process was laden with danger, but for the first time in his life, he saw its appeal ...

He was getting carried away, however. He ought to stick to his long-term plan: eating well, living cautiously, surviving for as long as he could.

Part of his regime involved a daily walk, and he liked nowhere better than the beach to battle high cholesterol. Aware that the tide would be out, he emerged in the late afternoon. It was no fun patrolling just the cliff-side; he liked to stroll on the sand, with wind from the sea full in his face. This made him feel alive, like the boy he'd been before many pressures from the world had descended upon him.

His first thought after spotting two new carvings on the beach involved jealousy. The words formed a name – a man's name:

PATRICK ARCHER

This was written with the same stick and surrounded by more of those inconclusive markings. Neil, marshalling errant emotions, felt his knees give way, almost toppling him to the sand and ruining the message from this lovelorn being.

If the author believed her respondent was male, it implied that she was female: a girl or a woman, her language pure and refined. For some reason, Neil immediately considered his audit systems at work. He'd never believed a person could inspire a similar sense of perfection, of unthreatening order, but whoever answered his comments was certainly achieving that ... But *who* was Patrick Archer?

Neil mustn't think of this man as a rival. That implied madness, and with his mother suffering dementia, he'd often feared the onset of such a condition. He'd heard a recent news report on Radio 4 about fish oils not having the positive impact on the brain experts had always claimed. Neil, his diet concentrated on vegetables, also ate as much seafood as possible ... But these thoughts were getting him nowhere, especially as he now recalled the gruesome images he'd viewed in Whitby's library.

Using his walking stick for support, he glanced a second time at the markings around the new shaky words. They couldn't be footprints, simply *couldn't*.

He turned away and moved as quickly as his ailing legs would convey him. He knew where he must go next.

*

He typed the name – Patrick Archer – into the library's online search engine, which stored electronic copies of every edition of the *Whitby Gazette* going back to the newspaper's inception in 1854.

Much material was returned, including articles about many Patricks and considerably fewer about people called Archer, yet still a fair batch. Neil began trawling, aware that time was not at a premium. The next low tide – along with another message, he hoped, from his covert informant – would soon arrive and he wanted to be equipped with all relevant information before it did.

It took him a few hours to look through the earliest editions of the paper. He found little of interest until the 1920s, and then only an article about somebody called *Peter* Archer, who'd run a factory in the town and donated a large sum of money to a local charity. A photo revealed a benevolent guy with a face full of smile-wrinkles, surrounded by people clearly suffering learning difficulties.

That was when community had meant something, Neil reflected, and tried to recall a time in his life when this had also been true. He failed with dismaying haste, but continued with his search.

And at five o'clock, just before the library closed, he found what he was looking for.

In 1964, a young woman – little more than a teenager – had gone missing in Whitby. Neil had located this story because the girl's boyfriend was called *Patrick Archer*, a good looking lad with a crop of blonde wavy hair. His picture was on a front page of the *Gazette* under an unimaginatively informative headline: TOWN SEEKS MISSING GIRL. He was standing beside one of the most attractive women Neil had ever seen.

She was slender and dark-haired, her skin pale and unblemished. Dressed in a knee-length skirt, her fine legs were dramatised by a pair of leather sandals. Her face was a tapered oval, the eyes wide and shining. It was apparent that the photo had been taken during summer, on the beach near Whitby. The North Sea glittered in the background, and the sand looked as pure as the girl's demeanour.

Her name, claimed a caption underneath this black-and-white snap, was *Gayle Greene*.

This young woman had been a local vicar's daughter and very popular in town. She'd carried out voluntary work for several organisations, helping deprived children and older people conduct their daily lives ... But then she'd met Patrick Archer, a less than community-minded person (or so the surprisingly frank journalist had claimed), who'd impressed her with his shiny new car and rock 'n' roll bearing. He'd come from a *nouveau riche* family of factory owners, and the whole world, as the proverb ran, was his oyster ... *A bit of rough*, Neil thought his mother might have described such a boy, and after reaching the end of the newspaper article, he couldn't help but feel disturbed.

The implication was obvious: the young man called Patrick Archer, '60s-heady to Gayle Greene's '50s-chaste, had got her in the 'family way'. And then, after she'd refused to have an abortion (her family being deeply religious of course), he'd bumped her off, presumably drowning her in the sea.

Shaken by all he'd learned, Neil continued searching electronic documents. Weeks after the first story, several more articles appeared about the missing girl, but none announcing any happy outcome. She remained missing, and after a few more entries of ever-dwindling column length, she'd vanished altogether from the local news.

Neil felt profoundly disheartened.

Nevertheless, entries for Patrick Archer didn't cease in the '60s, that seedy decade during which much had changed. In the early '70s, his high scholastic achievements were recorded in print; he was a good swimmer, apparently, and had represented his country in an amateur tournament ... This knowledge hardly lessened Neil's fear about what he'd begun to suspect, but he continued reading, paging through more stories until he reached a final one about his new subject.

In 2008, only five years ago, the aged Patrick Archer, now a successful London tycoon, had revisited Whitby and donated a large sum to a redevelopment programme intended to smarten up the quayside.

Had this been *guilt* at work, Neil wondered? In relative old age – his early seventies, similar to Neil's sick mother – had Archer been trying to offer something back to a town his selfish actions had once caused such grief?

"Oh, come on, come on," Neil said aloud, and a few people nearby, two librarians among them, glanced up to see what the disturbance betokened. Perhaps they thought he was mad. Nevertheless, he quickly added with similar audible necessity,

"You're running ahead of yourself, old man. You don't *know* he was responsible for the girl's demise."

He looked again at a photo, this one in colour, accompanying the latest article. It showed an ageing man, smartly dressed and with thinning blond hair, looking into the camera and surrounded by people who could only be his family. Healthy youngsters and ailing oldsters alike occupied this pack, each member looking genuinely happy.

Just as poor Gayle Greene had once appeared, clinging to the arm of dangerous Patrick Archer fifty years earlier.

But Neil shouldn't let such corrosive thoughts take grip of him. The guy might be innocent. He was clearly now a family man, using wealth to hold together his relatives in a way few bothered these days … including Neil, who'd neglected both his father and mother.

While heading out of the library, Neil began wondering whether his antagonism towards Patrick Archer and burgeoning feelings of affection for this man's former girlfriend arose from deeper reasons than inadequate knowledge about their case. He wondered whether, after half a decade on the planet with such a pathologically cautious attitude to life, he was changing, and whether this was a good or a bad thing.

*

That night he went outside at a foolish hour, with a cold wind howling and much rain lashing. He wanted to reach the beach before the tide swept in and prevented him from adding another message for his new associate.

Or his lover, he thought with delirious humour as he staggered down the path for the beach and then trudged across sand as sticky as mud. He had his walking stick to facilitate motion, and after reaching the spot still bearing the last message – PATRICK ARCHER – he jealously scribbled out this name and added a plaintive instruction:

LET ME HELP YOU

He retreated, back up the cliff-side to the road, where he stood for an hour in pounding rain to watch. Thunder rioted overhead. A few cars passed, including one whose driver had wound down a window and shouted, "Get inside, you daft old bugger. You'll catch your death out here."

He wasn't *that* old, and far from the end of his life. He could surely withstand a soaking, especially if this involved glimpsing the person he'd come to know as Gayle Greene.

But by the time the sea had reached his message, he'd given up hope. Perhaps she was always aware of when he was watching and reluctant to show what was little remained of herself. It had been nearly fifty years since she'd gone missing. Neil recalled incomplete footprints leading away from words written with a stick so brittle it might almost not exist ... But then his overstrained mind seized upon another concern.

How could the dead woman read his messages and then add her own? It would be impossible to do both at the same time, because the sea would also erase her reply. Each day, hers remained and his was gone. Did she scrub out his answers? But that didn't make sense. The sand was always too flat, with just scattered marks around the new words; surely only heavy water could create such a blank slate for inscribing.

Beginning to shiver with icy discomfort, Neil noticed movement on the beach. By this time, the sea was sliding back and forth over the message he'd left – LET ME HELP YOU – and now something was moving amid its frothing fringe.

Was it some kind of sea creature? At this distance, it resembled a pile of seaweed interspersed with oily sticks and wet rags. It was nudged further forwards by the tide, half-moored on the sand while possibly being fed by life-sustaining liquid. Perhaps it was even a bedraggled mermaid ...

Neil pictured in his tired mind the side of a fish with its innards hanging out, and then turned to retreat for his secure apartment. He tried telling himself that it was the chill he'd fled, but privately knew that the truth was far worse.

*

Today he'd put in a full shift.

That was his decision after waking the following morning. The delirium troubling him yesterday had departed, laying waste to his fears of suffering an early-onset mental health condition. Dementia might run in families, but he was too young to worry about that. His obsessive standards at work were exhausting, that was all, and he'd simply needed a proper break. The story about Gayle Greene had affected him more deeply than he cared to acknowledge, cutting to the heart of his psychological state.

But now he was back in a rational frame of mind and determined to deal with his main concern: the dead girl on the beach and what she wished to communicate.

If Patrick Archer, a prize-winning swimmer, had drowned her in the sea, that would explain why she came and went with its tides. She'd been down there almost half a century and might even rely on water to sustain her existence. Stepping gingerly down the cliff-side, Neil thought he'd worked everything out. When the tide came in, the girl would read what Neil had written. Maybe she believed these messages were from her former lover; perhaps she was unaware of how many years had passed since her disappearance. But neither issue really mattered. All Neil knew was that when the tide went back out, what little remained of Gayle Greene must carve her response.

He couldn't prove this; he'd only ever witnessed her incoming performance. But the explanation adhered to logic. He was a logical man, always had been, and went about his job like a ruthless machine. Difficulties in other aspects of life were negligible. In his twenties, he'd had only two liaisons with women, both living with other men at the time. Neil had felt safer that way, with a legitimate reason for refusing to commit to long-term relationships. Affairs were vulgar, and for some reason always put him in mind of his mother and the way she'd clung to him as a child, the way she still would if he ever got too close again ...

He glanced up, struggling to suppress his introspection, and found himself only paces from the latest message left only for him.

MEET ME

It was written in that same brittle hand, and Neil required little persuasion to heed such promising words. He quickly wrote in response:

I'M HERE

And then retreated to occupy huge rocks at the back of the beach, from where he'd get a good view of the girl's arrival ... and in far more detail than he'd managed last night.

Gayle Greene, a vicar's daughter, was chaste and innocent; she was also the victim of a terrible crime for which Neil was determined to seek firm evidence and overdue vengeance.

I'm here, he thought, hoping the girl would realise what he planned to do on her behalf. He wondered what his next message should be. One possibility was HOW DID HE DO IT? Or maybe WHERE SHOULD WE LOOK FOR YOUR BONES? Perhaps he could return with a camera and take pictures of these impossible communications from a watery grave ... But first he needed to see Gayle Greene as she existed now.

The day drifted by, and a few people came and went, chatting with the carefree attitudes Neil always envied in couples unlike his parents, whose marriage had unfolded in a tense coexistence. Hidden among rocks, he returned his attention to the sea, an icy mass of liquid advancing up the beach. Nobody else – neither resident nor tourist – considered it pleasant enough to stroll on the sand, and so he had the area to himself. When it got dark at four o'clock, the tide was near the spot in which he'd inscribed his latest communication, and then ... something could be seen, flopping in its foamy edge.

This resembled what it had the previous evening: a stack of slimy objects pasted together with oils and wrapped in threadbare cloth. But on this occasion, it failed to put in a full appearance, simply bobbed on the incoming water like a rotted wine cork. Then, after flitting briefly around the words Neil had etched, it moved elsewhere, under the sea, presumably to stalk other territory, places it knew best.

How had Patrick Archer prevented his girlfriend from being washed onshore? Had he loaded her pockets with rocks, the way Neil had seen thugs do in movies? He was uncertain what was real or otherwise, and as the sea made its final advance on the cliff-side rocks, he kept thinking he saw something moving under the surface, like pieces of bone drifting with its currents ... But the images dissolved, replaced by more choppy waves trying hard to reach him.

Then, many hours later, during which Neil occasionally nodded off with mental exhaustion, the tide began receding. It might have been the middle of the night when he regained clear consciousness. It was obvious that much time had passed, because the sea now slid down the beach with hissing, acerbic haste.

And it had left something on the sand.

Neil had to rub his eyes to get a good look at this thing, but even after doing so, he remained uncertain about what he observed. The figure – a mass of sticks, rags and emaciated meat – had ascended to stand on makeshift limbs ... insofar as the twisted, angular lengths of half-seen bone could be described in that way. The rest of it was bent over, the head or whatever passed for such a corrupted travesty pointed away from Neil, and one arm – moonlight made a mockery of its supposed covering: bone shone through wisps of skin and garments – performed its tenuous duty in the sand beneath.

Neil, terrified and fascinated in equal measure, moved forwards to get a better look at his respondent, but that was when one foot slipped on a ledge and stone rattled into gaps between the rocks.

The figure on the beach turned its sorry excuse for a face his way.

There was less to her expression than there was to the hand with which she'd carved a new message. Neil had been mistaken in thinking that she used a brittle stick; why bother when a single finger, shorn of flesh and nail, served the same purpose? Then the girl-thing hissed from a mouth boasting more ivory than lips, and came stumbling lopsidedly his way.

Did Gayle Greene – or rather, what little remained of her – think he was Patrick Archer, come to seek peace? Whatever the truth was, it was as much as Neil could do to focus on the young woman's disjointed body – slack sockets in slacker, age-stewed skin – moving inside clothing as eroded as she was. Either fish had chewed holes in her pockets, or this was where rocks had once been, holding her underwater for decades. Her face as she grew closer seemed aware of her captivity, the bulging eyes unsupported by lids. And although it was difficult to tell what emotion her expression betrayed – it might be insatiable rage or lascivious yearning – Neil quickly tried escaping his inadequate hidey-hole.

She was like a mermaid, and surely couldn't survive out of the sea for long. Nevertheless, while running across the sand away from her latest message, Neil's ageing frame offered little to gain advantage over her.

Then he noticed, at a hazy angle, what she'd written before detecting his presence.

I'LL COME FOR YOU

It was a pledge that was genuinely handwritten.

And while continuing to stumble along the beach, Neil wondered what he'd prefer the least: the creature pursuing doggedly in his wake to come and kill him … or to love him forever more with all the passion of cheated youth.

IN THE DEEP, DARK WINTER

Few seaside towns in the United Kingdom have suffered more from the decline of the 'holiday at home' industry than Morecambe in Lancashire. Despite its prominent position on England's northwest coast, Morecambe also once drew custom from Yorkshire and Scotland. But this didn't save it when the late-20th century rot set in. The resort was particularly affected by the loss of its West End Pier during a severe storm in 1977, while its Central Pier, already damaged by fire, was closed in 1992. When its fairgrounds and swimming pool followed suit a couple of years later, there was little left to offer in terms of entertainment.

Another casualty of this slow disintegration was the Morecambe Winter Gardens. Originally the ornate Victoria Pavilion Theatre, built in 1897 as an add-on to the pre-existing Winter Gardens, which basically comprised a seawater bath and a ballroom, it is now a sad relic of that elegant bygone age. Though in its heyday it played host to numerous famous artists – from Laurel and Hardy to the Beatles and the Rolling Stones – it ceased to trade in 1977, and even though the main theatre survived the demolisher's hammer that wiped away the ballroom in 1982, and is now preserved as a Grade II listed building, it still stands empty and desolate on the Morecambe seafront.

However, in 2008 the theatre achieved fame of a different variety when it was visited by Living TV's 'Most Haunted' team, who held two investigations over two separate nights, and apparently recorded a plethora of paranormal phenomena, including knocks, bangs and eerie disembodied voices. The aged structure appeared to be alive with unexplained activity, and it was sensationally revealed that it is divided down the middle, with a 'good side' – where benign presences lurk, and 'a bad side' – in which the atmosphere is darker and more sinister. The show's producers were so pleased with the experience that they returned again the following year for an eight-night live broadcast in the week leading up to Halloween, and the Morecambe Winter Gardens was pronounced "the most haunted theatre in Britain".

Local people do not disagree, and argue that the imposing Victorian edifice was always known for its scary reputation. Amateur ghost-hunters had long held vigils there, and afterwards would speak in hushed tones about the wide range of disturbed personalities they had encountered, including a violent *poltergeist who would pelt intruders with lumps of rotted plaster, a woman in an old-fashioned RAF uniform, a shrieking girl who may have been murdered on the main stairway, a former dancer who died heartbroken having failed to win stardom, invisible but viciously snarling dogs, a hostile shadow in the main bar, and even the ghosts of the theatre's two original architects, Magnel and Littlewood. One bunch of investigators reported weird mist-forms in the cellar, later suggesting that some kind of portal existed down there, possibly predating the theatre and maybe even predating Morecambe itself, which allowed nameless entities to pass through from a different world.*

Stories concerning the building's alleged good half and evil half are difficult to pin down, but appear to stem from the days when the theatre was in use, artists preferring to stand on one particular side of the stage while waiting to perform, some claiming that on the other side they had been pinched, slapped and even punched by unseen hands.

Theories range widely as to why an evil force may linger in this decayed but inoffensive structure, though most, on the face of them, seem fanciful.

For example, one name that has been mentioned several times by psychics is that of Buck Ruxton, a Parsi doctor who, in 1935, in the nearby town of Lancaster, murdered his lover, Belle Kerr, in a fit of jealous rage, and then, for fear of exposure, visited the same fate on his housemaid, Mary Jane Rogerson. Kerr died by strangulation, Rogerson by suffocation, but the murders were rendered particularly gruesome because, to prevent identification, Ruxton mutilated and dismembered the two corpses, scattering fragments of them over wide areas of northern England and southern Scotland. Ruxton was not by any means a serial killer – from the details of the case it sounds as if he was suffering from a severe form of depression, and on his arrest the following year, numerous former patients came forward to vouch for his good character. This did not prevent him being convicted and hanged in 1936, but the point is that, prior to these tragedies, he had no reputation for being an especially wicked man. Likewise, he was never a resident of Morecambe, though he was eventually traced because the newspaper with which he'd wrapped many of his grisly packages was recognised by the police as a Morecambe edition, while his second victim, Mary Jane Rogerson, was later buried in Overton, on the outskirts of the town. For all this, the link seems tenuous.

Other possible origins lie in local mythology. Lancashire has a colourful history of witchcraft – the trial of the Lancashire Witches in 1612, which resulted in ten executions, is one of the most detailed on record, though again these deaths occurred in nearby Lancaster, not Morecambe itself. In Roman times, a Celtic tribe, the Setantii, occupied England's northwest coast; they had a reputation for being warlike and rebellious, and for building forts overlooking what is now the Morecambe shore. They were also rumoured to be practitioners of human sacrifice, one preferred method of which was drowning – possibly just offshore. Not that deliberate violence has ever been a necessary ingredient for the loss of human life in Morecambe Bay. Mudflats, flood tides and quicksand have all played their part in innumerable accidental deaths. These in turn have given rise to ghost stories concerning the endless waterlogged sands. Rumours about the Lancashire boggarts – evil or vengeful spirits said to be particularly active around marshes and wells – abound in the Morecambe area, but again, though all of these things have been mentioned in passing reference to the Morecambe Winter Gardens, none have any kind of obvious connection.

Ultimately, folklorists and ghost enthusiasts may have to accept that Morecambe Winter Gardens is a spooky place simply because it is. A handsome, baroque building with an exotic history, but now empty and decayed – a symbol of faded grandeur and better times long forgotten – it was always going to attract the more romantic kinds of paranormal rumour: deceased actors waiting forever in the wings; lovelorn phantoms wandering the once elegant corridors; spirit doors opened to a spectral realm.

THE INCIDENT AT NORTH SHORE
Paul Finch

In some ways, Blair McKellan's escape from Lowerhall was a Godsend for Sharon.

Okay, it could never be good for anyone that a six-times killer was on the loose with an apparent agenda to continue the same grisly rampage that had seen him confined in the first place, and it especially couldn't be good for the police officers who were likely to have to pick up the pieces. But Sharon was getting to the stage where she needed more from Geoff Slater than a simple tumble in the back of his CID car, and this incident ought to create sufficient time and space for them to at least discuss it.

That said, in the first instance McKellan would cause nothing but problems. Sharon had just commenced night-shift when the call came through. The sound of sirens echoing across the darkened sea and the flashing glare of searchlight beams emanating from the distant, high-walled structure on the South Shore headland was immediately sufficient to attract patrols from all over St. Derfyn Bay. When news broke that it was Blair McKellan, and that he'd gutted one of the guards while making his escape, patrols had come dashing from neighbouring divisions as well, and even neighbouring force areas: Dyfed-Powys in the south, Merseyside in the north.

Of course, as a relatively junior officer, still with only a couple of years in the job, there wasn't much that Sharon could really do. She drove warily up South Shore Drive, the airwaves crackling incomprehensibly as radio messages rocketed back and forth, the black October sky reflecting the innumerable searchlights. But she'd only travelled half a mile before reaching the first roadblock. Somehow or other, PSUs had got there ahead of her. Two of their armoured troop-carriers sat at angles across the blacktop, their complement of tough guys standing around in visored helmets and Kevlar plate, some clutching PVC riot shields and hickory night-sticks, others – indicating that one of the carriers was in fact an ARV – with pistols at their belts and carbines across their chests. Local supervision was also on hand. Sharon saw Inspector Marquis in deep conflab with a man wearing the pale grey helmet and body-plate of the Lowerhall security team. Beyond the scene of chaos, the road curved on along the rocky coast, spangled all the way with spinning blue beacons.

A leather-gloved hand rapped at her window. She powered it down, admitting the face of Section Sergeant Pugh. He was a pale, severe looking man with short-cropped iron-grey hair, lean features and prominent cheekbones. Such a visage wasn't made for smiling, which was a good thing as he rarely did.

"What are you doing here, PC Jones?" he enquired.

"Wanted to see if I could be of assistance, sergeant," she replied.

"Well, as you can see ... the world and his brother have taken charge of this situation." He sniffed disapprovingly, never having been one to hold faith in specialist outfits like Tactical Support or Firearms Response. "Get back to the town centre please, and cover your beat until further notice. And if anyone else thinks they're going to toddle up here and spend the rest of the shift drinking coffee and chatting to their mates, you can tell them otherwise."

She nodded, powered the window up, shifted gear and spun the car around in a three-point turn. This was just what she'd been hoping for.

En route back to town, she passed another local patrol easing its way along South Shore Drive. She flashed her headlights and the vehicles pulled up alongside each other. It was PC Mike Lewton and his young probationer, Rob Ellis. Lewton was burly and black-haired, with a thick moustache, pitted cheeks and a flattened nose. But he wasn't the brute he looked and was usually good for a giggle. Ellis was younger, and even more fresh-faced than Sharon, but with a shaved head and jug-handle ears, there was something vaguely comical about him.

"Don't tell me," Lewton said through his open window. "Pugh wants us to pick up the scrag ends?"

"No work for us up there," Sharon said. "That's only for the big boys."

"Probably nothing to do anyway. Just come over the FR that McKellan's lifted one of the asylum security vehicles. He'll be half way down the A470 by now." Lewton pondered and shrugged. "Alright, no worries ... see you later, Shaz."

As expected, on returning to town Sharon copped for three jobs straight away. Routine calls had been backing up while the emergency on South Shore had been occupying the airwaves. The first was a complaint about a bunch of yobbos playing football against someone's front door, the second was criminal damage to a car, and the third a burglary. They each took her progressively deeper into what was known as the 'Back End' of town, where blocks of scabby flats and rows of run-down terraced houses alternated with boarded-up pubs, sex shops and tattoo parlours.

This was the sort of seedy district that the holiday programmes rarely focused on. Not that St. Derfyn Bay featured very regularly on holiday programmes these days. Who actually came to the seaside for a holiday in the twenty-first century? Perhaps there were one or two, but Sharon rarely saw them.

When she was a little girl, the town's seafront, which followed a slow, gentle curve of nine miles all the way from North Shore to South Shore, had seemed magical to her with its array of whitewashed, neatly-aligned hotels and guesthouses, its nautical-themed pubs and cafes, its theatres, casinos, pleasure palaces and amusement arcades, all done up in rainbow-hued neon. The neon was still there, loops of fairy lights suspended above the prom, while the prom itself was a pleasant enough stroll on a nice sunny day, but there was more litter around now than Sharon remembered, while a lot of the hotels had closed or been given over for the use of the DHSS. Sharon was only twenty-four, so in truth things probably hadn't been a lot better when she was a child – she certainly had no memories of the so-called golden age of the British seaside – while the close proximity of Lowerhall Psychiatric Hospital, a glowering edifice of black brick, originally constructed as a prisoner-of-war camp during the Napoleonic era, had always cast something of a shadow. But she never recalled St. Derfyn being quite as down-at-heel as it seemed to be at present. The town's former pride and joy, the *Jubilee Pier*, was still in use, but the pastel blue and pink colours with which it had originally been painted had long flaked away, leaving it a drab, skeletal grey, while the assortment of joke shops, puppet shows and postcard stands that had once made it such an attraction had long gone. Now there was only a tea-room at the end of it, and usually a bunch of desultory, middle-aged fishermen perched on the barriers, most of whom would be lucky if they caught anything other than a pair of dirty underpants or a used condom.

In actual fact, neither the beach nor the sea were in a particularly grubbier state here than anywhere else along Britain's west coast, but in poor weather, which seemed to be the rule rather than the exception these days, it made a bleak picture. It was difficult to imagine that Bubbles still lived off this coast. He was the mythical sea monster who'd supposedly been tamed by the original Derfyn back in the age of the Welsh saints, and had allegedly been sighted a few times since, on several occasions during the 1950s as a mass of bubbling turbulence several hundred yards offshore; investigating scientists had later explained this as harmless natural gases escaping from the seabed, but schoolchildren had preferred to think of it as their friendly local sea monster blowing bubbles. The name had stuck and he'd become a mascot for the town in its heyday, his smiley alligator head omnipresent everywhere, from the hoardings of fish-and-chip shops to balloons being sold on the sands.

Of course, Bubbles was a name from the past now. Much like the town itself.

Once Sharon had dealt with the burglary, she emerged from the Back End and was dispatched to a drunken dispute on the prom itself. She attended this scene with some minor trepidation, but she didn't expect the worst. It was midweek, and so was unlikely to be the usual story of a visiting stag party falling out with a posse of local cowboys. In fact, when she got there it turned out to be three retired men arguing about a disputed bowling score from earlier that afternoon. As soon as her white Opel Corsa complete with its Battenberg flashes pulled up, the anger drained out of them, and with all parties advised (and sent home with tails between legs), Sharon was at last able to concentrate on her real plans for this evening.

When she checked her phone, she saw that Detective Sergeant Geoff Slater had beaten her to it, having texted her over half an hour ago. His message read:

*Circus on South Shore – North Shore seems a plan.
Fun Land could be fun tonight.*

Fun Land, St. Derfyn's once-famous amusement park, was a good choice for three reasons. Firstly, as it had been closed since 2003, no-one went there anymore, apart from the odd tramp or drug addict, so privacy was nearly always assured; secondly, thanks to the *Diffwys* and *Cadair Idris* massifs lowering over the north end of the bay, it was a radio black-spot; few messages were deliverable to or from North Shore without chronic interference, so if Comms called her or Sergeant Pugh wanted a meet, she'd have plenty reason not to immediately respond. The other reason of course, as Slater had said, was that with South Shore the current focus of attention, North Shore would be quieter than usual – and it was quiet at the best of times.

There was no better personification of St. Derfyn and all its problems than *Fun Land*. As Sharon drove up there, the quality of the buildings on the seafront declined, the faded guesthouses giving way to derelict shells. There were still kiosks and cafés on the sea wall, but to a one they were more like rabbit hutches, sealed up with wire-mesh and corrugated metal. A couple had even been torched, as had *Captain Flint's Tavern*, the last pub on the last corner before the gates of *Fun Land*. As a child, Sharon remembered it teeming with customers – usually dads and granddads, whetting their whistles while mum and grandma took the nippers into the amusement park. Now its redbrick Georgian edifice was black and scabrous, its famous mullioned glass windows, what remained of them, hidden behind a fence of faceless wooden slabs.

There was plenty of opportunity for Sharon to leave the car at the front. There were no parking restrictions because, as a rule, no-one wanted to park, but it seemed a risk – it would be just like Pugh to make a pointless drive-by and 'catch her shirking'. Instead, she cruised down a side-street towards the park's rear, its south boundary delineated by an eighteen-foot wrought iron fence. Only darkness lay beyond this, the relics of rides and attractions visible as shadowy, shapeless outlines.

Fun Land had once been a huge draw for tourists from South Wales and the Valleys, but mainly from the English Midlands. While Rhyl catered for Liverpudlians, Blackpool for Mancs and Morecambe for Scots, St. Derfyn had found itself inundated each summer by Brummies, but the amusement park had eventually closed as part of the general downturn in fortunes suffered by the British seaside. By the 1990s fewer and fewer people were visiting it, and an increasingly rough crowd spoiling the atmosphere for families had led to the introduction of an entry fee, which had killed off even more custom. As a result there was under-spending and so dilapidation set in. A succession of miserably wet summers was the final straw, and even the ubiquitous Bubbles, who'd featured on billboards all over the park, and had walked around it every day in June, July and August, an actor enclosed in an ingenious rubber sea monster suit, complete with a bubble-blowing machine installed in his grinning, crocodilian snout (the bubbles emerging from his nostrils), hadn't been able to reverse that. When *Fun Land* had finally padlocked its ornate scroll-iron gates for the last time, there'd been a promise that new investments would be found at some point, and a revival project put into motion – hence the lack of demolition work – but there was no sign of that yet. Rumours abounded that the site was now for sale, but if so, no-one wanted to buy it.

To its rear there was an open space about the size of two football fields. This had formerly been a car park, but was now a wasteland of gravel and cinders. The odd forlorn structure remained: an abandoned caravan; a roofless brick shack that had once been a public lavatory. Geoff Slater's motor, a white Toyota Esprit, was also there – sitting unattended next to *Fun Land's* rear fence.

Sharon surveyed it through her headlights. It was tempting to park up alongside it, but again there was a worry that someone might happen along – not necessarily Sergeant Pugh, but maybe one of the other patrols. Then the idle tongues in the office would really wag, even if she *hadn't* had something going with the tough, handsome detective. In many ways Slater was a good catch, but she'd told herself again and again that it was a mistake to get involved with a married man. The moral issue nagged at her, not to mention all the practical day-to-day frustrations inherent to being 'the bit on the side'.

She depressed the accelerator and veered away. On the face of it, it seemed a bit pointless parking elsewhere – what matter if they were one yard apart or a hundred? It would still be obvious they were here together. All she could do was park the Corsa out of sight, so she pulled up leeward of the derelict toilet block, hoping that it would mask her from the road. She switched the interior light on and briefly assessed her makeup in the sun-visor mirror. She was a good-looking girl and always had been. There was something of the feline about her: green eyes; delicate, diagonal brows; a small, sharp nose; pink lips. Whenever she took off her ridiculous uniform-hat and unpinned her black hair, it fell in a lush wave to her shoulders. Oh, she had lots going for her, except that she didn't have Geoff Slater. Not totally. Not yet. And this was something they had to sort out tonight.

Checking she had her mobile and all her 'appointments' – her cuffs, baton, CS canister and torch – she climbed from the car, replaced her yellow 'high visibility' coat with a normal black anorak, and attached her radio to its lapel.

She locked the vehicle up, and walked around the toilet block towards the Toyota. It seemed odd that Slater wasn't here, waiting for her. She reached his car and peeked inside; from the blipping red light on its dashboard, it had been secured properly.

Peering across the windswept waste, nothing stirred – just a few rags of litter tossing on the sea-breeze. She pulled on her leather gloves as she looked to the fence. An explanation as to why Slater had chosen this exact spot suggested itself; at some time in the past a couple of railings had been bent apart, presumably by kids, and there was now sufficient space to slide through. Not that she had any idea why Slater would actually have wanted to enter the park. She fished out her phone and keyed in a quick text.

Where R U

There was no immediate response, which there probably wouldn't be given the poor reception in this area. She pocketed the phone, and approached the gap, sliding through it shoulder-first and emerging in a passage between two sheds, at the far end of which a rubbish bin lay overturned, disgorging a mass of refuse so old that it had coagulated into a solid mass. Sharon stepped gingerly around this, and entered the park proper. As her eyes hadn't yet attuned, its variety of once brightly coloured attractions was still a clutter of brooding, featureless structures. The breeze stiffened, droning between wires and girders and loose sections of clapboard, which tapped in response. To the west, she could make out the high gantry of the *Crazy Train*.

There was a creak directly behind her.

She spun around, torch in hand, beam flicked on full.

The loose shutter creaked again on the shed to her left.

A sign overarched what had once been its open frontage. The jolly crimson paint now turned to grey, read: *Hoopla*. She glanced at the shed on her right: *Buffalo Bill's Shoot 'Em Up*. A rifle range. The frontage to this one was still open, tatters of blue and white-striped awning hanging down over it. Again, the question bugged her: what was Slater up to? Had he got wind that she was after some kind of commitment from him? Was he playing a stupid trick? Overhead, the moon slipped out from the clouds – a reduced oval, but it cast a welcome silver glow, embossing the tarmac footways snaking between the attractions, though of course it created deeper shadows too, blotting out some buildings entirely, cloaking the black, throat-like alleys between them.

When Sharon suddenly heard a shrill clarion call, she almost jumped out of her skin. Swearing, she retrieved the phone from her pocket. The return text said:

Here. Where RU?

"For Christ's sake," she murmured, keying in a quick response:

Where is here?
Need a location

While she waited, she walked. She'd last been in here as a young teenager, and possessed no real knowledge of the park's layout, so she ambled in a vague northerly direction, trying always to keep the open sky over the sea on her left, though as she had to turn a few corners to do this, it soon became confusing.

She eased the volume down on her radio. She hadn't heard anything on it for quite a while, most likely because of the mountains; if not for that, she was certain the incident on South Shore would have kept the airwaves busy. But even so, she didn't like the idea that a sudden burst of static might announce her presence. This was a habit she'd fallen into while making night-time property checks; it was far better to catch the felons in the act than alert them you were coming. Of course, at this moment she wasn't trying to stop anyone doing something they shouldn't – it was the other way around, she thought guiltily.

She passed the *Flying Teacups* on her right and the *Surf Rider* on her left. They were grim relics of their former selves: jibs hanging, cables trailing. From what Sharon could see, any attempt to regenerate the park in the future looked doomed to fail. Everything she saw here was broken, begrimed, gutted. Where the *Dodgems* had once collided in time to a coordinated dirge of all the latest pop songs, silent emptiness yawned under a rotted iron pagoda. The billboard on top of it had once advertised the latest shows at the *Fun Land Emporium*; now it hung charred and soggy. In fact, arson looked to have been the sole reason anyone had visited *Fun Land* in the last few years. Though the lower section of the *Downhill Racer* was caged off, its main tower had been reduced to blackened bones, while a flame-damaged effigy of Bubbles wearing a scarf and bob-cap and holding a pair of skis, which had once stood on top of this, lay on the footway.

A short distance on, she accessed a timber boardwalk, which thudded loudly as she strode along it. This was partly due to the empty space underneath. It was one of the unusual features of *Fun Land* that, to facilitate drainage of the autumn rains or spring melt-water from the heights of *Diffwys* and *Cadair Idris*, numerous channels had been tunnelled underneath the park, leading eventually to the sea. Back in 1920, during construction, the park's original designers had made a special feature out of this: the *Fun Land Marina* had been built. This was a deep, octagonal harbour, about sixty yards in diameter, into which numerous of the drainage channels discharged, their vents carved into dolphin heads or the mouths of tritons and sea gods, but more importantly, from which motorised mock-Venetian gondolas would take paying guests out along the so-called *Royal Canal* for a ride around the bay, calling eventually at the *Jubilee Pier*, where they would ascend via a special stairway decked in a red carpet, then walk around for a bit and presumably buy a different brand of candy-floss from that on sale in the park.

Sharon crossed over the *Marina* via an arching metal footbridge. Rather to her surprise, the tide lapped against the aged pilings below. If nothing else, she'd expected the *Royal Canal* to have bogged itself up by now, but apparently not. There were even a few boats on view, though most looked like hulks banked in silt. As she reached the far side, a second clarion call announced that she'd received another text from Slater.

Haunted Palace

"What?" she groaned. "What the bloody …"
A voice she didn't recognise replied to her.
Sharon turned, surprised. The bridge arched away through moonlight. No-one was else was standing on it.
"No-one," she said.
The voice replied again, apparently mimicking her.
It was a long half-second before she realised she was hearing an echo, probably from underneath the bridge. Even so, for the first time her thoughts strayed away from what she wanted to do here onto whether or not this was a good idea.

Despite the moonlight, everything was so black and still. On all sides, the jumbled silhouettes of gantries, domes, wheels and monorails blocked out the horizon, reminding her how deep inside the park she was. She wouldn't easily be able to find her way back, and in addition she was now expected to locate the *Haunted Palace*. Enough was enough. Rarely in this relationship had she and Slater spoken to each other on their own mobiles; they didn't have a particular rule about this – it was just that texting was simpler. But now she called him and waited impatiently while the number rang out – until it switched to voice-mail.

She rang him again, and again. On both these occasions it switched to voice-mail.

So it was the *Haunted Palace*. Bloody great! Snatches of childhood memory recollected dark tunnels, staccato lights, booming laughter. Not the most salubrious venue for romance.

Not that she felt like giving him any.

She pivoted around, finally spying what looked like a set of battlements protruding above the *Pancake House*, and sidled towards them, glancing over her shoulder as she did – again she thought she'd heard something, though it was probably another echo. She zigzagged through a labyrinthine section, which had once been nicknamed the *Shambles* because it was basically a market filled with novelty stands, ice cream vendors and the like. It also contained the *Gobstopper*, an attraction that had freaked her out a little even as a teen. It comprised a row of clown heads and torsos – minus limbs – mounted on metal poles, each with a gaping mouth to serve as a target. Contestants stood behind a counter and pelted them with hard wooden balls, the idea being to get as many as you could through the open mouth of your particular clown and down into its belly. With each clean hit, the eyes would light up to the accompaniment of bells, whistles and hysterical 'Daffy Duck' giggles. Sharon had thought it an odd-looking thing even back then; she'd never been able to shake off an impression that the dummy clowns were screaming – and even now as she walked past the row of de-limbed figures, still sitting motionless under their canvas awning, she fancied their ink-black eyes were following her.

When she emerged in front of the *Haunted Palace*, it was initially no more than a gothic outline in the gloom, yet in that strange way of long-ago familiarity, it all seemed so recognisable. It was easy to recall the wild screams as one car after another shunted its way up the access ramp and vanished through a pair of huge, nail-studded doors. The *Palace* itself was mock-medieval, sponge rubber and fibre-glass doubling as heavy stonework, but when she shone her torch at it, she saw that it had decayed badly. Its griffins and gargoyles had dropped off, and fissures had snaked across it, exposing the framework underneath.

Of course there was no sign of Slater.

Sharon stood by the barrier and phoned him again. Still it went to voice-mail. "Geoff!" she said under her breath. And then, because frankly she couldn't take much more of this: *"Geoff, where the hell are you?"*

A voice replied. At first she thought it was another echo, though on this occasion it sounded as if it had come from inside the *Haunted Palace*. She ducked under the barrier and stood at the foot of the access ramp, on which only eroded metal stubs remained of the rail-car system. The door at the top stood ajar.

Finally, she ascended. It had definitely sounded as if the voice had called her by name. So it was Geoff. But if so, why didn't he come out? She approached the door, the glare of her torch penetrating the gaunt passage beyond but revealing very little. When she entered, it stank of mildew. The ghostly murals that once adorned the fake brick walls had mouldered to the point where they were unrecognisable. She ventured on, turning a sharp corner – no doubt one of those hairpin bends where, for their own entertainment, everyone inside the car would be thrown violently to one side – and stopped in her tracks.

A tall figure stood in the dimness, just beyond the reach of her torchlight.

"Geoff?" she said, in the sort of querulous tone the general public would never associate with a police officer on duty.

The figure remained motionless; made no reply.

"Geoff?"

Still no reply; no movement. She advanced a couple more steps, the light spearing ahead of her. And then a couple more, and finally, relieved, she strode forward boldly.

It was a department store mannequin, albeit in a hideous state: burned, mutilated, covered with spray-paint. Up close, its face had been scarred and slashed frenziedly; for some reason, she imagined a pair of scissors. When she tried to shove it aside, it swung back and forth. Glancing up, she saw that it was hanging by a wire noose, which, even given everything else that had been done to it, seemed a little OTT.

Another thought now strayed unavoidably into Sharon's mind, one that perhaps had been lurking on the periphery of her consciousness for the last few minutes.

Blair McKellan, the 'Night Caller'; a maniac who, for twelve terrible months in the north of England, had broken into homes during the early hours and, using whatever household utensils he'd found, had slaughtered the families sleeping there.

But it was impossible. McKellan had stolen a security van from the asylum, which meant he'd be far to the south by now. There was no possibility he could have driven north from Lowerhall; he'd have had to come through the town itself, which would have been too much of a risk.

Some vandals were responsible for the mannequin. Some bunch of stupid kids who had nothing better to do. But of course that didn't explain the voice she'd thought she'd heard, or why Geoff Slater wasn't here. Sharon made an effort to steady her nerve. More than likely those two mysteries were tied together. When she'd been a probationer, Slater had been one of several old sweats to play elaborate tricks on her – setting her up with a hospital visit for 'a prisoner with a crippling foot injury' who'd actually been an off-duty CID man under orders to dash off at the first opportunity, running her all over the hospital grounds. All the newbies were treated that way, but of course Sharon had been singled out for special attention because she was good-looking. Even now Geoff adopted the air of a guy who never took life too seriously, but surely he was past *this* kind of nonsense? Especially when she'd intimated that they had important stuff to talk about?

Suddenly irritated as hell, she stalked back to the front of the decayed building, kicking her way outside into the fresh air. She stabbed in another text message:

Stupid game
Not impressed

Heading back

It was more gung-ho than she felt, mainly because she wasn't sure it would be as simple as 'heading back' – she didn't know in which direction from here the gap in the fence actually lay, but also because she'd really wanted to sort something out tonight. All day she'd been psyching herself up to having this conversation – when she'd seen his Toyota and realised that he'd got here ahead of her, she'd felt certain they were about to resolve the problem. And now he was acting the goat.

That was when she saw him.

Or someone.

It was no more than a speck of movement in the corner of her vision. She squinted, and realised that she hadn't been mistaken. A couple of hundred metres away across the park, a diminutive figure was plodding along one of the high humpback gantries of the *Crazy Train*. Sharon was astonished. She still wondered if she was seeing things. But there was no doubt – someone was up there, a tiny shape picking its way along the track. A wino or drug-addict? Possibly. They came here from time to time and dossed down, but would they climb to the top of an edifice like that? *Could* they climb?

Of course not. It *had* to be Slater.

But again that question: what the heck was he playing at?

She tried calling him again. As before, it went to voice-mail. This time she left him a message: "Am I actually watching you on top of the roller-coaster? If it isn't you, there's someone else here, and that can't be good, can it? Call me back ASAP. And please, please ... stop fucking around. This is serious."

She glanced again to the distant gantry. The figure was no longer visible.

As baffled as she was unnerved, she walked over in that direction. Again, she had to sidle down passages between empty shacks that had once been stalls, and along tunnels piercing the guts of vast skeletal structures, which were all that remained of world-famous white-knuckle rides. At the foot of the *Flying Teacups* there was a deafening shriek, and a seagull with a wingspan of nearly three feet burst out through the long-smashed window of the booth and swerved around her, beating the air hard, before lofting upward and vanishing.

Sharon was still shaken from that experience when she arrived at the *Crazy Train*. Its waiting area lay beyond a wire-mesh fence, and was only accessible via a turn-style, which she now had to climb over. Beyond this, the temporary crash-fencing, which she remembered being arranged in rows so that riders could queue in orderly fashion, had been flattened. She stepped over it as she approached the loading platform. The moment she got up there, a figure was awaiting her with a grinning sickle of tight-locked teeth, but it only made her start for a second. In fact it was two figures, one standing in front of the other, and thankfully both were made from hardboard.

The taller one at the back was Bubbles, hence the toothy smile. The smaller one was a teeny boy in a stripy t-shirt. A notice above them read:

Unless you're at least as tall as Johnny here, sorry ...
you can't ride!

When she passed into the loading area proper, it was like a small railway station, the track-bed lying between two separate platforms where riders would either climb aboard or disembark. In either direction, only a matter of yards from the overhead canopy, the track, which was largely still intact, its rails gleaming with moonlight, rose up out of sight, though when she looked down from the platform's edge, she saw large gaps where the various cogs and gears comprising the brake-run had long ago been removed. An ugly black emptiness lay underneath those.

She moved first to the north end of the platform, and gazed up the shockingly steep incline. Its uppermost rim, perhaps a hundred feet overhead, was framed against the moonlit sky, but no figure was silhouetted there.

"Ridiculous," she said under her breath. "What the hell am I even doing here?"

She strolled the other way to the south end. From this direction, the track rose in a more gradual ascent, before levelling out at about fifty feet and twisting away. But this time she had to blink – she couldn't be sure, but fleetingly she'd fancied there'd been movement; a tiny blot slipping out of sight.

This was nonsensical. Whoever it was, he couldn't have seen her down here ... could he? If he *had* seen her and had ducked away, might that be because he was trespassing and she was a cop? Okay, perhaps it *wasn't* Geoff Slater – maybe yet another stupid teenager. Perhaps one of the firebugs who'd visited so often in the past?

Either way, it was time to assert herself.

She climbed down onto the track-bed. From here, she had to take extreme care as she advanced, balancing on the rails and sleepers, avoiding the black emptiness occasionally lying between. When she reached the foot of the incline, it was hemmed in on either side by steel-mesh netting, but at least she had a clear view up to the top. And if nothing else, all this gave her a good story.

"That's right, sarge. I was driving past Fun Land – no reason really, just routine – and I saw a figure on the Crazy Train gantry. I tried calling for support, but got no response on my radio. Black spot, isn't it?"

"Hello!" she called, waving her torch from side to side. "This is the police. You've got one minute to get down here, or I'm coming up after you."

There was no response.

"I've got more officers on the way. We're going to clean you lot out of this place."

She expected nothing this time either, least of all the echoing metallic *clack* that half made her jump. Sharon strained her eyes as she peered up the timber gradient, its two rails again glinting. That had sounded suspiciously like some kind of gear being thrown. Even as she watched, another dark blot materialised against the skyline, but this wasn't a figure – it was square and bulky, and it quickly vanished again, drawing numerous other squarish shapes behind it.

A slow panic went through her as she realised what this was.

Through fleeting patches of moonlight, she glimpsed a line of jostling carriages rushing downhill – right towards her. She stumbled helplessly backward. But the platforms were several dozen yards behind her, while steel mesh hemmed the narrow track in, so she couldn't even jump to the side. Sharon screamed as the speeding locomotive filled her ears with its ear-splitting clatter – and then dropped.

The train rattled by overhead as she plummeted through moon-stippled darkness for what seemed an eternity, and yet when she landed and the breath *whooshed* out of her, it was relatively easily – on a mound of wet sand.

Sharon lay groggy for a moment or two, vaguely aware of a series of explosive impacts overhead. Only long after this uproar had ceased did her surroundings swim into focus: a vast, empty space forested with pillars and supports, moonlight glimmering through it in crisscrossing shafts. Slowly, still dazed, she sat up. Similar dunes to the one she'd landed on stretched out around her, steams of water meandering between them. When she glanced overhead, she saw that she'd fallen about twelve feet, so it was fortunate indeed that she'd landed on sand. But no sooner had her scrambled thoughts reordered themselves than a particularly chilling one came to the fore.

The *Crazy Train* had rolled downhill because it had been pushed.

That was the only explanation. In the initial frenzy of her thoughts, she'd assumed that some kind of vibration might be responsible; that she'd triggered the coaster's descent by trespassing on the aged, flimsy structure. But on reflection that was quite ludicrous. It had to have been done manually. And would a bunch of vandals really do that when they knew a copper was waiting at the other end? Would they stoop to murder?

"Geoff ...?" she mumbled, hardly able to give full voice to the notion. She glanced around again. Her eyes didn't penetrate the further depths of these sandy, salt-smelling chasms. There was no sound, save water dripping from rotted woodwork or jagged, rust-eaten metal.

Geoff was her lover, and a great card in the office – but he was also a ruthless operator. He'd planted more than his fair share of screwdrivers to get villains sent down; several times he'd been investigated for alleged brutality. Murder wouldn't be too much of a leap for him. But why? Just because he'd had enough of his mistress? Because she'd been going to ask him to ditch the mother of his children?

Sharon spotted an upright ladder about thirty yards to her left. She hobbled towards it, one hand planted on her hip, which she'd clearly bruise during the fall.

Had Geoff got sick of her? And was he so much a shit-heel that rather than break it off and risk having a woman scorned muddying the waters for him, he'd try to kill her?

On the face of it, it seemed preposterous. But Geoff had asked her here, and yet hadn't responded coherently to any of her messages. She glanced over her shoulder as she reached the ladder, checking that she hadn't dropped her baton or CS canister. She continued to glance back as she scrambled up the rickety iron rungs, this time to ensure no-one was encroaching from behind. And then another thought struck her, and this one was such a shock that, briefly, she almost lost her perch.

Had someone been sitting in the front carriage of the *Crazy Train*?

It seemed incredible, and yet she'd kept replaying the incident in her head, and in that last petrifying second, as the train flitted through that final patch of moonlight, she could have sworn there'd been someone riding in the front of it.

She hung there in the half-dark, thinking hard, gradually convincing herself that she hadn't been mistaken. There was no doubt. Whoever had pushed the train downhill, they'd jumped on board to hitch a lift. Which, as the roller-coaster track wasn't functioning properly anymore and as there was no braking system left, meant they'd been dicing with suicide. So surely it could *not* have been Geoff Slater?

At the top of the ladder, she emerged through a square manhole into a dusty kitchen-like room, which astonishingly still smelled vaguely of hotdogs and onions. Through a broken window, she saw that she was just across the footway from the *Crazy Train* pay-booth. When she crossed towards it, she had baton in hand, snapped out to its full one and a half feet of flexible alloy. Warily, she re-ascended the ramp, and found the station area thick with dust and wood-splinters. She wafted her way through this, baton braced against her right shoulder.

"Geoff? You here?"

As the dust cleared, she saw that all twelve carriages had derailed on the other side of the station, plunging part way through its cage-work support structure. The train's inverted wheels still turned as the bulk of it lay arched and twisted over the track.

There was no sign of a body or any kind of movement, from what she could see – and she was damned if she was getting any closer – but if someone had ridden the coaster down from that perilous height, it could *not* have been Slater? It had to be someone else, someone with an absolute death-wish.

She leaned to the radio on her collar, knowing that failure to call this in wouldn't just be remiss of her; it would be an abrogation of duty. By instinct, she adjusted the volume control – and only now noticed that the device had been muted. On first entering the park, she'd turned it down low, but had not thought to turn it back up again later. She swore as she adjusted it, and immediately heard a crackle of static, and caught some cross-talk from elsewhere on the Division.

"That's confirmed," came the voice of Comms. *"It was reported that McKellan had removed a vehicle from the Security Pound at Lowerhall. It wasn't specified at the time that he'd removed one of the offshore patrol boats, over."*

There was further chit-chat, much of it incomprehensible, the messages broken, distorted. But Sharon was no longer listening.

A boat?

The Night Caller had removed one of the asylum's boats?

She turned dazedly in the direction where she thought the *Marina* lay. It was a hideous thought, but in a speedboat he could have crossed St. Derfyn Bay and moored amid the grimy ruins of *Fun Land* in next to no time. And yet – she glanced again at the piled-up wreckage of the *Crazy Train*. Deranged or not, Blair McKellan couldn't have survived such a crash.

On the verge of panic, she slid her baton away and scampered down the access ramp onto the footway, trying to get a radio message out, but almost immediately losing her reception again. She swore aloud, but when a piercing clarion call sounded from her pocket, snatched at her phone.

What game?

She tried to ring Slater again. It went to voice-mail. Turning the air blue, she tapped in a quick message.

Meet up now
McKellan in park
Maybe dead or injured
Call me!!!

But he didn't call. And she very quickly began to wonder at the wisdom of her last message. That was a hell of a thing to have told a fellow copper. Suppose Slater spread the word, and the whole circus headed over here, allowing the real killer to get clean away? She had *not* seen a body, she reminded herself. She couldn't even be sure that someone had been riding the coaster. Again she wondered if she might have tripped it herself. Or what about the bunch of kids she'd initially suspected? She'd had enough, she realised. This was going nowhere. She tried to call Slater again, but the call failed. She keyed in another text:

Heading back to car park
C U there

She'd no sooner sent it than something creaked behind her. She twirled around, and initially the breath caught in her throat – but then she realised what she was actually seeing.

Across the footway, in the recess between the *Hotdog Kitchen* and the *Penguin Skittles,* stood something like a children's theatre: a small upright cubicle made of timber or fiberglass. A pair of shutters that once enclosed the tiny stage had swung open, presumably in the breeze, revealing that a life-size figure was standing behind them. But it was the usual thing – Bubbles, probably an animatronic version, looking more than a little mouldy and saggy, his scaly hide mottled, his eyes like ragged holes in rotted fabric, his crocodile snout deflated.

Sharon ignored it, glancing back to the topmost tier of the *Crazy Train*, straining her eyes one last time for trespassers. It didn't feel like the done thing, heading away from this place when there may have been a fatal accident here, but regardless of the Geoff Slater fiasco, she needed to get the word out. There was no-one up there she could see, so she turned and walked away, passing the children's theatre on her left – and noticing from the corner of her eye that it was empty.

She stopped in mid-stride and pivoted around to face it.

At first she thought the Bubbles dummy had maybe slipped down out of sight. But how come the side-door to the theatre now stood open?

And then she sensed a figure on her left.

She pivoted again.

In its present state of decay, the Bubbles costume was quite the most revolting thing she'd ever seen, hanging raddled and desiccated on the strangely emaciated form inside. His right hand was raised, causing Sharon to involuntarily giggle as she remembered the way Bubbles used to wave to the cameras with his right hand as he walked through *Fun Land* on hot summer days, hordes of gleeful kiddies trailing after him.

But this time he held something in it.

It looked like it was made of steel; it also looked heavy and very sharp.

Even when she blasted him in the face with her CS agent, he swung this massive implement down – this cleaver, or whatever it was – aiming squarely at the side of her neck. With barely suppressed shrieks, she ducked away, jetting the CS spray into his face a second time, and hitting him dead-on – though perhaps the costume headpiece was masking him, because he spun after her, slashing again with his razor steel, knocking off her hat, her hair uncoiling every which way. She drew her baton again, snapping it open, trying to fend him off, but another arcing swipe caught it mid-stem, severing it in two. Blindly, she struck out with a different weapon – her torch, and this blow landed. The bulb audibly shattered on impact with her assailant's head, but it also drew a grunt from him and he staggered.

Sharon used the opportunity to run – in no particular direction.

"PC requires," she gibbered into her radio. "PC requires. *Fun Land* amusement park. Blair McKellan is here. I need back-up urgently ... I repeat, *urgently!*"

As before, there was no response. She turned along a side-passage, and found herself amid metal struts and under tarpaulin roofs. She was back in the *Shambles*, she realised, which surely was somewhere she could lose the bastard? She took turns at random, hoping to throw him off, constantly glancing behind, seeing no-one in pursuit – only to find herself confronted by the

Gobstopper, its broad front standing open on the darkened recess in which the mounted clown figures were just vaguely visible.

Her mind raced, thoughts tumbling over each other.

There'd be missile weapons in there, of a sort – those hard wooden balls. Okay, they didn't signify deadly force, but they would pack a wallop. She clambered over the counter and into the space behind, where she crouched low and fumbled on the floor, eventually finding two of the missiles – though they seemed much smaller and lighter than she remembered. Once in possession of them, she waited and listened, struggling to stop her teeth chattering. For a few minutes, even the wind seemed to drop – the only sound was Sharon's heart thundering in her chest as she scanned the surrounding maze of stands and stalls, through which moonlight spilled in various fantastical forms, making it difficult to maintain depth or perspective.

Nothing seemed to move.

Had she thrown him off? She hardly dared consider the possibility. No-one could second-guess a monster like Blair McKellan, the Night Caller; an out-and-out madman who left his victims like sides of butchered meat. But surely he wasn't completely demented? He'd retained sufficient of his faculties to lie low between kills, to evade the law for almost a year. If he'd identified her as a police officer, as he surely must, he'd be expecting her to call this in? Assistance would be en route. He'd be better running.

A few dozen yards away, a figure emerged through the moonlit haze.

Sharon sucked in a breath so tight it almost squeaked. She sank lower, only her eyes visible over the counter-top. But no ... now that he looked carefully, it wasn't a figure, it was just an awning, patterned with mildew, rippling in the stiffening breeze.

She allowed herself to breathe again, filching the phone from her pocket. She would try Slater one more time. It seemed futile, pointless, but he was the closest to her, the only who could provide immediate assistance. She prodded in his number – and immediately froze as she heard a tinny tune somewhere in her vicinity. It sounded like jazz; low, sleazy jazz played on a sax. And she recognised it.

Slowly, incredulously, she turned around, riveting her eyes on the dummy clown directly behind her ... except that, now her vision had attuned, it didn't even resemble a clown. Or a dummy. True, like the others it was only a torso; the legs and arms were missing, and the mouth yawned open to impossible width, and it sat upright on a metal pole, though possibly in this case that was because the pole had been jammed ten inches or so into the object's anus.

A warm trickle soaked Sharon's knickers and the crotch of her trousers.

What she'd first taken for clown make-up streaking the figure's cheeks wasn't anything like make-up; and those eye sockets, which now contained nothing at all, let alone electric bulbs, would never light up again. In the gaping mouth, where once there'd been a tongue, sat a small, flat device, juddering its jazzy tune – until it switched abruptly to voice-mail.

Sharon had some vague thought that it was a good job she didn't still have her torch. Because she last thing she wanted to see were the finer details of this atrocity. Even so it transfixed her. She could do nothing but sit there gawking – until she tasted something salty dripping down the front of her face and onto the tip of her tongue. Dazed, she craned her neck back to gaze overhead – and saw a massive rent in the canvas awning, into which a distorted figure was leaning, staring down at her. The fluid dripping from the end of his hanging snout was probably tears, or saliva, or nose mucus, or a combination of all three – a product of the spray she'd hit him with earlier.

There are times in every police officer's career when all sense of authority and decorum is lost. When you cease to be a stern pillar of law-enforcement, and revert to your natural state: a frightened, vulnerable animal whose main instinct is to run.

This Sharon now did.

With hysterical shrieks. Throwing herself over the counter and haring off along the footway, blathering incoherently into her radio – even though she expected no response.

Again, she ran in no particular direction, blindly, exhaustedly, threading between the stands and stalls, through moon and shadow, until she reached a broad thoroughfare, which, more by instinct than logic, she felt would lead her to the park's entrance.

It did. Right up to those towering, scroll-iron gates.

They were closed of course. And locked.

The chains holding them were thick with corrosion, the padlock fused into a lump of impenetrable rust. Sharon yanked on it futilely, tearing her fingernails, before glancing back. A figure approached along the main drag; at first it looked distant – was only visible through the intermittent patches of moonlight – but very quickly it assumed those grotesque quasi-reptile proportions. Its faltering, lumbering gait was also unmistakable; as was the glint of steel in its clenched right hand.

With more breathless shrieks, Sharon ran back into the park, veering right when she spied an open doorway. She had no idea what to expect beyond it, but immediately found herself in a complex network of passages, smoothly glazed walls encompassing her from every side. Phantom Sharon Joneses leapt and cavorted, bodies elongated, heads expanded; illusions rendered even more demonic by the refracting moonlight. Not that twists and turns were a problem for her pursuer. Somewhere close behind, mirrors exploded one by one as he put his shoulder to them. Billions of fragments rained ahead of his wild, bullocking charge. Sharon attempted the same, arms wrapped around her head. Despite her stab-jacket and the thick tunic beneath, flecks of glass wormed their way under her collar and cuffs, cutting, stinging. When she blundered through one already-broken frame, a hanging shard of glass drew a burning stripe across the top of her head, though in truth she barely felt this. She snatched the shard down; it was twelve inches long and shaped like a dagger – its edges sliced into her fingers, and yet she clung onto it.

With hot blood dribbling into her eyes, she now hobbled left, groping along a side-passage that seemed to lead to brighter moonlight, so desperate to reach this that even when another mirror disintegrated in front of her, and a brutal form blocked her path, she drove straight on.

Perhaps McKellan was more surprised than she was. He had a weapon, but now so did Sharon – and she was the one who struck first, plunging the shard into the top right side of his chest, puncturing the rumpled costume and the human tissue beneath – the glass grating on bone as she drove it deep, to half its length at least, before lodging it fast. Her foe made no sound but reeled backward, allowing her to shove past him and head on to the light, which, as she'd hoped, turned out to be a window. She kicked it until it fell to jangling pieces, and clambered through.

After the hallucinogenics of the *Mirror Maze*, the moonlight outside brilliantly bathed another thoroughfare lying straight and open. She'd staggered fifty yards along it, mopping blood from her brow, before glancing back. McKellan had emerged behind her, but now was toppling sideways rather than following. Even as she watched, he fell heavily to the tarmac.

She turned to run on, and slammed into a massive, iron-hard body.

Sharon screamed and lashed out with her fists, before strong, gloved hands caught hold of her wrists. Through fresh trickles of blood, she gazed up into the saturnine features of Sergeant Pugh.

"What the devil … PC Jones, what the …?"

"McKellan," she whispered. "It was Blair McKellan … he killed DS Slater …"

"Slater ... Blair McKellan?"

"But I killed *him*!"

"What ...?" Pugh looked perplexed. "What are you talking ... what happened?"

Aware that she was ranting unintelligibly, she tried to explain, not even attempting to conceal the nature of her relationship with the late detective. Half way through, Pugh – looking very alarmed – checked the gash on her scalp, and after mumbling something unsympathetic about it only being a flesh-wound, strode back along the thoroughfare, ordering her to stay close.

"No!" she yelped. "I'm not going back there!"

"Pull yourself together, girl! You're supposed to be a police officer!"

She stammered out a few more semi-coherent objections, but the sight of Pugh, stern as ever, unimpressed by anything, seemed to restore a half-sense of normality. And in any case, McKellan was dead. He *had* to be.

"How many other units are attending?" she whimpered, following from a distance.

"None, as far as I'm aware." Pugh's features tautened as he spotted the shape lying on the tarmac ahead. "No-one even knows where you are. It's pure good fortune I swung by North Shore and spotted your vehicle." He hurried forward, speaking urgently into his radio. Though Sharon fancied she heard a fizzing of static, she didn't hear anyone at Comms respond. He tried again as he knelt beside the casualty.

She halted a few yards away and held her breath.

Wasn't there a lack of blood? She'd stabbed McKellan deeply, and yet there was no blood spattered across the footway. How much of what she'd penetrated was McKellan, and how much was monster suit?

And where was the shard she'd used?

That last question struck her like a mallet.

She'd left it jutting from beneath the killer's collar-bone. Yet it wasn't there now – because it was in his left hand.

Sharon watched as, in seeming slow-motion, that long bayonet of glass plunged up and around, striking Sergeant Pugh in the left eye. By the time the steel blade appeared and sheared into the side of Pugh's neck, she was already running again. She only looked back once – but this was sufficient to show her supervisor's limp corpse being whirled around like a rag doll and launched into the *Mirror Maze* through its demolished window. It was also sufficient to distract her so that she blundered headlong into a low barrier, fell over it and landed upside down in a litter-filled concrete channel.

The blow to her already-wounded cranium was dizzying, but her adrenalin kept flowing, pumping her full of energy. As awareness seeped quickly back into her head, she sighted the costumed horror approaching the other side of the barrier. She lurched to her feet and staggered along the channel, following it through an arched entrance into another indistinguishable building. She ran blindly again, hands out in front. A single backward glance showed an ungainly silhouette coming relentlessly in pursuit.

From the next corner, she spied a downward shaft of moonlight. She tottered towards it – only to be stopped short by a fearsome face apparently suspended about twelve feet in the air. Heart-pounding moments followed before she recognised it as the face of an Aztec god, and realised that she was in the *River Caves*. What was more, now that her eyes were attuning, she saw a framework of scaffolding standing alongside the statue. At the top of this, some kind of trapdoor hung open. Without thinking, she climbed. He would know where she'd gone – the hollow bars rang and echoed – but would he be able to follow her in his monster get-up?

At the top, Sharon hauled herself through the aperture, which in fact was an old skylight, and found herself on a sloped roof greasy with moss. She slipped as she tried to turn around, landing heavily on her bruised side. As she lay winded, she peered down into the darkened interior. His twisted form was already ascending the scaffolding with no discernible difficulty. Just like he'd ridden the *Crazy Train*. Just like he'd survived a deep stab-wound in the chest. It was impossible, it made no sense – but it was happening.

Weeping at the unfairness of it, Sharon tried to scrabble down the roof on her buttocks and ankles, but gravity took over and she began to slide, rocketing over the edge and dropping a considerable distance before hitting another, lower roof. This one, apparently consisting of plywood and tar-paper, simply collapsed underneath her, jarring her left ankle and turning her upright again as she fell through it. Some seven feet below, her injured ankle blazed with even more pain as she hit a solid, cage-like frame, which possibly had once contained a motor or generator.

The collision flung her sideways onto an old mattress made sodden with decay – at least, she thought it was due to decay.

She sat bolt-upright as she realised that she wasn't in this dingy place alone. The moonlight shining through the shattered roof revealed a figure seated on the floor against the wall opposite – though the destruction wrought on this poor soul made even the combined agonies of her lacerated scalp and sprained ankle dwindle. Whoever he had been, someone had hacked and slashed his face and throat to a ghastly ruin. Sharon scampered away crablike, hands sliding in pools of clotted gore, clattering through empty bottles and cans, only to slam into a second figure slumped against the other wall. This one had been propped up in a musty, sleeping-bag; as it now fell over her, its head detached and bounced into the shadows.

Whining and weeping, scrabbling through newspapers and rags all slimy and foul, she wriggled free and had to use a wall of rubble-cluttered shelves to drag herself to her feet. Dust and cobwebs plumed into her face, clogging her nose and mouth. There was a thunderous impact on the roof, and splinters erupted downward. A black shadow blotted out the moonlight.

Gasping, she flung herself around the walls, trying to find the door, hammering into more obstructions, jolting her injured ankle, barking her shins. She twisted as she tripped, grabbing at another shelf. It tore away from the wall, showering her with bric-a-brac, which she wildly rummaged through, seeking any kind of weapon she could find. But all that came to hand was something like a stiff tube of plastic with a grip on one end. The idea struck her that, if all else failed, she could jab this at her tormentor, maybe take out his eyes the way he had taken out Slater's.

Dear God, Dear Christ ... Geoff!

There was another heavy impact, this time on the floor behind her. She spun, hefting the ridiculous tube as though it were a knife – and only then, in the better light, realising what it actually was. Even as she did this, the interloper rose to his feet and turned his crazy, crumpled face towards her – and lunged.

More by luck than design, Sharon fell to one side, the blade bypassing her and striking a large plastic object in the recess behind. Whatever this was, it burst apart, gouts of fluid exploding over Sharon, but also drenching McKellan, sloshing not just down his costume but around his feet. The chemical stench of it brought immediate tears to her eyes – *diesel*. The maniac had ripped into some kind of fuel container.

She scrambled back across the room on all fours, now through a slurry of mingled blood and oil. The blade slashed over her head as McKellan twirled, gashing a huge chunk from the wall.

The door, where was the fucking door?

Clambering over a corpse, she saw it: an upright crack of light. She jumped up and threw her shoulder against it. It shuddered in its frame, but resisted. With hoarse screams, she scrabbled for a lock, sensing the presence turning behind her. She found the latch, lifted it and yanked the door open. As she did, she spun back, pumping her thumb on the plunger built into the handgrip of the butane candle-lighter.

It had to work, it had to work ...

But it wasn't doing.

Until a tiny flame suddenly spurted to life at the end of the tube.

Sharon flung it at the monstrous vision – which in less than one second was engulfed in a curtain of roaring flames.

She tottered outside, still whimpering, still weeping, beating down on herself, imagining that she too had caught alight. Only by a miracle, it seemed, had she avoided this, but still she wasn't safe – she expected a fiery figure to come surging out. But if McKellan tried to do that, he failed, perhaps stumbling against the inside of the door, which now banged closed, entrapping what looked like a raging inferno inside the small outbuilding. Its grimy windows quickly blackened and shattered. Its wood and tarpaper exterior was already smouldering, flames licking out through every crevice.

Sharon continued to back away, not quite believing that her ordeal was over. As the fire spread over the hut's exterior, it burned so fiercely that the heat of it dried her tears, seared her sweat-sodden cheeks. And then a hand landed on her shoulder.

She squealed as she spun around – only to see the brutish, baffled features of Mike Lewton, with Rob Ellis standing a few feet to one side. Their patrol vehicle was parked behind them. Lewton still held the bolt-croppers with which he'd managed to secure access through the front gates, but he almost dropped them with shock when he saw the state she was in: her hair a tangled mop of gluey blood, her face equally stained but also dirty, wild-eyed.

"He's ... he's in there," she stammered shrilly, gesturing at the hut.

"*What?* Who ... Shaz?"

She shook her head dumbly, unable to say more.

The men pushed past her towards the blazing structure. Much of the hut's combustible material had been consumed, and the small building was now in the process of collapsing on itself. Flames still blazed at ground-level, but otherwise only a bare, blistered framework remained. Sharon stood numbed while her two colleagues tried to get closer, wafting at the pungent smoke. Ellis gave a sharp cry. "Christ! There *is* someone here!"

"I ... I lit him up," Sharon said, suddenly giggling.

Lewton stole an astounded glance at her.

"There's two of them!" Ellis blurted. "Bloody hell!"

The fumes had turned foul with the stench of charred meat, but the flames continued to recede and Sharon could distinguish two blackened shapes lying in the glowing wreckage. Lewton swung back to her, face pale. "Shaz ... what have you done?"

She shook her head, still giggling. "Not the winos ... *they* were already dead."

"You say *you* lit this fire? Why?"

"*He* was in there. *He* murdered them."

"Who?"

"He killed Sergeant Pugh as well."

"Who killed Sergeant Pugh?"

Lewton's expression was so earnest, so honestly mortified by what he was seeing here, that Sharon now thought it better to stop sounding so amused and actually try to assist. "Blair McKellan, obviously."

"Shaz ..." Lewton shook his head. "Blair McKellan was arrested forty minutes ago. His boat ran aground near the pier."

"Mike!" Ellis shouted.

Lewton darted back to his side. Sharon ventured over there as well, vaguely amazed by that last piece of news, though not necessarily mystified. The object of their interest seemed to be a square aperture in the middle of the hut's scorched floor. A steel grille lay to one side of it. That made sense too, now that she thought about it.

"If there *was* someone else in here, that's how he got out," Ellis said.

Lewton kicked a heap of embers aside and crouched to get a better look. "Shit," he breathed. "There're hundreds of channels and culverts down here."

"And they all lead to the sea," Sharon said. "But that's just about right." The two men gazed at her blankly, at which point she began giggling again, her giggles soon transmuting to full-blown laughter. "He's so, so angry."

"Who's angry?" Lewton asked. "Who the hell are you talking about?"

She made a big effort to control herself. "Who do you think? Bubbles."

THE WALKING DEAD

Berwick-upon-Tweed, on the Northumbrian coast, is the northernmost town in England. It is a scenic place, overlooking the estuary of the River Tweed and located close to the Anglo-Scottish border. However, it has an ultra-violent history, having witnessed bloodshed since its earliest days.

Founded in the immediate post-Roman period by the Britons of Brytech, it was eventually captured and fortified by Anglo-Saxon raiders, in later centuries to become the focus of immense power struggles between the Saxons and Vikings. But these affrays pale to insignificance compared to those in the Middle Ages, when Berwick was fought over by the English and Scots, changing hands repeatedly. In 1307, one limb and part of the quartered torso of the Scottish hero William Wallace was displayed over the main gate after his execution by Edward I, while in 1333 the town overlooked an even more gruesome event when the battle of Halidon Hill, fought just beyond the walls, saw the slaughter of 10,000 Scots at the hands of Edward III.

But the most grisly tale by far concerning Berwick-upon-Tweed is a supernatural chiller, which comes to us courtesy of William of Newburgh, a medieval chronicler well-known for the factual nature of his historical accounts, and famous for once berating his fellow clerics for 'encouraging' beliefs in ghosts and goblins – which makes it even stranger that he should be the first one to put in writing so eerie a story as this.

According to William's 'History of English Affairs', compiled between 1136 and 1198, and regarded by modern scholars as an invaluable early medieval source, the peace of Berwick was grotesquely disturbed in the year 1196 by the wandering revenant of a local merchant, who after leading a life of avarice and cruelty, had become convinced that his wife was committing adultery, and whilst spying on her as she lay with her lover, had fallen from the roof of his house and been killed. Within days of his death, the merchant, in an increasingly decayed state, was seen roaming the streets at night, banging on doors and window-shutters, and viciously attacking anyone he encountered. His breath was said to be so foul that those he exhaled upon would shortly succumb to a dreadful disease. He was also accompanied by a mysterious pack of snapping, snarling hounds, which were never seen during the day-time but at night would savage any folk they chanced upon – in due course, those bitten would also die from unknown but horrible illnesses.

Clearly some kind of epidemic was at large in the town, but William of Newburgh is quite clear that this was caused by the walking corpse, and that the good people of Berwick soon realised this and concluded that the monster must be dispensed with. Volunteers approached the merchant's grave during daylight, at which time – William tells us in a tone reminiscent of later vampire stories – the undead being "was asleep". The tomb had clearly been disturbed since the merchant's burial and the volunteers, who were armed to the teeth, were able to enter it easily. When they opened the casket, the merchant showed all the usual signs of vampirism: glaring eyes, extended teeth and claws, blood glutting his mouth, a ruddy hue to his flesh. Convinced they were in the presence of evil, prayers were said, and the volunteers went to work with their swords and axes, chopping the corpse into numerous pieces, which were later cremated.

This seems to have done the job, for, according to William, there were no further such incidents in Berwick-upon-Tweed.

Vampiric horrors of this sort rarely figure in English folklore, but this is not the only such instance the Newburgh chronicler records. He mentions a similar tale from Alnwick, just south of Berwick, and another from Melrose, not too far to the north in the Scottish border country, and all at around the same time-period – the end of the 12th century. For a reliable and rather dry historical commentator like William, this is an unusual little cluster of fables, especially as he attempts to pass them off as the complete truth and yet offers no explanation other than to say they were "the contrivance of Satan".

There is no obvious explanation. One might argue that a combination of contagious disease and superstitious fear led the villagers to open a recent grave and uncover a corpse rendered bloated and fiendish by the effects of putrefaction, but that does not account for the sightings of the undead merchant around the town – there were allegedly many witnesses – nor does it explain why several such incidents all supposedly happened in close proximity to each other at around the same time.

Scary stories spread of course, and panic breeds panic. But William of Newburgh was a shrewd judge when it came to matters of this sort, and rarely penned his records without investigating them further. In addition, if one looks back far enough, there is a vague precedent for this kind of myth on England's northeast coast. As already stated, Berwick-upon-Tweed – like most other towns on that rugged, windswept shore – was settled during the Dark Ages by pagan Vikings, who told *tales of the 'draugar', the zombified remains of drowned sailors who, if not laid to rest properly, would come ashore by night to terrorise the living.*

SHELLS
Paul Kane

"If you put it to your ear, you can hear the sea."

Aaron Marshall didn't really know why he'd want to do that; he could hear the sea already. They were on a beach, after all. Him, and another boy called Dean he'd made friends with the day after they'd arrived.

Dean was a local, Aaron could tell straight away by his accent. The way his voice rose and fell when he spoke, like the rest of the people in the little village not far away – the place they'd stopped off at for essential supplies (bread, milk, tea – the usual) before moving on to the camp site.

Aaron, his mum and his dad.

It had been his father's idea, this trip. They hadn't been to the coast in a long time, not in this country anyway. There had been trips abroad, but that was never the same. Of course, they hadn't been anywhere for a couple of years – not since his dad was made redundant and things got tight money-wise. But Aaron didn't mind the fact that they'd had to have a 'staycation' as it was now known, that this was the only holiday they could afford: borrowing a small caravan from one of Dad's old workmates. It reminded him of when he was very little, back before his parents had begun arguing over every little thing.

His dad probably hoped it would remind Aaron's mum of those days, too. Of happier times. But, so far, his parents had had three blazing rows – one even before they'd set off from home – and were now not speaking to each other at all. It was how Aaron had come to be at the site's tiny park on his own, sitting on the swings and pushing himself half-heartedly back and forth. It was how he'd come to meet Dean, who'd rolled up on his skateboard, simultaneously shielding his eyes from the sun's glare and pushing back that curly mop of his with one hand.

"All right?" he'd asked Aaron.

And that had been that.

It really didn't take much more at their age, barely into their adolescence and in no rush to become grown-ups. They'd both seen far too much of that world, as it turned out. And with very few other kids around because the season was only just beginning, Aaron had leapt at the chance to hang out with Dean, to be shown around the place. Dean, for his part, had grown bored with the company of his friends from the village. He wanted to hear tales of the big city – not that Aaron came from one, it was just that any place larger than a couple of streets seemed exotic to Dean.

"We're always the last to get anything around here," he told Aaron as they'd headed off walking together, swapping likes and dislikes – football teams, films, computer games. "It's like living in the Dark Ages," moaned Dean. "Half the time you can't even get a signal on your cockin' mobile phone."

Aaron had laughed at that. "Probably better off," he'd said. Personally, he hated the way his mates back home constantly texted each other, usually talking complete and utter crap. "I like it here."

And the more Dean had showed him around, taking him to places like the haunted cavern, the cornfields that seemed to stretch out for miles, and the lifeboat station – seeing it all through this newcomer's eyes – the prouder he'd become. In return, Aaron had promised to show Dean around if he ever found himself in his neck of the woods. "Except there aren't any actual woods, not like there are here."

No beach or ocean, either. Which is really what made this place so special, so magical for Aaron. The smell of it had come wafting through the car's open window even before they were anywhere near. His father, steering their battered old yellow estate – with the peeling paintwork – up one country lane and down another, had sucked in a lungful with a satisfied sigh; head back and eyes closed, if only for a couple of seconds. "Ahhh, sea air. You can't beat it, can you?" His wife had said nothing, just clicked her tongue and looked sideways.

He'd cast a glance back at Aaron and smiled weakly. Aaron had smiled back, saying nothing either. He didn't want to take sides. He loved his mum and dad equally, and it broke his heart to see them like this.

Another reason to stay out of their way, to spend more time with Dean. His father's face fell a little, though, when Aaron had told him he was going off with his new friend again today: the third morning on the trot. "I thought ... Well, I hoped we'd be doing more together. You know, as a family." As a family? That was a joke. Though this father got up early every day, before Araon, it was obvious he was sleeping on the small sofa in the living room of the caravan (just like he slept on the couch back home). There was no closeness anymore, everything was ... sour.

"Oh, for goodness sake! Let him have some fun with someone his own age, Michael," Aaron's mother had grumbled. Not Mike, as she used to call him. Michael, now. Always Michael – and even that was said with a bitterness she couldn't seem to mask. "Somebody should be having some fun on this holiday."

"I could always tell Dean we'll catch up another time," Aaron had said, unable to muster much enthusiasm for this plan. Seems she'd passed that trait on to her son, not being able to hide how you feel. You can hide things from people, but never feelings, as far as Aaron was concerned. He just didn't know how.

His father had stared at him for a moment, then mustered that weak smile again. Not even he could do it. None of them were very good actors. "No, no. You go and have a good time, like your mother says. We can all do something tomorrow, right?"

"Right," Aaron had agreed, regardless of the fact he knew Dean probably had something else in mind for the day after.

For today, though, they'd wandered up the beach, tracing the coastline itself, scouring it. Dean said he knew a place where there were loads of crabs. That they could maybe even catch a couple, take them back into the village and get Mr Ross at the butchers to boil and de-shell them.

"Ever eaten fresh crab?" Dean had asked. Aaron shook his head, and the other boy smirked. "You're in for a treat, then. Better than fish and chips, that is!"

It was as they were looking for this mythical place where all the crabs congregated – Aaron lagging behind and complaining that there was too much sand in his trainers, in his socks – that Dean paused. Then he broke into a wide grin. "Look at that!" Dean suddenly rushed forward, running towards whatever he'd spotted.

Must have been something unusual, Aaron figured, for Dean to take notice. He came here all the time. As Aaron joined him, he saw what had caught Dean's attention. To begin with, he thought it was the stash of crabs they'd been searching for, littered all over the beach. Because covering the sand were shells, loads of them, all washed up by the sea. Aaron had seen shells on the beach before, naturally – they'd walked past a few clumps earlier on. But not like this, not quite so many, and not spaced out like that, dotted about amongst the rocks.

It wasn't that there was anything particularly wrong with how they were arranged, it was just that they looked exactly that: arranged. Aaron couldn't quite put his finger on it. Maybe someone had already been here, tinkering with them, making vague patterns? A lot of folk collected shells, didn't they? Even made things out of them to sell …

These would have been good ones for that, very shiny, unusually patterned. They were all roughly the same size and shape, which also struck Aaron as odd; quite big and curved instead of the flat variety.

He didn't have any more time to ponder, however, because Dean was bending and picking one up. He turned it over in his hands, examining it – letting the light bounce off the ridges. That's when he'd said the thing about holding it up to your ear, about hearing the sea. Again, it was one of those pride things, passing on local knowledge.

But Aaron still didn't see the point when they were right next to the water, the waves lapping gently against the sand, foaming as they were dragged back out again on the tide. It would only be the blood pumping in your ear anyway, echoing. He wasn't that gullible.

"Go on," said Dean, proffering the shell to him. "Try it."

Aaron shook his head.

"What's the matter?" Dean asked, then laughed. "It won't bite, you know."

"I know, just don't see the point."

"You'll be able to hear the sea," Dean repeated. "It's just a bit of fun. Look ..." He moved his curly hair aside and placed the shell against his ear. Aaron could imagine the *whooshing* sound Dean would be hearing. His friend chuckled again. "Yeah. Really good, this one is. The best I've ever heard. I can –"

Dean stopped; his grin turning into a grimace, lips pulling back over teeth and gums, just like the waves were doing on the shore. His eyes went wide, the hand holding the shell was shaking.

"Dean ...?" Aaron moved forward. But before he could get any closer, Dean let out the loudest howl Aaron had ever heard. It grew more high-pitched with every moment it went on. Then Dean clamped his mouth shut again, growling and hissing through the gaps in his teeth; seething in pain.

It won't bite, you know.

Aaron hadn't known his friend for that long, didn't really know his sense of humour. Was he the kind of person who played tricks on people? Left buckets of water above doors or shook hands while he was holding an electric buzzer? "Dean, come on. Stop messing about ..." Dean just looked at him, pure terror in his eyes. "Please ..." Aaron begged him.

The hand holding the shell fell away – the casing itself tumbling from Dean's grasp to land back on the beach again. Dean dropped to the floor, convulsing. Shit! thought Aaron. Had he got some kind of medical condition Aaron didn't know about, epilepsy or whatever? Surely he'd have told Aaron something as important as that if it might happen at any time? Maybe it just hadn't cropped up, maybe Dean was embarrassed to talk about it with people he didn't know that well? Was even ashamed of it, though why he should be was –

The spasms were growing more violent. Aaron bent, not sure what he should be doing. Were you supposed to even touch someone while they were having a fit? He didn't have a clue. Dean was throwing his head back, the cords in his neck standing proud. He'd stopped screaming completely now, the only noises he was making through his closed mouth were muffled grunts. And there was blood, redness on the beach near Dean's head. Maybe from the fall? There were rocks nearby ...

Aaron needed to call for help; this was beyond him. Beyond most adult's ability to cope with, let alone ... Aaron reached into his jeans pocket for his phone, dialling up the emergency services without even looking at the screen. When it beeped angrily at him, he saw there were no signal bars at the top. Looked like Dean had been right about the reception around here. "Oh come on!" Araon snapped, looking left and right, then down again at the twitching Dean.

His friend's eyes had gone back up into his head now, the convulsions dying off a little. Perhaps it was ending, whatever this was. Any moment now, Dean would snap awake, start laughing and say: "Sorry about that, happens all the time ... Should really see someone about it." But then he started jerking again, even more violently than last time.

Aaron got up and backed off. Before he even realised what he was doing, he was running, back along the beach in the direction they'd just come from. Part of him was desperate to find help, recognised he was in over his head. He needed to share what was happening with someone – anyone. Get Dean some help, and quickly before –

But a much larger part was just running away from the scene, didn't want to witness Dean going through that anymore. As much as the stuff with his parents hurt, it wasn't as bad as this; wasn't as immediate. Aaron closed his eyes, which were tearing up, but he could still see Dean on the beach, his body jumping like there was an electric current being passed through it.

Then there, down along the beach – a couple by the edge of the water, holding hands and skimming stones into the sea. Thank God! thought Aaron. He wasn't alone anymore. They could help him. "Hey! Hey, help!" He'd stopped now and was waving his arms, trying to attract their attention.

The woman, blonde hair whipping about in the light breeze, turned first. Then the man. They looked at each other, saying something.

"Please ... My friend's hurt!" Aaron cried.

They started towards him, both breaking into a run. Aaron said nothing to them as they caught up, just pointed. His face, the tears, were enough to convince them this was urgent. For the woman to blurt out that her partner was a nurse.

But Aaron had already set off back to Dean again – now that he wasn't dealing with this on his own – and they followed quickly behind him.

*

Even before they got there, Aaron could see something was different.

For one thing, Dean wasn't sprawled on the beach anymore. He was standing, staring. Not at the approaching trio, but out over the horizon.

"Dean!" Aaron called to him, but the boy never even flinched. Just because he was standing, that didn't mean anything. He could be in shock, disorientated. "Dean!" More urgent, and this time the boy did gaze over in their direction.

Aaron looked at the couple he'd brought with him, the man – the nurse – frowning, the woman just looking puzzled. "He ... he collapsed," said Aaron by way of an explanation. "He was having some kind of seizure when I left him."

The man nodded, and they trailed Aaron again as he drew closer to Dean. That's when Aaron saw it wasn't just Dean standing upright that had changed. He was looking at them, but didn't really appear to be seeing them.

"Dean," Aaron said, more quietly this time. "Are ... are you okay?"

He opened his mouth to say something. Closed it again. Then he said, simply and clearly: "I'm fine."

It was Aaron's turn to frown. Fine? How could he be fine? "You ... Don't you remember what happened?"

Dean shook his head. "No ... Who are these people?" His tone was even, monotonous. No rise and fall that marked him out as local. No accent at all. Just words.

Aaron realised he didn't actually know who they were. "I – I brought them to help. You were – "

"I'm fine," Dean told him again.

"You're quite clearly not," Aaron argued.

"Look," said the nurse, "I'm not sure what's going on here but – "

"He was fitting," said Aaron, turning to him again. "He fell, hit his head. There was blood ..." He looked around him for the spot where the red had stained the sand, but saw nothing.

"I'm fine," said Dean once more.

"This really isn't very funny." The woman now, annoyed.

"It's not a joke," snapped Aaron. "He was ... Dean, tell them! What's the last thing you remember?"

Dean closed his eyes and opened them again slowly. "I could hear the sea," he said in that same flat way. "I can still hear it."

The nurse went over to Dean. "Let me take a look, if what he says is right you might be concussed." He reached out a hand, and Dean grabbed it by the wrist.

"I'm fine," the boy stated. There still wasn't any emotion there, not even anger. He let the nurse go and the man drew back, rejoining his blonde partner.

"Are you guys on drugs or something?" asked the woman.

"No," said Aaron. "'Course not. Dean, tell them. Tell them what happened. I'm not making this up."

Dean said nothing.

"Oh, come on!" Maybe he was playing a trick after all, but this was taking things way too far.

"I can hear the sea." Dean stared at them each in turn, and it made the woman visibly shiver. "Would you like to hear, too?"

"I've had enough of this," Aaron said with a grunt. "You're fucking mental." He turned and began striding off. Screw Dean; it was just as easy to break friendships as it was to make them. Aaron looked back only once, saw that Dean hadn't really moved. But then neither had the couple. Perhaps the nurse wanted to make sure ... Or they wanted to give him a talking to. Aaron was glad to be out of it.

Just before he faced front again, Dean caught his eye and it was a look that made Aaron shiver as well.

I can hear the sea. Would you like to hear, too?

*

"You're back early," his dad said to him when Aaron stepped into the 'van. "What's happened?"

His mum, who was sitting reading a trashy paperback novel on the couch, glanced up as Aaron closed the door behind him. "You've had a falling out with your friend, haven't you, hon?" His expression was giving him away again.

"Something like that," Aaron admitted. "I don't really want to talk about it."

He wouldn't know where to start. "If ... If you still want to do something, Dad, you know, go somewhere ...?" It was still morning, they had most of the day ahead of them.

"Great!" said his father, beaming. A genuine smile, not put on. "Maybe a walk on the beach or something?"

"No!" said Aaron a little too quickly. "I mean, maybe we could go somewhere in the car?" Anything to get away from here for a little while.

"Okay... We could go check out the pier?" That was at the town down the road; far enough. "Love...?" asked Aaron's father, looking over at his wife hopefully.

She waved a hand. "You two go, have a good time. I'm going to try and finish this."

Aaron's dad looked like he was going to try and persuade her, but then thought twice about it. He had his son, it was a start. One out of two wasn't bad. "Maybe tomorrow then, we'll all go for a picnic or something. Have an early start."

By now his wife was stuck into her book again, flipping a page and studying it intently. Not really reading at all, as far as Aaron could tell. "Dad, can we go?" he asked, tugging on his father's sleeve.

They said their goodbyes and left, getting in the car. "All right, Pilgrim." It was what he always called Aaron because of their shared love of old westerns. "Just you and me. Let's hit the trail."

He gunned the engine, guiding the estate off the grass area and onto the little road that would take them away from the caravan site. As they passed the small slope, the path that led down to the beach, Dean was walking up it.

At first Aaron thought he was alone, but the boy was soon joined by the nurse and his blonde partner, flanking Dean. Aaron pushed himself up in his seat, staring out through the car window.

The three of them dawdled at the mouth of the slope. Were those two taking Dean to see his parents – his parent, Dean was being brought up by his mother he'd told Aaron – so he could get the bollocking he deserved? Or maybe to the doctors, to get him checked out after all.

But something was ... off. Was it Aaron's imagination or did those two people now have that selfsame vacant expression on their faces; the one Dean had when they returned to him. And why were they all just waiting there? Not talking to each other, nothing. Like someone had frozen them in time.

Then they all looked over at the car, watching it almost as one. Aaron held their gaze for a moment or two, but couldn't for any longer. His eyes dropped instead to what they had in their hands.

All three of them – Dean, the nurse and his partner – were carrying something. Aaron's eyes narrowed, focussing. Yes, he could see now.

All of them were carrying shells.

*

They had a nice enough time at the pier. They went on a few rides, ate fish and chips – Aaron said no to the suggestion of crabs ... or cockles, mussels and whelks for that matter; they looked disgusting – and ended up in the amusements, though they couldn't spend too much money, Aaron was warned.

They also spent a little while eating ice creams and watching the fishermen on the end of that pier, dangling their lines into the water. Aaron thought about telling his dad about Dean, about the couple who he'd dragged into the situation, but realised how it would all sound. There was something different now about those people – but then he didn't really know them in the first place. How could he say what was different about them at all?

Only ... why did they have those shells with them when they came back from the beach?

It won't bite, you know.

Aaron stared at the ocean, at the rolling waves again. Thought about the creatures those fishermen were trying to catch, about the crabs he and Dean had been after. About the shells that had been washed in, that Dean hadn't seen before.

Would you like to hear, too?

"Something wrong?" asked his dad suddenly, licking the side of his cone. "I mean, apart from the falling out."

Aaron shook his head.

"Is it ... is it me and your mum?"

Another shake of the head.

"Because it won't always be like this, you know. Me and ... well, we're just going through a bad patch, that's all. We will be a family again, I promise."

Aaron nodded, licked his own ice-cream, and returned to his thoughts.

On the drive back, they called at the village again to get more supplies. They were almost out of tea and if there was one thing Aaron's mum could not do without, it was her tea. Aaron stayed in the car while his dad popped into the shop, and as he gazed out of the window again, he noticed more clumps of people just standing and staring out into space. They were on street corners, huddled together in twos and threes; not really joining in the bustle of village life. Set apart, waiting. All with that expression he'd seen on Dean's face. On the couple's faces. If Aaron and his family were useless at hiding their feelings, then this lot were the masters. Betraying nothing, not talking, not even smiling.

Aaron was so wrapped up in what he was seeing – apparently the only one to have noticed – that he didn't hear his dad return, and started when the car door was yanked open. "Hey, easy Pilgrim. I come in peace," joked his father, dumping a carrier bag in the back. Then: "What?" when he saw Aaron wasn't laughing.

"Nothing, let's just get out of here," he said.

When they got back inside the caravan, they found that Aaron's mum hadn't really moved. She was still reading the same book, didn't look up when his dad told her he'd stocked up on tea, and had even bought her some of those iced buns she liked. Didn't say a word when his dad suggested a game of knockout whist to pass the evening; she just gazed at her book, lost in a world of romantic encounters. Aaron's dad left her be.

Later, she got up and went to bed quite early, leaving Aaron and his dad to play ... and to talk. It was only now, biting his lip, that Aaron ventured, "Dad ... I'm not sure we should stay here any longer."

His father looked up from the hand he was holding. "What do you mean? Why?"

"There's ... I think something weird is happening here." His dad cocked his head, gestured for Aaron to go on. "I can't really explain it. You just have to trust me on it. Dean, the boy I was hanging around with. Something happened to him ... And now I think something's happening to the other people here."

"Something happened? You're going to have to be more specific, son."

"You'll ... you'll think I'm being stupid."

"Try me."

Aaron thought about it for a moment, then shook his head. "Please, can we just go home."

His dad looked at him, and could tell he was serious about this. Was frightened if anything. "We'll see what your mother says in the morning. Fair enough?"

It would have to do, Aaron supposed. Unless he was going to get into the whole thing with the seizure, the couple, and the groups of people back in the village – who weren't really doing anything wrong, were they? Standing about and staring? No law against that ... It was just the way they were doing it, like they were spaced out.

Are you guys on drugs or something?

It wasn't long before Aaron turned in as well, attempting to read a comic on his bunk and still wide awake at gone midnight in spite of the fact he'd turned off the light; his parents had always drummed that into him, let your body adjust, tell it you were ready for sleep. There was fat chance tonight, fat chance till they were well away from this creepy place.

Every now and again, Aaron would pull the curtain aside and peer out, the silvery half moon picking out the shapes of the other caravans on the site, not that many of which were inhabited.

It was about the third or fourth time he looked out when he saw them.

Shadows moving through the camp, from caravan to caravan, targeting ones that showed even a hint of light, or had vehicles parked next to them. The figures moved slowly, and in packs, in no particular rush. Aaron watched as someone – he couldn't really tell if it was a man or woman – knocked on a caravan door and waited. When it was opened, this person moved in, along with a few others, crowding the owner.

Aaron sucked in a breath. Not the kind his dad had when he smelled the sea air ...(*I can hear the sea. Would you like to hear, too?*) ...but rather the shocked and terrified gasping for air of someone who again knew he was in over his head.

For a little while he waited for the knock on their door. For the people to push their way into their caravan. Should he warn his father? Aaron didn't know what to do. His dad would be out there; would be sleeping out in the living room, like every other night since they'd arrived. Except by the time he'd plucked up enough courage to open his door and let his dad in on what was happening, he found the room empty. A light shone from underneath the door to the main bedroom.

As scared as he was, Aaron couldn't help feeling a little flutter of happiness at this: his parents together for the first time in a long while. Nothing was going to spoil that – nothing could. And as long as the door to their temporary home was locked ...

He crept back into his room and quietly closed the door. Aaron looked out again, but saw nothing else. And nobody knocked, even though he was still waiting for it; aware that he was just sitting there and staring out, that he looked just like them.

At some point he must have fallen asleep, though – couldn't keep his eyes open – and he dreamed of Dean, of the fitting. Of the shell he'd placed against his ear. Dean approached Aaron with one of them, raising it.

"It won't bite!" he said in a watery voice, gargling each word. Then he laughed, something he definitely hadn't done back on the beach. "If you put it to your ear, you can hear the sea. Go on ... Do it!"

There were people behind Aaron now, hands on him, holding him. The shell was being brought closer and closer. "No! Stay away, stay back!" He lashed out with his legs, because his arms were pinned.

"Don't struggle. It'll only take a moment. Then you'll see ... Then you'll be able to hear it."

"I don't... I don't want to hear it!" screamed Aaron.

In the distance, behind Dean, were those fishermen from the pier. They were casting their lines into the sea, but lines were also being cast out of it: slimy tentacles lassoing them like cattle in one of the Westerns Aaron and his dad loved so much.

Nearer and nearer, Dean's shell was looming larger in front of him. "It won't bite," the boy repeated. It was a lie, that thing *did* bite. There was blood pouring from Dean's ear now, down his neck and onto his t-Shirt – staining it, covering it. Coming from his mouth as well, cascading down his chin. "I don't bite," he was burbling. "We don't bite."

"Liar!" Aaron roared back, struggling to break free. Before they could turn him, before they could put that shell up to his ear and –

There was a glimpse, just a glimpse of something inside its dark recesses. Something squirming, something that looked very much like those disgusting cockles and mussels and whelks from the pier ...

It's just a dream, Aaron told himself regardless of how real it all seemed. Can't you see that? Your brain is dredging all the stuff from today up and rolling it into one big ball of a nightmare.

The shell grew legs then, suddenly had pincers. More crab than anything. Revenge for hunting them, for wanting to boil and eat its flesh. It snapped those pincers together. Dean held it closer. "Do you want to hear the sea, too?"

Aaron jerked awake, almost jerked off the bunk. Dull light was streaming in through the gap in the curtains. He was alone, nobody here threatening him, trying to 'turn' him – whatever that meant. And in those few moments, as he calmed down, he could actually convince himself that all this had been just a dream. There had been no shells, no fitting. No groups of people standing and staring.

He wiped the sweat from his brow, got dressed, and stepped out of his room – an urgent need to pee gripping him.

Aaron stopped dead in his tracks when he saw them.

His parents, sitting on the small sofa his father had slept on until last night. Before his wife had let him in, encouraged him to join her in the bedroom. Now Aaron saw why.

They were both gazing over at him blankly. He forgot about needing to pee, pinched himself instead to make sure he was really awake. He was.

"Mum …?" he said softly. "Dad …?"

No answer. Aaron stared back, trying to read them. But that was just it, there was no expression. No way to tell what they were thinking, were feeling, for the first time in his life. They weren't this good at acting … what, detached?

Ironically, they were sitting closer than he'd seen them do in a long, long time, side-by-side. No sourness now.

"Are … are you okay?"

Again, nothing.

Aaron's brow knitted. "Please, you're scaring me."

His father turned slightly, just a small movement to look at his wife. "I can hear the sea now," he said in a hollow voice. Hollow, just like he was.

"What … no …"

"Your friend called for you yesterday, while you were out." This was his mother; she'd never taken her eyes off Aaron. His dad faced forwards again. "He brought something for us." She raised her hand, palm open; resting on it was one of the shells. "This one is for you."

"No …" Aaron's eyes were misting up, he shook his head. "Not you two."

"We are going to be a family again," his father announced in that droning voice. "It won't hurt."

It won't bite …

That broke his dream, and Aaron called his father a liar. Because he knew how much it hurt; he'd seen how this worked, hadn't he. So much pain and emotion and then –

His parents rose together, and Aaron took a step backwards. He was half expecting people to be behind him, but of course there wasn't the room. His eyes flicked left to the main door.

"You will join us, Aaron," said his mother, proffering the shell. He couldn't tell whether it was an order, question or suggestion, now that there were no nuances to the tone.

They took a step towards him, and he ducked sideways. The door was locked, he remembered at the last second, yet it still took him by surprise. His parents were walking towards him, not at speed – not in any kind of rush – and there was something in that inevitability which scared him as much as the shell itself.

As much as what would happen to him …

Aaron fumbled with the locks, sweaty hands slipping on the metal. He looked over and across. His parents had passed the small table by the window where they'd played cards last night. They weren't far away from him now.

He closed his eyes, opened them again, taking a breath at the same time.

Ahhh, sea air. You can't beat it, can you?
I can hear the sea ...

With a final click, he undid the lock. Aaron knew he shouldn't, knew he didn't have much time left, but he looked again – and his parents were only inches away. Letting out a small whimper, he shouldered the door and half fell out of it, tripping on the steps and landing part on the concrete breezeblock below and partly on the grass where the car was parked. His knee was throbbing, and when he touched it he felt a rip in his jeans, wetness that could only be blood. It reminded him of the blood running from Dean's ear, trickling down his neck.

Aaron looked up – saw dozens of the zombie people, all standing and staring at him. When they saw him, they began walking in his direction. No urgency, not like in the dream – the nightmare – because that would take emotion. That would mean they had to feel something, and the shells had taken that away. Stolen it.

He scrambled to his feet, narrowly avoiding the arms reaching out behind him – his father's – and stumbled sideways. Aaron ran, gritting his teeth from the pain in his knee, going first left then right, spotting clumps of the staring people everywhere. It was like he was in an old computer game, one of those retro ones with the mazes. He just had to make sure he didn't get captured, didn't get eaten.

It won't bite.

He pressed himself up against one of the smaller 'vans, looking round the corner to see if he was being followed. It was then that he had the idea: to get underneath the caravan and hide there. He'd never been able to hide anything emotionally, just like his mum and dad, but maybe he could tuck himself away physically. You could hide things; you could hide people. At least until it was safe, whatever that entailed. It would be just like the settlers hiding under their wagons when the Indians attacked.

Aaron wormed his way beneath, fearing he might get stuck at one point because there was little or no room, and banging his wounded knee on a strut. He cried then, more freely than he had back at the caravan. More freely than he ever had in his life before, thinking about his mum and dad; thinking that no matter how bad it had been before, that it was so much worse now. That feelings, however strong they might be and what they might cause you to do – the rowing, the sleeping apart, the sourness – were so much better than not being able to feel at all.

He also had a pretty decent view from where he was, angled slightly on a hill. Aaron was able to watch as more somnambulant figure gathered, flooding in from the village. Victims of this ... what, virus? It had spread so quickly and in such a short space of time.

There were a couple of moments when feet passed by and his heart leapt into his mouth, but he was never discovered. And the more he watched their movements, the more he realised as the day wore on, that everyone affected by this thing was following some kind of plan. A calling, drawing them to the beach down that slope.

The sun was dipping in the sky, turning it an orangey-purple colour, before he decided it might be okay to come out. He'd not seen any activity on the caravan site for a while; the crowds had thinned, all heading to the beach.

Quietly, cautiously, Aaron yanked himself free. He should run again, try and find help – but he remembered how well that had worked out the first time with Dean. Besides, there were his parents to consider; maybe he could reverse whatever had been done?

Get them to see reason?

No sooner had he thought of them than he saw the pair, standing by the mouth of the path. Standing with Dean. None of them talking, just staring at each other as if communicating silently, then looking about themselves.

They're looking for me, thought Aaron. He was a little disappointed when they started walking down the path; that they'd given up on him. Part of him wanted to call them back, to shout and wave that yes, he'd changed his mind, he wanted to be part of whatever family they were talking about. That he didn't want to be on his own ... Maybe that's why he started to follow them, at a distance, though it was more curiosity at this stage. Wanting to see how this would all play out.

He kept his distance all the way along the beach, yet he needn't have worried – they never looked back once. Didn't look back even when they reached the spot where Dean had picked up that first shell. What had made him do that? Aaron wondered. If he hadn't, then ...

Perhaps something had forced him to? Aaron shook his head, but the thought was no more ridiculous than the scene unfolding in front of him.

There were no shells left on the sand. They'd all been used, the same number of people standing in their place now – and in the same spots those damned things had been. They were all staring out at the ocean. Seeing it; hearing it. Perhaps even hearing its voice?

His parents and Dean took their positions, the boy on the original patch where he'd fallen. They waited there a few moments, Aaron watching from another hiding place behind the cliff. Then they were on the move again, lifting legs together, moving forwards in a wave. Into the waves.

Aaron cried again as he watched his parents go with them – almost called out again, but fear held him back. And he thought about those fishermen from the pier, from his dream, being reeled into the sea, and wondered if that's what was happening. If something was fishing for people, throwing those shells up onto the beach as hooks?

It didn't matter in the end, because they were now hip deep in the water. Getting deeper with each stride: chest-height, then shoulders. Was it Aaron's imagination or did he see his mum and dad's heads turn a little, just before they sank underneath the waves. Before they vanished completely.

In over their heads ...

Aaron broke cover again, only now bellowing at the top of his lungs. Sinking down onto his knees, ignoring the pain, tears dropping and mingling with the grains of sand.

*

Aaron thought about that moment often, here in the home where he now lived.

Back in the city, away from the beach, from the sea – he didn't care if he never saw those again. Not magical anymore: cursed. They'd reported it in the news, naturally. Mentioned it in magazines and on TV shows about weird phenomena. Talking about the village where everyone had suddenly just disappeared. Leaving only Aaron behind, though he'd never told them a thing. Never spoken since.

Just stared at the policemen, the doctors. Saying nothing, feeling even less. Keeping it all locked away inside, just like they'd done with him. It was for his own good, they'd said, to try and help him. To force him out of the state of shock he was so obviously in.

But he'd think about that evening all the time. Think about how quickly that village, that caravan site had been taken by the shells. Turned into shells of what they once were. Then drawn back into the sea, never to be seen again.

Aaron thought about what might happen if they ever showed up again, those shells. The objects or the people. Remembered his promise to Dean that he'd show him around if he ever found himself in this neck of the woods again.

He often looked out through his one, single (barred) window, just like he'd done back in the caravan. Thinking he might catch sight of Dean. Of his parents.

You will join us, Aaron ...

We are going to be a family again.

Maybe even hoping to see them down there, in the courtyard. Carrying their shells. Carrying that one for him. To take away his longing, his pain.

And at times like those, he'd cock an ear. Convince himself that the sound was carrying as well. That if he listened closely enough.

He might, just might, be able ...

To hear the sea.

HELLMOUTH

Brighton, more accurately known as Brighton and Hove, is one of Britain's party capitals.

Located on England's south coast, but less than an hour from London, it enjoys a balmy climate, miles of 'blue flag' beaches, and has a flourishing pub, restaurant and nightclub scene. At night, its twinkling neon glow can be seen from far out in the English Channel. It is the last place where you would expect to find a 'Hellmouth', in other words a hidden access point to a darker realm, where evil, supernatural beings await their opportunity to slip through into our world.

In actual fact, the fun-loving Brighton we know today is a relatively modern invention. Previously a medieval fishing port called Brighthelmstone, it acquired its present status in the 1780s, when the Prince Regent, shortly to become George IV, began to take holidays there and built the Royal Pavilion. But in earlier times it was a far more spiritual place. During the Anglo-Saxon incursions into Britain in the fifth and sixth centuries, the county now known as Sussex, at the heart of which Brighton lies, was one of the first areas to be taken forcibly from the Romanised Celts. The Saxons who conquered this region were pagans, but very devout in their beliefs. When they discovered a number of coastal caves and woodland grottos where the native Britons had worshipped before they were Christianised, they recognised them as holy places and set about venerating them in the names of their own gods. Later stories would tell how the first Saxon settlers found evidence in these temples of cannibal feasts, and how they cleansed them of evil with special ceremonies, though this most likely was propaganda.

Whatever is true, the coastline we recognise today as Brighton and Hove was once sacred to three different societies: the early Celts, the Romanised Celts and then the Anglo-Saxons. When the Saxons themselves converted to Christianity, they abandoned their woodland sanctuaries to build chapels and minsters, though some better known shrines were re-dedicated in the names of Christian saints. One such was Annafreid's Well, a natural spring named in memory of an early Saxon Princess famed for her holy nature. The spring still runs and is now a feature of St. Ann's Well Gardens, a public park in the west of the city.

The main reason why former pagan temples were adapted to Christianity was to ease the passing of converts from one faith to another, but it was also to pin down any evil entities that might *linger there. If that was the case at St. Ann's Well, it appears not to have worked, because throughout the history of Brighton, this open public space has been regarded as a place of mystery and menace. Both locals and visitors have reported bizarre experiences.*

Two particularly frightening ones come to mind straight away.

In 1896, a partly of Brighton shopkeepers and their guests were strolling around the park after a business supper, when just ahead they heard the sound of children playing. This was unusual given the lateness of the hour. The adults decided to investigate, but as they approached the place in question there was an abrupt silence, and when they searched they found no trace of a living soul. They became uneasy and decided to withdraw, but as they were returning across the green they glanced back and beheld a group of diminutive figures in close pursuit. If these were children – and it was not possible to see clearly in the darkness – there was a strangely aggressive air about them; even more so when they came up close and revealed that they each possessed the slitted, emerald eyes of a cat.

The merchants fled to the safety of the lamp-lit streets, and stammered out the tale to incredulous bystanders. Someone wondered if the party might actually have disturbed a group of cats at play, feral felines being known for their belligerence when threatened. But the witnesses swore that the beings who'd followed them had walked on two legs.

The second tale comes from 1993, and is even more disturbing because the person who experienced it, a Japanese tourist, had no knowledge of the area's history. She was crossing the park late at night when a voice hailed her by name. The tourist was astonished that anyone here would know her, but she was also disconcerted. The voice hailed her again, and now she saw a figure moving parallel to her, but slowly closing the gap between them. The tourist stopped and asked if she could help. The figure changed course and came straight towards her. What she then saw almost drove her mad with horror. She fled from the park in an incoherent state. When she was finally able to speak she'd been taken to hospital, and she described her would-be assailant as an archetypical western devil, complete with goat's legs and hooves, a naked hairy torso, curved horns and a terrible face.

In neither of these cases is it inconceivable that what was seen was the mischievous use of fancy dress; but it is less easy to understand how in both cases the victims – grown adults – were so alarmed that they had no qualms about telling all and sundry. None of them were apparently worried about appearing foolish, because what they believed they'd encountered was worse still.

There are no obvious explanations behind the tales concerning St. Ann's Well, other than that it is a place associated with ancient rites, and that ghost stories only ever improve with the telling – for example, rumours that the well sits at the end of a ley-line and that famous occultist Aleister Crowley once performed rituals there have never been proved, but add great paranormal kudos.

The park is a well-known place for recreation, and no-one feels menaced there during the day. But at night things are apparently different. It isn't referred to locally as 'the Hellmouth' for nothing.

THE SANDS ARE MAGIC
Kate Farrell

After over thirty years the locals are used to her, though the newcomers have questions.

"Where does she stay?"

"Isn't anyone with her?"

"She gives me the creeps. Can't they get her to move on?"

She comes for the same two weeks each year, speaks only in shops and cafes to state her needs, and returns always to the same spot on the beach where she sits and waits. And waits.

*

It was 1977, and the Queen's Silver Jubilee, a good time to be away from west London, from the flat in Golborne Road.

"Why all the fuss?" Rob had asked. "We pay her enough. All she has to do is ride round in a big car, wave a bit and shake a few hands."

Sitting in the pub on a warm summer's evening, Carl and Annie, and the strange boy with the wispy beard had all agreed with him. So had Susan. "Yes," she said, "it's a fuss."

Rob had served with her husband in Northern Ireland, and was only yards away from him when a sniper in the Falls Road took him out. A single shot to the head. He and Bri had been friends, and he took it hard. Two years later and having left the army, Rob decided to look out his old pal's wife. He'd kept in touch during that time, and so it was no great surprise to her when he turned up armed with a duffle bag, a ghetto blaster, a notebook full of unpublished poetry, and not much else. He had hitched to London from Exeter after his discharge, about which he said little, and asked if he could sleep on the floor at Flat 12A Golborne Road until he got himself sorted. He tickled Lucy, then aged six, who protested that she was too big for such nonsense but loved it really; he tossed four year old Nick into the air, and pretended he was about to drop him, then at the crucial moment nestled the boy in strong, tattooed arms. That had been six months ago, in January. He was still at Number 12A, helping out, fixing things, and just before Easter had migrated from the futon in the living room to Susan's bedroom. She liked his attention. It was the first time since Bri that she'd let a man see her naked, touch her, enjoy her, and she reminded herself that she was still a young woman with needs, and not just the mother of Corporal Brian

Maynard's fatherless children. All the same Lucy and Nicholas had kept her sane in the dark days after his death, days when she had to deal with his mother's loss besides her own.

"You don't know what I'm going through," the older woman wailed. "Nobody should have to bury their child."

After the session in the pub, Rob put his suggestion to Susan when they were in bed. It was a sticky night in London W10 with hardly a breath of air. The windows were open and also the French doors that lead out to the back. Her landlord, the local council, referred to it as a patio, though really it was only a collection of paving slabs. There was enough space to hang out the washing, and a wall against which Nick practised his football skills. She had tried to grow geraniums in a few pots, but the neighbourhood cats put paid to them. Lucy and her brother would soon be too big to share a room, and Susan had requested a move to larger premises, without revealing anything about her non-paying guest. The DHSS might want to ask questions.

Rob said, "You asleep?"

"Too hot."

"Y'know what we were saying before, all that fuss going on in London?"

"Yeah?"

"You fancy getting away, getting out of town for a bit?"

Susan shifted to look at him. "What've you got in mind?"

"Cornwall. A holiday. Us four." He moved damp hair away from her brow.

"Lovely idea. What do we use for money?"

"Leave it to your Uncle Rob. We can borrow a mate's camper van I reckon, pack it with tins of beans and bags of crisps, get some sleeping bags and head off. I know just the place. Port Trewithan, it's called. I went there when I was about Lucy's age with my mum and dad. It was brilliant and I know the kids'll love it. It's not big like Newquay, it's quiet and the beach is small. The sea is deepest blue, nearly hurts your eyes just to look at it. But it's the sands that are magic; sometimes they're the colour of bleached bone, sometimes they're golden white, and other times they're like, oh I dunno, runny toffee. There's little bays and coves, and the kids can catch stuff in rock pools, and we can eat fish and chips every day. I've been giving it some thought. What do you say, Soos? If we're canny we can even park up for nothing. It'll only cost some petrol money and a bit of food, and we'd have to buy that anyway, wouldn't we?"

Susan shut her eyes and imagined warm Cornish sunshine instead of inner city humidity; she saw her children wearing shorts and T-shirts running barefoot, herself in a bikini, Rob tanned and strong ...

"It sounds wonderful, but I'm not sure." She heard a cat outside beginning its nocturnal serenade, and thought of listening to the sea instead. If only.

"No, Rob, we can't afford it."

"Come on, Soos. I've got a few bob. We won't need to pay for a hotel. We'll be like gypsies. A couple of weeks. What do you say? Hmmm?"

His hand found her own private cove beneath the sheets; the tide was in, and he began to work his special magic.

*

Three weeks later in mid-July when Lucy's school had broken up, Susan, Rob and the children were playing happy family in an ancient camper van. It was a relic from the 1960s, still painted in psychedelic swirls, and borrowed from Rob's friend from the pub, the boy with the wispy beard.

There was no charge, Rob only had to make a delivery to some people in Launceston, and take a small package back from them at the end of the holiday. Despite Susan's reservations, which were mainly financial, the children's excitement won her over and drew her in like iron filings to a magnet. The night before they set off they could barely sleep, and Susan lay listening to them chattering away in the next bedroom. On the morning of departure Nicholas and the normally calm and mature Lucy were hopping with anticipation once all their gear was stowed.

"Are the sands really magic?" the boy asked. The questions started before they were out of London, the same questions that had been asked once the children learned of their upcoming adventure.

"You bet," Rob said.

"Are they white gold or just gold?" the girl wanted to know. She had an eye for colour, and selected her own outfits with care from her small wardrobe. This summer she favoured mint green and pale pink.

"White gold at day when the sun's overhead, then just plain gold, deep gold you might say, when the sun goes down. Yes, deep gold." He lowered his voice in the style of an American country singer. The children giggled. They liked it when he did his funny voices. Nick was sometimes 'pard'ner' and Lucy he called 'ma'am.'

"And the sea? What sort of blue?"

Rob considered the sea, the hints of azure, cobalt and turquoise that it displayed from memories of his own childhood's Cornish idyll.

"The sea," he promised, "is every shade of blue you care to imagine," and he smiled at their mother. Susan settled back into the cracked upholstery of the passenger seat and let herself be seduced by thoughts of the magic she was sure would eventually unfold.

*

Once they departed London, heading further west they not only left behind the stuffy confines of the small flat in a baking summer, but also the sunny rays that penetrated the urban grime. The nearer to Cornwall they travelled, the cooler it became; the clouds lowered, and the dreams of every shade of blue were replaced by the reality of several shades of grey, from pewter to dove, via battleship and ash. Once they crossed the River Tamar the first stripes of rain streaked the windscreen, and Rob discovered that only one of the wipers worked. By the time they stopped in Launceston for him to exchange one large brown envelope for one small mystery parcel, the watery blobs had joined up to create a genuine Cornish downpour, and in the rear of the van the children's despondency hung like damp laundry. Lucy and Nicholas looked out of the windows, searching for the shades of blue and gold of their promised land, and the nearest they managed was the sight of a lady in a navy mackintosh running for the shelter of Boots the Chemist.

"Don't you worry," Rob said, "you wait. Tomorrow it'll be fine. You'll see. It'll be magic."

He was supremely confident, for it had never rained during the holidays of his own early years. Susan remained tight-lipped and consoled her children with milk chocolate buttons. That first night they all fell asleep with raindrops the size of golf balls bouncing off the roof of the camper van, which Rob had tucked in a corner of a municipal car park. He and Susan slept either side of the van on padded benches that also served as narrow beds, and the children were shoehorned together at the rear, behind the Formica dining table. Susan had cleaned the van when Rob brought it round the day before their departure – "No kids of mine are going to sleep in THAT," – she had announced, as she set to with Vim and bleach and a can of air freshener.

He tried to hold her hand across the gap that separated their sleeping berths, and she turned her back on him and faced the van wall. It smelled of Vim.

The next morning she awoke, stiff and cramped, in the same position. She looked at her watch: 7:15. The van was silent, its thin curtains drawn across the windows. The children were still asleep, no doubt worn out after the journey, the disappointment, and some inferior fish and chips. She turned towards Rob, but there was no sign of him, his sleeping bag was screwed in a heap on the opposite bench. She closed her eyes again and then became aware of a strange sensation, a bright light that dazzled her, even behind closed lids. Rotten sod, was he shining a torch in her face? That wasn't funny. The door to the van opened, an unaccustomed brilliance poured in and Rob shouted,

"Wake up, you lazy lot. Sun's up. Didn't I tell you it'd be magic?"

He wasn't wrong. That day and the next, and the one, two, three, four after that, and into the second week, the sun shone on them as if they were the chosen ones. Lucy and Nicholas turned from pallid West London basement dwellers to bronzed little berries. Susan lounged around in shorts and a bikini, and her blonde hair was lightened further from exposure to sun and sea. It developed the consistency of coir matting but she didn't care. Rob's tan deepened each day, his eyes a startling blue in his weathered face, and he let his beard grow. They drove to other areas and explored, they walked, they ate ice creams and the children were beyond ecstatic. For the adults only one thing was missing.

They had parked the van away from prying eyes in a quiet spot at the end of the town, where they'd not been before. The children were playing behind some boulders that led to a series of inlets and rock pools, each one revealing new treasures. It was amazing how much happiness could be achieved with a shrimping net and a couple of plastic buckets that cost only pennies.

Rob and Susan were stretched on a towel, within earshot of Lucy and Nicholas, while still managing some privacy. He stroked her bronzing stomach, which was flat and firm.

"Unlucky for some," he said, his hand moving to her thighs, rubbing ever upwards.

"What is?"

She wasn't feeling unlucky, even though their holiday was almost over. Since her husband had been killed she had acquired the knack of savouring each precious moment, and the past two weeks had been overflowing with them.

"Thirteen," he said, parting her legs just slightly.

"Thirteen?"

"Thirteen days we've been here, and that's thirteen days without a fuck."

"Rob, shhh!" She giggled, and trapped his hand between her legs.

"They can't hear me." He leaned into her until she could smell his warm, toasted skin, and let his beard scratch the side of her neck. "We could go back to the van, nobody to disturb us. Tell the kids we're going to have a lie down because we've got a long drive tomorrow. They can see the van from here. They'll be fine."

The cunning use of his index finger in the region of her pleasure dome convinced her. Susan sat up, adjusted her bikini bottom and put on her beach cover up.

"Lucy! Nick! We're going to have a bit of a lie down, got a long drive tomorrow," she said, echoing Rob. "You know where we are, you won't have to cross a road if you want me." Lust notwithstanding, their safety was always her main concern. "All right?"

Her children were intent on their latest discovery in the pool.

"I said 'all right'?"

"All right," said Lucy, without looking up.

"We'll leave our stuff here, so help yourselves if you want an ice cream from the shop." To keep the sand out of their belongings they had hung their gear on an old rotting wooden board. She shook out their towel and draped that over it too.

"All right," repeated Lucy, then she screamed as her brother threw a tiny crab at her.

Rob led Susan towards the van. "Won't even notice we've gone," he said.

*

Sometime later Nicholas had had enough of the rock pool. The shop that sold ice creams was shut for lunch so he wandered off to the next small inlet. It was unlike the others, a bare, flat bed of very dark sand, almost grey in colour and surrounded by tufts of coarse grass. He thought it was a good spot to build a sandcastle. He began by shovelling some sand into his plastic bucket, scooping it up and cramming it down with his hands. It was damp, not powder fine and dry, like the area where his mum and Rob had been. He knelt and concentrated, unaware of the rippling beneath him as he dug his knees in. Having packed several bucket shaped mounds together, he decided he needed some shells and suchlike to decorate them. Lucy could do that.

"Lucy! Come here, I want you."

Silence.

"Lu-cy!"

Sisters! She either hadn't heard or was ignoring him, so he'd have to go himself. He tried to stand and toppled. The sand wouldn't release him, so he made an effort to kick his way out which didn't help as his lower legs vanished into it. Next he wriggled a bit and struggled a lot and then found he was covered up to his knees. He didn't think the sands were magic any more, he thought they were naughty. Twisting his body towards the rock pool where his sister still played, he shouted her name.

"Lucy!"

The movement pulled him further down, until he was up to his waist. This time Lucy turned. She had known him all his short life and for once it didn't sound as if he was just being a pest. She scrambled over the rocks towards him, by which time only her brother's head and shoulders were sticking out of the lightly shifting mass. It looked as if the sand was eating him. He still held on to his red bucket.

"Lucy," he cried. "I'm stuck."

She was his big sister; she would get him out of trouble.

She trampled the coarse grass and jumped, launched herself onto the sand and reached for him, as he threshed and tossed and twisted and turned. A kick, a final lunge, and she managed to grab his shoulders though she was sucked down immediately by the force of her leap. He dropped his red bucket and clung onto her, burying his face in her neck. Their small thrashing limbs were no match for the relentless sand. It devoured Lucy and her brother.

"It's all right, Nicky, I'm here."

They were the last words she ever spoke.

As her eyes and her ears and her mouth filled with coarse, damp, grey grains, Lucy screamed; in the camper van her mother screamed. Neither heard the other and a red plastic bucket rolled on the surface as the sand settled. From nowhere the wind rose. It blew at the towel and the bags hanging on the rotting wooden sign, revealing some lettering:

AN ER U C SAN TA WAY

*

Thirty-three years later, Susan sits beside the sign on the beach. Her skin is puffy, her hair grey, and she holds an old red plastic bucket. She stays for thirteen days, unlucky for some, and the council has long since replaced the dilapidated wooden board with a new notice that is properly maintained, although the message remains the same. It is made of toughened, industrial strength plastic, perfect for all weathers, ideal to withstand seaside conditions, guaranteed not to chip or flake, warp or crack, and is graffiti proof. It is white with red and black lettering and shows a drawing of a flailing matchstick man, surrounded by a mass of speckles inside a red triangle:

DANGER! QUICKSAND. STAY AWAY.

WILD MEN OF THE SEA

The existence of free-spirited aquatic humanoids, or merpeople, is common to many mythologies across the world and throughout history. From the fearsome sirens of Greek legend, superficially beautiful sea-nymphs who would lure sailors onto the rocks and then devour their corpses, to the gentle and romantic merrow of Irish folklore, a traditional mermaid, long-haired, fish-tailed and wearing conches over her fulsome breasts, who would keep her human lovers in a permanently happy and enchanted state at the bottom of the ocean, there have been myriad stories hinting at the existence of a rival civilisation beneath the waves, occasionally sticking its head up to amaze and beguile us.

Even now in the 21st century, rumours persist and alleged sightings continue to be made, though an embarrassing percentage of those home movies appearing online purporting to show mer-folk are quickly and easily outed as fakes. Of course, in times past – particularly in the Middle Ages, when the sea was a vast, unknowable force – it was a different story, and among most shoreline communities there was a deep conviction that 'wild men of the sea' were real and existed close at hand.

Two particularly interesting accounts come to us from the Suffolk coastline, which are radically different in nature and yet have vaguely nightmarish overtones.

The first one has no specific dates attached, but is roughly traceable to the 16th century, and though its exact location is unknown, it has been placed in locations as far south as Felixstowe and as far north as Lowestoft. Both of these modern harbour towns were little more than fishing villages in the pre-industrial age, quiet hamlets where few events of note ever occurred. Yet this was the environment where, one day, very unexpectedly, a mysterious, dark-skinned foreigner chose to make his home. Nobody in the village knew who he was or why he was there, and they came to refer to him simply as 'the Italian'. The man kept himself to himself, but in due course made friends with a local fishing lad, and the duo were regularly to be seen walking the beach together, engaged in discussion. These days, this activity alone would arouse suspicion, but times were different then, children grew up more quickly and sexual impropriety tended to be ignored so long as it remained out of sight. In any case, there was no suggestion of anything more than a platonic relationship between the two, and when the Italian one day *announced that he needed to leave the village, he asked his young friend to accompany him. When the lad refused, the Italian requested that he look after his dog while he was away. The lad was surprised as he didn't know his friend owned such a pet, and when the animal – a large black hound – arrived at his house, he was even more surprised; he had only previously seen this beast hanging around on the village boundaries, and had thought it feral. The boy and the dog became friends and regularly swam together, but one day, when the lad had swum farther from shore than he'd intended, the dog refused to let him return, snarling at him in the waves. Frightened, the lad was driven into ever deeper and rougher water, until he glanced over his shoulder and was amazed to see that it was not the dog pursuing him, but the Italian, who now launched a vicious attack, gnawing on his neck with razor-tipped teeth. The boy was only saved when a passing fishing boat, whose crew witnessed the incident, came to his rescue. Enraged, the Italian plunged beneath the surface and was never seen in that locality again.*

Folklorists have long contended that this creature was none other than Black Shuck, East Anglia's infamous hell-hound, and in Suffolk in particular, Shuck, who normally appears as a black dog, has a reputation for being a shape-shifter, occasionally transforming himself into an evil monk. However, the Italian angle is bafflingly inconsistent with the other stories, while Shuck is usually regarded as a death omen rather than a man-eater. Another version of the tale explains the mysterious stranger as a sorcerer seeking an acolyte or even a human sacrifice (Reformation England regarded papist Italy as the natural home of the devilish arts), though the common opinion in East Anglia held that he was not an Italian at all, but a merman, whose foreign looks and accent were so unfamiliar to local folk that they had simply guessed at his racial identity.

The traditional merman myth would certainly fit with the bloodier aspects of this story, as medieval fisher-folk generally lived in fear of these undersea beings, whom they believed to be cannibals in possession of magical powers.

The second tale from the East Anglian seaside again hints at a remarkable clash of cultures, though this time it casts humanity as the aggressors. It was reported in detail by Ralph of Coggleshall, a thorough and studious chronicler, who placed it during the reign of Henry II (1154-1189), and described how "a wodwose of the sea" – literally a 'wild man' – was captured in the nets of local fishermen just off the Suffolk coast near Orford. It was not described as having a tail or gills, but as being large and hairy, with webbed hands and feet. Bewildered, the villagers took their captive to nearby Orford Castle, where the knight Bartholomew de Glanville took charge, though he plainly didn't know what to do with his prisoner. The thing could not speak, but by all accounts was friendly enough and ate whatever food it was given, though it preferred raw fish. Several times it was allowed to swim in the sea, but always returned of its own volition. Eventually feelings grew against this curious being, which had been taken to chapel several times but had shown no knowledge of devotions or interest in the service. When someone aired a theory that it might be the corpse of a drowned sailor in the possession of evil spirits, it was thrown into a tiny dungeon, and later hanged upside down and tortured. What such actions were expected to achieve is anyone's guess – by his tone, Ralph of Coggleshall clearly disapproved – but the creature survived this ordeal, and was finally released back into the sea. According to the record, it returned to Orford a couple times more, but unsurprisingly was no longer inclined to stick around, and eventually disappeared.

No viable explanation has been offered for this bizarre historical anecdote, except that some scholars have wondered if Coggleshall was rebuking his people for their casual misuse of nature – in medieval times woodwoses were seen as benign guardians of God's flora and fauna – but this would be unlike Ralph's normal form, which was to give straightforward accounts of real events, without subtext or metaphor.

Various images of the wild man are still visible in modern-day Orford, and the case is regularly reviewed by cryptozoologists, though most will admit to being perplexed by it.

BROKEN SUMMER
Christopher Harman

King Cole's harsh laughter expressed what was possibly the true opinion of the Pleasure Park regime as the smooth corporate voice informed Philip that in spite of a good interview he hadn't been appointed on this occasion. "However, Mr Earl, we'll keep your details on file and don't forget, we advertise in the Job Centre."

In the enclosure outside Coffee Island, Philip crunched his styrofoam cup, squeezed his phone with his other hand. A low-grade job, but the money would have helped. Under the razzmatazz, the Day-Glo colours the constant movement of bodies and machinery, the Pleasure Park was just another overbearing corporation. King Cole in his plexiglass cubicle, rocked back and forth on his gold-leaf throne and laughed uncontrollably at Philip's defeat. Surely on the payroll in some mysterious way; maybe the little black eyes had cameras in them to monitor failed candidates as well as troublesome holidaymakers. A nursery tale king with his plump red cheeks, the school-cap tilt of his crown, his parti-coloured, pyjama-like suit. His black eyes followed Philip as he left his table and went to the turnstiles, where he fed his complementary ticket into the machine and entered the Pleasure Park proper.

He felt the rumble of the great wheel carrying four concentric rows of mainly rider-less metal horses on the Derby Races. He walked on under the shadows of the Flying Machines, then was glancing queasily away from the Sky Rocket and its row of secured, seated passengers bobbing to assorted heights and depths.

Neither fun-seeker nor employee, he didn't belong here. He felt transparent until the sound of his name clothed him in flesh again.

It was Shop, with his usual open, amiable expression. Sleepy-eyed, he'd had a bad night or more likely a good one. His kinked, untidy hair was the same red as the teddy bears ranked in tiers behind him.

"Well? One of us?" he said.

"No. Now if I'd had a Polish accent." Before now they'd discussed half the staff being East European.

"Easier getting into Cambridge?" Shop wasn't trying for anywhere prestigious. He'd be lucky if he got into the catering college in Lancaster he'd put his name down for. Philip would know his own future in a few days when he got his results. Behind innumerable rides, King Cole laughed as if he already knew them.

"At least I won't have to listen to that all day."

"Listen to what?"

"King Cole." The laughter seemed to vibrate the forest of iron structures surrounding them.

"You stop hearing it after a while." Shop looked at Philip over invisible half-moons. "'cept when someone reminds you."

Philip shrugged. Five linked carriages thundered down a steep hump-back of the Big One, like something intent on feeding on the lowlier rides beneath. The ground trembled. A shuddering ran up through his legs. The Big One's struts looked as woolly-edged as pipe cleaners. The structure held as the carriages took the curve and soared upwards. Philip breathed. "Did you feel that?"

"Feel what?"

"Only a flippin' earthquake."

King Cole's laughter seemed to sound from just behind a queue for seafood.

"They must be quite a weight those carriages – does feel like an earthquake sometimes."

"I was thinking it was that fracking thing that's in the news."

Shop's grin could compete with King Cole's. He thrust out a spherical woolly missile. "Go on, free of charge."

Philip declined. "I'm off before that laughing drives me mad."

Shop was unfolding the rolled cosh of a copy of the *Gazette*. "If you need some cash, you could do worse than this."

A photo of a blonde with her face blurred out. She had a rolled *Gazette* wedged under her armpit. Miss Seasider would be strolling around resort hotspots this week. If you saw her, had that day's edition with you, with the voucher intact inside, you could claim a thousand pounds.

"I'm just not lucky that way," Philip said.

"In this town, miracles happen," Shop said, but didn't provide any examples.

"You should work for the Tourist Office."

Shop smiled as if he'd thought of that. As Philip was leaving, Shop reminded him of the party tomorrow evening.

Philip caught the bus inland to the college. Two emailed rejections; he wouldn't be a washer-upper in the steamy hell of the Terra Firma Restaurant kitchen, nor would he be waiting on tables at Yates Wine Lodge. Searching for other openings online meant he could put off his return to the Sea Lanes Bread and Breakfast until four when he let himself in with his own key.

On the low table in the street-facing sun lounge was a tiered cake stand; a card on a tiny easel said 'Help Yourself'. Philip scoffed a macaroon to the soothing surf sounds of the vending machine. Mouth full, he groaned at a banging rattle on the glass front door.

Neutral-faced, he made big vowel-shapes with his mouth – Not. Back. Yet. Miss Bridge mouthed back with equal unintelligibility. Philip unlocked the door and she blustered in like wind off the sea. "I know. She's crystal balling. I'll wait. It's important." An appreciative glance at the cake stand; a frown at the vending machine. "Do me a cuppa would you luvvie? Earl Grey, I know Rose has got some. Oh these shoes are too tight." Flesh bulged out between the straps.

Her eyes rolled as if she were about to faint.

Philip guessed she put on a similar display when she communed with spirits on stage. She dumped herself onto the sofa and looked similarly foam-filled. Wrist bangles jangled as she reached for an Eccles cake. Philip withdrew from her scent, which would reach the back row at the Winter Gardens, and prepared Earl Grey in Mrs Oliphant's kitchen. When he returned, Miss Bridge had the *Gazette* open in one hand, the Eccles cake, mostly eaten, in the other. A scree slope of crumbs on her acreage of bosom. Philip placed down the tea tray and said, "Well, I'll leave you."

She tapped a column of print with a purple-painted fingernail. Someone else thinking an encounter with Miss Seasider would benefit him? No, this was serious: *Students Stage Fracking Protest*.

The front-page photo had been taken outside the drilling site; it was less than a mile from the town and within sight of the college. Some of the laughing, animated youthful faces, Philip recognised. Earnest and politically aware, they instilled in him a secret shame.

"They aren't the only ones protesting," Miss Bridge said, looking at him significantly and sucking in her cheeks as far as it were possible.

"Yes, Tories, trade unionists, Women's Institute." Justified protests: extracting shale gas might mean cheaper energy bills eventually, but mini-earthquakes were a high price to pay.

"I meant people aren't the only ones protesting." Blue chip eyes in the marshmallow flesh of Miss Bridge's face.

"Chief Sitting Bull not happy?" he said, mildly. She should feel flattered he could be bothered to name-check her psychic helper.

"Chief Bright Cloud," she corrected, crisply. "Anyway, you've no time for that, Rose tells me." She looked him up and down as if the lack in his life were sadly plain to see. No, he had no time; didn't want to debate it either. "Not my thing," he said, smooth and awkwardly jovial.

"What is your thing?" As if she needed to ask. Her eyes were as tiny and angular as the windows of a toy car. Mrs Opliphant never cleaned his room but he strongly suspected she sneaked in when he was at college. He cleared away conscientiously after smoking hash, but the old sofa, stiff curtains and worn carpet harboured odours he noticed after spells away. She'd pass on her suspicions to her psychic friend, but not to her other friends – his grandparents. All smiles when they'd left for home a fortnight ago after their annual stay. It was their offices that had got him the top floor room at 'mates rates' while he was attending the college.

"What's my thing? Well, making money – one of these days if everything goes to plan."

*

In his room he opened the window. The air was only marginally fresher, and with a taint of fish and chips.

He read some of *Inherently Evil: Corporate Governance in the Twentieth Century*, then switched on his computer and toured the green quads and stone galleries of the university. The images on the screen were an antidote to the brashness of the resort. Centuries of history trumped six score decades of rapid expansion on dunes and bogs. His grades would be posted up on Thursday. And they'd be no matter for derisive laughter.

Grey light outside. He rolled his desk-chair on its castors and the mouldy brickwork and rusted fire-escapes of the resort's back streets approached in the window. He could see the glowing bulbs of the 'W' of the Winter Gardens sign in one direction; in another, a few grey strata of the Hounds Hill Shopping Centre multi-storey car park. Elsewhere, narrow thoroughfares blushed with the first blinkings of neon.

His flesh chilled as laughter moved in a nearby street. King Cole's merriment couldn't carry the length of the Golden Mile. A bit of tape played here at the north end of the resort must be generously publicising the rival attraction of the Pleasure Park in the south. A moving vehicle with a loudspeaker? The laughter seemed to hover at a point behind a corner roof gambrel covered in a root system of black wires.

He pulled down the window sash and it stuck, six inches short of the bottom of the frame. He pushed down, his face a grimacing mask. Still no give to the sash. He sat heavily, his hatred of the room renewed.

The laughter had stopped but he couldn't stop listening for it all evening. In bed he lay awake. The window offered no hindrance to the shrieks of hen night gangs and the answering cries of male counterparts. They exhausted themselves to a silence which seemed shaped for the series of rapid light impacts.

Rats. Plentiful as wildebeest in the crumbling housing stock, the ravaged back yards. He'd heard herds on slate roofs, seen a moving floor of them converge on restaurant waste in a back alley. These just now had moved away, leaving one straggler. Too fat, too slow? Maybe it had sniffed out rich pickings others had missed. None here, unless the faint stale odour of hash from the curtains, carpet and sofa was proving a lure. Philip sat up, eyes sharp for a fat hairy parcel to plop heavily through the glassless letterbox below the sash and scuttle for cover. He left his bed to stand guard at the window.

Nothing visible on the Alps of slate nearby. The tunnel of a ginnel gave onto two paces worth of lit pavement. The coloured lights of a basement club shone up through a glassed iron floor-grid, staining stilettos and calves of women tottering over it, the white trainers of a youth walking backwards and shouting aggressively. Elegance followed: a knee-length dress, sleeveless white shirt, a straight waterfall of honey-toned blond hair, rolled-up newspaper tucked under an arm. She walked back and forth on the grid but there was no sense of her waiting impatiently. At this distance, her face was as much a blur as in the *Gazette* photo.

She might be gone by the time he got there. And if not and he declared to the revelation of her face "You are Miss Seasider and . . ." And she wasn't?

See, gone even as he watched. A girl on a night out—must have spied her date. He should prevent his imaginings running off like a roller coaster. He returned to bed, thoughts stolid. No stray rats, no Miss Seasider. Here was another thought: he'd insist Mrs Oliphant put aside her crystal ball and get her friend Len to fix the window. He was a handyman but not seen here in a good while. With a chest-voice that could frack shale gas maybe his singing career was finally taking off.

*

A big, blowy, blousy sky the next morning. Frothy white waves raced to the beach, lace-sleeved the pillars of the North Pier.

Philip walked along the dense damp sands, noted ancient pebbles and yesterday's fag ends and fast-food packaging. Prints of foot, hoof, shoe and paw. Half a mile on, he was startled to discover himself at the centre of a pattern like a crop circle. Arms' width, splay-toed prints dug deep in a spiral; evidence here of monster footwear, worn presumably with a commensurately monstrous costume, all to publicise some indoor entertainment for the next rainy day – so there was no need for him to feel piercingly self-conscious, even downright uncomfortable enough to leap sharply out of the circle and hope nobody had seen.

He climbed the steps of the sea wall to the Promenade, crossed tramlines and the road to Madam Sospiri's premises. A minimal rent, if any, for quarters as wide and deep as a horse-box. 'Madam Sospiri: Palmist and Clairvoyant' in a flamboyant whirl of puce and glitter letters on the lintel. He entered, glad to be off the beach.

She was talking into her mobile phone. "Yes, fine . . . No, just the deposit. Yes . . . payable to The Sea Lanes . . . No, Lanes. Yes. Thank you . . . Goodbye." Mrs Oliphant snapped the phone shut and secreted it in her sash. She blew out. Her hoop earrings, three to each ear, jangled. "Sea Lions, Sea Loins. Simpler when it was the Rosa Dora." She looked abruptly embarrassed, as if uncomfortable at him seeing two sides of her existence conflated. She straightened her headband on her jet-black dyed hair, clutched her intricately woven shawl about her. "First time I've seen you here." Her smile faltered. "Something wrong?"

He immediately thought of those prints in the sand. "I was passing and thought I'd mention the window in my room. Won't shut."

"I'll sort it when I get back. Don't like doing B and B business here—puts me off doing this." She made a moulding gesture around the crystal ball with her liberally ringed brown fingers.

"Somebody could get in," he said.

"What? A cat burglar?" After a flash of her heavily made-up eyes, she relented. "I'll get onto Len. He'll sort it."

Philip caught a movement in the crystal globe, the shadow of something large passing behind. She'd noticed and wiped the ball with her sleeve.

"Come on. Sit down." She smiled with a quiet confidence, as if he'd inadvertently expressed a wish for a reading but was too proud to admit it. "On the house." A tiny house, a tomb with flock wallpaper, a seeing eye and other occult-looking junk.

"Better not. I'm a bit busy."

She peered as if mists were already clearing. "Busy, my eye. It'd do you good to be. The devil makes work for idle hands." A shrewd look, and he knew she knew about his surreptitious smokes. She hadn't let on to his relatives. A tolerant old bird – he should like her more than he did.

Philip sat, the globe between them. She swirled her fingers over it, peering as if it were a magnifying glass over minuscule print. "Oh yes, oh yes. Books hundreds of them. A slow river. Weeping willows. Lovely old buildings." Old fraud and flatterer. He'd told her he'd aimed high.

"Ah, here you are – and you're having a high old time." A slight edge on the word 'high'? A better class of drug maybe? He'd settle for better weed than the stuff Shop had supplied recently.

"Laughing, you are. Through gritted teeth. Can't see what at." She frowned, gave the crystal a rub with her lacy sleeve. "Can't see where you are. Sitting down. You're in a costume. You could be on a stage. Never had you down as theatrical. Can't make out the ones watching. Definitely you. though. Still got that silly dyed-blond thing." Like her silly, dyed black thing – though he had to admit it went with her handsome old face. He'd never asked if she actually had some gypsy blood.

She was staring as if at some incomprehensible ritual.

"Have I got a rosy future in there?"

His stiff humouring of her went unappreciated. A 'yes' would suffice. Her large eyes raised to him now. "You should take care."

"Any point if what's to happen is all done and dusted?" He twisted sideways to get out of the chair. Determinism and free-will, he might be discussing those in a seminar in a few weeks. "Interesting though. I might come again." A bit of teasing flattery. He said he'd see her at the Sea Lanes later. She made no reply as he left.

He kept to the town side of the Promenade. Seeing a crowd gathered at the Promenade railings, shortly before the North Pier, he wondered if some other curious markings were imprinted on the beach. He crossed and looked down to a police car and ambulance half concealed in grey shadow under the pier. "A body" someone said. A nearby ice cream kiosk was doing good business. Entertainment of a kind, Philip thought, moving away. A drunken reveller must have taken a dip and the cold sea had filled his legs with lead, shrunk his lungs, dragged him down then cast him to the land. No future there, Philip thought. Nobody's was guaranteed, and there were no sneak previews to be had in crystal balls.

Parts of a body, he learned from Radio Wave on someone's portable set, as he made his way home. He had his own switched on all afternoon. Other body parts found bobbing under the central and south piers. Not drowned, savaged it seemed. Teethed fish with stomachs like dustbins were a rarity in the Irish Sea – but if one had wandered to the shallows and snacked it was hardly likely the tide would deposit remains with such regard for symmetry.

*

The gruesome topic prompted merry laughter at the party. Alcohol and pot grew Shop's pad at the top of the house in South Shore extra floor space and a room or two to accommodate everyone. Voices piggy-backed to be heard over a recording of a local garage band. Philip moved from space to space, drink in hand, partly intent on finding Shop. Greetings exchanged with faces he recognised. Shrugs and head shakes on the subject of Shop. He felt confident enough to open a closed door. He withdrew, resealed groans and bed creaks.

A teenaged Falstaff handed him a spliff; he found a space on the floor and filled his lungs over and over. He smiled as girls' laughter tinkled like a slot machine win. Low chuckles clustered against a scabrous anecdote he couldn't quite catch and couldn't help laughing at louder than anyone. He didn't deserve unamused glances. "You all right, mate?" a youth said, disliking him for not being.

"Me? Yeah. Got a rosy future. Got myself crystal-balled today." His sniggers danced over mutters. Dullards, stuck in this declining resort. So many hard little eyes like fragments of bottle glass. Something said at his expense and his insides turned chill as ice cream. He got up; he wanted to get out and ignored complaints – he didn't intentionally kick legs and flanks. He pulled at a door-handle – any door would do to get him away.

Inside, a dead body on a bed. In a foetal position, it partly rolled to face him – pursed lips the wrong shape to "ha ha ha". Philip closed the door on the puffed-out red cheeks, the damp forehead, the eyes with pupils like the holes in pencil sharpeners. He doubted Shop was ever reduced to such shameless solo artistry. Popular, he could miss his own party and not be thought ill of.

Me, on the other hand. Gate-crasher, they're thinking – or worse. Evident in the tone of voices. The ice cream inside him was curdling. The walls vibrated with malevolence. He blundered out of the flat.

In the breeze off the sea, a taint of seaweed and sewage. A kiss-me-quick hat bowled by. Stretched clouds; stars like detergent bubbles on oily water. Great rags of white foam floundered on the tide-line.

Pan scrapes and irregular ticks approached. Philip waved his arms. Gold pillars, bass-relief cupids, scrollwork, painted metal curtains tied back by brass cords; the tram was a tiny Matcham theatre on tracks. He took his seat, the third passenger as the tram scraped onwards. A man in creams and whites lowered the rag in his nicotined fingers and sniffed at the seaweed and sewage which had boarded with Philip. The other passenger had a head of hedgehog spikes, red-rimmed eyes quivered at the screen on his iPhone.

Souvenir shops were fortresses behind metal shutters. Madam Sospiri's lair was an anonymous wooden box. Five-star hotels were ivory palaces; the concrete cladding of lesser establishments bore vomit-hued stains and streaks left by polluted rain. Outside Coral Island a gaggle of women wore white to set off spray-tans. Jeers and blown kisses at the tram. One showed her back, indifferent. A straight scroll of light gold-blond hair. Rolled newspaper wedged underarm like a sergeant major's baton. A delicate sketch of a woman next to heifer-builds with slack mouths and pork-crackling skin. He felt sick and sour, sweaty; a drummer played drunkenly in his chest all the way home.

*

Madam Sospiri dropped a plate behind her door. Entering through his, Philip saw she'd not bothered to get his window fixed. His drop-down bed received him with a wheeze.

Night sounds through the empty slot under the sash. A disoriented gull circled, its cawing like an appeal. Blokes laughed, dispersed, leaving one laughing alone. No – that was the gull, sounding like King Cole. Bastard Shop, dishing out that poor quality weed. Everything had been wrong since smoking at the party. His body felt stiff and stale as old clothes disinterred from a chest. The room resented him as much as he it.

The stuff must have knocked him into blackness, he realised, when the silence awoke him. The gull had flown off, or crash-landed. Fun-seekers were indoors, seemingly every single one who might otherwise have been audible. No scuttle of vermin. No lazy intermittent soft thump of waves which he fancied he could sometimes hear at the dead of night. Nothing – a vacuum.

A single hard knock had him sitting up in bed. If it had come from the other side of the locked door into the room he would have laid himself back down again. He couldn't deny the fact that the sound had come from the wardrobe, which dominated the room as it never had before. Common sense dictated that you didn't wait, trembling, and not immediately investigate such a sound. Conscious thought reduced to a pinprick, he switched on the ceiling light and was at the wardrobe door and opening it in one continuous movement.

Thoughts expanded, buffeted by shock as King Cole fell forward from an upright position and lay at his feet from where he grinned up at him, a chubby crowned kid in motley pyjamas. Philip hauled him up by the ruff around his neck, and cast him down again, violently, onto the worn carpet. Still the king grinned. Philip felt of a substance harder than the pot hands and head of King Cole. He aimed but didn't follow through with the kick. Shop deserved the kicking. The effort and logistics were almost admirable. And ingenious the way Shop had somehow succeeded in propping the puppet so that it had leaned against the inside of the wardrobe door, prior to him closing it. As for the knock—Philip supposed he'd imagined it, or heard some heating pipe or floorboard give voice.

If Shop had applied himself as ruthlessly to studying and exams as he did to partying and pranks he'd be leaving the town in September as Philip was even more ruthlessly intent on doing.

Philip grabbed King Cole and propelled him headfirst through the gap under the sash. The king tumbled head over heels, down successive slopes of slate, as if weights were tied into his puffed sleeves and curl-toed boots. Gone, into the black chasm of Back Bunker Street. He wouldn't be resuming his laughter for a good while – if ever. In bed, Philip surged like the Irish Sea. Words gathered behind his sternum like sick. He got up, grabbed his phone and keyed in Shop's number. Shop's self-assurance was about to falter.

He answered, his voice groggy.

"Thanks," Philip said.

"Phil? How are you mate? Enjoy the party?"

"Mate? All this matiness. I'm in better nick than King Cole for your information. Worth missing the party for was it?"

Shop smirked audibly. "Had my own little party going two floors below." Something about Cheryl being up for it "in spades", "Stuck my head through the door and saw you all Happy Face."

"Then what did you do?"

"Nothing much. Went out for some mixers."

"Oh yeah? To my flat, you mean. How did you get in? Hope you cop-it for nabbing King Cole."

"Your flat? King Cole?" Laughter in his voice and Shop sounded almost convincingly puzzled.

"Yeah, in my wardrobe. Go on – laugh."

"Go to sleep, you nutter," Shop said, with no particular vehemence. He hung up. Philip rang him again and he didn't answer. After that Shop's phone was switched off.

*

Morning came with a crash of beer crates in Back Bunker Street. A gull draped the shadow of its wingspan across the window. No exclamations had awoken him at the discovery of King Cole, contorted and grinning in the crumble and grime below.

Philip fried bacon on his stove then ate it between slices of Mother's Pride on his way down.

King Cole had gone. Immediately recognisable, he wouldn't be left to deteriorate like a shop manikin. A phone call – "you'll never guess". Dark suits and shades from the Pleasure Park flying up the Promenade in a limousine. In the poky alley, clipped words into slick mobile phones, "Yep, the King's here." The fantasy crashed as King Cole hadn't done from that high back window. The King in this dingy ditch between streets? He'd been as present as comely phantasms uttering confidences and admiration across Philip's pillow. No question he'd done Shop an injustice on that score. He'd had a bad reaction to cannabis the last time – a disconnectedness and an intense distrust of everyone. Whether dream or hallucination, this had been several degrees worse.

On the tram, formulating a face-saving set of words was difficult. Stepping off, he deserved the grating laughter of King Cole coming over the high wall. Entering the Pleasure Park, the clockwork interior entangled him. He was glad to get to Shop's stall. A chain of carriages on the Big One was plummeting, all hands raised. Philip raised his own in surrender and Shop's expression lost its wariness. "You're a mad bastard," Shop said, with something like affection.

"That stuff – where'd you get it?"

Shop looked sympathetic. "It's you, Phil. Remember the last time? Maybe you should lay off."

Philip disliked being singled out as the one who hadn't measured up, but figured Shop was right. His own brain chemistry couldn't handle it. It could handle inebriation now and then – he'd settle for that at uni.

They listened to King Cole's relentless jollity a moment. Some kids wandered up and Shop handed them furry blocks to throw at the coconuts. "Nailed down," Philip said, a friendly jibe by way of a farewell to Shop but nobody was listening. He headed away.

He crossed the Promenade and stood at the railings overlooking the high tide. The rapprochement with Shop felt good until the tide organ's moans nearly articulated words that mocked him. It towered, a fifty-feet high sculpture in the shape of an elongated wave with a curled-over top. It contained organ pipes which were connected to openings in the sea wall. He guessed an obstruction in the water intake forced that wet guttural sound, suggestive of the throat-clearing of something moist and unspeakable. Philip felt miles from the nearest holiday maker on the vast Promenade.

He walked northwards. Glitter on the ale-brown sea. He bought an ice cream and had eaten it by the time he came to Madam Sospiri's den. It was padlocked. Mrs Oliphant wasn't at the Sea Lanes either. His room kept reminding him of someone who hadn't even been present and King Cole didn't constitute a 'someone' in any case. He went to the library on Queen Street and read in the *Gazette* that test fracking operations would continue as there was little risk of a tremor large enough to damage structures or people.

He ate scampi and chips in the massive mausoleum of red brick at the base of the Tower.

Between chalk and coal-dust clouds, sunlight fell in a shower of gold coins onto the stone-washed blue of the sea. He left, wandered some more and ended up at the Hounds Hill Shopping Centre.

Shops were closing down in the arcades. In a poster, Miss Bridge's gaze toward spirit regions was rather qualified by chunky amethyst earrings, powdered cheeks, her ice-blue perm and glasses hanging from a chain. A man swept an industrial cleaner from side-to-side on the scuffed parquet flooring. On stools in a steamed window, some kids sipping milkshakes were like targets in a shooting range.

Philip had stopped before a window full of kitsch prints when he saw Miss Seasider through a plate glassed corner. He sprang in pursuit, glancing the while, greedy for nobody else to have seen her.

She was gliding away. No apparent fatigue after a day waiting for a hand on her shoulder. Now between blank plaster walls, passing out of sight around an island of cash machines and a keycutters. He followed, rehearsing in his head ("Hello Miss Seasider, I, er …") Past the island, no sign of her in the passageway but a door with a tiny symbol dressed in a triangle was closing.

Not a fantasy, Miss Seasider was answering to a human need. Philip hovered, keeping the door in sight. His stomach fizzed as if he'd glugged soluble aspirin. He took some deep breaths. Women never hurried this aspect of existence. He studied his watch, noticed his grubby trainers. She deserved a better dressed assailant but it was too late now.

It seemed minutes later when the door was pulled inwards. A 'Miss' emerged – another 'Miss' entirely. A magical reversal – princess to frog. Miss Seasider wouldn't be far behind.

Miss Bridge looked over her bullfrog chin at him and bustled over. "Got some shopping done." She lifted an expensive tooled leather bag with Red Indian iconography, tassels and the like. "I'm in a rush. Due at the Winter Gardens in an hour." She'd vouchsafed some information and now it was evidently his turn.

"Waiting for a friend."

"Friends," she huffed. "Been trying to get in touch with Rose all day – " A shutter rattled down over a shop window. Her cheeks wobbled as she shuddered. "Can't be living in this town any more. When you see her tell her I'm leaving."

"Me too in three weeks or so," he said abstractedly. "If everything works out as it's supposed to." He fervently wished she'd leave right now. His gaze swung to the Ladies – as sealed as a bank vault. Miss Bridge missed nothing. If she'd been about to go, she visibly changed her mind.

He felt suddenly unwell. The floor rocked like a pivoting paving slab. Reduced scampi high-kicked in his gut. Voices in the arcades became one threatening voice, low as the tide organ, reverberating off the tiled walls. The door to the Ladies tiptoed with deliberation on its bottom corners. Philip swallowed. Miss Bridge's globular cheeks and chin advanced.

"Been taking anything you shouldn't have?"

The damned woman was right. After the best part of a day, Shop's stuff was still working against him.

"You need a sit down," she ordered. "And some sweet tea." She pointed a fat ringed finger at a café entrance with faux-marble pillars. He was defenceless in the beam of those little eyes that could manipulate the bereft and the bereaved.

Inside, an ancient pinafore-ed waitress brought doughnuts and tea in an ugly china pot. Miss Bridge added milk and several sugars to their cups while Philip watched the passageway and the Ladies door. Miss Seasider must have left by now, probably missed her as they headed to the café. Gone as totally as a sea mist burned off by the sun. His frustration burst out in confession – Miss Seasider, the thousand quid that would have sat nicely with his student loan.

Miss Bridge took a bite of doughnut. "There was only me in there," she said.

Philip made a silent vow. He'd smoke plain cigarettes, suck boiled sweets for God's sake. She was looking hard at him. That was her trade secret, looking forensically, as well as listening, and she knew he hadn't lied.

"That's not to say nobody went in," she said.

Whatever that meant, Philip didn't want to know. Miss Bridge had a light stubble of white sugar from the doughnut. She chewed ruminatively, swallowed. "Need this, the day I've had. Heaven help me when I do my turn. I'll have to get by on sheer professionalism. The messages are all confused. There are folk coming through who aren't who they say they are. Chief Bright Cloud won't come near me. Says the town's corrupted. He's right. It's the fracking that's done it. The bone yards are in uproar – and that's just the half of it. Un-lives are stirring – that's my pet name for 'em anyway. Not belly-born, have never lived and will never see the insides of a pine box. That body divided between the three piers – what do you think did that?" She didn't wait for him to venture an opinion. "Those in the know, know. There's been a thing seen on the beach at sunset – like a ton of blubbery white tripe supported on turkey legs as long as sapling trunks. That's what's done it. And there's worse than that lurking – "

"Thanks for this. Have to go." The evening yawned, empty of content as Miss Bridge's forebodings. He stood, legs grudgingly dependable.

Miss Bridge worked her jaws. "If you see Miss Seasider again, you should leave her be." He sent her a weak smile; Miss Bridge he'd avoid, mad old witch.

*

As he got ready for bed, the town grimaced at him in the shape of the gap under the sash. Sounds found their way into his room; the mating cries of stags and hens, cheesy pop from an amusement arcade, the weird tonal distortions of a pub singer. In bed, he walked. Far away on the vast sands was the tide organ. Without approaching, he found himself closer; he could hear its brainless pitiless groans, see a tiny man dancing around it, kicking his feet, swinging his arms forward and back. Philip ran, woke to his legs kicking the duvet off.

By eleven the next morning he was on the upper deck of the bus heading inland. Outside town he could see across drab fields to a clump of nondescript white excrescences where drilling tests for fracking had been conducted. He could barely believe shale gas was extracted let alone entertain the crazy notion that the process had unearthed monsters and dead folk.

In the college entrance hall, stares at the lists – gasps, hugs and the odd slinking away. He felt no particular joy writing down the grades which would open the doors to his new life. A density of packed sand in his chest where his heart and lungs should have been.

The journey back to the coast was like a fractious Pleasure Park ride; the bus would roar down straights, take corners at speed. The sky lightened as the brick, concrete and tarmac began to predominate and greenery virtually disappeared. Road works and diversions took the bus down narrow ways. Backs of houses resembled the damp-darkened undersides of flat stones set on end. The sky offered no relief; it was like the blank reverse of wallpaper hinting at vivid and strange patterns on the other side. Beyond the concrete tomb of the bus station, the Tower was a tapering skeletal snout.

That night, the grin of invisible bared teeth under the sash was more than he could endure. He'd correct the warping himself if Mrs Oliphant could provide a chisel.

From the top of the stairs he could hear a faint patter of water below. He went down and found her door ajar. No answer to his knock, his call. He stepped inside, into the tenebrous past; antimacassars, a preponderance of heavy wood furnishings coated with dust. On one wall a formation of three ceramic ducks.

Not a hint of Madam Sospiri, other than the heavy flock wallpaper from which off-cuts had papered her gypsy den.

Falling water said his name. He went through a door, saw another restricted space. Water droplets and steam on the other side of frosted glass made for a greater opacity in which skin tones shattered and reformed, and two hands lathered a startling quantity of black hair. "Sorry," he mumbled inaudibly against the loud and bestial extended suck of water down the plughole.

He backed out, closing the door after him, and still he had to struggle free of the sounds from the bathroom that sought to pull him back like an undertow.

He lay on the bed and watched his locked door. The light tapping had ceased – a *blip, blip* like water droplets – unless those had been his name – "Philip, Philip". He ignored his buzzing phone until it oriented itself lengthwise towards him.

Laughter before the voice spoke, evidently close to King Cole's booth. A throb and surge rendered the woman all but unintelligible but for the word "interview" and a number "ten". A faulty automated message; it hadn't even given him the opportunity to confirm if he would attend. He thought about it:

never mind the money – menial tasks to occupy him during the day and pot-free evenings gaming or reading would ward off unhealthy perceptions and bizarre notions. He had to get the job first and hope his new qualifications didn't over-qualify him.

The rectangular slot breathed cold air at him. Later it had snaggle-teeth of grey roofs and vague chimney stacks. He faced away, waited for sounds to join the grey light. He was glad of them when they came – a rolled beer barrel, a hawking cough. These were snapped to silence by a sharp bang which echoed inside him. Uttering a shaky "shit" he looked.

The sash had snapped down, sealing the window.

*

The tram's overhead cables ticked like competing clocks, only in agreement that he had little time. His suit was the blue-grey of the clouds watching from far out at sea; he must have grown for it pressed as if he were fathoms deep. Hotel flags rippled, membranous, plates of patterned pale seaweed in slow currents. Sand smoked under car wheels, tried to ensnare the hooves of the ponies dragging traps.

Visible over the perimeter walls, the Pleasure Park's rides spun and sprang like parts of a single mechanism. He walked down a side-road. Sounds came to him as if through glass – a family unloading from a vehicle, the creak of a car park barrier coming down.

The Pleasure Park was run from an anonymous white block at a back corner. Philip pressed a button in a panel by an equally nondescript door. Metal mesh crackled and asked him his business. A muffled discussion followed his answer. "We're looking into this. No interviews today as far as we're aware. No jobs for that matter." He told them what they should have known – of the call last night. He was asked to wait and he heard steps come up to the door.

The woman had a strong chin and hooked nose. She watched him closely as she said they were investigating, if he'd "care to wait". Not in the admin block, which she led him through. He supposed he should be grateful for the free entry to the Pleasure Park.

Too early for the crowds. Young men in smocks bearing the corporate logo picked up litter. A young woman yawned, canopied at the centre of a merry-go-round of leaflets. Again, not holidaying, not working; he couldn't decide if his surroundings felt unreal or he did.

Under the forest of their poles, clustered cars were stationary in the dodgems arena. Gloom beneath the mesh ceiling, fruited with unlit bulbs. One car had an occupant waiting for the others to be filled. Bowed forward as if reading or sending a text. Now sitting back. Forward again. Clutching his stomach, as if in pain, or was it a silent paroxysm of laughter? Neither. Philip was convinced the man was trying to push himself up out of his seat. Before he might be embarrassed by a request for assistance, Philip left and moved on past stalls in which nobody showed signs of seeing him.

But someone watched. From the dodgem cars as it turned out, just inside the perimeter, and a child to judge from the figure's stature. Carriages plunged with a din of metal down a nearby incline of the Big One. No screams, no shouts from the occupants, who all stared in the same direction into the Park as if something close to where he was standing engaged their interest. Philip could make out wild, wind-ruffled hair, but no faces. They could have been dummies on a maintenance run. Looking back at the dodgems he saw the watcher had gone.

Shop wasn't manning the coconut shy but Philip lingered a moment. The coconuts had coarse thinning hair. One was crowned with a band of yellow paper cut into points in some tribute to King Cole. Philip fancied taking aim and knocking it for six. Instead he faced outward, and understood why sounds puzzled him. He was hearing them without interference from King Cole's laughter.

Essential maintenance? A new laughter track being prepared? A new outfit to replace that dusty patchwork of colours? A completely new resident for the narrow glass enclosure? That'd be no bad thing.

Shop appeared behind him, Styrofoam Coffee Island beaker in his hand. He looked listless. Was a function of King Cole's laughter to energise staff?

As Philip opened his mouth to speak, Shop said, "The king's been nabbed. Don't look at me though. You didn't put ideas into my head." Face rubbery as he manipulated it with one hand.

Philip mentioned the job. "What job?" Shop said.

"Exactly," Philip said. 'Some mix-up. I'm jinxed."

Shop surveyed their surroundings, the motionless rides, mostly empty thoroughfares and plazas. "I'm going to be around a while yet. Got my results." Philip's silence on the matter told Shop all he needed to know. "So you'll be leaving then?"

"Can't bloody wait," Philip said with feeling. He realised he didn't want any job here, even unaccompanied by King Cole's laughter. "First, I'm going to take a look at an empty throne. Always been a bit of a republican myself."

There was more activity at the main entrance. Holiday makers gawped at the empty throne in the glass booth as they never had when it had been occupied. A couple of grey suits with the Pleasure Park logo on the lapels talked to a police officer. His sense of detachment must be this place preparing itself to become an unsatisfactory memory. Stepping out onto the Promenade, he cast away the Pleasure Park for good.

The tide was far out, the tide organ silent. Road and Promenade strove for the blankness of the sea. A few distant dots on the sands. Philip wanted the human dimensions of his room, and before that a tram compartment. One was approaching.

*

With the lower deck full, he had to stand. Heads and unwashed windows to see past didn't give a reliable measure of the slow-billowing vertical length on the bright white tide-line. A voluminous garment on someone disconcertingly tall, unless the flea leaping around it was not a dog but a kicking donkey. He looked the other way at the interminable tableau of hotels. Madam Sospiri's kiosk was a padlocked crate. In a telephone booth a greatly amused person rocked back and forth on a stool, head tilted to secure the receiver between chin and shoulder.

Ahead the Tower and North Pier, a forefinger and thumb in a reversed 'L'. Crowds were in a hurry on the pavements. Clouds darkened the colours of bobbing balloons, turned to old ivory the snow-white of a carriage pulled by ponies. Pink rock and pink skin dulled. People ran in white trainers no longer pristine, and were soon erased by dashes across the tram's glass.

Philip alighted and ran through puddles. The Tower steamed with cloud. Heavy rain disguised the streets and filled his eyes, but he found his way to the Sea Lanes.

In his room, he cast off his ridiculous drenched suit and towelled himself dry. Rain fizzed and smoked on black rooftops. Rivers in roof guttering, white waterfalls where they overflowed. Neon colours leaked from tubes.

Philosophy for Dummies took up a few hours. Best not to arrive at university a complete novice. Later he logged onto *Zombie Hell* but saving the city and being hailed for it was getting boring. The view from the window was less so.

Roofs gleamed in tones of ebony and lead. The short stretch of pavement at the termination of the alley was floored with mirrors laid end to end. A blink and it was as if Miss Seasider had burst through the inverted mirror world to walk restlessly back and forth on the flags.

Somebody had to win the thousand. He was as entitled to a piece of good fortune as anybody. His exam results weren't that – they were the end product of hard work. He could afford to smile at a notion, worthy of Madam Sospiri, that this and those previous sightings were all portents preceding the reward of an actual encounter – but that was no reason to ignore them.

*

By the time he'd donned his waterproof, rushed out of the Sea Lanes, taken several corners and reached the shining slabs, she'd gone. He walked up and down on them for a moment, frustrated before realising his declaration would have been worthless without a copy of the *Gazette* to present. He bought one on his way to the Promenade.

It was a huge empty plaza. A few pedestrians leaned into the wet wind or were pushed by it. Fewer cars hissed by, their dim colours reflected in wet tarmac. The low sun spilled behind tower blocks of cloud. Dressed in bedraggled fleeces, waves rolled in. Rain vapour writhed around the heights of the Tower. Far below, Miss Seasider passed through the main doors in the Tower's monolithic brick base.

Philip pinched his collar, leapt the water course of a roadside gutter. A cold rain of sweat on his brow. Dry air and light from chandeliers would solidify her. Early evening, there would be few visitors amongst whom she could conceal herself, should she spot her pursuer and try to evade capture.

The entrance foyer was deserted. He paid at the end of the switchback queuing system. Nobody in the shop with its forests of mini-Towers, its Towers in paper-weights and fuzzily stitched onto tea-towels. Stately home opulence in the wide plush-carpeted stairs, the crimson and gold flock wallpaper. On the first floor, round tables in a row before windows looking out to cloud and sea; a pear-shaped couple chomped scones decked in clouds of clotted cream.

On the next floor a door opened onto an upper tier of the ballroom. Some elderly pairs stepped with careful grace to the dove-tailings of a soporific old tune played on the Mighty Wurlitzer. Miss Seasider wasn't visible amongst the seated spectators, one of whom rustled a *Gazette* while others chatted. Spaced at regular intervals around the base of the vaulted ceiling, bosomy gold-leaf goddesses leaned down, watching with golden, blind eyes.

More rococo gorgeousness on the floor above. He entered the deserted mini-theatre to find it wasn't currently running the advertised 'Tower 3D Experience'. Next door, the history of the resort ran on an encirclement of screens interrupted by lift doors. Nobody waited for a trip to the top. Philip pressed the button and heard the twang of cables and a growing rumble. A *ding* and doors opened.

He stepped inside and felt weightless as the lift rose. Stuffy in the dimly lit box; he didn't realise the sides were windowed until he saw red oxide-painted girders scrolling down, the town sinking and broken in a series of frames.

Dank, dim streets, like rock ridges on the seabed. Vehicles were slow snails with matte-coloured shells. Neon-stained haze outside nightclubs. Spectral steam from vents in the back walls of restaurants. On the beach, roped donkeys looked as furred and leggy as spiders.

Another *ding* and the doors opened. A covered space; he walked around it to the strengthened glass floor. Nobody on the Promenade footpath hundreds of feet below. Life would have been a terrible joke if Miss Seasider had been smiling up at him.

Seagulls hovered, wingspans half the horizon, their caws declaring there were morsels to be had up here. Over the sea, great diaphanous fins of rain dangled from clouds coming nearer.

A scrape behind him. An ankle bone rose out of sight on the narrow iron stair. Philip moved quickly; ascending, he felt as light as she had seemed, his chest an empty cage. He'd sound disembodied when he said the words.

He stepped onto the higher platform. Girders caging him were blistered with droplets. Wire netting above the perimeter waist-high barrier reduced the town to a beach of blackened stones, strewn with lights.

She was sitting, facing away, on a backless bench. Not so enticing this close with her drenched shirt clinging to the bones of her shoulders; as well as wispily frayed at the waist, it was grey at collar and cuffs – as if in days of treading the streets there'd been no time to change. A pool under the bench – something worm-like wriggled.

What to say now? He'd kept his *Gazette* dry inside his waterproof. It didn't matter that hers had disintegrated and lay glutinous on her muddy shoes. "Miss Seasider? I …"

Her head ducked between shoulders thrust up to bony points. Rummaging in a bag on her lap, or inside her shirt. Whatever she found she raised to a few inches above her forehead.

The fat cold breeze filled Philip's open mouth.

A crown, a simple gold band with raised triangular points. She lowered it, crowning herself with great ceremony. She stood. Philip was backing to the stairs. She turned and he'd dreaded a worse face, but King Cole's was shocking enough. His heart and brain chilled.

Crown, mask, and, he could see now, a blonde saturated wig.

Nothing real above the neck. Below, soiled water ran and smeared in the discoloured fabric. Laughing now—a cracked old recording secreted about him. Not King Cole either. Knowing it was Shop didn't temper his intense need to get away. Unreasonable fear at the mask. Fury buried deep he'd give vent to at another time. He'd been manipulated: dodgy hash, Miss Seasider dangled like bait, King Cole in the wardrobe. He whirled around for the stair. Shop had turned up the volume of the laughter – Philip wanted that to be the case. Unbearable, the thought of Shop getting nearer.

He descended rapidly on the narrow metal steps. Their steepness and slipperiness a side issue – until his foot slid back. His other leg collapsed under him and he fell forward. The shock of instant flight, then pain – elbows and shins striking metal edges. So fast, nothing to spare to cry out. An obliterating impact against his skull – blackness.

The blackness paled. Cold faced, not bloody faced when he checked with his fingers. No pain at all. He'd fallen astonishingly well, and to the bottom of the stair.

The daylight dimly amazed him. Must have been out cold for hours on the metal floor. He climbed the steps and surveyed the upper deck. No sign of Shop. A blacker blot on Shop's soul for stepping over him on his way down the Tower.

Philip went into the lift and descended. He felt jittery, a lightness as if he'd not eaten in many days. Grey mist in the streets below, like disturbed sediment on the seabed. Bewildering that he could make out the Pleasure Park at this distance, even the squirms and motion of individual rides. At this early hour it could only mean a mass testing of machinery.

He stepped out of the lift onto empty carpets. No tourists, no officials. From the vault of the ballroom, the bosomy gold-leafed goddesses observed pools of shadow on the floor. As he turned away, he felt their blind gold eyes flicker towards him.

The lower floors were deserted too.

No indecision on the matter. He'd leave town – now.

He walked out onto the Promenade. The air felt like he was still inside, neither warm nor cold. Nobody anywhere. His digital watch had stopped at 6.50pm. Early morning, he reminded himself, though with a quality of desertion that seemed too absolute to be solely attributable to the hour. Waves were sluggish, their crests strung with white like spit. The awning over a confectionery stand flapped like a dying thing in no discernible breeze though recently one must have gathered beach sand into mounds variously browed, nosed and cheek-boned.

He went to the Sea Lanes first and packed things into his holdall. His room felt like a platform with paper-thin walls. In the window, buildings were blackened shells as from a distant era. Nobody crossed the bit of flagging at the alley-end. If she had, he would have ignored her this time. He'd been fooled by Shop and wouldn't be again.

He went downstairs and onto the empty street. Shop windows were filled with the sky, a grey white-wash. Dank tarmac and brick, as if a phenomenal high-tide had risen over the chimney stacks and since retreated, taking residents, holidaymakers and shop-owners with it. Doors were open – and windows. Curtains and nets hung out like denuded tongues. He looked up towards bleak cries. Seagulls glided, stiff-winged, schematic, and just about whitely visible in the cover of grey cloud.

He was heading for the railway station. A shock to find the Promenade filling the street end. He returned to the Sea Lanes and set out again on a different route and again he was facing the sea with the Tower in the foreground.

A taxi would circumvent his faulty navigation. He'd close his eyes until the cabby informed him of their arrival. He walked. Parked cars might as well have had bricks in their wheel arches; windows were en-grimed with sand – roofs, boots and bonnets ridged with it. He'd gone a hundred yards and not seen a taxi nor any other vehicle in motion.

He pulled out his mobile phone. The taxi firm number in the address book dated from his arrival in the town two years ago. Gone bust, he guessed when his phone died on his completion of the dialling. But here was a telephone kiosk.

He felt vulnerable within the plate-glass sides, though nobody was visible on the street. His first piece of luck was the card above the wall-mounted receiver – the second an answer following his dialling.

"Tom's Cabin Cars." A woman's voice. He didn't speak. He looked through the grey haze. Which street was this? He couldn't see an end to which he could run and read a street sign. A sensation – it was like sand blowing inside him.

"Hello? Tom's Cabin Cars. Can I help you there?"

He slumped to the floor between the towering glass panels. Fear, like the snapping and cracking of the wooden frames of deckchairs. It gathered in his throat – and he recognised it for what it was. Not fear at all. It had a sound. And he had to laugh. He'd been in some scrapes before – but this ... Funny that humour was saving him – it had never been his strong card. Now it was deriding the confused, weak person he'd been. What a commotion he was making with his laughter! Little wonder the street was no longer deserted. People were coming from all directions to stare. Muddy people, bony people, people clad drably, some in dusty Sunday best, some in mouldy sheets, others in cerements. And intermingled there were ones he recognised as not bed-born nor destined for box or casket – stranger than imagination could have made them.

All his people, nevertheless. He stood. No need to laugh anymore – time to speak. In the faint mirror of the glass he adjusted his crown to a frolicsome tilt, then, with the curled toe of his booted foot, he kicked open the door.

SOURCES

All of these stories are original to *Terror Tales of the Seaside* with the exception of 'The Causeway' by Stephen Laws, which first appeared in *Terror Tales #3*, 2005, and 'The Entertainment' by Ramsey Campbell, which first appeared in *999*, 1999.

FUTURE TITLES

If you enjoyed *Terror Tales of the Seaside*, why not seek out the first four volumes in this series: *Terror Tales of the Lake District*, *Terror Tales of the Cotswolds*, *Terror Tales of East Anglia* and *Terror Tales of London* – available from most good online retailers, including Amazon, or order directly from http://www.grayfriarpress.com/index.html.

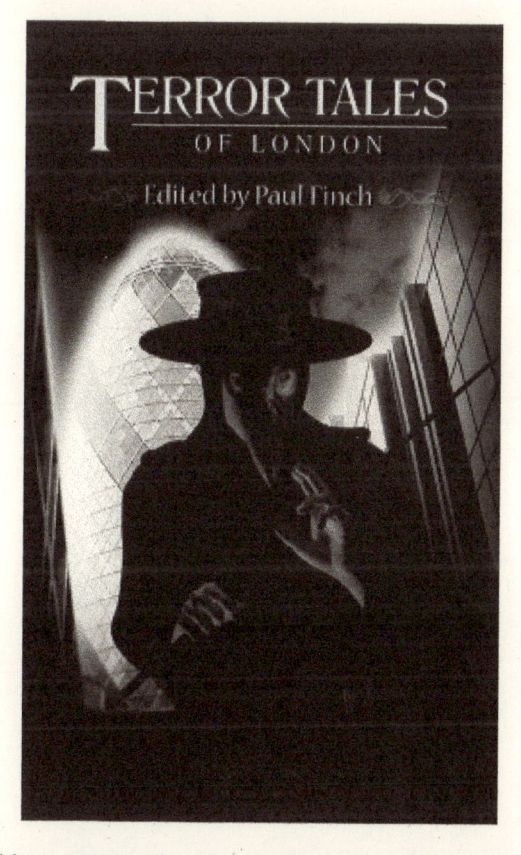

In addition, watch out for the next title in this series, *Terror Tales of Wales*. Check regularly for updates with Gray Friar Press and on the editor's own webpage:

http://paulfinch-writer.blogspot.co.uk/.

9 781906 331375

Printed in March 2021
by Rotomail Italia S.p.A., Vignate (MI) - Italy